FORGED IN CRIMSON

Book one of the Silver and Crimson series

Sarah Eriksson

BONUS CONTENT

Congratulations! In purchasing this book, you access the hidden content within the pages! Whenever a character steps into an important new setting, you, as a reader, can follow along by scanning the QR code on the page. Bonus content such as descriptions, art, and even some soundscapes can help immerse you into the Silver and Crimson universe.

ACKNOWLEDGEMENTS

My Husband, Ian

Since the moment we started dating, you have guided me through self-doubt, insecurities, and fears. You pulled back the veil that separated me from my dreams. Words seem petty in showing you my appreciation. I can start by writing; you rescued me and my creative babies. You believed in me, supported me, and gave me many headaches throughout the journey. Thank you for pushing me and making sure this came true.

Thank you.

Jag älskar dig.

To my Mom and Dad

I want to thank you from the bottom of my heart for everything you have done and sacrificed for me. You are the reason I am alive in more regards than one. It is hard to describe what you mean to me but all I can say is that both of you fill my life with light, warmth, and care. I am truly blessed to have you as my parents.

Thank you.

Jag älskar er.

The Wall of Heroes

With the support from each of you beautiful souls, this book found its way into the real world. Thank you for backing the Kickstarter and making this dream a reality.

HanzHalfelven	Jiiiiiimiiiii	
Tobias Stenwall	Sigge Fabiansson	Mårten Anduri
Anna Layton	Liza Södergård	Martin S
Ludvig Orvegård	Oliwier Radke	Johanna Södergård
Linnea	Johnny MacIsaac	Ian Pendleton
JS Apgar	Emelie Dahlskog	Alex Moulton
Mats Eriksson	Michael Howe	Victor Teddy Tedeman
Casper	Wyatt Kelley	Isabella Wade
Torti	Niklas	Mordechai Gofman
Elin Kothe	Anh	Brenna Greenfield
Gabriel	Ashton Lambert	Tyler O'Donnell
Magnus Olsson	Sofia Rydén	Jakob Lundgren
Ichan	Zalith	Lars-Göran Holmgren
JP Murray	Dave B	James A. Buckhorn
Erik Wahl	Wildcrown Productions	Emma Nordström
Elijah Rawson	Emily Macgregor	Denice
Mikael Wahl	Catrin Thorin	

Settler's Bay
the Gray Waters
White Rock Strand
ECKROS
the Iron Pinnacles
Icoun
Avaora
Centhos
Swaroth
Moldir
Tuqour
Ahoca
ACKR
Preon
Vegdir
BURROUS
Estunc
the Rogoth Mountains
Barra
the Wary Waters
the Fire Isle

the Cursed Seas
Cylar
Kingsay
the Shivering Hills
Bronzefold
GOLDFORK
VESILIA
Longview
Lord
Hart
the Dawnview Heights
Lake Ember
Levent
Rostain
Nedox
Thorne's Town
sk Highlands
the Rugged Spines
the Boundless Ocean
Stiller
Soriec
the Shallows
Bleakwind
Havenreach
MORBURN
Fryn
DRELORN
Endhill
Firebay
Grimshear Heights
N
The Continent of Caldril

The Scarlet Stream
The Blushing Channel
Hawk's Ridge
Oaken Ridge
North
Riverview
Graceview
West Point
Bayside Point
Westview
Stonelake
Glasshou

LEVENT
Capital of Vesilia
Mudward
KeelHeart
Rose Lane
Main Street
Lower Grove
Lake Ember
Ember Gate
Secret Outlet
Copper Passage
OK

A Solitary Witness

Death clutched Liam's hand with its pitiless misery. Stubborn as ever, he endured and recoiled from the alluring presence beguiling a respite from the pain searing through him.

The stench of pine, mud, and blood bombarded his nostrils as proof of his survival. He must have hit a rock with his fall as an opponent's swift sword hilt bashed into his face. The chaos of battle: cries, steel on steel, flesh tearing open, all of it silenced along with his consciousness. He let his ears hone in on the surroundings, expecting the chaos to return. Wistful stillness ensnared the glade. Liam's gaze examined the nearby forest. A hushed breeze shuddered the lank tree trunks reaching toward a misty-grey sky.

It must be dawn, Liam explained. The battle ended hours ago, or perhaps it had moved further into the enemy's forest. He cursed. A wince escaped past his blood-filled lips once his body shifted. Again death sirened near, filled with promises of peace and ease. A chunk of blood followed an unfamiliar and foreign cough as he refused death a second time.

The battlefield had turned into a gruesome garden filled with wilted flowers. The Vesilian soldiers bloomed red. The iron-reeking sap felt cold against his exposed fingers. He did not know what he expected, laying on a heap of dead or finding a fallen opponent. The sight revealed the verity behind the agony keeping him on the ground.

Like the pine trees sprouted from the ground, so did a spear from his belly. Dread fogged his thoughts and ceased his efforts of moving. A dead soldier's half-closed fist rested atop Liam's belly near the weapon. The slain foe was probably the one who invited death to approach Liam. A cough, wet and tenacious, aired his vulnerability. A shiver gnawed through his aching bones. The sight of his woe notified his brain of the struggles facing his being.

"H-help." His faint call was scarcely loud enough for himself to hear over his rushed breath. "Help."

The gruesome garden answered his plead with silence, a strange occurrence in a forest basking in the first light of day. Birds chirping, crickets singing... where were they? Where were the wolves and ravens who would ravage the garden's wilted flowers?

Where was the Keeper in these, Liam's desperate last breaths? Where was the pure light from her sword that held evil at bay? Had none of the Almighty come to claim him?

He calmed his worried mind. He was alone. Nightbringers, the Beast's servants, had yet to approach. Their predatory stare had yet to descend on him. His time was yet to come. The forces of malice and benevolence had yet to claim him. A weak smile pulled his dry lips apart.

The Unborn's protection extended to him, keeping him safe. Safe may have been an overstatement, but alive, which meant someone would come for him. Someone would hear his call and return him to his dearest. Home to the vast open plains where grass and sky nuzzled. Back to the Riveroak's side as their protector. Not that he minded the campaign. The lands to the west needed protection, and he would supply it.

Dawn gathered clouds of mist over the forest. Gorges and valleys blurred with fog while dew formed droplets in his thick beard. It could have also been blood, though he chose not to linger on it. At the slightest sound, he twitched and called for attention. The silence was smothering.

The mist spun by an abruption further up ahead where the glade began. Liam focused his rambling thoughts on the disruption of silence. Another man stepped into the garden. An ashen grey cloak coated with crud trailed the owner. Equally somber rags clothed the man, except for his feet. Dirt soiled the stranger's bare feet, gently tasting the moss covering the forest floor. The stranger's presence could have gone unattended to the unobservant as if one with the forest.

If the stranger were a foe or friend did not matter. Liam's ragged voice intruded on the peace. "H-help. Sir, I need your aid."

Like a spirit, unresponsive to the other side of the veil, the stranger focused his attention on the newly departed, the wilted flowers. Attention... perhaps not, but his curiosity. The man came to a halt, feet away from Liam.

"Sir, I need a hand," Liam said in Vesillian but contemplated speaking the few words of Eckrosie and Burrousie he knew.

Wrapped with indifference the stranger's head turned to lock eyes with Liam. Beneath a hood, the man's pasty skin stayed shielded. An angular face ending in a sharp chin peeked forward. The man was no different from any other. Stubby ebony hair strands rested beneath the hood, and no facial hair grazed his features. However... a crimson horizontal streak reached from ear to ear across cold blue irises. It seemed to hold every shade of blue known to man, from the purest sapphire to a deep sky-blue tint. The colors fused in harmony in a synchronized dance. Upon further scrutiny, Liam witnessed an infinite misery carrying the weeping souls of the departed inside the stranger.

Nay. Inside the Wanderer. Liam's tired eyes widened at the sight of the Almighty's vessel. It had to be. That was the only explanation for the absence of its sisters, the Keeper, and the Unborn. The soul of the Wanderer walked the continent to keep the forces of nights at bay.

"You... are you the Wanderer, aren't you?" Liam stretched his bruised hand toward the stranger, seeking his guidance and empathy.

The stranger did not move.

"I beg of you, Almighty," Liam said despite each breath inflicting increased ache. "Please take pity on my soul. The Unborn must have blessed me. No one has come to claim my soul, but now you're here."

Again, Liam's words carved through the silence. The Wanderer knelt to the fallen soldier by Liam's side, letting the departed steal the focus from the living.

"Where are the souls walking by your side, Almighty?" Liam spoke, ignoring the annoyance he might cause the stranger. "Please. I need help, and I don't want to die. All you need to do is help me on my feet."

The utter indifference... the fact that Liam tried to plead for mercy and it fell on deaf ears awoke an annoyance he had carried for many weeks.

The dead soldier's leather armor that failed to protect his torso followed the stranger's forceful tug as he inspected the wounds closer.

"I'll pay you whatever you want. I'm sure we can work something out. For fucks sake, help me. You can see me with a bloody spear sticking out of my belly. I'm a person. I fucking matter!"

"You find a doe in the woods." The stranger spoke. The voice was flat, void of emotion, yet appealing. He kept probing the wilted flower while focusing his gaze on Liam. "It's limping, barely holding itself upright. You hear its' ragged breathing. You try to save it initially but notice you will only prolong its suffering."

The frigid attention his blue eyes pinned Liam with made the hair at the back of his neck curl. This was not the Wanderer. This was different from the Almighty he had heard stories and tales of.

"Tell me, Liam, would you save the doe?" The stranger said calmly as though they were old acquaintances.

Liam hesitated. The throbbing ache coursed through his being, yet it subsided with the mystery surrounding the stranger. "How... how do you know my name?" Seeing as the stranger awaited an answer, Liam grunted through the pain. "I'd try saving it. It has a second chance at life and isn't ready to die."

The stranger's jaw tightened, and a quiet snort followed. The cloak unfurled with its owner's rise. All attention fell upon Liam. Like a disgruntled parent, the stranger towered over him.

"It was never fit to live. Life is suffering and writhing. A vicious evil we force upon each other when punishing souls with life." The stranger revealed a frugal knife along with wounded wrists.

The blade ascended to the man's skin and cut into his flesh. His gaze refused to leave Liam. "The vile act of keeping the doe alive when all it needs is rest... is not mercy. The same goes for civilization; only we let the doe suffer."

Fresh red sap bled onto the moss. But accompanying it... Liam could swear he saw tar pouring out of the stranger's wounds. The tar propelled to the ground, but in mid-air, it took flight like black smoke rising from a pyre.

A deep-toned vibration spread through the glade. A consistent, growing, and frightening growl, Liam believed only thunder could supply.

The general spoke to them often of the brutality of war, the unforgiving battlefield, and the fear it would bring. But witnessing creatures made of smoke leaving the stranger felt like staring into an abyss of malice. *What the...*

He was not alone in his fright. The moss came to life with insects penetrating the ground. They writhed in pain, trying to escape whatever threat approached.

The stranger's stare remained as yellow, green, and white eyes appeared in the smoke. Nightbringers. The servants of the Beast had laid their eyes on him.

"Do not fret." The stranger's voice carried through the rumble. "Your being wanders onward, nourishing the living while granting you peace of eternal oblivion."

The spear kept him pinned to the ground as the monsters descended. The smoke twisted and turned like a windless whirlwind. Claws, nails, and teeth tore into his flesh, ripping and tearing it asunder.

The stranger conquered the ground his naked feet touched. Firmly standing only feet away. Unwavering. A solitary witness to a feeding frenzy.

Liam's final glimpse of the land of the living ended with the stranger's cloak swinging at its owner's bare feet, leaving Liam to his fate.

～❈～

Watching the creatures of the dark devour the gashed man was nothing the stranger relished. Each step across the soft moss leading him further from the dying man's scream weakened him. The sudden urge for a long and peaceful slumber called him. However, the peace he bestowed on Liam remained far from the stranger's grasp. There was still much to be done. He could not linger further by idle distractions. Perhaps not distractions, it was necessary to complete the puzzle. Although hard to admit, he had enjoyed it—a lot.

And there it was. A growing rumble not caused by either thunder or rain. A hum matched by nothing the forest had heard before. The dying man's words silenced, and for a moment, the stranger heard nothing but steady rain pattering against his bleeding skin. He stopped his advance and tilted his head towards the blackened sky, waiting. He inhaled.

The cries settled abruptly, and the rumble dispersed.

It was the reassuring sound of death.

CHAPTER ONE

Lord Riveroak

The winding path leading through lush gardens up a hill to the grand estate denied the boy's longing gaze from seeing Laim return home. Each day the road let him down as he studied the surroundings from the valved windows of his bedroom.

"Lord Aiden?"

Aiden heard his name repeated from behind by his educator, but ignored it again. Beyond the closed windows, the Riveroak estate spread down the hill it occupied, all the way to the Red River and the rest of the estates of Thorne's Town. His lord father, accompanied by other lords in colorful robes, rode toward the estate through the gardens.

"Lord Riveroak," said the thrall, Sonya. "I really must insist you pay attention."

Aiden threw a fleeting glance at the top of the book's page, headed "*The Crown and Its Duties*". Sonya's questions returned to him.

"It is the Crown's duty and honor to supply its citizens with the resources and means to further the welfare of Vesilia."

Aiden heard her surprise and needed not turn around to see her accompanying smile. "So, you did listen?"

"Why does Liam refuse to return?" Aiden uttered, more for his own benefit than for Sonya. Heavy snowfall had brightened the steep cliffs on the outskirts of Thorne's Town last they spoke. No later than summer had been Liam's promise. Months without Liam's brutish charm and booming laugh left Aiden's everyday a bit duller, not to mention the secret sparring sessions he missed out on. Fighting the marble statues in the mansion could not replace the fighter's teachings.

Sonya breathed in the calming scent of books, probably searching for another string of words to ease Aiden's worry.

"Who's that?" Aiden pointed to his father and the lords and ladies, letting their horses trudge the gravel road leading closer to the estate.

"I thought you were paying attention, little lord," Sonya said, her smile vanishing just as fast as it had appeared. Reluctantly, she rose from her cushioned chair and joined Aiden by the arched window he leaned up against. The hefty layers of cloth making up her attire rustled with her stride. Despite a somewhat bowed back, Sonya carried herself with a subtle poise befitting a servant. She sat by his side, and Aiden could not help but get distracted by her most defining feature— a thick nose slightly crooked from an old injury.

"Black and blue," she said. "That's the—"

"The Riveroaks. I'm not dense," Aiden sighed.

"What about the red and white? Or white and green?"

Aiden shrugged. "The Thornes and the . . . Tallstags?"

"Thornes? Now you are playing dense, my lord. Thornes wear silver and blue."

He knew that. A new day, but the same boring lectures. Regardless, teasing Sonya by making her believe he did not listen gave him some pleasure. By the Almighty, he needed it—anything to feel like a child. At times, he forgot. Endless lectures with Sonya driveling history, long and tedious dinner parties with other noble houses of Thorne's Town—it was enough to have to neglect the  joys of riding his pony Adventure and practicing with swords together with Liam.

Aiden brought his knees to his chest and blew out his cheeks. "The Tallstags and the Holdens. They will join us for supper, and again, I need to pretend that I care."

"My lord, that is quite rude." Sonya wrinkled her broad nose, making it appear even bigger than it already was. Though her youth may have left her skin creased and marked by years of labor under the harsh sun, Sonya exuded a certain wisdom and experience.

"So? You cannot tell them. You are just a thrall."

Whether she took offense or not, he did not notice. The arriving guests passed the thralls' quarters, three one-story buildings with polished stone and orange tiles. After a growing silence, he focused on Sonya, who clasped a book in her hands as if it were a shield to protect herself with.

"I am sorry, Sonya. I—I just want to have someone to play with."

Sonya closed the bindings and placed it in her lap. "No offense taken, my lord." A quick ogle to the bedroom door preceded her words. "I understand the age difference between you and your brother is cumbersome, especially since there are no other little lords your age nearby. There is a boy about nine years old working for your family, however. Perhaps you could play with him?"

Aiden pulled at the sleeves of the uncomfortable blue doublet his parents required he wear for dinner. Getting a friend sounded great. He gave Sonya a smirk and a hasty nod.

"Tell you what. Let's read something less dull." Sonya scurried over to one of the bookshelves and returned with a book with tattered bindings. The dry pages separated and welcomed them with stories.

"Last time, your father wrote about the war in Eckros and described how he retreated back to his home in Levent," Sonya said. Only halfway through Lionel Riveroak's stories, and he had already achieved great deeds.

Aiden leaned his chin against his knees. "I want to be a hero, just like my father."

Sonya threw a gaze his way. "You will be, of that I am certain."

A curl of Aiden's ash-brown hair poked at his eyes irritably. He flipped his head to the side to rid the irritation. "Slaying the Following once and for all, and protecting the realm of Vesilia from filthy Eckrosie. Do you think I can do that?"

"Yes, my lord. I believe you can achieve anything you put your mind to. As does your lord father and lady mother."

"But . . . what if I fail?" Aiden said. "Mother and Father will be furious and disappointed."

"Yes. That is why you need to read to get smarter and continue learning. Getting to know your enemies will help you defeat them."

He would not disappoint them. Even though he wished to do other things, Aiden had to focus on becoming greater and more heroic than his father, the hero of Riverview and the defender of the city of Levent. No matter the cost. He merely wished Liam would nudge him along.

Aiden tugged at the snug corners of the doublet. The heavy brocade turned him into a butterfly against the white surroundings of the Riveroak dining hall. Once the lords and ladies stepped through the double-doors, Aiden felt the silliness of his attire seem to lessen. He was used to standing alone with the dull dressed thralls for comparison.

"...and please take a seat." Aiden's father, Lionel Riveroak, ushered their guests into the hall. A joint gasp of awe filled the room as ten or twelve guests took a look at the dozen paintings clinging to the windowless wall, from the floor to the ceiling. Aiden's eyes fell upon the portrait of his lord father. Although the painting had to be at least ten years old, the painter captured what Lionel looked like in the present day, although he was missing a few limbs. The Lionel in the painting stood among a violent crowd. Sunlight illuminated the man as he thrust his shimmering sword into the air. Aiden had often heard the tales of how his father stood tall in Riverview at the top of Levent, fighting against the city's rioting savages, the people who had come to call themselves the Following. The strife had cost Lionel a foot and an ear, but he ignored the pain from the battle and kept on going strong.

While the lords and ladies studied the paintings, Lionel approached his eldest son. Aiden straightened and gave his father a respectful bow. Lionel's cane, dressed in silver and gold, scraped the hardwood floor. His right stump where his foot used to be followed as he walked. Although Lionel's body was lanky and unstable, he moved with as much determination as the other men nearby. "The hero of Riverview" suited his appearance well. His leathery and battle-worn skin told stories of a past life on the battlefields of Eckros and the sequential fights against the Following. Each time he approached Aiden, the boy could not help but envy his father's realness. Thankfully, he had gotten the same intense emerald eyes his father now looked down at Aiden with, as well as his ashen-brown hair. He could not wait until he grew the same heavy facial hair covering Lionel's squared jaw.

Lionel leaned on the cane and whispered, "Sonya has taught you the correct greetings, son. Now, I wish to see you pay the lords and ladies the proper respect."

That he would. If he would take his father's place one day, he needed to prove his worth. The lords and ladies stepped up to greet him. Their unfamiliar faces blended along with their names, one face older than the next, until suddenly, a girl stepped forward.

"Son, this fair maiden is Lady Clarissa Holden," Lionel told him.

The lady had been fitted with a plump pine dress that looked like the thick stem of a flower. It seemed he was not alone in wearing uncomfortable clothes.

Aiden bowed lower than ever and struggled to find the words. "My.. my lady."

"My lord." Clarissa's voice was sweet and kind. Her sharp cheekbones, long pointy nose, and high brow flared warm against her already reddish-brown skin. Long charcoal hair twined along her small, yet revealing cleft.

"This is my first-born son, Aiden," Lionel explained to Clarissa, who did not let her stunning teak eyes flicker from Aiden. "He is eleven years old."

"And I am fourteen, my lord." Another bow followed her words.

"Show her to her seat, Aiden."

Aiden gave a nod and held out his hand to the lady. Although all the prancing around felt unnecessary, he escorted her to a seat at the long table where the older lords and ladies sat down. Sonya and other thralls rushed around the table, preparing the feast.

Lady Riveroak, Aiden's mother, stepped into the hall. The others rushed out of their seats to welcome the lady of the house with great respect. Emilia swayed toward the table. A black-and-golden evening gown draped the floor behind her like a shadow. Her long, raven black hair was pulled back into a tight bun. Whatever tiny wrinkles her face used to display were tugged with her hair, revealing a clean and almost youthful woman.

By her side, Aiden's little brother, Eamon, squeezed his mother's hand tight. He, too, had been forced into an uncomfortable shirt and trousers, which he tugged and ripped at, making no effort to hide his discomfort. It was to be expected, though. A child that young did not understand the world like Aiden did.

Potatoes, venison, and fresh mushroom sauce found their way to the table with the thralls. Aiden dug around the sauce in hopes of—well, he did not know. Perhaps some sort of distraction.

"I don't know about all that, my Lord," Lionel said to a man farther down the table.

"Your modesty, Lionel, is for bards to sing and tell," Emilia said. "Speak freely. I am certain everyone is anxious to hear about your experiences."

Lionel squinted before resting his elbows on the table. He gave a half-smile, the same way he did when Aiden asked him to tell a bedtime story for the third time.

"There is a certain simplicity to life when one lives on the edge of it. Things we take for granted here and now are not given a second thought out in the fields. But one thing is for certain: bathing is always on one's mind."

The table of grown-ups joined in laughter at Lionel's story.

A man with a hideously ugly beard, nearly reaching the tabletop, huffed. "Not only did you fight the savages to the west, but you raced home to protect your king and country. If that is not bravery and courage, I cannot fathom what is."

The man peeked past the other people sitting along the table until he sought out Aiden. "You have quite the reputation to uphold, Little Lord. The son of the hero of Riverview."

Aiden gave a grin, but feeling the food squeeze through his front teeth and start spilling, he hastily stopped and chewed instead.

The supper continued, and for some reason, with each word he uttered to Clarissa, he fumbled until he fell silent. It could well be the unfamiliarity of neither speaking appropriately like he did with adults nor speaking more simply like he did for his brother's sake. Finally, another person his own age sat beside him, but he choked under the pressure.

Eamon tugged at his mother's dress, like the five-year-old he was. Food covered his entire face as if he had fallen asleep in the potatoes. "Mother, can I go?"

"Of course. Sonya, show Eamon to his room."

Sonya rushed over to the head of the table and grabbed Eamon by the hand. She escorted Eamon away. Perhaps that was a sign for Aiden to ask the same.

"May I also be excused?" Aiden called out across the table.

Emilia folded a napkin and placed it in her lap. "You may not. The Holdens and Tallstags have graced us with their presence. As a lord of this household, you must tend to our guests."

"Then why does Eamon get to go?"

A slight tug pulled at Emilia's lips. "You are no boy, dear son."

He was testing her, but he figured, why not a bit more? "May the lady and I be excused in that case?"

The uncomfortable smile on his mother's face disappeared. An eyebrow lifted with disappointment. Her teak eyes shrunk and fixed in on Aiden.

"Come now, Lord Aiden." Clarissa's caring voice called to them. "We are perfectly fine dining together, you and I."

Emilia released her gaze from Aiden and turned to another lady at her side.

"How fare your interests to the east, Lady and Lord Holden? We have heard of great harvests in the mountains," Lionel said to start up a conversation.

Aiden stuck his fork into a potato, only to repeat the same thing over and over until it was riddled with holes. As he did, the eyes of Clarissa followed every movement until she finally broke the silence. "What do you enjoy doing, my lord?" Clarissa said.

"Riding, fighting, going into the woods with Father. You?"

"Riding, fighting, and heading into the woods." Clarissa smiled. "But also reading stories about adventurers."

Aiden stopped. The fork was deeply entrenched in the potato. "Me too." His sulk turned into a grin. "I love the story about Keldra and her adventures in Caldril."

"Oh, she is my hero." Clarissa directed her body to face Aiden. "Once, when my family visited Nedox, we stopped at the Ancestors' Square and placed flowers at her statue."

"What did she look like?"

"Regal. She looked like a princess, but not like Princess Trelinda. She was big and tall as any man, and by her side, she had her wolf Marrion standing watch with her."

"I would like to see that one day. I've only been to Levent and seen a couple of boring old men and women," Aiden sighed. His lady mother saw to it that he would only see Levent and Thorne's Town. Venturing beyond the comforts of her home in any way seemed to frighten her.

Clarissa placed her soft and delicate hands on his and gave a gentle whisper. "I shall take you there someday if you would like, my Lord."

Perhaps the evening would not turn out as dull as he had thought. He gave her a warm smile and let their conversation continue without giving another excuse to leave a second thought.

Aiden let out a loud and wide yawn. Eamon and his new friend, another little lord, played on, ignoring Aiden's loud protest completely. Both the five-year-olds declined Aiden's ideas of running around the mansion playing peek-a-boo and tag. Instead, they insisted on playing with Eamon's toys in the bedroom next to Aiden's. The other option was for him to join his parents and yet another visiting family. But sitting next to them, listening to their endless conversations, was not really enticing either. Usually, it did not bother him, playing with his little brother, but he could not help but feel excluded and aware of their great age difference when Eamon and the little lord laughed about something.

"Aiden!"

Eamon dragged Aiden back to the floor, where wooden toys littered the colorful carpet. "Now stop us, because you are evil dragon."

Aiden held a carved dragon and danced with it in front of the other boys. "Grrr . . . I'm the mighty dragon, Thesul. Prepare to die and fear my flames!"

Eamon and the other boy squealed with delight.

"Attack!"

Both of them attacked the dragon using their puppets to hit and slash the defenseless beast. Aiden gave a final dying screech and collapsed on the carpet. "How could this be? You're only human! I should slay you!"

"Move. You're dead, stupid dragon," Eamon said, and passed Aiden. "I want an apple. Can you get it?"

Aiden threw a gaze around the room to find they were alone. No thralls answered his brother's request. Perhaps that was for the best, seeing as the boys were done with Aiden's part of their game.

Aiden shrugged. "Sure."

Their giggle carried with Aiden down the stairs. The adults sat in the dining hall, nibbling and chatting about something. Aiden snuck past. For some reason, his parents had let him leave supper early, and he had no intent to question their decision. Instead, he rushed through the mansion, down the grand stairs leading him past the dining hall and the library. He swept past the kitchen's door, where the smell of spinach wafted over him. Pots and stews spewed out piles of mist into the kitchen, where at least six or seven thralls competed for space. He hurried through the kitchen and out the backdoor of the mansion.

The sun hid behind thin clouds, rushing in from the Rugged Spines. He skipped out to a gathering of apple trees. The hot evening's air cleansed his lungs as he let in a deep breath. The apple trees stood in bloom, their sweet aroma covering the backyard. Beyond the Riveroak estate, a several-story high building constructed from different brown bricks and with a deep orange roof, lay the Rugged Spines. The mountain range was anything but spines, though, as their peaks shot high into the sky. On good days, the snowy peaks of the steep cliffs glimmered in the sun. Aiden wondered what he would see from up there, high above Thorne's Town. Would he see beyond the Great Grasslands all the way to Levent? To the south of the mountains lay the neighboring country of Drelorn. Thankfully, no one had ever been bold enough to send an army through to claim the town as theirs. But if it did, Aiden would bravely defend his home by his lord father's side. Nothing would compare to that honor—riding into battle, wielding the sword Lionel received from the king himself.

A twig broke nearby, and a boy with crazy brown curls reached for a branch beneath the apple trees. Aiden had noticed him around, as he appeared to be Aiden's age, but never on his own. He walked up to the boy. Eamon and the other kid could wait. Maybe this was the boy Sonya had spoken of the other day.

The boy gazed up at Aiden with blueberry-shaped eyes. He was smaller than Aiden in height and frame, with arms as thin as the apple trees' branches.

"Hi, I'm Aiden."

The boy rushed to his feet and bowed. "My . . . my lord."

"What is your name?"

"Nyle, m-my lord."

A bucket of red apples stood by Nyle's feet, though only three or four fruits rested at the bottom. Aiden smiled at an idea to help Nyle with the tedious task.

"Want to race? Whoever picks the most apples wins my dessert."

Nyle threw a glance at the mansion's back door, where steam from the kitchens lunged out into the summer air. He gave a quick nod and threw himself onto the nearest tree, where he shook the branches.

Aiden darted to another tree and clawed his way upward. It was not a long climb, but at least ten or fifteen feet off the ground. He rocked the branches with his weight and knocked down whatever apples he saw. The apples, some red, some green, all different shapes and sizes, rained to the ground with tiny thuds.

Nyle took Aiden's approach and climbed a tree as well. "But how do we know when someone has won?"

Aiden halted, the branch creaking beneath him. "I did not think about that."

The clouds could be a way to time their task. Or perhaps a few riders approaching the town's gates from the north. Aiden pointed to the riders. "When they reach the gate, we stop."

Nyle did not waste any time. He flung his hands toward apples while keeping a close eye on the dots moving toward the gates.

For years, Aiden had searched for a person his own age, but never once had he thought about one of the thralls working at the estate. Most of them always acted kindly toward him, even if they could be a bit dull company (he was thinking about Sonya in particular). Sure, there was Clarissa, but being a lady and a couple of years older than Aiden, he could not see them playing together and climbing trees.

Aiden reached for the top branch, which buckled from all the apples hanging there. The thuds of the orbs dropping to the ground continued with his violent shake. He did not really wish to win, but he would make sure it was challenging to compete against Nyle.

"Stop," Nyle shouted when the riders reached the gates. They gathered beneath the trees.

At a quick count, Nyle gathered twenty red apples beneath his tree while Aiden counted thirty-five by his.

Nyle pointed and laughed at Aiden's pile. "Those don't count. Only ripe ones, silly."

Aiden scratched his head. "Really?"

"Yes. But let's take them to Sonya, she'll decide who wins."

Aiden gathered his pile into an empty bucket. It weighed heavy in his grasp, but he refused to give up, so he dragged the apples after Nyle to the backdoor into the kitchens. Aiden and Nyle snuck inside and put the baskets down by a workbench.

Sonya caught a glimpse of the boys. She hurried over past the thralls chopping potatoes and stirring stews.

"My Lord Aiden, what are you doing here?" Sonya rushed and wiped her hands on a handkerchief.

"We picked apples," Aiden said, and stood proudly above his contribution.

"You helped Nyle? But my lord, that is not something you are supposed to do."

"I felt like it. Who won?"

Sonya's eyebrows touched with confusion. She peered into the baskets, looking over the red and shiny ones in Nyle's and the mixed colors in Aiden's. "Both of you did well, my lord, but you picked the most."

"No, these don't count," Nyle said, grabbing one of the green apples. "They're not ripe."

Aiden had seen that look before. The face thralls gave when they disagreed with their superiors yet put on the facade that they agreed. He would not have it.

"Darn," Aiden cussed, and bowed to Nyle. "You will get my dessert as agreed." He gazed up at Sonya. "Can I help?"

Both Sonya and Nyle blinked.

"Can I help you? I do not wish to be with my brother and my parents . . . they are boring."

Sonya kneeled to his level. "My lord, are you playing games with me?"

"No, no. I want to help. Well, I want to stay with Nyle."

"A lord does not need to learn to serve. There are other things your lord father and lady mother want you to learn," Sonya said. "I am glad you met Nyle, but perhaps play with him once he has done his chores?"

Aiden crossed his arms in defiance. "Well, you cannot force me to leave. So I will stand and watch."

"But, my—" Sonya began.

"Leave it be, Sonya. Once this one wants something, there's no stopping it." Jarred, another thrall and Aiden's close second favorite, walked up to them. He gave the boy a quick wink. The thrall exuded an aura of strength and experience, similar to Liam.

Sonya sighed. "Fine. But you will have to explain this to the lord and lady."

"Will do." Jarred grinned. As Nyle and Sonya carried the baskets into the kitchen, Jarred leaned near Aiden and whispered, "You trying to seduce a certain woman with pie?" The well-groomed eyebrows arched slightly over his chestnut-colored eyes.

Aiden's face turned red. "No. I . . . she was nice, but I do not want to give her a pie. Or do you think she likes pie?"

"Only one way to find out, my lord."

Once Sonya got talking about food, she did not stop. She showed Aiden through the area. "These apples need to be scrubbed from dirt. After that, we chop them up into little pieces."

She picked up an apple from Aiden's pile and inspected it. "I am sorry to say, my lord, but this cannot be used. It is too early, and not ripe. When they turn red, that is when you put them in a pie. We do not wish to serve any sour food, do we?"

In awe, Aiden followed around the kitchen. Chopping apples into pieces, steering pots, and kneading dough together with Nyle brought some hope back to him. He did not need to be alone. There were friends to be found right at home.

CHAPTER TWO

The Slums of Keelheart

"Wake up, sweetie," Leah's mother's gentle voice called through her dream.

A lonely candle sparkled. Leah opened her eyes and quickly shielded herself from the light. She rubbed her eyes, and the scratchy linens rustled with her defiant twist as she rolled over to the other side of the bed.

"It's early, I know, but you've gotta wake up." Her mother nudged and caressed Leah's shoulder. "You need to get ready to go to the Halls."

The lone cracked attic window showed no signs of daybreak. Leah snuggled deeper into the bed.

"I'll get you a treat if you get up now," Jaida teased her daughter.

Okay then, Leah thought, and bounced up to greet the new day. She slipped into some garment her mother had scrunched up for her, letting it fall over her shoulders until it touched her bare feet, hugging the chipped wooden floor.

In the corner of the cramped attic room, Leah's little sister buried her bunny-like nose into a pillow while stretching out across the entire bed. Another garment passed Leah's head and hugged her neck in a strap. A second strap tied behind her waist. Leah looked down to see something looking like a sack of potatoes on her. She giggled and sat back down on her bed. 

Jaida plucked a stray of red hair and tucked it with the rest behind Leah's ears. "Remember what I said?"

Leah folded her hands in her lap. "Why can't I stay? Work with you?"

"Sweetie, you shouldn't. You're too young to stay downstairs. Besides, Miya needs her big sister."

"Okay." Leah rolled her eyes at the answer that never changed, no matter how many times she asked.

Her mother tugged at the sleeves of her own dress. In the sparse light, it became difficult to tell the different brown shades. The dress was dyed deep brown, while the wild curls framing her round and gentle face glowed like bronze.

"What have I told you?"

Leah squinted. "Ne'er let people touch me if I don't wanna?"

"Exactly." Jaida poked Leah's nose, making Leah's face wrinkle. "And if they ask about me?"

"Do you think Ida will give me clay to play with?" Leah burst out excitedly upon seeing her latest attempt at making a clay horse. The clay lay atop their only dented shelf where a few clothing items rested.

Jaida took Leah's hand in hers. "Leah, I need you to promise me that you're listening."

"Okay, pinky tap?" Leah lifted her pinky and touched her mother's pinky. "I promise that if someone asks about you, I say your name is Walda."

"I love you, my little rascal," Jaida said, and embraced her before she headed over to Miya to wake her up and clothe her.

Leah leaped out of bed to head out, holding her mother's hand and following her and Miya down the staircase. Compared to the attic, the rest of the house came to life at night. People wrestled inside closed doors as usual. But this was morning, and the house was quiet. Before heading out, they passed the pantry, where Jaida picked up a wrapped bundle with bread. She handed it to Leah and continued into the streets of Levent.

Leah never liked walking the streets when the dark hugged every crack and nook of the red clay houses. Upon seeing the black sky shading to deep blue, Leah let out a loud sigh of relief. Dawn was upon them, and soon the monsters and beasts that crawled in the night would retreat. They cut a corner into a narrow alleyway, where Leah had to let her mother walk first in order to not get stuck. Thankfully, the windows and doors into the shelters were closed. That way, she did not need to come upon someone unfriendly.

By now, the dawn's red light made all the houses blood red. Her mother's stormy brown hair shone scarlet, almost like Leah's. Jaida was without question the most beautiful woman ever. Leah didn't seem to be alone in thinking that. The few people outside this early passed them and looked over their shoulders to glance at Jaida once more. Leah could only wish that she would get the same orange-brown skin that almost reflected light because of its softness. Leah rubbed her cheeks again whenever Jaida looked away, trying to get rid of the small freckles that lived there.

They moved through rows of beat-up houses and shelters until they came to the district square of Keelheart. There, unlike any of the damaged ones around it, a building stood like a proud statue. No holes peeked through the facade except for big, tall windows that reflected the dramatic morning sky. Leah had visited the district square before; it lay empty, except for an open carriage with two horses pulling it. A couple of people got inside the barricades and sat down on 

benches. Young girls and boys, the same age as Leah, but also grown-ups rubbed sleep from their eyes.

"Where are they going, Mother?" Leah caught up with her mother and sister.

Jaida grabbed Leah's hand. "Silly, you already know. They're going to Riverview, Main Street, and other districts of Levent."

"Why?"

"Because they work. They're thralls, and work for the man who lives in that house." Jaida pointed to the beautiful house nearby.

"But, are you a thrall then?" Leah said.

"No, Leah. I work by myself. A thrall is owned by the Rosses, and they decide where the thrall works. I can choose where I work."

Leah began asking the same question she used to, but she let the words fall silent with her breath. If only Leah could work like others, then maybe they could move into the beautiful castle she couldn't take her eyes off. One day, she would help her mother. One day she would work and get money to buy something. Still, she could not escape feeling down. What if she wasn't good enough to work? She didn't know a lot of things, after all.

Reluctantly, Leah hurried after her mother and sister to get to the Halls, the place of worship for Wanderers. The eight-sided house of red clay shone brightly in the dawn's light as they arrived. The doors swung open, and a familiar woman stepped outside, pulling a young boy roughly Leah's age.

The boy struggled against Guide Ida's grasp around his rugged collar. "I can sing for you. What do you wanna hear? How the Keeper killed thousands of Nightbringers?"

"I'm sorry, boy." Ida released the boy, who brushed off his torn clothes.

"Name's Gil. Not boy." Gil puffed out his chest to look bigger than he was. "I will become the greatest performer Levent has ever seen." He gave Ida a roguish smile and rubbed the top of his shaved head. It seemed kind of strange to Leah, a child her age not having any hair, only a shining brown scalp.

"Listen, Gil. I'm sorry to have to do this, but the Halls are not meant to house people. If you don't have a place to stay, visit the Rosses, and they'll take good care of you," Ida said, her always-calm and hushed tone remaining.

"Fine." Gil rolled his blueberry-shaped eyes. "Oh, before I go, can you point me in the direction of Rose Lane?"

"Straight across the bridge, you'll find it."

"Many thanks." Despite being tossed out of the Halls, the boy took a bow in front of Ida before leaving. Jaida pulled Miya and Leah with her to greet Ida.

Ida, dressed in long gray robes from shoulder to toe, turned her attention to them with a gentle but somewhat surprised smile. "Jaida, you're quite early. Did something happen?"

"Giana needs me to help out around the establishment." Leah's mother sighed and brushed off dirt from Miya's skirt as Miya made the fabric twirl in a circle. "Is it alright for them to stay with you awhile? Gets boring for them at home."

"Of course they can stay. You deserve all the help you need Jaida, given your great work for the Unborn. Who knows, I might even rustle up some food for these two as well," Ida said, and pinched Leah's plump cheek.

Jaida tied her fingers together. "I hope the Wanderer watches over you."

With a quick embrace and kisses to her daughters, Jaida hurried back to their home, leaving the two sisters alone with Ida. Leah didn't hide her disappointment at the sight of her mother disappearing through a growing crowd.

"Miya, why don't you run inside, and I'll be right behind you with your sister?"

Leah sighed, and her shoulders slumped.

"What's going on, Leah? Are you sad?" Ida leaned forward with a crooked back to look Leah in the eyes. "Today is going to pass before you know it. You'll see."

"Mother doesn't think I'm good enough to help her," Leah muttered. Her gaze swept across the crowd of Keelheart in search of her mother's wild hair.

"What kind of talk is that?"

"I . . . I wanna work, but she always says no. She doesn't think I'm good at anything."

"That's not true. Jaida doesn't want you to worry about that. You're a child, and children don't work. They take care of their family and have fun."

"No, all the other children are thralls. I wanna be one too."

Ida grasped Leah's shoulders, forcefully first but the grip softened quickly. "Listen here. The other children don't have a choice. Their parents . . . their parents are dead and can't protect their children. So instead of losing their home, they work for the Rosses to have a place to stay. Your mother works to make sure you don't have to. It has nothing to do with what you are good at or not."

Leah tore her gaze from the town square and back to Ida's wrinkled smile.

"You know . . . I think I need some help today. Do you know if someone can help me?"

A smirk pushed away Leah's frown, and she bit her lower lip to reveal a playful grin.

Visitors of all ages came and went. The Halls of Keelheart stood open for anyone needing to speak with the Guides, the ones who could talk with the Almighty. Leah dragged her sister along to follow Ida around the strange-shaped building, even though Miya yawned in protest. Within one of the rooms, adults rested on mats, coughing and sneezing. Ida offered a blessing to the sick. Together, Leah, Ida, and Miya prayed for the Wanderer to watch over the suffering people. No answer came from the Wanderer, but Ida explained to the girls why that was:

"The Wanderer watches over those it can. It roams the lands of the living and protects us from the Beast and the catastrophes the Beast tries to release on the living. But the Beast has thousands of Nightbringers looking for vulnerable souls to take when the Wanderer is unable to see." When both Miya and Leah gaped widely, Ida continued. "Don't worry. That's why the Wanderer has a sister called the Keeper. She fights Nightbringers and brings the souls of the dead to the Wanderer's side."

Inside a big room, on a tiny plateau, Ida stood next to a man and a woman. Miya and Leah squeezed through a growing crowd that had gathered to witness the ceremony, something Leah never had never seen before. Adults budged as Leah brushed against their legs. The couple standing before the crowd held each other's hands and didn't let go of their gaze on one another. It was a look like the people at home gave her mother before going away to another room—a kind of happy and playful look.

Ida held her hands on the man and woman's foreheads and spoke loudly. "Unborn, we turn to you. Please bless these souls and keep them safe through strife. Let this Enfolding be a confirmation of their willingness to take on the burdens you shall bestow on them."

It made her wonder. Did Jaida join this binding of souls with her and Miya's father? Probably not, because the only answer given to her was that Jaida didn't know who their father was. It didn't matter.  They had their mother there, and that was what mattered.

Miya tugged at Leah's droopy dress. "I'm bored. Can we play?" she said out loud, although she must have attempted to whisper. Leah smiled at her bright-eyed sister, her blonde hair tussled from running around.

In the middle of the Halls, they stepped out into the gardens. The walls of the Halls circled the green and colorful courtyard, an uncommon sight to see in the dirty streets of Keelheart. Miya rushed past a group of people sitting beneath an oak tree and climbed up on a warm boulder. Leah followed, and within a few minutes, they clapped their hands together in a song their mother sang to them.

There're dangers in the West, wherever you will go
They do not fear death, the people of the West
There're dangers in the west, wherever you will go
Look away from the rising sun, or they'll take you away
Away, away

A woman leaning against the nearby tree chuckled. "Where did you learn that?" Compared to Jaida and other women, this middle-aged woman wore a short-sleeved beige tunic and simple pants instead of a dress or skirt. Wide-legged, she grasped a knife, which she forcefully carved into a piece of bright wood in her hands. By her side, a pile of toys rested beneath the shade of the tree.

The lady must have noticed Leah's interest in the toys, as she asked, "Do you want one?"

Miya didn't wait. She leaped to the lady and ripped through the pile. A wooden horse, a wooden sword, and a wooden soldier fell to the ground at Miya's feet before she settled on a cute goat. Leah grabbed the sword and weighed it in her hands, biting her lower lip and running her tongue on the back of her gappy teeth. Of course, she wanted it, but wanting something never did anything good. It only left her disappointed.

"It's yours if you want it," the woman said with a kind smile through gapped teeth. "We have hundreds of toys back at the Rosses' Haven. If you ever want another toy for you and your sister, all you need to do is ask. Do you have parents?"

Oh, she's asking about Mother. I have to do the lie. Leah panicked, afraid of Miya saying something else, but her sister had already gone away to play with her toy.

"Our mother is Walda," Leah mumbled.

"Walda? That's great. Well, my name is Selene. What's yours?"

"Leah."

Selene carved into the wood again. Somehow, she created a new thing by cutting. The bright wood spliced and twirled on itself, creating funny loops. Leah wanted to release her stare, knowing how rude it was, but she couldn't.

"Tell your mother that if you need toys or food, come to the Rosses', and we'll take good care of your little family," Selena said.

Leah extended the wooden sword to the lady, who placed a hand, riddled with calluses on Leah's. "No, it's a gift. Take it. It's yours."

"Thank—thank you."

"Your mother should be happy to have such a great girl looking out for her little sister."

"Okay." Leah touched the wooden sword. It almost felt as soft as skin. How could that be if it was cut out of wood?

Selene stopped her work. "You wanna try? I'll show you."

Unlike the other people of Keelheart who smelled bad, Selene smelled like some kind of special flower. Her clothes were not dirty or had any holes in them. Leah did not shy away from the woman.

Together, Selene and Leah carved what looked to be a leg of a dog. Selene handed the small knife to Leah, the grip still warm from her hand. On the blade, spots of red and brown disturbed the otherwise silver coating of the metal. For a time, Leah forgot about her sister, who ran around the gardens singing and shouting. Before long, Ida came and got them to bring them to their mother.

"Take the knife as well, Leah. Then you can create toys." Selene smiled.

"Are you sure?"

"You take care, and I hope I'll meet you again."

All the way back home under the setting sun, their mother didn't seem too excited about what they had done during the day. She pulled Leah and carried Miya back home so fast that Leah needed to take quick steps.

But as soon as they got home and put Miya to bed, everything was back to normal.

"What's that? Did Ida finally get some toys?" Jaida asked when Miya fell asleep and cuddled beneath a blanket.

"No. A woman gave me it," Leah said and brought the sword over to the lone candle.

Jaida toyed with a lock of Leah's hair. "A woman? What woman?"

"I don't know, it was a gift. I met her in the Halls, and she was very nice. She taught me to make toys with this." The knife looked scarier in the dark attic than during the day.

"Leah, you . . . can't accept these things from people."

"I can't keep it?" Leah's brow scrunched up.

"Of course you can, sweetie." Jaida leaned in closer and pinched Leah's cheek. "I just . . . I just want to protect you and your sister.

The Wanderer and the Unborn are keeping you safe, but I have to protect you too. Did the woman say something else?"

Leah jumped up beside her mother on her bed. The wood creaked at the sudden disturbance. "Ehm . . . she said we could come to the Ross house and get food if we want to."

"The Rosses? Listen, I don't want to scare you, but . . . the Rosses are dangerous. They do the Beast's work. They try to lure good people to join the Beast."

"But she was nice," Leah mumbled as she bit her bottom lip.

Again, her mother's soft hands twirled Leah's hair and put it into a bun. "Do you remember the story Ida once told you?"

"The one 'bout the handsome man who lured people into the wild?"

"What happened to those people?"

"Something bad."

"Don't trust everyone, even if they are nice to you, Leah. Get to know them before you trust them."

Leah couldn't help but feel stupid . . . or rather, dumb.

"Cheer up, sweety. As long as you don't use the knife when I'm not here, it's okay that you keep it. But I'll have to find some wood for you to carve."

"Thank you, Mother. I love you."

"And I love you."

Chapter Three

A Stray Songbird

Beneath a stone bridge, gatherings of tiny fish glistened in the sunbeams piercing through the swift surface. Gil leaned over the bridge's barricade, the stone burrowing into his ribcage. Men and women passed behind him to enter and exit the slums of Keelheart. Already, only a few feet across the bridge, the air felt cleaner and fresher. The vile stench of feces and mold-infested buildings lessened in Rose Lane. It made him question the decision to sleep at the Halls of Keelheart, but the bruises from when the town's guards beat him to a pulp gave him a painful reminder. The pain was worth it, made him focus on why he went to Keelheart of all places. A troupe of actors he had followed began their performance there. Next up, Rose Lane.

Gil followed a cobblestone street into Rose Lane, one of Levent's better areas, as far as he could tell. The streets were clean and tidy, and the general public just the same. Gil tucked his wide, unfitted tunic into the loose trousers that wrapped around his thin waist, tied by a hempen rope he stole off a bag of wheat months ago. He found that presentation was all that mattered, all that differed rich folk from the rabble. A particular determination and sense of pride powered the rich folks' steps. Why could it not power his as well?

A fresh smell of baked goods wafted into the air. By the outskirts of Rose Lane, a sign hung with a loaf of bread carved into the wood. His belly growled and churned at the aroma. *If only food wasn't necessary, life would be pleasant,* he thought.

Gil stepped into a bakery where shelves displayed food. Bread, mostly, but also colorful cakes with whipped cream that made Gil's mouth run. He stepped up to a counter where a slender woman wiped the counter clean.

"Welcome," she uttered kindly.

Gil rummaged through his pockets in his ashen and patched-up trousers. He gave her an uncomfortable grin. "I could've sworn my father gave me coins."

The lady drew a long sigh, "Aha . . . and what's your father's name?"

"Turner. Canden Turner," Gil said with faked confidence shining through his wide smile.

"Nice try, urchin." The lady returned to her chores behind the counter, brushing the floor.

When at first you don't make it . . . Gil thought and lowered his head while peering at the lady with pleading eyes. Many trials had perfected his innocent and beady-eyed plea. "Please, madam, I don't wish to return to my father without bread. He'll beat me half to death if I don't."

The lady ignored him and brushed past him as if he were not there.

Gil rolled his eyes. "Fine, you've got any burnt bread or crumbs I can get?"

"What do you think?" Her nostrils widened with her puff. "I don't burn bread. Now get out."

Gil avoided the increasingly aggressive broom-strokes by tip-toeing around it. "What if the Wanderer's soul lives in me? Would you refuse it food?"

"That doesn't work, boy. Maybe out in the country, but I have a family to feed too. Now go."

Gil's jaw tightened. "Fine, I'll go. Might I ask where the Shields of the Moon troupe are?"

"They're up by Rose's Square."

"Much obliged. Eh . . ."

Gil didn't get time to speak before the lady hurried to explain. "Straight forward, and follow the street five blocks. You'll see it."

All the groveling and begging would meet its end. Of that, he felt certain. Once an acting troupe or a guild of performers took him in, everything would fall into place. No more hustling for the next meal, no more scavenging to find a place to rest. At least, that was what powered his steps through Rose Lane. Half a year ago, when the rains came for Levent, the poorhouse of River's Brook cast Gil into the streets to live by himself. It had been an endless cycle of survival, yet now when setting sights on the actor's troupe, he was close to getting all he wanted—a family.

Gil stepped into the town square of Rose Lane. Like other districts, the square used to house a large market, but now it held bales of hay lining up toward a stage. Merchants' stalls found a new home pushed against the two-story clay buildings surrounding the square.

At the stage, a large canvas draped from a beam suspended above a plateau. Stitched to the middle of it, Gil recognized a shield surrounded by a starry crown, the sigil of the Shields of the Moon.

A couple of men and women by a set of large wagons were deep in a discussion, it seemed. They gestured as they spoke, loud and clear. It dawned on Gil that they were performers rehearsing. Without their beautiful costumes, they could have been any other merchants or people from Main Street with the men in their simple trousers and shirts, the women wearing long dresses in meek shades.

Cautiously, Gil sought out a lone hay bale to listen to the troupe's discussions. A couple of men in their thirties stood in the sun, speaking their lines. Gil could not help but admire and envy them in their embroidered tunics and colorful unbuttoned shirts. Waking up each morning in a new place yet surrounded by people one knew, or perhaps even a family, seemed like a faraway dream. But looking at it now, he could not but hope for the same thing. They gave one another warm smiles, and hugs to any newcomer. It looked like everything he dreamed about.

Somehow, he needed to get their attention. If indeed his wish was to become one of them, he had to be of use. Builders by the stage seemed to be all but done as they took a breather beneath the vast canvas. Having never held a hammer or built anything, that was probably not the right way. His focus drifted back to the actors and performers.

Hours later, the bells of Riverview rang loud, and its sisters soon followed across the city of Levent. The market stalls closed for the day, and the square filled with curious people wanting to see the performance. As the sun set, the stage came alive with torches and lanterns. The night may have started its intrusion, but the torches kept it at bay.

A woman dressed in elegant, tailored attire that kissed her skin slickly stepped onto the stage and took a bow. The crowd's murmur hushed.

"My ladies. My gentlemen. Our troupe, the Shields of the Moon, welcome you to our performance of *The Hero of Riverview.* We invite you to relax and enjoy. And as always, we appreciate whatever support you would bestow on us this evening so we may continue telling these thrilling tales. Thank you."

A couple of performers in their fancy clothes walked among the rows of viewers. Merchants, tailors, parents, and people from every place of society rummaged through their pouches, and coins rattled plenty. Performers collected contributions, and a tall man with long dark curls tied into a bun reached Gil's row. The chiseled fellow's angular face came face-to-face with Gil, and the man hunched over and offered him a pouch.

"Take it," the stranger said.

Folks next to Gil emptied their pockets and showered the performer with coins into a rugged hat. When no words left Gil, the man spoke. "It's been hours, and you haven't moved. This is the least we can do for an admirer."

"Thank you," Gil said with tears gathering. But as he looked up, the man disappeared into the crowd.

Hidden in the bag, a gathering of sausages and salted pork greeted him. Wasting little time, he devoured it like a starved wolf, which was quite a shame, as once he finished it he could only savor the rich, lingering taste of smoke and salt.

The play commenced with ten actors taking the stage from behind the curtain. The man who'd offered him food glowed in his performance of the fisherman turned noble and hero, Lionel Riveroak. The play depicted the call for adventure and glory to the west, where he fought for Vesilia and its king, Canden Thorne. But upon Lionel's return home, there was an uprising stirred in Levent by the Following and their pretentious leader, Lord Rick Haven. The play ended when Lionel defeated the lord, and the king made Lionel a Riveroak by arranging an Enfolding to the Riveroak's daughter, Emilia.

Gil found the moments where the characters faced hardships during the play even greater than in the last show. Perhaps it was just because of his new appreciation for the man playing the main character, but he enjoyed it immensely. So too did the surrounding crowd, save for a few onlookers commenting snidely after it ended.

"Like expected, the Crown forces poor actors to indoctrinate and tell their twisted fantasies," a woman said, not far up ahead from Gil. As she conversed with a man at her side, she exposed her face, where her left eye was missing.

"What'd you expect, Lady Presider? It's either this or performing at executions. Besides, having them perform here gives us opportunities to question the Crown's actions."

"I suppose you're right."

The couple followed the queue leading out from the square.

Gil lingered. Where else would he go? This way, he could follow the troupe to their next destination. One day, he would know the play by heart, and by then, no one would be able to ignore him.

~❖~

Over the coming days, Gil avoided standing out to the troupe. He refused to be known as the needy urchin using the group. So he hid in the shadows and the crowds. Each performance, he ensured the actors did not spot him, while soaking in every aspect of the play he could. From the slums of Keelheart to the merchant's district of Main Street, the troupe traveled. Performing, then packing their things and setting up for the next show. Some bakeries and shops would be charitable once Gil sang a quick tune for them, giving him food to survive each day.

Today, the troupe's horses pulled three carriages up the increasingly steep hill of Levent. On the trudge up the city, Gil glued his eyes on everything passing by. The houses became prettier the farther up Main Street he got. Here, the red facades had been smoothed, making the houses look soft and inviting. Markets filled with people and stalls displayed colorful garments that ladies and men bought.

Up ahead, where rough cliffs rose above the street, separating Riverview from the rest of the city, the caravan halted. Guards inspected the troupe, and Gil took shelter behind a large birch tree. Below him, the city lay at his feet. Everything was so little. Houses, streets, and people were small dots in the distance. But the strangest sight had to be the glistening lake beyond the city's walls—and the ships. How could ships as big as those look so small? He put his thumb in front of the lake, and an entire ship disappeared behind it. Beyond the lake, a vast green landscape stretched in every direction. At the edge of it, the Rugged Spines rose into the blue sky miles away.

The caravan moved and entered the upper city and its beautiful mansions, large as ships. He counted five, six, and even seven stories tall, white buildings grasping onto the cliff above. Compared to the rest of the city, the district seemed to be covered with flowers and trees.

Gil moved to the guards to gain entrance. As expected, the men stepped in front of Gil, blocking his path. "Where do you think you're going, urchin?"

"I am no urchin. I work with the Shields of the Moon."

"Nice try. Head off before you get hurt."

Gil grunted. "You're going to beat me?"

The men exchanged glances, their helmets probably boiling their heads in the intense sunshine. "We do not hurt children. Trust us, it's for your own good we won't let you in. There're lords and ladies in there who won't let you wander around."

"But I'm a performer. Listen!" Gil sang: "Wherever the Keeper goes, the Nightbringers her foes, she shall strike them down with a vow."

"Boy, you're not getting past us," the pair interrupted with a sigh.

Gil turned his heel and proceeded to a patch of grass nearby to sit. "Fine! If I can't go there, then I'll wait until they're back."

A day and a half, he waited. The sole entertainment source came whenever a carriage of thralls entered Riverview in the morning and left at dusk. The guards switched shifts, and every attempt Gil made to pass failed. The guards stationed in front of a giant gate were nothing like the ruffians patrolling the lower districts' streets. They were always polite and never threatened with a beating. They even let Gil stay nearby, in the shelter of a tiny natural cave burrowed into the high cliffs.

It fascinated him how the bells of Riverview rang, and the city answered its mother's call. Finally, the troupe's colorful caravan left the upper district and hurried to the less busy streets of Westview, where middle-class citizens lived in the shadow of Riverview and the giant building called the Precedents' Court.

Following at a distance became increasingly hard for the spent boy. His stomach growled loudly, making him keel over to hush its complaints. The troupe traveled in vast hues of blues and reds, though, so they were quite hard to misplace.

The usual routine commenced by another district square. The builders raised wooden beams and tied the canvas with their sigil on it. This time, Gil saw little purpose in hiding from the troupe. He approached a hay bale and lay down to rest his eyes for a bit.

Actors stepped in and out of the wagons. They rehearsed, it seemed. Quite strange, since they performed each and every night. But it looked like one of them was adamant about rehearsing. At first, Gil had not given the woman nearby a second glance. Her coal-dark hair contrasted finely against her pale skin. She muttered something to herself through her puffy lips. "Then let it be known, the brave hero shall find my embrace and . . ." she said louder.

Gil scratched his scalp, correcting every line in his head.

". . .and I shall . . . love you? What's the line?" She slapped her high forehead.

"Then let it be known, the brave hero who sacrificed all shall find my embrace. For there is nothing greater than family I can offer you. As the Unborn protected you and I from sickness and death, we shall carry out her wishes," Gil called out.

The people standing nearby fell silent. Gil felt eyes on him but refused to let it turn him away. He had gotten their attention.

"Looks like you've got an admirer, Zahna," the chiseled gentleman playing Lionel said as he dressed.

The lady known as Zahna gave them a gentle smile and strolled over to Gil.

"You've seen our performance more than once?" Zahna tugged at her earlobe, where silver earrings dangled and chimed.

"A couple." Gil rolled his shoulders.

"Then you know the king's response?"

"'I pray the Almighty bless your Enfolding, as I have. You shall hereby be named Lord Lionel Riveroak.' Then Canden approaches Lionel and presents him with a sword," Gil said.

Zahna gathered her wavy hair and tied it into a ponytail, and chuckled. "Can you read?"

"I can certainly try." Gil winked.

"Seems as though the Wanderer has led you to us. It so happens that our script-reader has lost her voice. What do you say to fill in for her for a couple of days?"

By the Almighty, say yes! Gil's thoughts shouted at him. This was his chance to prove himself. It was a way in. But he could not let his joy get the better of him. To get the excitement out of his body, he pulled and tugged at his filthy trousers. "That's an interesting offer. Though I feel it lacks something."

"A bed to sleep in and food?"

Gil grinned. "When do we start?"

"Right now. My name is Zahna."

"Gil. It's an honor to meet you."

Chapter Four

In the Ancestors' Shadows

The Ancestors' Walk sent shudders along Aiden's spine. He could walk among the massive and detailed statues hundreds of times, and the feeling would remain. Kings, queens, and generals peered down at the visitors along their cheekbones, reminding everyone of their greatness.

At the bottom of their gray pedestals, bouquets decorated most of the walkway. Some statues stood alone, their memory tainted or forgotten. Although Emilia Riveroak chose to observe the favored statues, Aiden read the bronze plaques of the forgotten. It was a walk through history and time. Reading about them would never cease to amaze him, but standing before them felt different, greater.

His mother had decided to visit the Walk with Aiden despite his protests to leave Nyle. However, strolling through the memorial and tribute, he nearly forgot his earlier reluctance. His grandfather, Lord Heathon Riveroak, peered at his daughter and grandson when they placed a violet bouquet beneath him. By his side stood his sister, Queen Layla Thorne, the current king's mother. Her plaque read, *Queen Layla Thorne of Vesilia. Reigning year 363 to 366. Died during childbirth.*

"Was she your aunt then?" Aiden asked his mother as she lingered by the statue.

With weaved hands, she turned her torso elegantly. "Yes. She was my aunt. Our king, Canden Thorne, and his brother Serril Thorne are her children. That makes you and the prince and princess second cousins."

"Have I met them?"

"Definitely—a few years ago, when you were Eamon's age." She swayed back toward their mounts and the thralls. Jarred stood dressed in Liam's refitted guard's uniform. Dark armor, almost black, wrapped around his torso with the Riveroak sigil hammered into it. The sigil was a midnight blue oak tree standing in the middle of a river. Jarred's dark brow glistened, yet Jarred did all in his power not to show his discomfort in the scorching heat. Aiden could barely stand it himself, and yet he only wore his usual set of embroidered tunic and gray pants.

"Serril has no children. If somehow the Thornes would . . ." Emilia paused and hushed her voice some. ". . . meet a tragic end, that means you will become king of Vesilia."

Woah . . . me? King? Aiden thought, his eyebrows touching by his frown. On reflex, his teeth bit the inside of his lower lip to figure out what that meant. After some thought, Aiden reached for his spotted pony and its reins. "Why do you not become queen first, and father king?"

"Your dear father was not born a Riveroak. As for me, no one desires to see a tired old lady ruling. Therefore, I would pass the crown onto you."

Jarred assisted Emilia onto her brown horse's saddle.

"Do you think something bad will happen to them? Even to the prince and princess?" Aiden asked.

"By the Almighty, no. But in such an event, we must stand prepared to do what we must. An unprepared king is a manipulated king."

Adventure, his mare, took a couple of hesitant steps forward at Aiden's command. "But is that not why King Canden has father as an advisor?"

"All rulers and people of higher status need advisors, dear son." Emilia steered her horse down the main road of Thorne's Town. Trinkle and splashes emanated from the fast-flowing river dividing the town into two parts, west and east. The Riveroak estate, with its orange roof and grey bricks, stood on the northwestern hills. Behind them, straight beneath the steep mountains surrounding the valley, the Thornes' mansion lay. Aiden thought his home held thousands of flowers and bushes, but it withered with shame compared to the Thornes'. Whenever Lionel met with the king, he returned home with endless improvements for their estate. Not that Aiden complained, seeing as it provided him with large bookshelves filled with stories.

～❀～

A frog breathed fast in Nyle's grasp. Its chest compressed and expanded while gazing past Nyle's fingers. Black and red stripes marked its damp skin.

They approached a stream where reeds grew thick and tall. This would be a perfect home for a frog. Together, they unmounted Adventure and let the mare munch on nearby grass next to the broad road leading through Thorne's Town.

"Why do you think she found her way all up the hill?" Nyle asked Aiden.

"Maybe a bird took her and dropped her?" Aiden shrugged. "Birds are stupid sometimes, when they fly into windows and stuff."

Nyle giggled.

Pebbles crunched beneath the shoes of people passing by. Judgmental glares came from nobles when they saw Aiden and Nyle kneel in the river's muddier part. A young lord and his thrall, playing together as equals, was not a common occurrence from what Aiden could tell.

Nyle placed his hand among the reeds and unfurled his fingers. But instead of hopping off into the wild, the frog sat still, questioning where it was. Aiden poked its butt, yet no reaction.

"I think she likes me," Nyle smiled, revealing the gaps in his teeth, the same that Aiden himself had.

"I think so too. Maybe she wants to stay with you?"

"We can keep her." Just as Nyle said that, she jumped away. Her long legs shot her high into the air and carried her into the shelter of the reeds.

"Or not . . ." Aiden muttered, disappointed.

On the way up the hill, Aiden let Adventure gallop. The wind caught her mane and whipped against Aiden's face. Behind him, Nyle held on tight, and through the clopping of the hooves, his laughter carried loud and clear.

They dashed past the gate leading into the estate. The guards, clad in the Riveroaks' usual blue and ebony armor, jumped out of their path. If Nyle thought it was fun to ride fast, Aiden knew he would enjoy jumping over hedges in the gardens.

Adventure followed Aiden's wishes and soared into the sky to clear a hedge. For a moment, they were flying, and his stomach tickled. Adventure snorted after each leap, and after a couple of jumps, she started getting worried. She came to a sudden halt, refusing to let them play around anymore.

"Aiden?"

Aiden heard his mother approaching. He gestured to Nyle to hide nearby and saw his friend throw himself into a gathering of bushes.

"Did I not tell you, no more fooling around?" Emilia delved her nails into his chin to make sure he looked up at her. "These animals are no toys, Aiden."

They stood together in the estate's gardens. Bushes as tall as Aiden blocked the sun, but only reached halfway up his mother. The sun illuminated Emilia clearly. The hooves of Aiden's spotted pony scraped against the gravel path he had followed.

The pony pulled against the reins in Emilia's grasp. "If you teach it bad behavior, you fall off the saddle and hit your head or get kicked. You control the horse. You do not play with it. Do you understand, son?"

Aiden wiggled in her grasp. "Father plays with his horse and rides really fast all the time. I was fighting the mountain monsters."

Her nails left chinks in his chin as she let go of him. "By the Almighty, Aiden. If this is another game you and that thrall play, you stop it right now. You are a lord. Not some half-witted peasant."

She tugged Adventure to move. "Now, where is the boy you played with?"

"I played alone, Mother."

"You are as terrible a liar as you are a Lord. Step out now, thrall," she snarled at the surrounding bushes.

The gravel crunched with Nyle's obedient approach. His brown curls lit up as the sun shone upon him. "Yes, my Lady?"

"Were you playing with my son?"

Aiden shook his head to Nyle and mouthed to him to be quiet behind his mother's back. Nyle looked at both of them and folded his hands in front of him. "I was searching for some apples for dessert later tonight, my lady."

"Then why are you in the garden when the apples are outside the kitchen?"

Aiden stepped up beside his friend. "Mother, we picked apples together. I helped him, and he was done with work for today, so we started playing. We found a frog, and we brought it to the river. I thought that was fine."

"Come," was all Emilia said as she nudged Adventure with her. Nyle and Aiden followed her obediently.

They traveled along the gravel path through neatly trimmed hedges and roses. Bees and flies buzzed. They passed the thralls' and servants' quarters, four one-story buildings in beige and gray stone. Behind stood the large Riveroak estate with towers and spires reaching high into the sky. The orange tiles of the roof twinkled in the sun after the heavy rain the day before.

"Do you want to play after supper?" Nyle whispered to Aiden.

"I'll take some apples from the kitchen and my wooden swords." Aiden snickered at his mother's ignorance.

Nyle gave a toothy grin, and Aiden returned it.

"Jarred," Aiden's mother called out once she reached the yard outside the thralls' quarters.

Jarred wiped the sweat off his glistening brow. "Yes, my lady?" He kept a firm gaze on her, completely ignoring Aiden's playful gestures of approaching monsters behind his mother's back. Unlike the day before, clad in the guard's outfit, Jarred wore his usual functional breeches and shirt.

"Aiden is no thrall," Emilia said, and handed Jarred the reins. "You better stop encouraging him from assisting servants and focus on helping him with his reading. You know I do not like to ask twice."

Jarred took a bow. "Of course, my lady. It will not happen again. I will ensure the thralls will stay out of the lord's way."

"Good. Secure the horse and bring me a whip," she said.

Jarred's brow wrinkled at her request. Still, he did as he was told and returned quickly without Adventure and with a whip in his hand.

Emilia handed Aiden the whip. "Punish the thrall and flog his back."

Aiden's hands gripped a tightly bound whip. The leather straps wrapping around the whip creaked by his touch. A couple of ropes sprouted from the stick, looking like a bear's claws, long and sharp.

"What do you mean?" Aiden gaped.

Jarred snatched Nyle's thin pale arm and dragged him to a boulder, right outside the thrall's quarters. Another thrall, a man, helped Jarred prop Nyle up against the boulder and held him in front of Aiden.

"But . . . Nyle is my friend," Aiden mumbled. Many months had passed since Aiden last witnessed his father whip a thrall. This reminded him too much of that day.

"He's a thrall, and he works for our family. He is not a friend."

"But Mother, I . . ."

Her teak eyes became the only thing he could see. They became like the sun, enormous and observing everything. She was tall and angry, just like the Nightbringers he knew lured in the Rugged Spines. It could not be his mother staring down at him.

"Go on, son," Emilia snarled, and nudged Aiden forward.

"Do I have to?" Aiden gulped.

"You have to learn to rule. Ruling requires a firm hand and discipline. Do not disappoint your father and me."

Aiden looked to his father, sitting on a fallen tree nearby, reading a book like he used to. He leafed through the pages while the paper-thin thrall Lacey sheltered Lionel from the scorching sun with a canopy.

"Aiden. Carry on, or I will be forced to punish you. I will lock you into the cellar," Emilia said in the background.

The cellar. One trip there was more than enough. A dark and quiet cage where Nightbringers tried to eat children . . . No part of him wanted to return there. But seeing Nyle bending over the boulder, waiting to be punished, scared him more.

Emilia grabbed Aiden's arm. "Fine, into the cellar . . ."

Aiden pulled away. There was no way he was going back there. Aiden unleashed the claw on Nyle. Nyle knew how it was in the cellar. He would understand.

At least, that was what Aiden hoped.

Every time the whip lashed over Nyle's back, a spray of blood followed. The strikes juddered up Aiden's arm, similar to how a horse's reins would jerk whenever he forced it into a gallop. Aiden did not count the lashes, but he heard every one of them crack the air. He listened to the onlooking thralls' distraught gasps with each strike. Yet whenever he looked their way, all of them nodded in agreement with what he was doing. Nyle deserved to be punished; that was what they all said whenever Aiden hesitated and let the tail of the whip hang loose at his side. His cheeks puffed, and his eyes grew hazy.

The whimpers leaving Nyle reminded Aiden of a suffering deer he had found with his father in the forest. It had lifted its head a few inches off the ground before slumping back down, exhausted. After each stroke of the whip, Nyle lost his footing, but Jarred and the other man kept him aloft.

"Did I tell you to stop?" Emilia jeered.

Aiden rubbed tears away with the edge of his sleeve. Everything within him begged to quit and leave Nyle be. But the commanding glare of his mother overshadowed his desires. Nothing else could be done other than finishing the deed and satisfying her.

An inky veil of darkness and shadow covered Thorne's Town once the sun disappeared behind the mountains' sharp peaks, which glowed in a golden shimmer. Hopefully, the frog they'd found was better off than Nyle. Although Nyle was down by the thralls' quarters, Aiden could still hear every whimper and scream leaving his friend, echoing within his mind.

The blood on Aiden's hands felt like it still stained him. He rubbed his fingers over his palm to rid himself from it, enough to peel the skin off and create a scrape wound. The pain was nothing compared to what his friend had suffered.

Once Nyle had passed out, Aiden followed his mother to the estate. She gave him words of comfort and encouragement, but nothing she said nudged the pile of guilt resting inside Aiden. To affirm his attention to his mother, he gave an occasional nod, but the hurt he caused Nyle was the thing that kept repeating itself to him. If this was what ruling, leadership, and lordship entailed, he would not take part in it.

Under a candle's light, Aiden desperately attempted to read. Dry pages scratched his crisp fingertips, and the words jittered in a jumbled mess. Again, he focused on the top of the page. *On that day, Leandra marched forth with the blessing of fifteen settlements. The unity of Vesilia would come to fruition at the dawn of the second day.*

"Aiden?"

By the doorpost, Aiden's parents studied him, dressed in nightgowns. Aiden put the book down to make space for them on the bed. Lionel's cane scraped against the hardwood flooring, and the bed caved beneath their weight.

"Are you upset?" Emilia uttered.

Aiden scratched the book's chunky bindings.

"Please understand, I never wished to upset you. Thralls are not appropriate to form bonds with."

"Why not?" Aiden mumbled, his focus resting on the book.

"They work for us and are paid to serve our needs. We are sorry you have not found other friends, suitable friends. You were the first to be born in Thorne's Town. Only now are the other families catching up. But you always have Lady Holden."

"You have told me not to play with her. And Liam has not returned. I tried to play with Eamon, but he is . . ." Aiden shrugged.

"He is much younger than you," Lionel said. "We understand. You need friends your own age. And friends who are appropriate for you to associate with. That is why your mother and I have decided you will attend Soldier's Discipline."

Aiden gaped at his father, who gave a small smile in return. "You need to learn to rule and lead. I learned much during my days as a soldier. But more importantly, you will learn to lead from the best. My dear friend, Captain Hutton."

"He will teach me to fight?" Aiden scooched closer to his parents, ignoring the book he read.

Lionel clicked his tongue. "I suppose he will, but he will start your path into becoming a general. You are destined for greatness, son. If the Thornes were to meet an . . . unfortunate end, you could become king. Even though that might not happen, and should not, you will carry our name and perhaps even become the Lord High General who sits on the King's Council. Captain Hutton will help you achieve this."

Emilia brushed her hands against the linens hugging Aiden. Everything Lionel said was followed with a slight nod from her.

"Jarred will be responsible for your safety and will accompany you to Camp Wintersmore every day," Lionel said. "He will teach you things a lord should know, and at the camp, Captain Hutton will teach you to become a general. There will be plenty of friends for you there."

"Does this feel fair?" Aiden's mother asked, and stroked his cheek. "All we want is for you to be happy."

Aiden scratched back at the aching wounds on his hands. Maybe they were right. They probably were. There was a reason for his parents being a lord and a lady. They worked hard to ensure they had all they did: the house, the estate, and their thralls. The thralls were there to work for them. Although it did not sit right with him, torturing other people, he understood the argument they made. Aiden was supposed to become a great lord. He had to trust his parents.

"Thank you. I will try to make you proud." Aiden embraced them both. They were there for him, and he had to be there for them.

✦

The sun heated Aiden's back. Pearls of sweat rolled from his neckline down his shirt that kissed his skin tight. The sun had only been up for a few hours, yet it was as hot as midday. Aiden tightened the reins in his hands to steer his spotted pony, Adventure, back onto the path. He'd sure picked a suitable name for the animal. At any opportunity, she veered off to stride the forest aimlessly in search of an adventure. Aiden could not blame her. He had half a mind to head into the rows of tall tree trunks himself and leave his father and Jarred behind. However, he was a bit curious to see what the camp they were heading toward had in store for him.

"Will I learn to fight?"

Lionel pulled the reins to slow his silver horse. He rotated in the saddle to look at Aiden. Pearls of sweat glistened over his high brow beneath the streaks of gray hair sprouting out. "You will learn to fight with the sword, with the spear, and with bow and string. More importantly, however, you'll learn to lead."

Adventure neighed at the command from Aiden, but stepped up next to the silver horse.

"What if I do not want to lead?"

"Those who wish to stay clear of it are the natural-born leaders, my boy. I never wished to see myself commanding others, giving orders, but I needed to step up to do what I was born to do. So will you."

"But I do not know anything about it."

"That is what education is for, son. Most receive education through life, like I did. Others, like your mother, study what they need to learn. Under Captain Hutton, you'll receive both. And with Jarred, who will teach you during your travels."

Jarred caught up with Aiden and leaned forward on his black stallion. "That's right, my lord. I will accompany you and ensure that the lessons you had with Sonya are maintained."

Instead of his usual clothes, a simple shirt and trousers, Jarred had on chainmail that rattled with his sways. Lionel wore the same, but with the Riveroak coat of arms decorating it, a large oak tree.

They stayed on the northwestern path that cut through a vast oak forest until, finally, a pillar of smoke rose to the sky. A wooden barricade encircled a hill in the middle of the grasslands that took form once the treeline stopped.

They moved closer to the camp.

"Who goes there?" a man shouted through the barricade.

"My name is Lord Lionel Riveroak. I bring my son, Lord Aiden Riveroak."

The gate flew open, and they mustered their mounts through.

Inside, the camp sat on a tiny hill. A large tree stood at the top. Around the base of the hill, there were thirty or so cream-white tents. Not many people were around from what they could see. But they heard some mutter and speech farther ahead.

Emerging from the shade of a tent's canopy, a surprisingly lanky, dark-skinned man with scars covering half his face stepped forward to meet them. Three distinctive claw marks etched a rough path from his brow to his strong chin. The scars almost testified to the Captain's tenacity and determination in battle.

"Welcome, welcome." When the gentleman spoke, a trimmed mustache bounced on his lip, looking quite comical.

He took a bow in front of Lionel and paused once he laid eyes on Aiden. "Green eyes, sharp features, chiseled jaw, and short ashen-brown hair. Ah, that's your boy if I ever saw one, Lionel. Though a bit younger and a lot more handsome. Girls must be throwing themselves at your feet, boy."

"If they did, the poor kid would not even notice," Lionel said, and dismounted his mare. "That's for the best, I assume. Captain."

Lionel leaned on his cane once he found his footing and took a gentle bow to the captain, who did the same. Aiden remained in his saddle.

Two older boys threw a quick gaze their way but returned to a nearby tent just as hastily. When the canvas separated, it revealed an area where rows of benches lined up together. Other men sat inside, dining, it seemed. The smell of cheese, bread, and butter lay heavy in the air.

"Come, my lord," Jarred instructed Aiden. He gathered the reins of their horses and tied them up to a post.

"Lord Aiden Riveroak. It is a pleasure to meet you." The captain smiled down at Aiden once he got off Adventure's back.

Aiden took a bow. "Thank you for taking me in, Captain."

"It ought to be me thanking you." The captain laughed and patted Aiden on the back. "A Riveroak serving by my side once more, I didn't think I'd see the day. Yet here we are."

"This is Aiden's thrall. He will act as Aiden's escort."

"Ah, that." Captain Hutton's face wrinkled, and his thin lips parted, exposing the lack of two front teeth. "I mean no offense, but is it possible to keep the lad here? All this back and forth may not be the most secure."

Lionel leaned on the cane even more and drummed his fingers on it. "You're most welcome to explain this to my lady. She needs to keep her eyes on the boy. Ever since our oldest passed, she . . ."

"Understandable. Alas, no need to worry. In a few weeks, this lad will best even the strongest. Lionel, please make yourself comfortable, and I'll show Aiden around." The captain led the way for Aiden. They closed in on the encampment while his father stayed behind.

Rows of triangle-shaped canopies welcomed Aiden. He rushed in under a canvas stretching over one of them to catch a break from the terrible sun. The captain seemed to be drenched in sweat, but he did not let it show to the men hiding in the shade. Instead, he walked, back straightened and head held high, just like Emilia would.

Hutton separated the white cloth and let Aiden take a glimpse into the dining area. "Here's where you'll feast. Make sure to be especially kind to Rosa; she prepares the best food. Be careful, though—she doesn't enjoy smartmouthing."

Men of all ages, young and old, peered up from their plates and bowed their heads at the sight of their captain. A couple of them uttered his name before they returned to dining.

The youngest ones had to be at least five years older than Aiden. Nearly all of them had stubble or beards of different lengths on their chins and cheeks. At the sight of Aiden, some of them raised an eyebrow. Aiden cowered by the captain's side as he continued to show the camp.

"This is my tent, and the smaller ones around here are the ones for the soldiers."

At the captain's belt, a sword's pommel twinkled in silver. The hilt was wrapped with leather, and the crossbar seemed to be silver or iron as well.

"You like swords?"

Aiden bumped his head enthusiastically.

"You'll get one in time. Perhaps even your lord father will hand you the one the king bestowed on him."

The one above the mantelpiece? Aiden thought. A vision of the outstretched blade with a curved crossguard, bejeweled in rubies, flashed before his eyes. He loved to study it where it decorated his father's library while listening to the thralls' tales of the hero of Riverview.

"And here is where you'll learn to handle weapons. You'll train each day with a practice dummy."

"A doll, Captain?" Aiden scoffed. Months spent in front of a practice dummy Liam had assembled a year or two ago, had been dull enough to fight. He held no desire to digress.

An open area where years of feet had stomped the ground stretched out before him. It looked nothing like a battleground, not anything Aiden had envisioned.

"Don't underestimate it. They won't hit back, but they're the opponents you have to face. Meanwhile, you'll see me work with the others. Pay close attention to that, and it might go fast for you."

Aiden sighed.

"Actually," the captain said, and marched into the trampled field where a casket with wooden sticks stood. He withdrew a stick and held it out to Aiden. "How about we start right now, little lord?"

Aiden's fingers wrapped around the stick. He had the advantage. With a flick of his wrist, he whipped the captain in the side with the stick.

Hutton grinned and took a step back, holding a stick in his hands. "Very well. Disarm me."

Aiden kept his guard. The weapon near his body protected him from any incoming attacks, just like Liam had taught him. He lined up sideways and kept a firm eye on the captain, who, for some reason, stood casually with his guard down.

Aiden flinched, causing the captain to react, but the boy switched his balance to his left foot and lunged the stick straight at him. Hutton parried the incoming blow, and Aiden surged forward, releasing the grip of the stick. He slammed a fist into the captain's side and lunged at him, incapacitating what defense his opponent had.

Hutton grunted in surprise and grabbed Aiden's wrists to make him stop. "Easy there, soldier," he huffed. "Seems like I did the underestimating here. Come."

The sticks stayed abandoned in the dirt. Upon reaching Lionel, sitting on a tree stump, Hutton gave a loud laugh, resonating from his stomach. "You sly Nightbringer you, Lionel. Why didn't you tell me about the boy's talents?"

Confusion riddled Lionel's face, and then the captain's as well.

"Who taught you that?" the captain said.

Aiden shrugged. "Liam and I have been practicing in secret." At the realization of his words, Aiden corrected himself. "I did. Not anymore, Father."

Lionel parted his lips to speak, but Hutton beat him to it.

"Whoever taught him . . . I wouldn't recommend the conventional approach, Lord Riveroak. With your permission, of course, I will teach him a more roguish method. A boy with this talent does not appear often. The sucker who chopped your ear . . . your boy has that in him."

What little was left of Lionel's ear caught Aiden's attention. A couple of uneven bulges rose from the dark hole at the side of the skull. Aiden realized how it might have happened— a knife could have easily slipped past his father's defense and sliced it off. Was the captain saying that Aiden was capable of that sort of cheap fighting, the kind of style Lionel despised?

Lionel rubbed his fingers against his beard like he used to when in deep thought. His eyes traveled from Aiden to the captain and back several times before he finally spoke. "As long as he learns leadership, I cannot see a reason why not."

"Please, have a bite to eat, and I will get started. Aiden, let me introduce you to the other boys," Hutton said. Aiden smiled at the invitation.

CHAPTER FIVE

Awakening

The sun stood high in the bright blue sky, but unlike on other days, Jaida sat together with her daughters underneath the sanctuary's giant oak tree in the middle of the Halls. Miya played with fallen sticks while Leah rocked back and forth with anticipation. Ida stepped out again from the shade of the building. She wiped sweat off her brow and knelt to Leah.

"It's your Soleday today, Leah."

Leah smiled at her mother.

"Happy Soleday, sweetie."

Leah took off her foot bracelet and gave it to Ida, who hurried back into the Halls to replace the old with the new. Not that it was necessary. Not really. Leah made sure to always protect the leather from cuts. She wanted it to stay as pretty as the day she first got it.

"What's a soulday, Mother?" Miya asked as she pressed two sticks tight together.

"You silly. You know what a Soleday is." Jaida's hand ruffled Miya's bright hair. "It's Leah's Soleday, the day when she began walking with the Wanderer, five years ago."

"Is Leah only five years?"

"No," Jaida chuckled. "Do you remember what five plus four is,

Miya?"

Miya looked away.

Leah broke the stick she was holding into pieces and counted them. "See . . . five sticks. Then comes . . .?"

"Six?"

Leah smiled. "Yes, then seven. . . then . . .?"

"Two."

"Eight. Four years the Unborn protected me. Then the Wanderer began protecting me. So I'm nine years old, but only a wanderer for five years." Her words flew over Miya's head, which didn't surprise Leah.

Sitting without the anklet was odd to her. She felt naked, or like something was missing. Luckily, it would return to her once they engraved it.

Ida rejoined them and sat down in the uneven grass. She waved her fingers to Leah to bring her close. Leah extended her left foot.

Ida wrapped the leather strap around Leah's ankle and locked it tight. The brown leather shone brightly. "Thank you brave protector and walker among people. We wish that you continue to keep Leah safe and in your protection from the Beast and the shadows."

Ida and her mother pressed their hands gently against the anklet and uttered together, "Blessed be your walk by the Wanderer's side for another year."

Her eyes sparkled. The Wanderer had saved her before. It had reached out to protect her and her family, of that she felt sure.

"Where is the Wanderer?" Miya tilted her head. Her blueberry-shaped eyes dilated at the sight of Leah's new jewelry.

"The Wanderer could be anywhere." Ida gestured widely to the surroundings. "It walks among us, forever keeping a watchful eye on all of its children."

"But she doesn't fight the Beast?"

Jaida brushed against Miya as if she was trying to stop the girl from asking the question. "I'm sorry, Ida, I'm trying to teach her, but . . ."

Ida gave a dismissive wave of her hand. "No worries. You see, Miya, the Wanderer is one of the Almighty, but it doesn't have a body. So it's not a woman or a man. Sometimes the soul of the Wanderer steps into a person. The adventurer Keldra, she had the Wanderer's soul inside of her. The Wanderer used her body as a vessel."

Miya shrugged. "Is it in Leah now?"

"We don't know. It could be." Ida pinched Leah's cheek. "That's why we shouldn't turn strangers away if we meet them in the wild. If you say no to the Wanderer and don't help it with food or rest, bad things can happen. But the anklet is to help the Wanderer find its followers and kind-hearted souls. People without an anklet are usually shadow-walkers. Bad people who serve the Beast."

Miya picked up another twig to fool around with.

"Let's go home, girls. I have a surprise waiting for us," Jaida said, and thanked Ida before bringing them back to their home in the attic.

Leah rushed up the stairs to their room. Whatever the surprise was made her skip with joy all the way home from the Halls.

"Take a seat on the bed," Jaida said to Leah, who gazed at her mother. Jaida rustled Leah's wild red hair. "I've been working extra to make sure we could celebrate you, Leah."

Jaida unwrapped a pie that tinged the room with tempting strawberries. Crust hugged the dessert and kept it in place. Leah had seen pies in windows along Main Street but never tasted one. The three of them gaped at the enticing treat.

"Strawberry tart," Jaida said at the sight of their longing gaze.

"You've earned a treat, Leah, for your Soleday."

They cut the pie into smaller pieces and ate at the same time. Leah wanted more. Whatever it was that tasted so good and made her squeal with happiness had to return to her.

Leah risked another piece to make the happiness return. Together, they smiled and chuckled at their luck to be together and eat treats.

Many days passed. Their mother went to work downstairs fairly early and returned home late at night. Even if Ida and Jaida talked to Leah about not being afraid of the dark, she could not help but keep her eyes away from the darkest corners of the room when they were going to bed. She wanted to look strong for her sister, but sometimes it was difficult. They told stories about Nightbringers, the Beast's servants who tried to take souls away from the Wanderer. Whenever she looked into the dark a bit too long, her stomach twisted and made her turn away.

The days, however, were good. Sure, it could be boring some days. But most days, Miya and Leah found fun things to do.

"Where's my sister?" Leah said in a sing-songy voice, and tied her fingers together, sneaking back into the room. "Hmm . . . not in the corner. But what about the bed?"

Laughter burst from Miya. She huddled up in a ball as she tried to escape Leah's tickling. The giggle was infectious, revealing the gaps between Leah's teeth. It was the kind of laugh that, no matter what, did not stop.

"Where's Mother?" Leah said once they settled down.

Miya shrugged and attacked Leah with a surprise tickle.

A loud bang joined Miya's fall off the bed. Leah looked to her sister, who held onto her knee. Her lips quivered before tears burst from her big eyes. Blood wept from the wound. No matter how much Leah wiped the blood off her sister's skin, it kept coming. She knew her mother was working, but this was something she couldn't stop on her own.

Leah wrapped her arms around her sister and helped her down the steep stairs. They reached the back door into the rest of the house.

Leah hadn't set foot in there in a long time. They entered a large room filled with sofas, pillows, and tables. Candles and torches made the red clay of the house shine, like the blood on Miya's knee. The tables held bowls of fruit, wine, and cups.

A wave of heat hugged them as they stepped into the busy room. Ten or fifteen people sat together, kissing and hugging. Their mother's beautiful hair was nowhere near.

"By the Almighty, come here, child. Let me help." A woman, with silver hair reaching down her exposed back held, out her hand to Leah and Miya. Sitting alone at a bar she seemed to be enjoying a drink of some sort. Just like the other women and men, the woman dressed in loose-fitted clothing that exposed much of her bare chest and legs.

"Did you hit your knee on those awful stairs?" she asked, and placed Miya in her lap.

"We played, and she jumped off the bed and hit the floor," Leah said while holding Miya's hand. The people around them didn't seem to care. They kept on kissing and hugging. "Where's Mother?"

The silver-haired lady pressed a wet towel on Miya's knee. "She's . . . speaking with a man. She'll be back soon, I think. Your name is Leah, isn't it?"

Leah nodded.

"Jaida has spoken a lot about you two. Don't know if you remember me, but I'm Giana. Your mother works for me."

A couple of heavy thuds carried through the building.

"Do you want some fruit? We have apples, strawberries, and pears," Giana said, and pointed to the table where the adults gathered. Leah grabbed an apple and munched on it while Giana took care of Miya. Some of the couples stopped kissing, throwing a gaze at Leah, but quickly continued when the woman or man sitting next to them grabbed the other by the chin. Their kissing looked messy and wet, very different from what Jaida did when she kissed Miya and Leah on their foreheads.

"Can I work with you?" Leah bit through the ripe apple and grabbed Miya's hand again, to keep her safe.

Giana's patting of Miya's knee stopped. "Eh . . . Why are you asking? You're a child. You should have fun and play with your sister."

"I know, but . . . I wanna give Mother something. Something beautiful."

"You're a sweet soul, caring for your mother. But I swore to Jaida not to let you work here. Why don't you talk with Cidron Ross? He can always put you to work."

Leah's gaze lingered on the floor. Ross. That was the bad people her mother warned her about.

A curtain, separating the large room from connecting ones, slid to the side, and Jaida stepped through. She held a bald man by his hand, but upon seeing her daughters, she let go and rushed over to them.

"Girls, what did I say about coming here?" Jaida asked, and grabbed their hands.

"Miya hurt herself," Leah said.

Her mother paused and turned. "Oh . . . thank you, Giana."

"Did I do something wrong?" Leah asked.

"No, no, it was good that you got help." She pinched Leah's cheek. "Giana, can I come back in a minute?"

Giana straightened her loose-fitted blouse. "Take your time. Others can cover for you."

When evening fell, and cute little snorts and snores left Miya, Leah carved on a log her mother gave her. But she did just little enough for Jaida not to suspect Leah using the rusty knife alone. At the moment, she didn't know what it would become. Maybe a guard dog, the kind some city guards brought with them. Big and hairy with large teeth. Or it could be a horse. Not that she had seen many, but she knew how they looked.

Most of all, she liked the way the metal separated tiny slices of wood, which twisted in funny-looking curls. A pile of wood shavings gathered on the floor, which she hurried to gather and hide beneath her bed when the footsteps of her mother neared from the staircase.

They saw less of their mother each day. Leah learned it was useless to ask to help. The question always got the same answer. With a quick smile and a kiss, the question went ignored. However, Leah found out why Jaida worked so much when they got dressed for Miya's Awakening.

For the first time ever, the colorful and bright textiles from downstairs found their way to the attic with Giana. Bright violet skirts wrapped around Leah and Miya, while their mother wore a bright green skirt under a rope belt. Leah hugged the wool back. As they went to the ceremony, she nearly tripped all the way because she was determined to refuse to let her gaze leave the expensive clothing. Within the marketplace, Leah glared at anyone daring to bump into either of them right outside the Halls. Them disrespecting the hard work and money going into getting the beautiful skirts made Leah's skin crawl.

"Miya, are you ready for your Awakening?" Ida asked as she knelt in front of Miya, whose wild hair was tied into a bun.

Miya shielded herself behind Jaida and blushed.

"Silly, you know Ida," their mother laughed, followed by a cough. "You shouldn't be nervous."

"What . . . what if the Wanderer doesn't like me?" Miya sniveled.

Leah snuck a peek behind Jaida and grabbed Miya's hand. "The Unborn has to get her rest from keeping you safe. It's the Wanderer's turn to watch over you. It watches over me too."

Miya rolled her eyes teasingly and followed them into one of the gathering rooms, where an Enfolding was taking place. Leah held up her skirt and took a seat on the cool stone floor beside her mother. Miya followed Ida up the small stage.

Jaida dragged Leah close, and together they watched the ceremony begin. Ida and Miya faced the east, where the high city walls blocked the bright sun rays.

Ida gathered Miya's tiny hands in hers and spoke. "We thank you, Unborn, for the care, nourishment, and protection you have offered this child and all children of the world. You have kept Miya safe to offer her the gift of life. We are forever grateful for the kindness. Like mothers and fathers must let their young leave, so do you. We ask of you to release this soul from your watchful gaze and bring her into the realms of the Wanderer."

On a moss and lavender bed, Ida presented Miya with a leather anklet, which she tied around Miya's left foot—her first wanderer's foot link. Both her sister and mother beamed with pride.

"The one who wanders the realms, we bring our voices unto you. We beg for you to guide Miya on her journey through life. Protect this soul from the clutches of the corrupted, the wicked, and the foul. Once she departs, we pray you guide her as she walks the ground beside you."

Miya leaped over to her family and gave them a great hug. They were all wanderers now. Protected by it from the Beast and his minions. Leah didn't remember when she became a wanderer but . . . she thought Miya would look different or sound different. Nothing changed, however. She still had small baby teeth hidden behind her giant smile and the same cute giggle.

Miya showed off her foot link. Not a single scratch marked the smooth leather tied together by strings. Some sort of marks had been carved in, just like on Leah's and her mother's. It looked a little different. Jaida said it was called writing— a secret language that some people could understand.

"Thank you, Ida. Truly, I don't know what I'd do without you and your kindness," their mother said, but not with the same cheerful tone. Something quivered in her words.

Ida approached. The same gray robes she always wore swayed with her. "We do what we must, and do what we can. Your family deserves much more than what life has given you. I'm simply here to make it a bit more cheerful."

"And you do. You've saved us countless times."

Miya pulled Leah's focus with a poke to her stomach. She started a tickle fight, but Leah would not let her win. She chased her sister, who giggled loudly, almost enough to make her lose her breath. Meanwhile, Jaida and Ida talked before they gathered to leave the Halls.

"I need to head back. But let's get some food first."

They stopped underneath a merchant's stall, outside the Halls, with a green-and-white-striped canvas protecting the merchant from the heat. The large, hardened man greeted them with a toothless grin.

"How much does this give me?" Coins rattled in Jaida's hand.

The man clicked his tongue before mumbling, "Two slices, filled with lettuce, tomatoes, and fish."

"Very well, sir." The silver coins left her hand, and she received two giant slices of filled bread. Miya snatched one from her hand and munched on it.

Jaida gave Leah the other.

"Mother, you can eat mine." Leah pressed the crusty bread back, although it smelled and looked delicious.

"No, my dear. You eat that. You need all the food you can get, so you can grow strong."

But I don't work or do anything for you, Leah thought while twisting the bread in front of her mother. "But you look hungry."

And she really did. Usually, the hard parts of Jaida's soft face did not show, but now they did. Large, swollen lumps hung beneath her beautiful eyes and revealed the truth to everyone who wanted to see. She was tired.

Selene, the lady who gave Leah and Miya presents weeks earlier, approached them fast. Leah pulled at her mother's skirt to introduce them, but Selene was quick to speak. "Let me get that for you."

Selene paid the merchant and handed Jaida a third loaf of bread. Jaida accepted the stranger's gift with a faint smile, but it vanished as soon as Selene spoke. "I'm with the Rosses, and we'd love to help you, seeing as you can't feed all three of you. Your children can always—"

Jaida held up a finger, interrupting Selene. "Good for you, but like I've told Cidron, stay away from my daughters. I enjoy Cidron's company, but his practices are immoral, and he treats people like wares. We'll stay far from it."

Recognition dawned on Selene's face. Her mouth opened wide, and her eyes flickered. "Oh, you're one of Giana's girls. Yes, he's talked 'bout you. Of course, we'll respect your wishes. Sorry for bothering you, ma'am." Just like that, Selene returned to the Halls, leaving their family alone.

Jaida placed the bread given to her within her armpit and grabbed both daughters' hands, hurrying back home to once again leave Leah and Miya alone in the attic.

Panic struck deep in Zahna's eyes. Hopefully, the audience standing a good couple of feet away would not notice, though Gil did. Her already-pale skin drained of color, and the corners of her wide eyes twitched whenever the words accompanying her actions flew past her.

Gil mouthed the lines she'd misplaced with grand gestures beneath a little hide-out at the edge of the stage. These last days, the casket-sized space, concealing him from the audience, had felt larger than in reality. He was living his dream—well, close to it anyway.

"Then . . ." Zahna whispered, but immediately spoke clearer once the words came back to her. "As the Unborn protected us from sickness and death, we shall carry out her wishes."

Next, the actor playing Canden Thorne stepped up to Dorian, who performed as Lionel Riveroak. Dorian rendered Gil useless. Made him another set of admiring eyes of the many. Sure, all the actors and performers of the Shields of the Moon were spectacular and inspiring, but Dorian managed to steal the admiration from the others.

Zahna showed great compassion and kindness once Gil accepted their offer of joining. All fifteen performers shared space in four wagons. The others complained of the lack of space, but Zahna welcomed Gil into her part of the caravan. A sea of pillows, pleads, and blankets. Each night, she drifted off to sleep in a different position. For some reason, though, she ended up sleeping diagonally, putting her feet near Gil's face every now and then. Not that he could complain, or even would, for that matter.

Rain dribbled against the multicolored tarp Gil hid under. A bleak sky cast the yellow, green and blue colors on Gil's fingers as they moved along the neck of a spruce lute. Mere months earlier, he dared not believe he would hold an instrument in his hands. Yet here he was, sitting in one of the actors' caravans, listening to the rain and trying to imitate it. How the water dripped on the canvas and ground sang a tune to him—a merry yet somber tune.

> *"Round the forest-grounds it swelled,*
> *with quite the call it bawled to 'em,*
> *a warning for all to heed."*

He paused. Around him, the actors and performers huddled up in private discussions. Zahna, closest to him, received a waterskin from Dorian. Gil shot Dorian a quick gaze. Something was pulling his gaze in, similar to a siren's song. Gil had seen paintings where each brushstroke was refined and intentional. Dorian's face and toned body were just the same. Each line and sharp curve appeased every onlooker. Gil enjoyed observing the crowd's adoring, nearly mesmerized gaze once Dorian took the stage with a blue cape complementing his fallen-leaf skin. Or it could be his husky voice . . .

"Want some?" Dorian offered Gil a waterskin.

The lute came to rest in Gil's lap. An involuntary cough left him once an alarmingly bitter taste coated his tongue. Not wanting to

ruin the moment, Gil let the liquid heat his belly and ignored the body's request to throw up.

"So, your parents," Zahna kept interrogating Gil as she leaned closer.

Gil continued plucking strings, ignoring Zahna's and the other's advances.

"Come on, Gil. Everyone comes from some sort of messed-up background. Look no further than my parents, who were sent to Nedox because they joined Lord Haven's rebellion. Look at me now—I'm the actress portraying the Hero of Riverview's true love, and I mess up every show."

"You don't," Gil lied. Zahna gave him a meaningful raise of her slim eyebrows. "Fine. But I think that's because of the material. You don't believe the words. That means you can't remember them, right?"

Zahna wrapped her arm around Gil's neck and nestled him near her bosom, and rubbed his scalp where strings of the boy's natural blond hair started to show. "You're a smart one. Why didn't I figure that out?"

Gil wrestled his way out and pulled at the tiny stubs of hair. But it refused to bend to his will. The roots shot waves of pain around his scalp with each mighty yank he gave. "Can you just shave it off? I hate it."

Another performer wiggled across Zahna's collection of pillows and pulled out a sharp knife. "I can. If you want to?" Each word dragged with the man's speech.

"As the Beast you will." Zahna yanked the blade from the cross-eyed, long-haired bard, who collapsed head-first onto the floor of the caravan. "Hold still, Gil."

He did as requested. Her fingers traced along his scalp, and the blade followed. Outside the caravan, on the cobblestones of Stonelake, Gil's tiny strands of hair scattered in the rain.

"So, again. Your parents, who are or were they?" Zahna asked.

"I don't know," Gil shrugged.

"They're like mine who died fighting Canden's stupid war in Eckros?" Dorian chugged whatever drink he had.

"At least you know their names," Gil let slip. He drummed his fingers on the floor of the wagon.

"Ha! Pay up, Dorian." Zahna slapped Dorian across his shoulder. "Told you he had that look about him."

"Sorry, kid. This is as close to gambling we get. Please, continue." Coins rattled from one hand to the other. Dorian leaned up against a pole that was holding the canopy of the caravan in place.

"I don't know. Not much of a story, really," Gil said.

"Nonsense." Crow's feet appeared with Dorian's grin. "Everything is a story depending on how you present it."

They awaited Gil. An additional group of performers hidden from the rain in the caravan was buried in private conversations.

What will it harm if they know? Gil sighed. "What's there to tell? My parents probably couldn't afford to look after me. A poorhouse in River's Brook took me in, so I grew up there."

The shaving stopped, and the knife stowed away. A tug of his lips accompanied the touch of his shaved scalp. Finally, he looked presentable.

"Let me guess, the poorhouse tossed you out a few weeks ago," Zahna said.

"Pretty much."

"Sorry to hear that."

"We won't ditch you, Gil." Zahna nudged Gil's side. "We're a family, and you're part of it now, especially with that talent of yours."

His lips pulled apart to make room for a smile. If what Zahna said was true, everything he'd ever wanted was his. The rain did not feel as depressing any longer.

"You won't be an actor, but with a voice such as yours and the way you connect with instruments, let's just say we'll make good use of your talents. Won't we, Merry?" Dorian called out.

Merry, a scrawny and shaking bard, directed his attention to the three of them and gave a goofy, contorted smile. Gil met odd people around the city, but not as unusual as Merry. The man was frightened and intimidated even by a stray kitten. Once he got on stage, a completely different person wore his skin and surprised everyone as his powerful song reached far and wide. If spending time with Merry was what had to be done for Gil to achieve greatness, he would happily accept.

Gil had witnessed spectators who stayed after the performances and insisted on meeting the performers. After one performance up in Northrun, a young girl even approached Gil, asking him whatever questions she could about the play and the story. To hear that what he was doing impacted the girl's life spurred the fire burning in Gil. He was going to achieve greatness and make the world a better place, or more pleasant at the very least, no matter the cost. The people in the caravan would help him get there. They were his family.

CHAPTER SIX

A Sundown Greeting

"You should have seen it, Father. The captain is an artist. He says you were just as good and even better." Aiden bounced around Lionel's study, from the desk where his father sat, back to the mantle above which the sword Canden Thorne had given Lionel for his efforts in Riverview hung.

"There is truth with some exaggeration," Lionel said, and reclined into his stuffy chair. Compared to the last few months, he looked rested and fresh. The bags under his eyes were now tiny lumps. The way the quill scratched ink into the paper was swift and determined. Despite being occupied with his duties, he focused on Aiden throughout the boy's retelling of the previous day.

Aiden leaned up against the desk to ask his father. "Can I go back tomorrow?"

"If the weather allows it, of course you will."

The rain poured outside. Clouds concealed the surrounding mountains around Thorne's Town as they descended on the valley. Aiden sighed at the sight and focused again on his father.

"Father, can I live in the camp?"

"Oh . . ." Lionel paused and let the quill dip back down into the ink. "I'm merely taken aback, son. I thought you wanted to stay here."

"I—I still do."

"I wish I could oblige your request, but it is not possible. We need you here with us."

Aiden toyed with a curl of his ashen-brown hair, twirling it around his finger. "Why?"

"You are a lord. When I was a soldier, I did not have a family to return to. I barely had a home. But you live with us, and you are to become even more than a general. You will have a seat at the king's council as lord high general. That implies you can fight to protect yourself, yes. Still, it is also important you learn to lead, read, write, socialize with other nobles, and care for our family's interests and investments in the lands we own."

Aiden collapsed into an armchair, letting the pillows swallow him. "But, it sounds so dull."

Lionel gave a dry chuckle and applied the quill back on the paper. "Being alive usually is. We have our place and duties and family. Who are we to question what the Almighty has bestowed on us? Come, son, sit by my side."

Aiden sighed and pushed the chair from the large room's corner over to his father's desk, which stood by one of the tall arched windows. Lionel reordered the pillows of the chair to help Aiden see over the tabletop.

"You see here—" A slip of paper found its way to Aiden. "What do you think this is about?"

Honorable sir Freedale,

I, Lionel Riveroak, hereby acquisition the agreed-upon amount of forest and land in Kingsay. I trust in your abilities to acquire and secure the Riveroaks' interests in this matter and return to us once the deal is struck.

SINCERELY, LORD RIVEROAK.

"Acu . . . ?"

"Acquisition—it's a fancier word for saying buying."

"Why not say buying if it's easier?"

"Trust me, how one speaks and writes is crucial to nobles and merchants. It's what separates them from farmers and thralls. But the true master is he who speaks with both the rich and the poor."

The note stacked on top of a pile of papers. Lionel handed Aiden the quill and a new sheet of paper. "Here, write what I tell you."

Aiden leaned forward and bit his upper lip with concentration. The tip dipped into the black liquid.

Honorable Lord Supreme Judge Dahle,

I, Aiden Riveroak, the firstborn son of the hero of Riverview, ask for an audience in preparation for my coming of age, when I shall make Levent my homestead.

Sincerely, Lord Riveroak.

The ink slobbered each time Aiden stopped to think about the spelling. Once he'd completed it, the paper looked like a spotted pony. Lionel carefully explained each word and helped spell it correctly.

"Homestead? Are we moving to Levent?"

"You will. This is in preparation for such a time. Lord Dahle is the person to turn to; he knows the nooks and crooks of the capital." Lionel rubbed his chin. "A real pain in the arse, if you ask me."

Aiden snickered but was instantly reminded of what his father was saying. His parents had already made plans for him, and they would tear him away from his family. His father never seemed to like signing letters, attending meetings, and holding dinners. Why was he forcing it on Aiden? Especially now, when he'd begun to learn to fight and saw how good he was.

"I want to be a soldier like you, Father. I want to see the world and help people."

"You will."

"I want to see Drelorn and Eckros, maybe even Burrous."

"Drelorn is just the same as Vesilia. And Eckros, there's nothing left to see of that place."

"But I want to visit the Sea of a Thousand Swords. Is it true what the captain says, that there are a thousand swords there?"

"Yes. But did the captain explain why there are swords and how they ended up there?"

Aiden shrugged.

"I guess you're old enough." Lionel nudged away the things on his desk and rested his head in the palm of his hand. "Hutton and I were there twenty years ago, in a big, open field. It was beautiful, at first. Green mountains surrounded us for miles and miles. It was in a wheat field, golden streaks wherever you looked.

"The Vesilian troops arrived first. We were quick back then. Soon the Drelorn forces and the Burrousie showed. All the kingdoms wanted Eckros and their abundant lands, where food grew plenty and gems the size of my hand hid in their mountains.

"What you need to know is that the Eckrosie had been massacred by the Burrousie, who occupied their lands. We were in Eckros to lay claim to their land. The Burrousie army was depleted and ripe for the taking."

One of the thralls passed the open door to the study, but Aiden listened strictly to his father's story.

"Hutton and I were skilled. We sliced our way through the armies, staining the wheat with blood and viscera. But that's when the sky went dark from smoke and ash. No one thought about the Eckrosie. Burrous had taken everything from them. So a few Eckrosie surrounded the three armies and set fire to the fields. Five or six thousand people died. The fire was so hot that I had to remove my armor so it would not roast me alive.

"I don't know how I survived, not really, nor does Hutton. Together, we wandered across the burning fields for miles. Four entire days we walked back home. Has the captain told you this story? Has he told you about the Eckrosie refugees that are still out there?"

"No."

"Oh, he will. That's where the real battle is. Eckros does not exist anymore. They destroyed their own country and made Vesilia, Drelorn, and Burrous their home. They're trying to destroy Vesilia, mark my words. That is where you will excel, dear Aiden. You will put an end to the Eckrosie wherever they're hiding in our nation. The great wars are over. But I know you will become Lord High General and will put an end to those monsters from Eckros. That's why alliances such as the one with Lord Judge Dahle are important. He may be an arse, but he wants the Eckrosie destroyed as much as we do."

Aiden bit his nails in deep thought. "But . . . why are they dangerous?"

"Ten of them executed more than six thousand soldiers in one day. Think about what one of them is capable of."

For some reason, staying inside their mansion was not as bad as Aiden had thought. It felt safe sitting beside his father, listening to the rain drizzle outside.

"I did not mean to frighten you. You need to know," Lionel said, and placed a hand on Aiden.

"Will Eamon learn this too?"

"Yes, in a couple of years. His place is different, though. Once you become a general, Eamon will manage our lands and resources and what I am doing. He won't learn to fight."

Aiden smirked. Suddenly, their plans for him did not seem as dull as he had thought.

"My lords, supper is being served." Sonya bowed at the sight of them.

Lionel pushed out from the chair. Aiden provided him with his cane, leaning up against the fireplace. Together, they traveled down the stairs to join the others.

Candelabras on the dining table, the shelves underneath the paintings, and the ceiling helped light up the massive hall. Eamon sat on the floor with toys spread out. Their mother greeted Lionel and began speaking.

Toys carved out of wood were littered around Eamon. A couple that Aiden had once played with lay there. While the thralls served dinner, Aiden played along with his brother, ignoring their parents' dull discussions.

"What happened to Olivar's arm?" Aiden pointed at the toy soldier. One of his arms had been cut off.

"I dropped him," Eamon said, and grabbed Olivar.

The place where the shoulder connected with the rest of the body had been ripped off. Repairing it would be easy. "You know, I think we can make him feel better. Do you have his arm in your room?"

"No."

"Okay, tomorrow, we will go through the gardens and find him another arm."

Eamon nodded, and his bright curls bounced. "A better arm?"

"Yes! A sword-arm. We can give him an arm that's just a sword."

"Can we do it now?"

"After supper?" Aiden asked, peering toward the table.

The room smelled delicious. His peeking revealed an entire fish lying on a plate with dead eyes.

"Come sit with us, Eamon," their mother said when Eamon lingered.

"Not hungry," Eamon sighed. The figures tapped the floor with his play.

Her smile faded. "You need to eat something, son."

"No." Eamon snapped back at her.

"Please?"

Eamon sat still and ignored Emila until he hummed a tune and sang, "Mean, mean, mean, mother's hair smells like beans. She'll never be a pretty queen. She's busy being obscene."

The room went cold and silent. Within seconds, a winter's firm grip sealed the room.

"What did you say?" Every word dragged as Emilia spit them at Eamon. "Eamon, come here. What did you say to me?"

"I'm singing a song," Eamon said, looking up at their mother. But at the sight of Emilia's angry eyes, he shrank to a little ball.

Emilia sighed and raised her hand above her head. The slap echoed through the hall, and the thralls momentarily stopped their duties. Jarred placed silverware next to Aiden.

Eamon's face blazed red, and his eyes pleaded to Aiden. But he was old enough to understand and learn not to upset their mother or father. With each whimper his brother gave, Aiden's stomach churned. Even though Nyle's pleas had been much louder, Aiden could not help but remember the day he'd punished Nyle.

Aiden averted his gaze to the fish and the thralls cutting into its flesh to serve them supper.

❧

"Don't tell your father I'm teaching you this," Captain Hutton mumbled under his breath while Aiden manipulated metal components within a lock. The metal slipped in his sweaty palms.

"I believe this will come in handy when you find yourself in a pickle."

The sun hid behind smudged clouds, though the heat was great still. A nearby clash of dull blades interrupted their conversation. The camp's other soldiers parried, advanced, and practiced while Hutton kept an eye on them from beneath a lone oak tree's shade.

Weeks had passed quickly in the captain's company. Although Aiden held hopes of befriending other soldiers his age, he remained unsuccessful. Most of the people staying at the encampment looked much older, given their facial hair and tall, bulky bodies. Perhaps it was for the best. Each journey home, Aiden's mind cluttered with information from the day. Not that he complained. Learning to fight and pick locks, and listening to Hutton lead, gave more to him than any short-lived friendship. Even though no one would agree, Aiden could not help but see Hutton as a new friend.

"Why does my father not approve of this?" Aiden asked. The lockpick slipped back into the lock.

"Cheating mostly, or that's what he'd say." The captain took to his feet and bellowed at the soldiers. His mustache gave a disoriented quiver on top of his lips. "Bron! Did I tell you to quit?"

"No, sir," a large, bulky youngster replied.

With the captain's yell, Aiden noticed again the two front teeth missing. The physical imperfection could have changed his authoritative voice but only added to it. It symbolized the sacrifices he had made for the kingdom, just like Lionel had.

"Then, by the Almighty, get back to it, or I'll send you to Nedox and the Beast's Gate for utter laziness. You wanna spend time there?"

The lock clicked, and the hasp opened. Aiden displayed it to the captain, a broad grin plastered on his lips. Hutton reclined to the stem of the tree and crossed his arms. "Again."

Aiden rolled his eyes and drew a deep breath to protest. Upon seeing Captain Hutton's determined gaze, Aiden shut the lock to start over.

"You'll thank me one day. You learn to pick a warded lock like this one, you can pretty much open all of them. The issue lies in whether or not you've got a lockpick to match it."

Hutton leaned in closer and plucked the lockpick from Aiden. He fiddled and teased Aiden with it. "What happens if you lack the tools? What if someone took it from you?"

Aiden shrugged.

"Well, go find something to improvise with," the captain said.

Something he could bend but was hardy enough to pick a lock with . . . Aiden scoured the camp. In tents, beneath trees, in beds. The kitchen tent turned up the most results. Metal of different kinds, such as dining ware, entered a pile in his hand that he brought back to the captain. On his way back, a barrel obstructed the path. Nailheads protruded from the gnarly wood. He pulled one and managed to wrench it free before he returned.

"Pick the lock with one of those."

The pile shrank and created a stack nearby instead. Neither spoons nor twigs worked. The nail, on the other hand . . . Aiden put the nail beneath a stone and stepped on it with his boots while pulling the head upward with all his might. The metal bent, and shortly after, the lock clicked open.

The captain lifted an eyebrow. "Alright. Whenever you have time on your hands, make sure you have a lock in your hand and learn all its secrets, little lord. Like with everything else, practice is key. But what would've happened if you were locked up and didn't have access to any tools?"

Aiden bit his lip, trying his best to come up with an answer.

"Could you hide a lockpick somewhere, perhaps?" Captain Hutton glanced at Aiden's boots and handed him the proper pick from earlier. It wound up wedged between the sock and the shoe's bottom. Unsurprisingly, it chewed the soles of his feet like a dozen stones taunting him.

"There're tricks you pick up through life. I am pleased to have someone to pass them on to." The smile on Hutton's face faded fast. "Not everyone had your father's fortune finding a lady as great as your mother."

Aiden could not help but agree. His father was fortunate. Or maybe it was simply his time to be awarded for the hardships he endured during the war and the Leventie uprising. Years of walking in the shadow of the Beast paid off once the Wanderer and the Unborn protected Lionel. Aiden's father decided not to die or slip into the Beast's domain. He rose up to become the hero of Riverview. He deserved some fortune.

"Captain, did you find a partner?" Aiden hesitated to ask, but did anyway.

The lord looked at the boys and men fighting in the roaring heat. "I did, though it lasted but a few months. I will not blame the Almighty for her passing, though I believe the Unborn turned her gaze from us for but a moment."

"I am sorry for your loss, my Lord," Aiden replied.

"As am I. She was a wonderful woman to the very end. Taught me the value of protecting those who cannot stand up for themselves. Fighting is easy. Protecting is where hardship lies." The captain combed wisps of brown hair from his scarred face. "Come, little lord. Time to work on that maneuver of yours."

Another day at camp Wintersmore passed. Jarred and Aiden ventured along a forest trail back to Thorne's Town. Jarred kept a watchful eye on the thick growth of oak and beech stems while Aiden fiddled with a lock in his pocket. Their mounts trotted along the trail as the evening grew late, and the sun began its descent.

A stream nearby caught Aiden's attention as the dribble teased his bladder. He pulled the reins of Adventure to dismount. "I need to take a tinkle," Aiden explained to Jarred, who gathered the reins of both horses.

"As you wish, my lord."

The forest welcomed him. Robins and swallows chirped nearby, and the gurgling caw of a raven disrupted the calm. He followed the stream calling to him and let Jarred and the horses disappear behind a hill.

After taking a leak, his dry mouth reminded him of the water nearby. A reflecting pool of tranquil water swallowed the hues of green leaves, suspended above the forest floor, deceiving him into believing the forest expanded way beyond the ground and sky. The steady, happy chirps of robins and swallows continued singing as Aiden touched the water's surface. The water chilled his fingers and froze his parched gullet. Heavy gulps accompanied each sip of the mossy, yet refreshing water. The horses knickered back by the trail.

Ripples disturbed the surface with his touch and radiated farther into the brook, where they met another set. Aiden traced the ripples with his eyes until they came upon the opposite side of the round creek. Another hand disrupted the pond.

The small warm-white hand belonged to a girl with bushy hair, similar to the forest's wild bushes, but black as the darkest night. Her unkept tangled hair cascaded down to her shoulders, framing her round, smooth face that crinkled up into a welcoming smile. The locks had a life of their own, bouncing and swaying with her every curious tilt and move. She looked like any other girl, but there was something special about how she looked at him.

Aiden focused on her and gave a silent wave her way. "Hi."

She dried herself off on a simple dress made of linen, looking like thralls back home.

"Who are you?" Aiden asked.

She leaned closer to the water, using the reflection to gaze at him. "Ayla."

He muttered her name to make it flow naturally. Given her lack of a last name, she might be a commoner or, at the most, a merchant's daughter. Surnames were only of importance to those who could use them.

The water splashed with her sudden disturbance. The surface swallowed her ankles and moved to accompany her trudge closer to Aiden. Jarred was only a shout away, but something about Ayla calmed Aiden. Perhaps it was her slowing approach once she noticed him drawing away, or maybe it was the constant smile lingering on her lips.

"Ayla." She placed a hand on her chest. "Means . . . giving."

A cluster of blueberries rested in the palm of her hand she offered to him. A dry chuckle escaped him, but he accepted her gift.

"What your . . . meaning?" Ayla sat next to him in the moss, nearly sliding into the brook.

Meaning?

Again, she placed a hand on her chest. "Ayla."

"Oh, my name is Aiden Riveroak." His family name gave him a straighter back as he uttered it proudly to the stranger.

"Aiden means?"

Aiden's brow furrowed. She did not give the proper respect his name merited. No one, save for his family, used his first name, especially not a stranger. Yet this did not faze her, for she sat patiently waiting for an answer with her hands on her knees.

"I do not know. I am a lord."

"Of what?"

"Of . . . of my family."

"Why?"

"Well, I—because my mother and father are noble."

"But who are you?"

"I told you. I'm Aiden Riveroak," Aiden repeated. Her misunderstanding should have disturbed him. However, connecting with her captivating, jewel-like hazel eyes, flecked with golden strings, scrambled his critical thoughts telling him to be upset. Aiden drew his lower lip between his teeth to hide his wacky lips from losing control.

"You choose name?" Ayla said after a lingering silence. "You choose, Aiden?"

Aiden shook his head.

"You don't change it?"

"Why would I?" he asked. "Can I?"

Ayla flashed her aligned teeth with a wide smile. Her golden, freckled cheeks filled with color. "I chose Ayla. Means giving. I like the word. Do you like your name?"

Aiden scratched his head. "I have not thought about it. But can you choose any word and have it as your name? Ayla is not a word I have heard of before."

"*Oayla Aiden siemru.*" Every word flowed beautifully past her lips. Whatever she said, it sounded like the song of a robin, gentle and soft.

Upon seeing Aiden's wide gape, she giggled. "*Oayla* means 'I give.' Aiden, that is Aiden. *Siemru* means 'berries.' I give you berries."

"What language is that?"

"Eckrosie."

His lungs turned icy with panic, and his fingers dug deep furrows in the moss. He shrank back in fear, keeping a close eye on the surrounding trees, which became tall, dark figures staring at him. Eckrosie. *Think about what one of them can do*, his father's voice echoed in his mind. Jarred was nearby. A quick shout and safety would arrive.

"Jarred!" Aiden shouted, pushing past dryness consuming his throat.

The thrall appeared over the rise concealing Aiden from the path. "My lord?" Jarred's call carried through the forest along with the cold ring of a sword leaving its sheath.

Despite Aiden crawling to Jarred, who stood at the ready to protect his lord, Ayla remained. The smile disappeared, replaced by a sad grin as she looked at the sharp sword.

"Are you hurt, my lord?" Jarred pressed Aiden, who hid behind his tall figure, using it as a shield.

"No, I . . . she's Eckrosie," Aiden stammered.

The sword in Jarred's hand lowered. "Did you come alone?"

Her dark curls bounced with her nod. "I am Eckrosie, but I do not wanting to hurt Aiden."

"That is alright. We will not harm you. What is your name?" Jarred secured the sword in his belt and approached Ayla. The fear that had struck Aiden subsided to make room for the confusion taking hold of him.

"Ayla."

"Nice to meet you, Ayla."

"What are you doing, Jarred?" Aiden muttered under his breath. "She's dangerous."

Jarred knelt between them and looked Aiden straight in the eye. "Was she dangerous before she revealed she was an Eckrosie, my Lord?"

"I do not think so. She gave me blueberries," Aiden said, displaying the now-squished mess in his hand. "But Eckrosie are dangerous and evil."

"My lord, I know your family has been telling you as much, but consider it. Vesilia, Burrous, and Drelorn eradicated their people. They are the ones without a homeland."

"That is why they want to kill us to get revenge."

"Does a wounded deer seek vengeance against the wolf, my lord? They wish to survive. It was our fault they came to our country, yet we decided to treat them like rats. I understand your lord father's disposition to the Eckrosie after the horror he suffered in Eckros, but have you heard of Eckrosie being behind a single bad thing since then? The uprising in Levent had nothing to do with the Eckrosie. Vesilian uprisers harmed your father."

Aiden looked over to the girl. She looked nothing like he'd thought an Eckrosie would. An average human without sharp teeth or an evil stare. She was just like him, a child looking for a friend. But at the same time as the thrall's words spoke some sense . . . he could not ignore the tales from his father.

"Give it some thought, my lord." Jarred returned to the horses and the nearby path.

"I am sorry," Ayla whispered to Aiden. "I see you pass, and you look lonely, like me."

Aiden sat back down near her. "How do you speak Vesilian?"

"My family teach me. My sister lives in Levent and acts. We must speak with you and others, not always live in the forest."

"Your family lives in the forest?"

Ayla nodded.

"But why are you here, now?"

"I . . ." She seemed to search for words. "Look for food. Berries for food."

"Oh." The berries were mushed in his hand, making it look like blood in the growing dark. "I'm sorry. You should take this back."

"*Oayla Aiden siemru,*" she repeated in Eckrosie, and stood up to head back into the forest.

Her spell let go of him, and Aiden raised his voice. "Will you be here tomorrow?"

She opened her arms wide. "Maybe."

The journey home could not have gone quicker. The whirlwind of thoughts clogged Aiden's mind from the moment he watched Ayla disappear into the forest to the moment they emerged out of the woods. He'd met an Eckrosie and lived to tell the tale. A more mind-boggling thing was Jarred's calm disposition at meeting an Eckrosie girl. Maybe he was right. Ayla was just another girl. Well, not really. There was something special about how she calmed Aiden and made him smile at the thought of her.

"My Lord," Jarred said as their horses trotted along the trail. Thorne's Town spread out over the grassland beneath the mountains. Lanterns and torches lit the paths as the sun disappeared behind the snowy caps of the mountains. "I will not utter a word to the lord and lady of the household unless you ask me to, but I wish to offer words of caution. If they find out about Ayla, your friendship will be short-lived, my lord."

A knot tied in his stomach. His grip on the reins tightened. Jarred spoke the truth. If indeed Ayla could become a friend of Aiden's, his parents could not get wind of it. Not after what had happened to Nyle. "You are right. Let it be our secret."

"Understood, my lord. And of course, if you at any point need my protection, I will do anything to ensure it," Jarred added.

After a moment of silence, Aiden spoke. "What does my name mean?" The birds quieted down, and crickets resumed their nightly ruckus.

"Your name? Well, I suppose you ought to ask your parents why they chose that name for you."

Aiden gave an acknowledging nod and kicked Adventure into a gallop down the hill, racing back home to his comfortable bed.

Chapter Seven

The Keeper

"Ladies and gentlemen," the herald Joanie called out on the other side of the curtain, her voice thankfully at a great distance from Gil instead of right next to him as had happened many times before, leaving him deaf in one ear for the better part of an afternoon.

Actors and tellers bumped into each other, half-naked, with bosoms and stomachs showing behind the huge curtain that separated a crowd from the performers. Gil couldn't help but risk a quick peek at Dorian's abs and smooth chest before they hid beneath a white tunic, hardly giving his body the justice it deserved.

"Be careful of that," Zahna whispered to Gil. She pulled a dress over her shoulders.

"Of what?" Gil said, and helped her with the lacing at the back.

"It might seem like nothing, but if the wrong person sees the looks you give Dorian, there might be trouble."

"I just looked at him," Gil explained.

A pained wheeze left Zahna at Gil's pull of the lace. He slowed and let her grow comfortable before tightening once more.

"I mean, I don't judge. Just be careful. Especially near the Halls, you'll find folk who'll want to cleanse you from certain thoughts."

"What do you mean?"

"People who disrespect the Unborn, as they call it, those who choose not to create children. Well, they're made to suffer the consequences. Most get an eye cut out if they don't do their duty and sleep with the other sex."

Gil's thoughts shifted to the lady he'd witnessed at one of the performances while he followed the troupe. An eye was missing. Perhaps she'd suffered consequences . . .

"Ehm . . ." Gil cleared his throat. "You got your lines?"

"Nah—or kind of. Got you there for me to count on." She chuckled once Gil patted her on the back to notify her his work on the dress finished.

"Shit and darn," Vinny, the storyteller with a bouncy mustache, swore nearby. "Where's Merry? Anyone know where the bastard went?"

The scrawny bard with thick blond hair was nowhere close. The performers standing at the ready to go on stage looked puzzled and shook their heads.

Joanie was wrapping up her introduction. The crowd applauded, and Gil moved to the hanging canvas.

"Gil!"

Gil stopped and turned to Dorian and Vinny down below. Joanie passed Gil. This was his cue to hunker down in the trap door at the edge of the stage.

"You'll take Merry's place. Come and get dressed."

Gil seemed to be the only one stunned by the demand as performers passed him and stepped onto the stage. Gil did, after all, know the song and the marks Merry made after watching the performance for months. He followed Dorian, who stepped in and out of Merry's untidy part of a wagon where shirts, blankets, and instruments littered the insides. An elegant shirt, made from silk, felt like water against Gil's brown skin. The gray fabric lay perfect against him. He tucked it inside his trousers with the aid of Dorian.

"Make us proud, Gil," Dorian said.

Gil took his place in line for the act. His heart kicked into his ribcage, and his stomach heaved. It was one thing to step on stage and hide from the audience, but this . . . this was entirely different. What would happen if he couldn't sing? Would they boo him off the stage? No, this was the moment, his moment to shine.

He took a deep breath and listened to the actors and the storyteller speaking from a few feet behind the curtain. Laughter washed across the crowd in the redecorated marketplace of Rose Lane.

The curtain parted for him. He brushed sweat from his shaved head and took his place on the wooden plateau. His footfall was the only sound that could be heard. Hundreds of eyes followed his every move. He knew it ought to bring him fear, but instead it calmed him. They saw him, he existed, he was important. Finally, he stood where he belonged, on stage with friends.

> *"As bright as day,*
> *as night is gray.*
> *She stole his heart,*
> *and it tore apart."*

His voice echoed across the crowd and into the surrounding red buildings of Rose Lane. He started out a tad higher than expected but managed to save the rest of his song while Darla and Dorian acted out the scene where the lovers parted for the Great War.

> *"In the hay they lay,*
> *to late midday,*
> *where they made art,*
> *with their body parts."*

A joint chuckle spread through the audience.  Their gaze filled him with adrenaline and excitement. Feeding off the audience, he understood what the others spoke of. It was a strange feeling, one not found anywhere else.

The beat increased, and Gil stomped hard on the floor, a steady thump as he sang. The audience followed his lead. Soon, hundreds of hands clapped together with him. There was a strong possibility of his voice being lost in the commotion, but it mattered not. He raised his voice and sang until his vocal cords ached. He was going to be remembered.

Once the show finished, as Dorian's character met with the king and became a Riveroak, all the performers took a last bow for the crowd. A couple of people whistled and hollered while winking at Gil.

Two days and two shows later, the joy remained. The troupe searched for Merry, but the scrawny man stayed away, leaving Gil room to sing and thump with the crowd. Though others grew concerned, Gil couldn't help but be somewhat thankful for Merry not being there. Not that he held anything against the bard and storyteller, he just feared what would happen once he came back. To return to the shadows wouldn't please him. Gil had touched the sun and now refused to leave.

Exploring Levent from the caravans and surrounded by friends differed significantly from trudging the streets alone. Unforeseen shouts and noises nearby faded into the lively ruckus of the city. The sight of city guards, dressed in padded armor embroidered with the double-headed hawk of the Crown, didn't send shivers of terror through him. Guards visited and enjoyed their shows just as much as other citizens.

The troupe's caravans tilted upward with their ascent of the hill to reach Riverview. Gil held onto a pole inside the carriage to keep himself steady against the rocking and tossing as the wheels moved over the uneven cobblestones. The guards who'd refused to let him pass weeks earlier didn't give Gil a second thought when he was traveling in the troupe's company. They moved past the guard post and reached the top of Levent.

"Don't get comfortable here and believe you're one of them. They'll lecture you if you even look at a lord or lady strangely," Zahna said, interrupting Gil's astonishment at the sight of all the glorious mansions. Beyond an archway, buildings at least four stories tall and just as wide surprised and amazed onlookers. Compared to the lower city's red and clustered houses, the mansions had ample room and space, with several displaying grand entries and gardens.

"Why do we come here, then?" Gil managed to reply.

Zahna leaned closer to Gil, also keeping an eye on the spectacular details of each wall. Intriguing columns and decorative windows created one unique building after the next. "If we're to perform in Levent, we need to put up a show in Riverview for a review. We get to perform for free on stages if we are seen as approved entertainers. If not, then we need to pay higher taxes and, well, start paying for every stage."

An enormous building revealed itself to Gil as they turned a corner. A gasp left him as he saw the Precedent's Court of Levent. The top of the giant dome was so tall it could have touched the sky. In every corner, every street, the court scrutinized people from its high vantage point, a sturdy reminder to all who looked upon it of the Crown's everlasting presence. On the brightest days, the court shone like a beacon over the city and the grasslands below. Some days, the polished facade's intensity made people shield their eyes the way sailors avoided the sun bouncing off the water.

Beneath it lay a town square with a big empty platform. The few people moving around nearby looked like ants next to the court's gigantic structure. Gil gulped and uncocked his neck to answer Zahna. "But the stages are just empty anyhow."

"Yeah, I agree. Save for when it's a flogging or a Victim's Will."

"You've ever seen one?"

"Flogging?" Zahna said.

"Victim's Will."

"A couple." Zahna sighed. "One down on Main Street and one in Keelheart. Nothing I'd recommend, especially not for a boy."

Gil's focus drifted to Zahna. "Is it true that the Crimson Wights are spirits of the dead or the victims, and that they disappear when the Victim's Will is finished? Or that the reason they hide their faces is that the Beast can't see them and can't kill them for killing someone else?"

Zahna's glossy eyes gazed at the cloudy sky.

Dorian answered in Zahna's stead, from a jumble of pillows and blankets inside the caravan. "They're not wizards or witches like the stories you've been told. They're just executioners. But yes, they hide their identities from the Beast. Their pearl masks are actually said to reflect the victim's faces to the criminal right before they die."

"You think they'll like the play?" Gil said.

"Better hope they do. They didn't seem to mind it last time we showed it. But without Merry . . . we'll have a harder time selling it, maybe. He's one of the writers, after all."

The caravan stopped, and they sprang to work, putting up the things needed for their performance. Each time Gil got stuff from the wagons for the show, his gaze went to the top of the dome, where a flock of birds soaked in the sun. He had finally made it to the top of the world.

"Mother?" Leah whispered, and placed another damp towel on Jaida's burning forehead. Her mother's eyes blinked slowly. "Giana's here. You wanted to speak with her?"

Giana leaned up against the attic doorpost, keeping Jaida and Miya at a far distance in the tight bedroom. Leah nudged her mother.

"I'm—I'm on my way," Jaida stuttered. The damp sheets she had sweat through slid to the side, but again she fell asleep. Leah nudged her again.

"Yes, sweetie?" Jaida gave a weak smile.

Giana jerked her fingers toward herself, calling Leah over. "She can't work. I'll send word to the Guides over by the Halls. Maybe they'll help."

"Help with what?"

"Getting your mother and sister better. I told Jaida to take it easy and not work herself to the bone. But she wouldn't listen," Giana muttered, and went downstairs.

Only days before, both Jaida and Miya had been, as usual, happy. Miya had run around, showing off her anklet to anyone nearby. But now, both of them lay in bed, barely able to even look up at Leah.

Leah squeezed a towel tight, just like her mother had taught her when the illness took over Miya. The droplets made the trapped water in the bowl bounce. Was it like Giana said? That her mother got sick because she worked too hard? What if it was true? Was the Wanderer punishing Leah because she didn't work?

The staircase creaked, and Ida stepped into their home, giving a long and burdened sigh at the sight of Jaida and Miya sweating and shivering.

"Ida's here." Leah held her mother's hand tight.

Each breath they took sounded terrible. A wheezing sound came from both of them. What scared Leah the most was how weak her mother looked. Her skin, which used to be beautiful and olive, looked pale and sweaty.

"You've been doing really good, Leah. Taking care of your mother and sister—they're lucky to have you," Ida said after long thought.

"What's wrong with them?"

"I'm not a healer, but . . . this looks like the sweats. They're burning up. But I'm sure they'll pull through. The Wanderer is trying to keep them safe. Leah, how are you? Does it hurt to breathe?"

Leah shook her head fast.

"Good. But we'll need to bring them to the Halls. Sometimes a healer visits us, and I know he'll help."

The journey to the Halls went smoothly. With the help of other Guides and a carriage, they reached the house of faith. Inside the oddly shaped circle, uneven beds provided Jaida and Miya a resting place. Six or seven other sick people rested nearby—all of them with the same kind of wheezing breath.

People dressed in long gray robes gave Leah's sister and mother food and water, though it ended up sitting by the beds, getting cold. Miya closed her eyes and refused to wake up to eat. Her mother, though, let the Guides feed her soup. Everything about it, watching her strong mother being fed like they'd fed Miya a few years ago, felt wrong and strange. There was someone else living in her mother's body. There had to be.

"When did this start?" Ida asked from the end of Jaida's bed. The intense light shining through the windows made her gray hair shine bright.

"After the Awakening. Mother coughed, and then she couldn't work. Is it because of me that they're sick?"

Ida leaped in to grab Leah tight. She stroked Leah's unkempt hair. "Hush, child. This is not your fault. Sometimes, people get sick. The Wanderer is trying to keep its eyes on everyone, but sometimes the Nightbringers sneak past to hurt good people."

A squeeze back from her mother roused Leah. She threw herself on her to listen. The woman's beautiful soft voice was just a whisper. "Don't be scared, sweetie . . . you're a great girl."

"How are you?" Ida leaned into Jaida. "Do you have problems breathing?"

"I'm tired . . . can I sleep now, Mother?"

Tears filled up in Leah's eyes. Mother? She thought Ida was her mother?

Ida placed a gentle hand on Jaida's chest. "Yes, but . . . what happened, Jaida?"

"I don't know . . ." Leah's mother shut her eyes but continued speaking. "Some guy may have made me sick . . . I'm just so tired."

A man approached them. His hairline was retreating, although he looked young.

"Andyr, praise the Wanderer. These two are sick and have been like this the last few days," Ida burst out to the man, who touched Jaida's forehead and then Miya's. "She's working at the pleasure house."

Andyr clicked his tongue. "Probably contracted it from a patron. Been going around lately. They've got a fever. Eating anything?"

Leah had never heard a person speak as quickly as the man did. Somehow he could form all the words before spitting them out. Maybe that was why his hair was missing?

"Ain't much to do but have 'em contained. You're the daughter?"

Andyr looked at Leah with hazel eyes. His dark skin glistened like water in the sun.

Leah gulped. "She's my mother. That's my sister."

His hand shot out and touched her forehead. "You're feeling alright?"

She frowned. "Are they alright?"

Andyr forced a smile. The kind of smile that her mother would give to say everything was fine even though it wasn't. "I don't know. This fight is between 'em and the fever. No one can help now. But keep 'em in the shadow and give 'em plenty of water."

Ida and Andyr moved on to other people in their beds, leaving Leah. But she wasn't alone. Her mother held her hand tight. Leah put a towel in water again before placing it on her mother's brow. Moments later, the heat was back, and Jaida's skin felt like it was burning. Both of them wheezed and simpered. All Leah could do was sit and listen to them. Even when Leah caressed them and talked to them, they didn't answer. Sometimes, though, when she said funny things to her sister, Miya gave a weak smile.

Night came, and the Halls emptied of people. Andyr left almost as fast as he arrived. But Ida stayed through the night, sitting nearby, helping Jaida and Miya drink and keeping them cool. Sometime during the night, when the moon shone bright, Leah fell asleep, and she didn't wake up until sparrows chirped nearby.

Her hand was already gripping her mother's hand tight. She felt cold. She touched Jaida's forehead, and Miya's as well. Their wheezing had stopped.

"Mother?"

No answer. She was colder than Leah and did not respond when the girl poked her and caressed her. Ida woke up nearby.

"Wake up . . ." Leah nudged her mother.

Jaida looked peaceful. Like she was asleep, dreaming a good dream. Her head tilted to the side, her hair covering the pillow she rested on.

"They're with the Wanderer," Ida said after several attempts to say something.

Leah looked at her family. "But . . . no . . . I can see her. She's right here." She touched her mother's soft face.

"Sweetheart . . . her being isn't here. I'm sorry. The Wanderer couldn't save them. The Keeper has carried them with her."

Everything Ida said brought tears into Leah's eyes. She shook her mother and her sister gently, wanting nothing more than for them to wake up. She couldn't be alone. Who was she going to play with? Who was she going to giggle with? Who was going to protect her?

Leah crawled into the bed to lie next to her mother. She wrapped herself around Jaida and smelled her soft and comforting scent. Nothing would harm her as long as her mother was there. With her mother, she was safe.

～❀～

"How do you say, 'I like playing'?" Aiden asked Ayla.

A couple of creases appeared around her cute nose when she giggled at his last pronunciation. Whenever Jarred and Aiden passed the brook after an intense day, Aiden ran back to learn about Ayla and her tongue. Fortunately, she met up with him every day.

Jarred kept his word. He let Aiden stop and meet Ayla on their ride home from the camp. Either he was becoming stricter with time, or time flowed quicker when Aiden spent it with her. Jarred called out for Aiden, his voice traveling through the foliage, alerting him of them having to leave.

"*Oantè ecquarie*," Ayla said once she stopped giggling. "You remember, we say 'I' as part of the word. *Antè* means 'to like.'"

"Where do you live?" Aiden asked after repeating her word a few times.

"*Oseda i gouro,*" she said.

Aiden leaned in closer. "Wait! Don't tell me . . . you live in . . . forest? No, farther in?"

"*A,*" she confirmed.

"My lord? We cannot linger unless you wish for the lord and lady to grow weary," Jarred called out again.

Ayla nibbled on her lip, a tick she did whenever she gathered her thoughts and the proper way to convey them. He cocked his head to the side, waiting for a continuation.

"Is Jarred your . . . slave?"

His breath caught in his throat. No. A slave was different. A slave would not have any say in their life. A thrall was simply a person who signed a contract to serve a particular household. There were no restrictions on them leaving or finding another place. At least, that was what his parents had told him.

"No, he's a thrall. He works for me."

"*Dasla?*" Ayla said.

"Because . . . he wants to."

"*Dasla,* why he calls you lord? Are you better person than Jarred and me?"

"Well, I . . ." Aiden halted. Although he knew he was supposed to be referred to as lord, her argument held some value. Was he better than Jarred and Ayla? And why? Was there really a reason for others to call him a lord other than solidifying the belief that some people were better? He'd never questioned it before, but the more holes he poked in its armor, the clearer it became; nothing hid behind the protection. "I'm not better than you or anyone, I think."

"Everybody is the same." She put a hand against her chest, then on his. "Eckrosie, Vesilian. Nobody is above. In family, nobody is lord or lady. Everyone is a you."

His heart jumped when her hand brushed against his chest. He gaped up at her, nearly forgetting what she'd just said. There was an invitation hidden in their longing gaze to get to know each other better. His entire being tingled to stay near her, but when Jarred called out to him a third time, he pushed the feeling aside.

"I see you tomorrow?" Aiden said after some self-deliberation.

"*A. Olera nivera Aiden.*"

Aiden gave a lopsided grin while figuring out what she'd said. *A* was 'yes.' *Lera* probably meant 'to see.' Perhaps *nivera* meant 'tomorrow'?

The ride home became more of a trot because of the growing dark. Jarred kept close to Aiden, keeping a watchful eye on him. In silence, they rode past the town guards clad in the Crown's emblem.

Aiden took a step inside the well-lit entrance of his home, where his mother and father rushed to get him in their arms. Jarred snuck through the door behind him and took a bow.

"Where were you? Are you hurt, my son?" Emilia asked, and shook Aiden. "We have searched for you."

"The captain decided to let me stay a bit later today, that is all," Aiden lied.

Lionel drummed his fingers on the cane. "Why would he do that? We specifically informed him to ensure your return by sundown."

Aiden threw a quick gaze back at Jarred, who stared at the polished floor.

"I asked to stay late to get more practice." Aiden brushed off his pants, smeared with dirt and grass stains.

"We are pleased to hear of your fondness of your studies," Lionel said. "But you need to respect the rules we have discussed with the captain. Traveling at night is dangerous and not something a little lord should do."

"Jarred," Emilia said. Something about her tone chilled the entrance hall. "Have we made our position regarding Aiden's safety unclear?"

Like always, Jarred was ready with an intelligent answer. He bowed until he showed the entire top of his gray hair. "Definitely not, my Lady. Serving your family is a great and noble task. I would gladly give my life to protect the lord."

"Then why did you not escort him home earlier?" Emilia said.

Aiden risked a peek at his father. Lionel seemed to long for an answer just as much as his mother. He leaned down on the cane keeping him aloft.

As the silence thickened, Aiden spoke in Jarred's stead. "It . . . it's not his fault. I asked him to let me stay."

"Have you not listened to us, Aiden? Jarred is just a thrall who works for us. He follows our command," Emilia snapped at her son.

There it was. The thing Ayla spoke of.

Aiden scratched his fingers tight and mumbled, "I'm not better or more important than he is."

Emilia let in a sharp breath and huffed at Jarred. "What have you taught our son?" She grabbed Aiden's shoulders to bring him close, shielding him from Jarred. "You are everything. Jarred is just a thrall we pay, while you are destined for greatness."

"Jarred, we need a word with you, in private," Lionel uttered, and patted his son's head. "You are late for bed—do not let it wait for you even more."

"But . . ." Aiden mumbled. "It's not his fault. A friend of mine said everyone is the same."

Crap, I have to make up another lie. They can't take Ayla from me, Aiden thought. His fingers gathered his trousers' fabric into a tiny ball, creasing it and folding it on itself. Their stares penetrated his heated skin.

"And this friend. Who is this?" Emilia said, letting each word drag.

"A . . . a friend at the camp. He is a son of a merchant."

Another frustrated huff left her. "Such a terrible liar. Now go to bed. Do not make me ask twice."

Aiden backed away to the staircase. Along with Jarred, his parents disappeared into the dining hall. He could do no more to convince them, but a sinking hole bore deep in his chest. What if Jarred got into trouble because of Aiden? What else was there to do?

He would not stop seeing Ayla. What if he could go there during the morning and be home before supper? Not every day, of course. Studying by Hutton's side meant a great deal of fun. But every now and then, he could meet Ayla and spend time learning more about her.

Aiden rushed up the staircase and passed Eamon's chamber, where a thrall watched over his little brother while he slept. Soon, the linens hugged Aiden's body tight. Sleep did not claim him. Ayla's contagious giggle echoed in his mind. He could not wait until they met again.

Chapter Eight

A Hidden Place

A week of performances across Levent's markets and squares followed. The sun stayed with them and offered plenty of crowds for Gil to entertain. Once he stepped off the stage, he nearly rushed back on to keep the adrenaline pumping. Nights in the caravan were not boring; still, he dreamt of the next day's performance and what could be improved to make it even better.

Zahna slept nearby. Her hair, the only thing visible beneath a sea of blankets, she hoarded to keep warm. Gil pulled his blanket tighter and stared through a slit in the canvas to watch the dark clouds sweep the skies above. The lute sang a lullaby in his lap, and Zahna's soft snores accompanied it.

Thoughts of his parents usually didn't linger and keep him up at night, but for some reason, they did now. What if they had seen him on stage? Had they gazed at their boy and felt any regret for leaving him? He didn't know much of them. No name, no address, and no words of comfort. Nothing. The poorhouse had told him the story many times while Gil waited with excitement, hoping it would yield a new ending. But it was always the same. One morning, Ulthal, one of the poorhouse workers, found a baby, wrapped in a blanket, on the doorstep. No one came to claim Gil as their own.

At least Zahna knew her parents. After their imprisonment in Nedox, they'd settled down in Rostain, a smaller town on the opposite side of Lake Ember. It wasn't hard to see her parents being tailors and selling the clothes they created. Whenever a dress, shirt, tarp, or belt split, Zahna was the first to put her fingers to use and repair it. When Gil asked what made her want to leave her parents, she replied with a shrug. "I didn't choose my dream to be an actress. My dream chose me."

Gil couldn't help but agree. The thought of working as a bard, singing and playing music, was not a dream he could let go of. Even when he'd try, it would haunt him and chase him down until he came back to it.

Morning came. The tarps of the caravans parted to let in the bright sun. Bells of the city called for trade to commence. Right outside, stalls with colorful canvases lined up in the town's square where only yesterday they'd performed.

A loaf of bread landed in Gil's lap. Zahna smiled his way. "Good morrow, sleepy-head."

Lettuce and ham mashed in his mouth as he took a big bite. "Good morrow. Any sign of Merry?"

"Not yet. Don't get your hopes up, but you might wanna prepare to perform the next set of shows."

A voice within Gil squeaked at her words, but he kept a composed face and brushed off some crumbs from his shirt. "I'll be ready in that case."

The men and women of the Shields of the Moon ventilated their sleeping wagons and put on their working clothes. The horses were watered, downing two buckets each in big gulps. Gil wiped sweat from his glistening brow.

Five guards dressed in padded linens, layers and layers of it, stopped by the caravan as they were about to travel to Main Street.

The sigil of the Crown, a two-headed hawk, was stitched into their chest pieces. Despite the day only beginning, their protective padding displayed dark stains of sweat on the bleak fabric.

A tall, hairy man removed his helmet. "This is the Shields of the Moon troupe, isn't it?"

Dorian and Zahna stepped forward. Gil gathered the reins to a horse and kept it taut.

"We are, good sir," Zahna addressed the soldiers.

"As procedure dictates, once a member is charged with crimes against the realm, so too is the troupe."

Everyone was equally perplexed by the guard's statement. Charged with a crime? Did this have to do with Merry's disappearance? An odd situation arose between Gil and the horse when it seemed to calm him by bumping its head against the boy's.

"Who among us has been charged with a crime?" Dorian asked.

The guard shifted his weight, uneasy at their questions. "Please, let us escort you to the District Court, and they'll answer all your questions, sir."

"No. You'll answer us right now," Zahna said. Her charm and cunning were snuffed out, replaced with a demanding growl. "For all we know, you might as well be thieves planning to steal from us once we comply and follow."

The guard rolled his eyes. "Merry, your bard and playwright, was found guilty of spreading dishonesty and ill-will. He is also guilty of safeguarding an Eckrosie. Because of this, your troupe is charged with dishonesty and ill-will."

Dishonesty and ill-will? Gil scratched his head. Sure, the play probably wasn't telling a true story, but to call it dishonest was going a bit too far.

The guard took a step toward Zahna. "Now, can we do this in an orderly manner? Two guards will remain here to ensure the safety of your belongings while we go to the Court."

"That sounds reasonable, sir," Zahna muttered.

The troupe gathered what little they could bring. Gil didn't have anything save for his lute he'd borrowed from Merry. The boy followed the rest of the group as they gathered.

"Where do you think you're going?" Zahna sneered at Gil once he joined her side.

The guards glanced Gil's way.

Gil gave a lackluster grin. Where else was he going if not with them?

Zahna grabbed his arm and tossed him aside. "You're to watch the horses like always, boy."

He struggled against her firm hand. "I'm coming with."

The main guard raised an eyebrow their way. "Is there a problem? If he is part of the troupe, he must join."

"He's not one of us. He's just a thrall."

Gil's insides seared at Zahna's words. A knife that always hid in his chest ever since his parents abandoned him delved deeper at the denial.

"No, I'm not." Gil was quick to say. "I'm part of the troupe."

Zahna faced the guard. "He's been hoping to have a place here, but he's here to care for the needs of the group."

"She's lying! I'm part of the—"

A slap from Dorian silenced Gil. He looked up at the actor and put a hand against his cheek, feeling the tingle from the sudden hit.

"Watch over our belongings, or I'll grace you again."

The troupe left the market, and Gil standing motionless at the edge of it. The two guards left behind gathered the horses as instructed and kept an eye on the belongings. Even long after they'd gone, Gil stared after them.

The months of laughter, companionship, and shows didn't really matter, as it turned out. Once it came down to it, they really didn't care. No. They did care, but once again, he failed in keeping them interested in him. Gil's brow wrinkled as he thought hard of the last months. Did they not like that he had stepped into Merry's role? Didn't they like when he fiddled on a lute under the starry sky? Had he been too talkative? Too cheerful? Too much . . . ?

"Chin up, kid." Gil jumped at the sudden intrusion into his thoughts. One of the sweaty guards stood by Gil and removed his helm to reveal a curly, messy hairdo underneath. "Might not feel like it, but your friends just saved you."

"Saved me?"

"You know, I've seen you on stage. You're a great singer. So I know you're a part of the troupe. They saved you from meeting a court and being punished. Thank them when they come back."

"But we didn't do anything wrong."

"Just some advice." The man shrugged his shoulders and joined his friend.

Midday came and went. His feet grew sore from standing, so he jumped inside Zahna's wagon, where her sheets and pillows littered everything inside. If indeed they'd saved him, Gil better understood the role Dorian had played when he struck Gil. The head of the guards needed to believe Zahna's words.

The lute sang with his fingers walking along the strings. A song the troupe hymned at night played in his mind. A somewhat sorrowful yet optimistic melody lingered through the song.

The evening's bells called through the city. Not until the last ring left and the merchants packed their wares did the troupe return.

Zahna walked at the head of the pack, her shoulders hunched and weighed down. So too was Dorian's posture. At the sight of Dorian, Gil felt a sort of resentment leaping forward, but he reminded himself that it had been an act.

Zahna and Dorian neared Gil. Gil jumped out of the wagon to greet them.

"Take a seat, Gil," Dorian said, and showed him to a barrel nearby. Cloth was wrapped around both actors' left hands. Zahna rubbed hers, pain filling her dark eyes.

"We . . . we've been disbanded."

Gil blinked. Zahna filled him in. "Meaning the troupe is finished."

"Finished?"

"If we don't move our separate ways . . . we'll be flogged, or worse. It means we can't continue together."

Dorian bit his upper lip nervously, like he did before a performance.

"What did they do to your hands?" Gil asked, and reached out to inspect them closer. Dorian pulled away.

"They branded us," Dorian said. "To make sure we'll never work again."

"But just cover it up and . . ."

"No, Gil. You might not understand it." Zahna grunted. "But no other troupe will dare hire someone with this brand. We'll only act on stage at executions, and that's something I refuse. I'm heading back to Rostain and my family."

Gil's mind clogged with questions. His mouth tried to ask them, but his tongue didn't manage to form any proper words.

"This is goodbye for now. I'll stay in Levent. I'm not above performing at executions. It was only a matter of time." Dorian gave

Gil an embrace, which he barely was able to register before the moment passed. "You'll achieve great things, Gil. Make sure the crowds remember you, and I'm certain we will meet again." Dorian's sway led him to the troupe, where people emptied their wagons.

Tears glistened in Zahna's eyes, threatening to spill at any moment.

"W-what happened? Did we do something wrong?" Gil finally uttered.

The tears spilled. "You didn't do anything wrong. Unfortunately, we were careless, thinking nobody would punish us for a silly performance." She contemplated the wound. "Live and learn, as storytellers say."

"Can I come with you?"

"To Rostain? Trust me, there is nothing for you there. Your talents are far too great for a small town. You belong here, where you'll make a difference and inspire hundreds if not thousands with your words and song."

He couldn't be left alone again.

"Here." A coin pouch rattled and settled in Gil's hand. "To get you started. It's not much, but it'll give you food and shelter. And the lute. It's yours."

The leather straps of the pouch felt dry against his fingertips. "But what about Merry?"

"He won't use it where he's at, I'm afraid. I know he'd want you to have it."

Gil grabbed her hand and squeezed it in his. "You can't leave me. Everyone does. Take me with you, and I'll help you in every way I can. You don't even need to feed me or—"

Zahna silenced his rant with a hug. His brave facade broke, and her shirt dampened with his crying.

"Sweetheart, I'm not leaving you, not really. It's only a temporary farewell. Keep singing and playing, and I promise, you'll find a home and a family. Besides, a true family is still a family, even miles apart." Zahna struggled to smile, but did it anyway. "Promise not to tell anyone, but . . . I'm not going to Rostain. I'm heading back home to be with my people."

"Your people? But . . . we are your people."

"If only. I can't explain it, but my family isn't exactly accepted here. I haven't met my sister for at least two years, and she needs me. Gil, don't you ever give up. You are magnificent."

Ayla moved swiftly. She pounced between rocks, branches, and shrubbery. Like a brisk, beautiful doe, she led Aiden and Jarred farther through a thick forest. Ancient oaks and beech trees with massive roots reached out to trip them, but Ayla maneuvered the path nimbly. Sparrows chirping among the branches bounced between trees, seemingly following their morning spurt.

Jarred huffed behind Aiden, who did his best to keep up with their guide. The entire morning, from when they left the mansion till they reached the brook, Aiden had worked to convince Jarred to let him stay with Ayla through the day. Though he did not enjoy it, Jarred was left with no choice once Ayla grabbed Aiden's hand and escorted him away from the path. Jarred's sheathed sword clanged against boulders and stalks, with sudden curses following thereafter. For once in a long time, the sun hid behind a thick, dark gathering of clouds.

Stepping farther into the enchanting forest felt like entering a land full of wisdom and age: the trees thick and gnarly, probably survivors from hundreds

of winters and storms. The same kind of protective feeling the portraits in his home gave as they watched over him, the trees did here. Twists and sudden turns confused Aiden. He decided to simply follow Ayla, no matter where she led them. She shouted out in Eckrosie. Only a few words registered with him.

Ayla stopped at the outside of a glade. Aiden joined, his breath shooting his chest up and down. A hidden gem in a small clearing, full of life and voices, made his jaw drop. Amid the ancient forest, where nature grew wild and uncontrolled, a dozen wagons stood beneath an emerald canopy. The presence of the chirping birds still overpowered the voices of the people nearby. This was truly a hidden place. The forest floor had barely been disturbed by the wagons and people in the quaint dwelling. Like a herd of deer, the people's disturbance to the surroundings was minimal.

"Welcome to Stysen," Ayla said to both Aiden and Jarred. She took another step along the moss-covered ground and peeked at them over her shoulder. "Leave sword. We have no weapons."

Jarred drummed a finger on the sword he carried, but with a quiet sigh, he did as he was told and removed it. The sword and the scabbard found rest within a tree's bulky roots.

Oddly enough, their arrival did not disrupt any of the people of the settlement. Twenty or more shared the area, some young like Ayla and Aiden, some older like Jarred. Some people attended to chores of different kinds, sitting on blankets and mats spread out over the uneven ground. Others dangled their feet from open bow-top caravans. The caravans reminded him of odd merchant stalls and wagons he'd witnessed in Levent, uninspired and straightforward. Or actually, as he studied the scene further, he realized the wagons were made to be inconspicuous just like the rest of their living. There were no fires spewing smoke into the sky, nor were there free horses. The horses, Aiden assumed pulled the wagons, were kept inside a makeshift pen provided by thick ropes wrapped around a tree gathering. It became clear to him why they had not been discovered. Ayla's people were vagrants. Unarmed, unprotected vagrants.

Aiden, followed by Jarred, stepped into Ayla's home. He studied each smiling face carefully to seek out her parents but quickly remembered that her parents passed long ago. Just like the thralls at the Riveroak estate, this home was a place for all kinds of people. Some pale like a lonely cloud on a sunny day, and some ebony like the beautiful trees in the surrounding woods. Although their encampment may not have been the most decorative, all their attention and creativity seemed spent on their hair.

Lords and ladies Aiden met strived to achieve the intricate and luscious hairdos these Eckrosie refugees managed, and they were probably not going to a ball or banquet even. Men and women alike had long layers of hair put into buns and braids. Decorative pearls and stones, even the occasional silver spirals, added to the beautiful aesthetic. Compared to the others, Ayla's hair was simple, even looking unkempt. Perhaps she did not waste time on such things?

"*Meevra,*" Ayla uttered, and dragged him along. Jarred huffed behind them.

Buckets of berries, blueberries, raspberries, and other golden ones rested next to a couple of people. An elderly lady sat on a colorful rug and smiled at Ayla as they approached. She seemed to be an important person. When Ayla spoke to the lady, whose silver hair reached far past her hips, Aiden bowed to greet her.

"Do not bow," the lady said, and extended her hand to him. "We are the same here."

"*These are my friends Aiden and Jarred.*" Ayla spoke slowly to respect Aiden. He winked at her kindness.

Her wrinkled hand embraced Aiden's. "My name is Sheila. Happy to meet Ayla's friend."

"This is my grandmother, Sheila," Ayla said.

Aiden prepared to greet Sheila with a courtesy but stopped his tongue just in time.

"*Ayla teller oh Aiden.*"

Aiden blinked, sorting through the few words he remembered.

"*A, oteller oh Aiden.*" Ayla spoke slowly to make sure he followed.

An uncomfortable embarrassment snuck its way to his lips, and he displayed a strange grin. "You said something about me?" he guessed.

"Teller means speak, tell story. I told story of you."

Aiden hesitated, looking around her home. "Are you sure we should be here? If the wrong people find out where we are . . ."

A toothy smile met him. "You are not wrong people."

Even Jarred's retorts had dwindled once they set foot in the Eckrosie village. Both of them were busy following Ayla and Sheila around. Unlike in the stories told to Aiden, these were not savages and uncultured people. People of different ages, young and old, played games of tag, just like Eamon and Aiden did when the opportunity presented itself. Instead of bows and titles, the Eckrosie greeted each other with hugs and smiles despite Aiden and Jarred being outsiders.

"*Aiden and Jarred hungry?*" Ayla managed to make Aiden understand after a long series of belly-rubbing gestures. She waved them with her to a wagon in the very middle of the settlement. Around the wagon's outer walls, pots of tomatoes, kale, and spinach grew. She plucked a handful of leaves and handed it to Aiden.

Midday meals at the mansion involved meats and different kinds of root vegetables, but no such thing made it to the bowl in Aiden's lap. Along with Ayla and Jarred, they picked what they needed to eat from the forest. He could not help but notice a skinned deer on a spit hanging above a fire pit nearby. The fire was snuffed out.

"Daytime we eat this. Nighttime, we eat deer," Ayla explained.

"Because of the smoke?" Jarred commented between gulps of vegetables. "That is why you do not have any fires during the day, to prevent people from finding you?"

Ayla tossed her fluffy hair around in agreement.

"And you move around the nearby forest, am I right, to not linger in one place?"

Again Ayla smiled.

As they ate, Aiden came to realize this was the first time he and Jarred had dined together. As they consumed blades of kale and spinach, Jarred was no thrall. Such a simple, trivial event spread joy within Aiden. And apparently, it did in Jarred as well, as he finished his bowl before any of them got halfway. It was just like they said. Here, everyone was equal.

Gil tilted his head at another couple, stopping to gaze upon one of the many gray statues in the area. The woman grasped the man tightly by his arm as he explained who it depicted. But Gil would be taking over the story. The strings on Merry's lute rang.

"Who was he?
the one with all such glee
Sir Horner the builder
these streets, these buildings,
oh Levent, how he filled her."

The man chortled at the sudden shift of the song. The woman gave Gil an uncomfortable smile.

The rattling of coins joined the lute's dying sound. The man held out a couple of silver pieces to Gil. "Well played, boy. Although it's far from the truth."

Gil scratched the top of his head, where his hideous curls began to grow. Whatever the plaque read, he couldn't decipher it. "It's called artistic freedom, sir."

A pouch departed with additional coins and found their way into Gil's hand. "Whatever it's called, keep it up."

Ten silver crowns. Not bad for one couple. Gil shoved the coins into his trousers to conceal his sudden wealth. With this, he'd be able to stay a night or two at an inn nearby and get at least two dinners. *Don't get greedy*, Gil cursed his mind for trailing off. He had to save it. If he was to find another troupe to accompany, he needed the lute intact. As of yet, nothing unfortunate befell it, but as with everything else, things never lasted.

It was hard to tell how many days had passed since the Shields of the Moon was severed. He did his best to keep his mind occupied, as it only brought tears to his eyes thinking about it. After Zahna had left, Gil traveled to nearby taverns where he sat down to sing and perform. He learned fast that the innkeepers didn't enjoy his presence. His hopes were for someone to let him into their establishment to sing, but they turned him away and chose an older and more familiar singer to perform in his stead each time.

Luckily, he found his way to Main Street's Ancestors' Square, a place of worship and remembrance. It was a secluded area that hid from sun and rain beneath a large canvas stretching over twenty statues like a house without walls. People visited the monuments to pay their respects and take a walk through history. Gil listened to others reading the bronze plaques that seemed to describe who was carved into the lifelike stone figures. Kings and queens, but also merchants and local heroes stood there. Beneath the statue of a woman, dried flowers decorated the base. From what he'd heard, she was an accomplished healer during the Great Wars and saved hundreds of people. One day his statue would stand there, keeping a watchful eye on visitors. Gil would have flowers dropped at his feet by people of all ages. No matter what, he would find a way to be remembered.

Like other urchins of the city, Gil ended up in Keelheart or, as Gil called it, Levent's shithole. After continual refusals from inns, they banded together, finding a guard to escort him from the district. Once night came, Keelheart showed both its sides. Lanterns lit a few taverns and inns, but the rest of the area fell dark. Young people and older ones hid in cracks between buildings, which looked ready to collapse at any moment. Just as Gil thought he'd found a spot for him to rest, someone hissed at him threateningly. Doorkeepers ensuring the safety of patrons of inns glared at Gil if he approached. He could not blame them. Looking down at his hands and arms, he saw layers of dirt and rind.

"Get lost, kid," a doorkeeper shouted after Gil. His hurried steps led him to another inn. Again, he brought up his lute in the hopes of being invited to entertain patrons.

The doorkeeper, a huge lady with hunched shoulders, gave him a grin and listened to Gil's song. She patted his shoulder but eventually sent him away.

"Boy," a voice called after Gil on his way to the next inn.

Gil cast a quick glimpse over his shoulder. A figure, dark and tall, followed him into a cramped alley. Gil's feet tapped the muddy street faster, soon reaching a half-sprint to get rid of the unwanted attention. His heartbeat quickened at the uncomfortable thought of being left alone with a stranger. He cut corners, not knowing where he was heading. The footfalls behind him closed in.

"Kid, I ain't gonna hurt you," the man's voice called. Despite the words, everything about the tone told Gil to keep putting distance between them.

Gil squeezed into a gap between two buildings. A stench of piss and excrement overwhelmed him in the tight space. He cradled his lute to keep it safe.

The figure stopped feet away. He twisted and turned to get a glimpse of Gil, but Gil pressed against a wall to be one with the shadows. He didn't know the figure's intentions. Was it to rob him? Rape him? To kill him?

"Listen, boy. I won't hurt you. The only reason I followed is 'cause you'll be somewhere else come morning. I wanna offer you a place to stay so you don't have to sleep in the streets." The man's harsh and raspy voice filled the alley. Somehow, Gil couldn't help but believe him.

"I'll let you hold my dagger if that'll feel better while I bring you there."

Metal chimed. Why would a man give up his weapons if he wanted to hurt Gil?

Gil took a couple of hesitant steps toward the stranger. The dagger was still warm from the man's body heat. Gil pointed the tip of the dagger toward the man. A shaved head, just like Gil's used to be, caught what little light there was. He dressed like a merchant, a somewhat fancy vest on top of a regular shirt and trousers. Tall boots hugged the man's feet.

"Who are you?" Gil said.

"Name's Cidron Ross. You?"

"Gil."

"Nice to meet you. What do you say we get inside, get you some new clothes?"

"Are you a Guide?"

Cidron snorted. "No, I'm a merchant who helps kids like you and anyone who wants help."

"So an innkeeper?" Gil lit up.

"Nah, not really. Better if I'll show you." With that, Cidron walked back the same way they came. Gil followed at a distance. Wherever they were heading had to be better than the reeking streets.

In the middle of the slums, a misplaced house stood. The building was intact and large. No holes on the roof, the walls looked whole, and lanterns of different sizes lit up the town's square. It was a palace trapped in a nightmarish place.

No expense had been spared inside, just like the finer inns and taverns up on Main Street Gil had glimpsed into. Carpets rolled out over hardwood flooring, and even an occasional painting decorated the pinkish walls. Once Cidron entered the house, a bow and a curtsy that only nobles were given met him. Other adults living inside looked like ruffians with crooked noses and rough faces.

Cidron pointed into an adjacent room, where beds and chests were lined up in neat rows. Gil peeked inside and was greeted with snoring and sleeping people hidden beneath blankets.

Up close in the light, Cidron came off even more intimidating than before. He stood at least six feet tall, easily two of Gil on top of each other. His egg-shaped head was battered and blemished. His ears pointed outward, and both his nose and lips curved to the right in a slight drop as if someone had recently punched him. He was not a handsome man. Not any longer, at least.

"You work for me, you'll never gotta think 'bout where you're sleeping or what you're eating. We'll even keep your lute safe, or get a new one if you want."

At this point, Gil lowered the dagger. Whatever fear he'd felt before washed away. "Really?"

"I'm a man of my word. Seen hundreds of kids like you getting tossed around and stepped on. Here, you'll have everything you need—and a home."

A home . . . were they like a family within this palace? Gil pouted, deep in thought. "Where'll I work?"

"Possibly with a merchant in need of an extra pair of hands or two. But if you'd like, I'd have you sing and perform for my close friends. We'd love to hear you sing. Heard 'bout you."

"You've heard about me?" Gil cradled the lute.

Wide-legged, Cidron peered down at Gil. "Yeah, saw your shows here and at Main Street a couple times. Quite a voice you've got."

Gil turned his gaze with his growing smile from the compliment. "Will I be a thrall?"

Cidron crossed his arms, which were thicker than Gil's entire head. "If you wanna put a label on it, sure. But I don't see it like that. You're a partner and a part of our family, where we make sure everyone is taken care of."

Thoughts fought for Gil's attention. He hadn't known a place such as this existed, but here it was. All of it was within his grasp: a bed, friends, and the opportunity to sing to people who appreciated it.

Cidron noticed Gil's hesitation. "Think it over. My offer stands. Come back if you want to take me up on it. Take a bed tonight, and in the morning you can eat all you want. You're free to leave if it doesn't feel right."

Cidron patted Gil on his back and retreated to another part of the house, leaving Gil alone in the hallway. A bed for the night didn't sound bad. Gil walked into the room with the sleeping people.

Young adults such as himself, perhaps older, cuddled tight in blankets, sleeping peacefully. Sleeping in a bed would beat sleeping in the streets again.

A bed greeted him and hugged him tightly. It reminded him of his aching bones from the nights before he slept outside in the chilly night. This was sublime. He cradled the lute and drifted off to a night of deep sleep.

CHAPTER NINE

Never Forgotten, nor Forgiven

This was it, an opportunity for Aiden to show his father and zealous spectators what he'd learned during the past months. He swung a dull blade in his grasp, getting a feel of its weight, and reach. Three opponents, men with layers of padding, stood in his path separating him and the captain, who patiently waited for a fight to ensue.

A grand party with lords and ladies from all over Thorne's Town was underway in the Riveroak estate gardens. Rows of scaffolding lined up along the gardens' riding pen, creating the perfect viewing grounds for the spectators of melee tournaments taking place in Lionel's honor. Warriors dressed from head to toe in plate armor swung at each other all day under the scorching sun. However, Aiden paid little attention to that, as it felt like insects gnawed his stomach making him nauseous with anxiety to prove himself in front of all the judging eyes.

A bard called out to the viewers in a yell. "My liege, my lords, and ladies. The honorable Lord Lionel Riveroak is proud to bring you his son, Aiden Riveroak, in this fight against our own Captain Hutton and his ruffians. May the lord's legacy follow in his flesh and blood."

On the scaffolding, their faces mixed into a bewildering blur, making it near impossible for Aiden to locate his family.

The three men stepped up to attack Aiden. He leaped into one person's range and swung his sword wide to distance the person from him. He moved onto the next, and repeated this over and over to spread them out and ensure they could not attack him all at once. They made half a circle to protect the captain in the back, but they would go down fast once Aiden got the upper hand.

The smallest guy sprang forward and cut with a dull blade from his head downward. Aiden escaped the strike by leaping past his guard, smacking the man's side with his sword. One down.

The remaining men made their approach as one. Again Aiden chopped to separate them, letting him take them on one on one.

The captain approached, unexpectedly to Aiden, and joined the duel. The two other guys placed themselves on opposite sides of Aiden, where they lunged at him. Using their momentum against them, the boy wrapped his fingers around one of their arms and pulled the person closer, straight into an incoming strike's path. Before reflecting on it, Aiden let the fallen opponent swing Aiden around, where he thrust the dull blade upward toward the man's torso.

Risking everything, Aiden dropped his sword and leaped toward the captain, where he managed to break past the defense. Aiden withdrew a dull knife from a sheath hidden at his lower back and stabbed it into the captain's abdomen. Layers of cloth creaked with each jab.

The crowd erupted with cheers and salutes. With their decorative attire, lords and ladies moved like a field of flowers caught in a windstorm.

Hutton and his students took deep bows to recognize Aiden's talents, bringing a bright smile to the boy's lips. On the scaffolding, he caught a glimpse of his mother mirthfully applauding with the rest of the crowd. But his father . . . his father was nowhere to be seen.

The bard ushered them from the grounds to hide in the shelter of the platforms above that creaked and moaned beneath the weight of the onlookers. Aiden handed over the dull knife to a squire standing nearby, as did the captain, who retrieved his proper sword. He secured it at his belt.

"Dedication and patience pays off in full, little lord," Hutton said, and patted Aiden on his shoulder. "I did not know what to expect, but sacrificing your blade to get close was definitely a stroke of genius."

"Do you think Father saw?" Aiden asked.

Hutton's face suddenly turned ashen. "Bow, Aiden, it's the king," the captain breathed, and bowed as far as his creaking back let him.

Aiden took a deep bow. But the saying of the Eckrosie that everyone was equal rang in the back of his mind. He bent even lower, anything to hide the fact that he was associating with the king's enemy. Even so, Aiden could not help but feel a smidge excited to be seen by the ruler of Vesilia.

Pointed leather boots stopped before him, and the familiar drag of his father's cane halted.

"My liege," Hutton said, which Aiden mimicked before ogling their king.

Canden Thorne stood at least a head taller than Lionel. A chest-piece wrapped around his torso, armor polished enough to reflect Aiden's wide-eyed gape back at him. On the beautiful silver, the two-headed hawk, the sigil of the rulers of Vesilia, decorated the piece in fine golden lines. A dark blue cape hugged the king's shoulders tight and trailed his movements.

Canden looked down his sunken cheekbones at Aiden. He looked like any other lord, with a square, clean-shaven face, a broad nose, and thinly curved lips. His hooded eyes hid in the shadow of two caterpillar-like eyebrows. Aiden expected there to be a crown adorning the king's wispy hair but was left disappointed.

"You are a tremendous warrior, Aiden Riveroak. The captain has taught you well," Canden said with a breathy strain as if each word leaving pained him. But his expression told a different story as the corners of his mouth turned up.

Hutton gave a modest chuckle. "Natural talents go a long way, my liege. Heritage as well, undoubtedly."

"Thank you, my king," Aiden squeezed out, knowing he had to recognize the compliment somehow. A blush bled onto his face as he interrupted the captain.

"It has hardly come as a surprise, my liege." Lionel filled in the captain's thoughts. "The lady and I caught him with sticks destroying our statues before he could talk."

There it was. The thing he wanted most of all. Lionel's eyes sparkled with pride and affirmation at Aiden's achievements in front of the king of Vesilia, the same king who'd acknowledged Lionel as the hero of Riverview. Aiden held in a scream of excitement and joy with all his might.

The king peered over his shoulder. "Pay close attention, brother. This little one may end up as your successor as Lord High General, seeing as the prince and princess have yet to reveal interest in these affairs."

A third man, who hid behind the king and Lionel, stepped forth. The two-headed hawk covered the blue doublet he wore. Without having to look twice, Aiden figured it to be the king's younger brother. Serril Thorne had squinty blue eyes, the kind that looked like he observed the world through narrow blinders. His boxy face was neatly framed by a few days' growth of dark beard and a head of neatly combed hair.

Serril gave a mirthless laugh and locked eyes with Aiden. "And I look forward to that day, little lord."

Again Aiden bowed. The Lord High General, the highest-ranking general of Vesilia, was speaking to him. The honor of being in the presence of four great men became almost overwhelming. He could not wait to tell Ayla.

Canden wrapped an arm around his brother and turned to head back the way they came. "Now, tell me, brother, how are you going to pay off the debt, seeing as you lost three bets in a row."

The moment Canden and Serril disappeared behind a corner, the smile on Lionel's face turned sour and disgruntled. The grasp of the cane's pommel intensified and turned his knuckles white.

"A hero fights with honor. A coward fights with tricks, Aiden," Lionel sneered.

His insides plunged at the disappointed expression written on his father's face. A coward . . . was he a coward? He thought that defeating Hutton and three others in an uneven duel would suffice for Lionel's approval. But he was wrong.

Captain Hutton wrapped a protective arm around Aiden as if to shield him from an onslaught of hungry wolves. "Do not let those words bring you down, Aiden."

Lionel refused to let his glare falter from the captain.

The captain's scarred face frowned at Lionel. "How do you think you stayed alive? You used tricks during the war and the rebellion." He must have caught his own indiscretion as he continued right after the insult, "I do not wish to sound insensitive, my lord, but not all are granted their father's talents. I believe Aiden would excel in being the unseen man sent behind enemy lines to save soldiers' lives, using subtler means."

Lionel's grasp of his cane tightened. "This is not a discussion. My son will not use cheap tricks and will not become an assassin, hiding in shadows. He is a lord, not a common farmer's or fisher's boy."

Hutton raised an eyebrow high at the mention of Lionel's father's trade. Before he became a lord after the wars and Riverview, Lionel was a simple fisherman's son himself. Aiden tugged his lips into a grin but hid it from his father.

"He is your son. I will make sure to teach him leadership if that is your wish." Hutton cowered under Lionel's commanding stare. "I apologize for bringing you shame on your Soleday of all days."

"The Great Wars may be won, but Drelorn is still of concern to this nation. So also is the Following, who uses the kind of devious and appalling tactics you teach my son. The Crown needs capable leaders to combat all enemies."

Aiden hesitated at first to enter their conversation, but asked anyhow, "What is the Following, Father?"

Lionel snorted in the Captain's face. "The former lord, Rick Haven, the man who rebelled against the king: he has gathered like-minded traitors in Levent and is trying to overthrow the Crown. These are the types of things you need to know." Lionel turned to Hutton. "I assume you have not discussed or spoken about the Eckrosie either?"

Aiden's heart skipped a beat. He wanted to escape the conversation but figured it would only draw more attention to him. Aiden crossed his arms and looked up at the Captain to hear what he had to say.

Hutton's usual grin and uplifting demeanor changed. "Believe me, my lord, such a thing has not been forgotten. He will learn of their deceit and understand why they need to meet a swift end. I trust you did not forget those days we walked home from that wasteland."

Their deceit? What deceit? Ayla and her people had had nothing to do with the attack in Eckros, where six thousand died. To hear them discuss killing his friends sent horrible shivers down his spine. He had to be careful not to expose them.

No matter what, he had to protect Ayla.

"Change your teaching, or we will have a problem." Lionel snatched Aiden and returned to the festivities, leaving Hutton alone beneath the cheering crowd.

"My lord? Aiden?"

Clarissa, the beautiful lady from house Holden, swirled her pitch-black hair while attempting to retain his attention. Aiden blinked to bring himself back to their stroll in the gardens of the Holdens' estate. Trimmed hedges and bushes created a maze of sorts for them to steer through. From the outside, the Holdens' mansion looked grandiose, but a tad bit small. Not truly small, just humble in comparison to Aiden's home across the river. The house had been built from gray stone with mahogany wooden nooks. Tall, narrow windows looked out over the trimmed hedges and the reeds growing in the fast-flowing water nearby.

In front of them, Lionel and Emilia strode with Lord and Lady Holden, apparently speaking about the gardens. Nearby thralls followed the company, carrying cushioning for them if the mood struck to sit. However, even Lionel managed to keep going for what felt like hours.

Aiden focused on Clarissa instead of the forests past Thorne's Town, where he knew Ayla was waiting. "You don't need to say that."

"Say what, my lord?" Clarissa squeezed Aiden's arm tight.

"Lord. You don't need to call me that."

A faint but uncomfortable smile formed on her lips, along with a stiff chuckle. "Of course I do. You are a lord, and I, a lady."

"But we're more than that." Aiden pried a rough leaf from a bush they passed and picked it apart. "Titles don't really mean anything. It's only a tool to separate us from others."

"That is the point. We are not the same. We are more sophisticated than common people without titles, my lord."

"Not really. We shit and piss just like them." Aiden shrugged. The curse came out louder than expected, and soon his mother halted along Lord Holden's side.

Clarissa stayed quiet when they reached their parents. Lionel and the other lord, Berric Holden, scratched their beards at the sudden stop.

"Please excuse us for a moment."

Even as his mother escorted him away, an unnatural smile lingered on her face until she stood with her back turned to the others. She peered at Aiden, down her narrow nose. "What are you doing, son?"

Up ahead, Clarissa twirled her hair, throwing him an occasional smirk.

"I said she didn't have to call me a lord."

"Why would she not? Until your Enfolding, titles matter," Emilia said, and brushed off some disposed leaf from his jacket. "And speak properly in her presence. Jarred seems to have fallen behind with his teachings as of late. Now act respectfully, and tonight I will bring you a treat."

Aiden rolled his eyes but nodded. Who was he to turn down whipped cream and pie?

Their stroll continued until they reached the ends of the grounds, where they turned to head back for supper. Clarissa walked beside him once more. To make sure he pleased his mother, Aiden extended his arm to allow Clarissa close once more, just like the men did. Soon Clarissa's emerald dress brushed against his shins.

"You were spectacular the other day, my lord," Clarissa said after a long silence. "We watched you defeat your opponents with ease. I believe even the king was impressed. You are quite the swordsman."

Aiden's shoulders sagged at the reminder. "Father does not think so."

They fell behind the adults and out of earshot of others. "I believe your lord father is proud, despite denying it. It would defeat the purpose if he granted you a glimpse of his pride."

"He just told me he did not like it," Aiden said defeatedly. "Said that cowards fight with tricks."

"If one considers Lord Riveroak's position, it becomes apparent. You are not to become a soldier, following orders. Your lord father seeks greatness and a different life for you than what he had."

"How do you know?" Aiden combed his fingers through his thick hair, which reached well past his shoulders.

"You have your swordplay. I have mine." Something chilly followed the way she said it with her silky voice. "It is a matter of understanding a person's gestures. You, my lord, you hold a secret, do you not?"

Shit . . . shit. She knows about Ayla? But how could she? I haven't told anyone, and Jarred promised not to tell. Aiden's mind surged, and his face turned scarlet with Clarissa's commanding stare. No amount of distraction could stop Clarissa's piercing teak eyes from seeking him out. A stone fell deep in his stomach.

"Do not fret, my Lord Aiden. I shall not reveal it unless you beg me to."

Aiden kneaded the back of his neck. There was no way she knew about Ayla, at least not the specifics. Jarred and Aiden had been careful not to reveal it to anyone else. To redirect the focus from him, Aiden cleared his throat. "Can you tell me yours?"

"Would not be much of a secret if I did, my lord." Clarissa tucked a lock of her hair behind her ear.

The way she caressed each word spoken left him wanting. What that wanting was, however, eluded him. Being in her presence rattled and excited him, siring a strife of emotions within.

"Father, may we be excused so I may show the lord my venture?" Clarissa said.

Without realizing it, Aiden stood within the confines of the Holdens' estate. Compared to his home, Clarissa's was cramped and small. The hallways and the larger rooms were shaped like boxes, the ceiling within reach for a very tall person. Although the sun shone brightly outside, the rooms were lit by lanterns and candles.

"Of course. Supper will be served in a little while. Do not delay too long," Berric Holden said hastily, and returned his focus to describing a mural by the dining hall.

Clarissa pulled Aiden with her into the indoor maze. Sharp turns and a few steep steps brought them to the second floor and a library with a single window peering at the surrounding mountains. Squared, wooden beams supported the ceiling, and the walls were littered with memorabilia and paintings of dark skies. Bookshelves cut in half outlined the room, and a cloud of dust overwhelmed his senses, making it difficult to breathe.

A thrall stood dressed in what had once been a shirt and pants but was now a collection of foul, raggedy pieces of fabric hanging from boney shoulders and hips. His face hid from the world beneath a burlap sack. Aiden realized it was not the room that reeked; it was the thrall.

Another thrall, a female, bowed at the sight of the lady. This thrall wore a simple dress, with not a stain on it. "My lady. My lord," she said, and headed right into a previous discussion, it seemed with Clarissa. "As requested, my lady, he has stood perfectly still."

Clarissa left Aiden by the doorpost and circled the thrall. "Splendid."

The hardwood flooring glowed beneath the man. A pool of sticky blood hugged the thrall's feet, and with Aiden's slow approach, he witnessed the man's ruined back. Like with Nyle, flaps of skin hung loose after a vicious lashing.

"Father brought this as a gift from his journey to Kingsay." The tops of her fingers grazed the man, whose legs trembled and buckled beneath him. "This thing understands Vesilian but refuses to speak it. You see, he was an Eckrosie refugee, but now he is my thrall."

Aiden's blood clogged, and his breathing grew stuffed. "Oh . . . that . . ." Aiden coughed. "What a great gift."

Standing at the man's side, she wrapped her fingers around his arm but kept a firm gaze on Aiden. "Did you know that Eckrosie ignore hierarchies? They believe all are equal and that titles are a vicious social construction. And apparently, you agree with them, my lord."

A monstrous blow carved terror through his being. With a few words, she'd stripped the veil. He had been careless, believing no one would find out. Fear choked him and tied heavy chains to him. He stood bare, naked before Clarissa.

"Hush, my lord." Clarissa hurried to his side and wrapped her arms around him. "I will not tell. Trust me, I understand the need to become familiar with the enemy to get under their skin, but do not let them under yours."

Her touch sent bolts of pain coursing down his spine. Seeing no other choice, he answered her embrace, though it made him sick to his core.

"You will be the hero of Thorne's Town if you manage to rout out whatever Eckrosie live nearby. I have gotten word of their kind lurking about, whispers of them seeking to do us harm."

Aiden straightened his jacket and kneaded out the pleats in the fabric, disguising his tremble. "I . . . What are you doing with this one, if I may ask, my lady?"

"Certainly." Her focus shifted to the hooded thrall. "I wish to break this one. I know I am getting close. But he only repeats one phrase if I order him to speak in Eckrosie."

Clarissa peered up at the damaged thrall and whispered, "Speak."

The thrall stayed silent.

"My lord, do you wish to partake?"

"Partake?"

"Hit him."

He could not back down. Although every part of him screamed to head in the opposite direction and leave the thrall be, he could not risk Clarissa's attention on him a second time. Aiden dragged his feet. Without lingering hesitation, he thrust a closed fist into the thrall's stomach.

Then another. And another.

The man hunkered over with each blow, his knees growing weak. A silent mutter left him when Aiden stopped.

"*Never forgotten . . . nor forgiven,*" the thrall repeated in Eckrosie, giving Aiden time to translate the words in his head.

Clarissa shrugged. "I have yet to discern what it means. Anyway, supper?" She grabbed Aiden by the arm, allowing him to escort her back to their parents waiting downstairs.

The meaty and perfectly cooked venison did not end the bitter taste the afternoon had left him with. His knuckles pulsated from the repeated strikes against the thrall. Every part of him felt it was wrong to harm an innocent man, but he was surrounded by people who did not understand his sentiment. Clarissa munched on the food seemingly without care or pause. She was dangerous, and he had let her get too close.

CHAPTER TEN

Before the Plunge

Gil was doing it. Cidron's offer the other night had been too good to turn down. Gil wiped tears from the lute, which rested in his lap. One hundred silver to replace the strings was a price he could not afford. The fifty silver he carried in his pouch had been hard enough to earn. Spending all on new strings simply would not work. Cidron's offer would give him food, drink, shelter, and work. Living on the streets, fighting for each night and day, was too much for him. Sure, he would end up a thrall, but it was better to be that than an urchin living in constant fear of someone robbing him, or worse.

The streets of Keelheart were not as crowded during the day for some reason, or perhaps it was just easier to move around when the sun was up. Gil squeezed past rowdy adults and children playing on his way to the Rosses'. The castle-like house looked even prettier in the light. Pots with giant flowers stood outside, something uncommon to see in the reeking slums.

Gil moved toward a lady sitting outside the entrance. Her tired gaze wandered up and down. "What?"

"I'm here to speak to Cidron."

"Why?"

Gil hesitated. "'Cause I want to be a thrall and live here."

The woman slid over on her chair to let him pass.

The bedroom to the right stood empty, with no thralls sleeping. Gil passed the room and followed the grand hallway. Chandeliers with half-burned candles hung above him, but large windows on the opposite side of the house lit the way during the day.

The dining room, where Gil had eaten a spectacular breakfast the other day, was also empty, but the smell of crisp bacon, eggs, and cheese lingered. Chairs leaned up against ten or fifteen tables, where plates and sleeves remained from the last meal.

By one of the windows, Cidron ate, standing up, dressed in the same baggy clothes as the other day.

Gil stepped into the light. "My lord."

Cidron turned to look at him. His hard exterior melted as he faced Gil. "Pfft... don't call me that. Only pompous shits in Riverview call me that. Just call me Cidron, and we'll be fine." Cidron leaned up against a table, crossing his arms. Even though he didn't have good looks, he appeared very manly and tough. "You've given my offer a thought?"

"Yeah. My lute broke. Or, I mean, the strings did."

Cidron wandered over to Gil and flickered the broken strings. "If it's because of this, I'll give you some money and send you on your way."

"No, I... I want to stay here. I'm tired of the streets. And you said I could perform for you and your friends."

"I did. But you understand you'll work as a thrall? That I get to send you to anyone who needs help."

Gil nodded.

"Great. All I need is for you to sign a paper. I'll be right back."

Gil stood alone. Soon he would belong again. No part of him regretted his decision. With the Rosses, he would be safe.

Cidron returned with quill and paper. He set them down on a table after removing the leftovers of the previous dinners. A paper uncurled. Scribbles, incomprehensive lines, and circles marked the page, mocking Gil. "I . . . I can't read," he stammered.

"No worries." Cidron patted Gil forcefully on the back. "It's a document that basically says you'll work for the Rosses, and you can't go working for someone else. Judge Dahle up in Riverview made this stupid law, where I have to get thralls to sign this paper."

The quill drew lines on the paper. Cidron wrote things on it. "What's your full name? Do you have a last name?"

"Gil."

"Hmm . . . we'll need something that means you and not another Gil. What do you think about Gil the Singer?"

Gil bit the bottom of his lip. "What about Gil the Great?"

Cidron clicked his tongue and dabbed the quill at him. "Like your attitude, kid."

The quill came to rest in Gil's fingers. Cidron placed a gentle hand on his and moved the quill on the paper. "Sign it by just letting it move on the paper."

The ink left the quill, creating a puddle at the beginning of the scribble. The quill moved in Gil's hand as he pulled it to the right. It was fun to watch each tremble trace to the paper and how the ink soaked into it. Three different sheets of paper found him as he signed his name on them. It was short, with half a circle and two vertical lines.

Cidron gathered them and shook Gil's hand. "Glad to have you with us. There is, however, one more thing for you to do. Real sorry, kid, but a paper ain't much to go on. To get into our family, you've gotta have a token that you belong with us." He grabbed the top of Gil's shoulder. "It'll hurt, won't lie to you. But it ain't for long.

Afterward, why don't you go get that lute fixed at the same place that turned you down?"

"But it costs one hundred silver crowns to get it fixed," Gil said with a tremble in his voice.

A coin pouch rattled, and Cidron counted it roughly before handing it to Gil. The pouch weighed heavy in his palm. "You're part of our family, and we look out for each other."

"Thank you," Gil said weakly, but then repeated it with more courage.

"Now, you'll get one of these." Cidron pulled the neck of his shirt to the left. On his already-blotchy white skin, a bulky mark rested above his heart: a circle and a star within it. They were going to brand him? Like Dorian and Zahna were branded?

"Did I do something wrong?" Gil asked, pulling the annoying strands of hairs beginning to sprout from his scalp.

"Almighty, no. This isn't like the Crown, where they mark people and sentence them. Trust me, I know," Cidron said, and revealed another mark, but this one at the bottom of his neck. Black ink stained his skin with writing of some kind. It looked like the way Gil had signed the papers.

"They put me in Nedox and made sure to mark me. Ever heard of Nedox?"

Gil gulped. "That's a city where the Crown sends criminals?"

"Yeah. But I ain't a criminal. I was a kid like you, sent to work for fifteen years. That's what the brand is for." Cidron leaned up against a table again. "What we need you to do is different. Instead of marking you an outcast and criminal, we have this as a sign of family and union. That sound fair, Gil the Great?"

How could he say no? "Sure, I'll do it."

"Fantastic. Let's get you to Barb."

Cidron showed Gil through other parts of the house until they reached the back. Under the shelter of a wooden roof, a woman, looking more like a man with her bulky and enormous figure, poked an iron into a burning stove.

"Barb, got another one here."

Barb glanced at Gil, clicking her tongue before shoving an iron into the fire. "Right."

Cidron placed Gil on a wobbly stub. "She's a bit grumpy, this one, but don't think 'bout her. I've learned to ignore her."

Gil handed the lute to Cidron. If it would hurt, he didn't want the pain to break more of the instrument. Somehow Cidron made Gil wish to do this without any fuss or complaint. It would probably hurt a lot, but he didn't want to show it. He didn't want Cidron to think of him as weak.

The iron left the fire. The air sizzled around the circular end of it, where glowing red and orange waves danced on the metal. The mark looked to be as big as the palm of Gil's hand. He grabbed his trousers and dug his nails into them.

The woman's rough hands slid his shirt to the left. His shoulder wanted to pull away, but he forced himself to stay still. Every muscle, bone, and hair on his body tensed when the iron dug into his skin. It screamed, and he twisted to get rid of the pain, but Gil remained determined. Cidron's eyes pierced Gil's soul and fueled it with resolve. Yet the boy couldn't stop a pained whelp from escaping. Ravenous dogs tore his skin apart, and Barb didn't seem to care about his discomfort. She held the iron against his skin long enough for the burning smell to reach him.

The metal hissed in a bucket of water nearby. Gil breathed heavily and looked down at the burn, his skin already red and swollen, pulsating and itching.

"You're a fighter, aren't you?" Cidron laughed, and handed Gil back his lute. "Let it breathe for a couple of days, and don't let stuff touch it."

Gil nodded. "Right."

"Go to fix your lute, kid, and we'll talk later. Welcome to the family."

Gil's new home rose above him. Already it gave him more than comfort and community. The pouch with coins weighed down his trousers. He pulled them up and headed into the streets of Keelheart to repair his lute.

Leah waited for the beds in the attic to hold her mother and sister. But no matter how much she wished for it, they stood empty. Their bodies had been burned a few days ago at the Halls after Ida showed Leah many times that they wouldn't wake up. She wanted to see her mother and sister jump off the pyre, but they kept on sleeping even when the hungry flames burned them.

A knock on the doorframe startled Leah. Standing in the opening, Giana, the silver-haired lady from downstairs, greeted Leah with a hug, the same way she had done for days. Today, however, she didn't hug for long or as gently. "Leah, you know how sorry I'm for your loss. Words can't explain. Do you have any relatives or family you can stay with?"

None that she knew of. Leah stared off into the distance.

"I . . . I don't know what to do for you. But . . . you can't stay here any longer."

"Why?" Leah sniffled.

Giana kneeled and leaned against the wall. "Your mother is with the Wanderer, and . . . I've got other people to look out for, other families who need to live here."

"I can work for you. I'll do what my mother did."

"I'm sorry, Leah, I am. I know you could, but I made her a promise. Your mother made me swear to never let you work for me."

Leah wiped her nose with the end of her sleeve. "But I'm . . . I wanna."

"No, the thing your mother did was not a job for a child."

"But . . . where should I live?"

Giana pulled her hair behind her ears, her skin flushed red. "Well . . . I have an idea where they'll watch over you and protect you."

In the middle of Keelheart, where rucked buildings with leaking roofs and damaged windows lined up, a house unlike the rest stood. Red clay and several stories high, the building towered above the rest of the slum. It was the house that her mother had warned her about. Leah carried a bag with a few things she had from home. Clothes, a gray blouse her mother had worn, a toy she had played with Miya with, and the anklets from both Miya and Jaida. Leah pulled the bag closer whenever a person passed her and Giana.

At the entrance, a mean-looking woman with a grumpy and crinkled face looked down at Leah. She let them pass when Giana said they were there for Cidron Ross.

The Rosses? She was going to the Rosses, the people her mother had always warned her about? She tugged at Giana's skirt. "I don't want to be here," she whispered.

Giana ignored her.

The house's insides were just as beautiful as the outside, with many doors connecting with the hallway they walked along. Farther down in the candle-lit hallway, they heard singing and people clapping so loud that the house shook.

They found their way into a large dining room. The tops of heads bobbed along with a beat that the entire room kept alive. Had it not been for their smiles, the adults would have scared her with their bulky, scarred, and aging faces.

Standing on a corner stage, a boy sang a song, and the adults in the room clapped their hands. The kid, with a shaved head and glittering blue eyes, watched the people clap and shout. He didn't need to smile for her to see how much he enjoyed staying on the stage. There was something different about him. Maybe it was how he stood on the stage, commanding the room with his performance, or maybe it was that he smiled while he sang. Whatever it was, he looked happy, and people loved it.

Giana grabbed Leah's hand and guided her along rows of tables and benches. It was like walking through a busy crowd in a market but with more joy. People sang and toasted together.

In the middle of the gathering, Giana stopped in front of a man with hard features. He looked like he had been carved out of stone that stood out in the open, beaten by wind and rain. His nose was crooked, and his brow dropped over his dark eye sockets. The man looked at Giana and stopped singing.

"Giana." He smiled. His voice was just as hard as a rock. "Long time since I saw you. And who's this?"

Leah stepped up to the man but kept close to Giana.

"I didn't know where else to turn. She's the daughter of one of my girls, Jaida . . . and she passed. I promised her I'd not let this little one work for me, but I can't afford to pay her living expenses."

"You did the right thing. Taking care of children and giving them a home is what I do." The man rested his elbows on his knees to peer straight at Leah. "I'm sorry for your loss, little one. I'm Cidron Ross, and you are?"

Leah shrank before him, but somehow he seemed to not be as bad as she'd been told. "Leah," she stuttered.

Cidron's eyes sparkled with excitement. "Leah. Well, I'm going to give you the same choice I give everyone seeking my help. You can work for me, wherever I'll send you, and you'll have a home and family right here. How does that sound?"

Leah fiddled with her mother's foot-link. *I want my mother and sister back*, she thought, keeping the tears at bay.

Giana patted Leah on her back. "See. Lord Cidron will take care of you. I wish you all the best, and I hope to see you again."

"But . . ."

Giana was gone. Leah cradled her bag tight while fighting back the tears.

Cidron seemed to notice, as he scooched over to make room on the bench for her. "I'm very sorry for your loss. I actually knew your mother."

Leah accepted the seat. "Really?"

"She was kind and always spoke about you. She was very proud of you. Now, I don't know what she said about me, but it's not my will to cause you any harm. If there's anything you need, you come and talk to me."

She scrutinized the surrounding crowd. He might not have looked nice, but he did seem nice. He offered her bread and butter, which she was quick to accept and eat. The party kept going, and the boy kept singing. Or at least, she heard him start a song before the others took over and sang it with him. Cidron spoke to Leah and asked her about her home and the things she liked to do. After a while, she dared to show him the anklets of both her mother and sister, which he offered to keep safe. He reached around his neck, where a leather band hung. He tied the anklets to the necklace and placed it around Leah's neck. Both dangled against her chest, always close to her.

No words could describe how good it felt to have them near. She gave him a half-smile to hide how pained she felt inside. Everything hurt. Breathing, speaking, living. Everything was hard to do, but she had to be strong. She had to be brave for her family. Even though they didn't live, they still walked beside her, thanks to Cidron.

~❀~

The hooves of Aiden's mount caused the surrounding mist to swirl along the forest trail. Adventure knew the path as well as Aiden, and she trotted mindlessly past the thick growth. The boy gathered the thick fabric of his jacket to keep the morning's chill at bay.

Jarred kept a watchful eye on Aiden. Once they'd reached the pond and the usual meeting spot for Ayla, Jarred slowed his mount. Adventure came to a halt beside the thrall.

"Aiden?" Jarred asked. Until recently, Jarred had never let slip any courtesy, but after Aiden's request, he'd called him by his first name whenever they left the mansion.

Aiden did not answer. The reins squeezed the blood from his hands.

"What happened with Lady Clarissa? You have been silent for days," Jarred muttered.

"I . . ."

Ayla leaped out of the shrubbery, her eyes glistening like morning dew at the sight of him. As soon as he looked upon her, the dread that cloaked Aiden dissipated. Her hair smelled of honey and lavender. Her skin heated him with their close embrace, an embrace he never wanted to leave. Wrapped in her arms, nothing could harm him. Not the fear of discovery, nor the disapproval of his father. Near Ayla, everything else faded into a distant nightmare.

"*Always great day when Aiden is here,*" Ayla whispered in his ear, sending a pleasurable trickle down his neck.

He burrowed his nose deeper into her wild hair. "I missed you."

Nearby forceful snorts and clopping from horses carried through the forest.

"Hide," Jarred said, and nudged Ayla from the trail, breaking up their hug. She did not need much persuasion, as she pranced into a gathering of bushes and got low to the ground.

"Get back on your horse," Jarred commanded Aiden, who did as he was told.

Three horses with riders appeared from the thick forest, trotting the trail. A black stallion neighed with its master's sudden tug of the reins.

Lord Berric Holden, Clarissa's father, pulled up to Aiden. Two thralls in similar armor as Jarred's halted behind their Lord.

Lord Holden, with protruding tawny eyes resting under arched eyebrows, scrutinized Aiden. The thin lips hidden in a goatee moved to make room for a hasty grin. "My Lord Riveroak. I have been riding as fast as my mount could muster to catch up with you."

"My Lord Holden." Aiden bowed his head as he was taught and tightened his hold of Adventure's reins as she began pulling. "I . . . we . . . My saddle was acting up, but it's alright now," Aiden stammered.

Unsurprisingly, Berric's superiority shone through with his complete disregard of the two thralls traveling with him. He urged his horse to move up to Aiden. "As luck would have it, I will be accompanying you to Camp Wintersmore. I have business to attend to with the captain."

"That is fantastic," Aiden managed to lie while keeping his gaze fixed on everything save for the bush where Ayla hid.

"Lead the way." Berric ushered Aiden forth, and the boy could only do as he was told. His meeting with Ayla would have to wait.

Thankfully, Berric was the kind of person who enjoyed long stretches of silence. Throughout the journey, not a word was spoken. They listened as the horses' hooves hit the well-traveled path, which led them outside the forest where the camp lay. The wooden gate parted, and a stableboy gathered their mounts.

Captain Hutton seemed to have tired of the intense heat the summer provided. He approached them with a short shirt that revealed his dark skin and countless scars adorning his arms. The sleeves rolled up as far as his muscular shoulders allowed.

He took a bow to acknowledge Lord Holden.

"A pleasure to meet you, Captain." Berric bowed as well. "Lord Riveroak has sung praises of you back in Thorne's Town."

"The pleasure is ours, Lord Holden. Would you care for some refreshments?"

Berric Holden gave a loud sigh and withdrew his hands from a pair of riding gloves. "No need. I would prefer to get started."

"Right away." Hutton waved a hand to signal Aiden to follow.

Aiden trailed along, without knowing what to expect. They headed toward the training grounds. Perhaps Berric was there to ask for Hutton to take in Clarissa as another student. But it did not seem likely, since the well-dressed and well-spoken girl did not accompany her father. Relieved by not facing Clarissa, Aiden's shoulders relaxed from the tension that had sprung up upon meeting Berric.

A couple of crates were lined up by the dull practice swords, as usual. But unlike other times, one of the crates rattled upon their approach. The captain and the lord took no particular notice as they halted before it. Five holes, too small for Aiden's hand to fit through, opened into the dark container.

Hutton bashed his hand against the lid, and again it rattled. "For lack of proper accommodations, we made do with the materials at our disposal, my lord. I hope this does not affect your work."

"Far from it." The corners of Berric's thin lips curved upward. "Rather enhances it."

Hutton undid a latch keeping the lid locked but stopped to speak his mind to the lord. "Here's the truth: torture doesn't work. Or at least, it doesn't work like we want it to. This man won't give us details on where he's from no matter how much torment you put him through. Meaning no disrespect, of course, my Lord Holden."

Aiden blinked. A man? A grown man was stuffed away in the crate? The crate barely reached the top of Aiden's head. Was it one of the soldiers perhaps, who lived at the camp? Aiden's gaze lingered on the crate while Hutton continued, "Drelorn forces kept me prisoner. They wanted information about our army, and I didn't give them the information."

Again, Berric drew a loud sigh, making it clear that he'd heard the arguments before. "Trust me, you did. Thankfully, the Drelorians were foolish and incompetent enough for it to slip them by unnoticed."

"You question my honor?" Hutton said, an unflattering and unusual snarl crossing his face.

"On the contrary, captain. No one can hide their darkest secrets once they are truly desperate. Of course, a lot of false information is given, but the truth hides within the cracks. The process may take months if not years to uncover, but in the end, it will be divulged."

The same kind of dread that had wrapped around Aiden during his last visit to Clarissa found its way back to him with the lord's confidence.

Hutton tugged at the end of his mustache. "My only concerns are the methods. Why deny a swift death?"

"Our king has bestowed the burden on my family and me to root out the Eckrosie vermin hiding in our country. This one is not alone, I can promise you that, and once I learn where they are, the honor of bringing them to justice will belong to you."

"This is not a question about glory. I merely ask you to show mercy."

"Why did you send word to me if that is the case? It is hardly a secret that I am the Crown's torturer."

Aiden gulped, and Hutton too. Berric was not there for pleasantries.

"Very well." Hutton tipped the barrel on its side. Out crawled a man, or at least, what looked to be a man. A horrible reek of sweat and feces followed his escape from the barrel. Stained clothing belonging to a merchant kept the man dressed.

His ashen hair was stained with dried blood, and it whipped behind his head as he slithered in the dirt to escape. Berric's thralls cornered him and yanked him from the ground to face their master.

"P-please don't hurt me. I have nothing to say. I was only heading to Nedox, and I—"

The air exploded from his lungs with a brutal onslaught of punches and jabs. Hutton grabbed Aiden forcefully and escorted him to his tent, away from the torture about to commence.

They could not escape the grunts, pleads, and screams even as they snuck into the large tent. Hutton sat down behind a shabby desk and sorted through piles of paper in no particular order; it was a distraction to lessen the commotion happening nearby.

"Sit," Hutton grunted, pointing to an adjacent chair next to a locked chest. "Make scrolls out of these papers."

Aiden did as he was told. Now hardly seemed the time to contradict or question the captain. A collection of scrolls followed

Aiden's work. An occasional crease followed the boy's uncomfortable twitch at the sound of a heart-wrenching scream.

"Captain?" Aiden risked asking.

Hutton released his focus on the papers and gave an acknowledging grunt.

"Why do people hate the Eckrosie?"

"You want the honest answer, or the right answer?" A quill clinked against an inkwell. "To be honest, there ain't no good answer, only interpretations of the same fact."

"My father hates them because they killed the soldiers at the Sea of a Thousand Swords."

A sudden burst of joyless laughter left the captain. "He hates them because they humiliated Vesilia and because we are taught to hate them. Once the wars came to an end, people saw the problems right here in Vesilia. What better way to unite people than to give them an enemy? The Eckrosie aren't any threat. They're made to look like they are to keep folks' minds occupied."

He shook his head.

"Eckros has never been a threat. The great countries used their fertile lands as a battleground. They were always occupied by other countries and used as slaves. Yes, a couple of Eckrosie attacked our armies and killed thousands, but honestly, we deserved it. Do you know how the Ashes of Penance were created?"

Aiden bit his lower lip, trying to remember.

"Eckrosie burned their own country. That's what truly desperate people do. They killed our soldiers and drove us out by making their lands uninhabitable. I honestly detest and despise the Crown for inventing this story of a people out for revenge that are trying to kill us all."

It was a different side to the story, one that none dared speak of, it seemed. The captain sweated and let out several frustrated snorts with his quickening discourse. Once he stopped speaking, however, his gaze widened and he winced, as if frightened of the words leaving him.

Aiden leaned forward. "It's alright. I'm not going to say what you said."

At this, Hutton seemed somewhat relieved.

Aiden dampened his lips. "May I ask why that man is being harmed if you don't hate the Eckrosie?"

Hutton rested his head in his palm. "He … a few of my men attacked his caravan. They saw an easy target and decided to inspect his belongings. A woman accompanied him, and well, things took a bad turn, and she left. My men noticed that they spoke a different language and brought him here to question him. There are rumors of a nearby settlement of Eckrosie. The person who uncovers it will be rewarded by the king. My men wanted part of the glory, I assume. That's why they sent word to Lord Holden."

The nearby settlement. The village. Ayla had let Aiden enter, despite the massive threat. His scalp burned and gnawed with the rising anxiety. He shuffled a couple of scrolls into a neat pile and avoided the captain's gaze.

Another scream tore through the camp. Uncertain whether or not his worry spat the words or if he accidentally thought out loud, Aiden spoke again. "Sir, you said we need to protect those who cannot protect themselves. Does that not include the—"

A crash sounded, followed by a sickening pop. Next to Aiden, the chest caved in as the prisoner slammed into the lid. Neither Aiden nor the captain had heard or seen his approach.

The reeking man looked as surprised as they were. He moaned and dragged himself off the chest, several long splinters latched deep into his skin. He brushed his hair from his face, which was shiny with new gore. Aiden gasped at the unrecognizable swollen features.

"*I need to leave . . . I have to,*" the man moaned, stumbling. He reached out to Aiden and clutched him to not fall. "*Please . . . don't let me talk. Please, make them stop.*"

"I'm sorry . . . I can't," Aiden whispered back in Vesilian.

"*Please, I will do anything, but please . . . do not make me talk. I cannot survive longer, I—*"

Hutton unsheathed a knife from his back and slit the man's throat.

A spray of blood washed over Aiden as the prisoner lost his footing and dropped to the ground. The thick fluid was no hotter or cooler than his own skin, yet each drop felt like rain. Disgusting, reeking drops.

Blood gushed from the dying Eckrosie at his feet. Aiden wanted to move, help him, do something, but his body stood frozen.

"If you want to stay alive, tricks are necessary," Hutton huffed, and turned the limp man on his side. "Let me do the talking, little lord."

Sounds left Aiden, but nothing coherent.

"You wanted that brute to prolong his suffering?" The captain pointed the knife to the outside of the tent.

Aiden trembled. Of course not. But the alternative seemed much better than the finality of death.

Footsteps drew near. "Where did he go?" Berric yelled outside the tent.

Hutton cleared his throat. "In here, my lord."

The canvas parted to let in Berric and his thralls. Unsurprisingly, his clothes were stained red from the blood of the prisoner. He halted at the sight of the corpse, quickly observing the slit throat, and turned to Hutton.

"You . . . killed him?"

"Self-defense. He showed up and threatened Lord Riveroak's life. I did what needed to be done."

Lord Holden scoffed at the absurdity even Aiden caught upon.

Hutton wiped his blade on the prisoner's clothes and put it back into its sheath at his back. "How could you let this happen, my lord? Did you let him go?"

"He . . . did something impossible." Berric kneaded the back of his neck. "He disappeared. The thralls kept him in place, and suddenly he vanished into thin air."

"And traveled into my tent in an instant?" Hutton raised a curious eyebrow. But what the lord said made some strange sense to Aiden. Neither of them had heard him approach. Suddenly he was just there.

"I am not certain what I witnessed, my lord, but he managed to escape regardless. Luckily, he did not get far. Well . . ." Berric sighed and combed his hand through his stubby hair. "It seems you have not lost your touch, Captain."

Everything closed in on Aiden. No matter how careful he was, the world found its way into his lies and secrets. What if this was the future waiting for Ayla? He could not risk it. Her life meant more than anything. The surrounding conversations, their removal of the body, all of it faded in the presence of the growing worry.

This could not be her future.

CHAPTER ELEVEN

In a Family's Servitude

As soon as they reached the brook, Ayla popped back out. She rushed to Jarred and Aiden's side.

"Hi, I missed you," she said, and strolled alongside the horses with her hands knit together mischievously.

Aiden blinked the confusion away. The Eckrosie man's blood was washed clean, and Jarred had scrubbed Aiden's garments, but the unsettling feeling remained.

"*What is happening? Did I do wrong?*" Ayla asked.

"No, I . . ."

Jarred steered his mount across the path, creating a blockade for Aiden. "Aiden, the horses need rest to take on the remainder of the journey."

"So what? I . . ." Aiden stopped, realizing what Jarred implied. "Oh, well, great. I'll just . . ."

He slid off the saddle and handed Jarred the reins before heading off to the pond with Ayla. All the while, Aiden kept a close eye on the surrounding trees, bushes, and shrubbery.

"*Are you angry?*" Ayla brushed her tangled hair, hiding her beautiful eyes. "*What happened?*"

Aiden stuttered in an attempt to buy time to find the correct words. "*No, you have never made me angry. I need to protect you.*"

"We protect each other," Ayla said, and grabbed Aiden's hand lovingly. A tingle sprang loose in his stomach.

He squeezed her fingers back. "Everyone's looking for you and your home, Ayla. The man that came here . . . he tortured an Eckrosie and he—they killed him. I don't know what to do to protect you."

Ayla brushed a strand of his hair behind his ear. "We are fine. Nothing will hurt us. We know it dangerous to go outside forest, but inside forest, we are safe."

Unable to control it, tears rained, glistening as he wept. All he wished was for them to live as one and share even more beautiful moments. The world wanted to tear them apart, and it was succeeding. With his tears, his soul ripped open. He loathed the words forming in his throat and hindered them from being spoken, but what other choice was there? His parents would punish Ayla, the Holdens would torture her, and the soldiers would kill her. There was no other way.

"If we don't meet, they can't find you." Aiden repeated the words between sobs. "Believe me, I want to stay with you, but not if that leads to you getting hurt."

Ayla gathered his hands in hers. She peered deep into his eyes. "It hurt more not seeing you."

If only the pain could escape. Instead, it strangled him with a sickening embrace he would do anything to evade. How could she not see what this was doing to him? But as he looked at her and the tears threatened to spill yet again, he understood: she was saying goodbye as well.

The sun disappeared, stressing the fact they needed to part. As the forest's shadows turned blue, Jarred tore them apart. At first,

Aiden wanted to hurt Jarred for doing it, but he was doing them a favor. Neither of them wanted to leave, but as Jarred guided Aiden back to the path, he followed voluntarily, leaving the most incredible girl and friend alone in the ever-growing darkness.

Another dinner, and new company. The Holdens and Tallstags sat together with the Riveroaks at the massive oak table of their estate. The three families dined on the food the thralls had prepared— mashed potatoes with venison.

Aiden picked at the tasty meal, barely enjoying any of it. Word of the event at the camp had reached his parents' ears fast and gave him an excuse to hide his tears and sorrow behind. The trail each day lay empty. He wished to see Ayla, but she stayed away, which was probably for the best.

Once again, Clarissa accompanied him to supper. Each time they met seemed to bring her dresses farther down her bosom and expose a bit more of her breasts to him. It grew mighty distracting how she leaned in closer whenever he said something that caused her to giggle. Although she was a girl, bordering on young adulthood, she was dressed like the older ladies, in laced tops and skirts reaching the floor.

Aiden pried his gaze from her chest when Jarred's hand distracted him. Jarred gave a sly smile at Aiden before putting away the boy's empty plate.

The lady leaned close to him. "Would you be interested in taking a ride with me through Thorne's Town in the morning, my lord? I know some trails where you can see far. At times, one can spot Lake Ember and Levent when the weather is clear."

Aiden gulped some water. "I . . . I mean, if I'm not at the camp, then sure." He caught a glimpse of his mother, who clearly was listening to their conversation from across the table. "Eh. I mean, of course, my lady."

"You seem nervous, my lord. Are you feeling ill?"

He had to say something smart to get back into the conversation and to fight off the onslaught of sorrow squeezing his throat tight. "Well, I . . . how can I not when I have a beautiful woman at my side?"

Next to him, Eamon poked around his plate, imitating the Tallstag boy sitting nearby. Aiden could sympathize with his little brother's boredom, as he shared it as well.

Lord Berric Holden took to his feet and rang his glass to silence the table. Everything about him frightened Aiden after their last meeting. Today he was clean-shaven, suiting him much better. It showed his robust features instead of hiding them behind a thick beard. He cleared his throat. "I would like to propose a toast. To our future couple, Lord Aiden Riveroak and Lady Clarissa Holden, who will bring our two families together."

Aiden accidentally spat juice back into his goblet. It spewed over his face, which he hurried to dry. Future couple? Him and . . . Clarissa? Of course, she was beautiful with her teak eyes and delicate features, but he did not know much about her. All he knew was that she enjoyed the stories of heroes and explorers like Aiden did, but who did not? And, well, the disturbing amazement she obviously took in tormenting thralls. Compared to how he felt about Ayla, his feelings for Clarissa did not extend further than acquaintance.

"May your coming Enfolding and union bring us closer and inspire us with your love."

The adults clapped at the announcement while Aiden loosened the collar of his doublet from strangling him.

Clarissa stood up. Her dress caressed her slim figure, revealing much of her hourglass shape. She looked at Aiden. "I offer my gratitude to Lord and Lady Riveroak and my lord father and lady mother for making our union possible. I am counting the days until we may join and forge our own household."

It was a good toast, one Sonya was probably applauding back in the kitchens. Aiden clapped with the rest of the room.

All eyes searched him out. His knees wobbled beneath him as he stood to speak. Sonya had taught him words of courtesy and common sayings for these occasions, but his mind blanked . . . this was not what he wanted. He hardly knew Clarissa and did not wish to become as close with her as he had with Ayla. Then he understood. Aiden was a name put on him, never chosen. He was not in control of his own life. Ayla and the Eckrosie had decided for themselves, but as a noble lord of House Riveroak, he had no say. Even now, they decided who he was supposed to love and cherish. They tried to make him into someone he did not want to be.

But now was not the time for such thoughts. Ladies and lords awaited his reply. It reminded him of a story he'd read. A lord who fought to claim a lady's hand. He could not think of anything else, so why not take it as inspiration. Aiden turned to Clarissa, her hands folded in her lap. "My lady. I cannot wait until the day I can call you my nearest. You are my lady, and I will do everything in my power to support you and ensure your happiness."

Lionel and Emilia gleamed with pride, though they'd at first scrunched their noses, concerned where his speech would lead.

Clarissa took his hand and gave him a peck on the back of it. Reluctantly, Aiden returned the favor.

"Mother?" Eamon uttered. People took to their feet and cheered for Aiden and Clarissa. Eamon and his friend, the little Lord Tallstag, remained seated.

The chairs scratched the floor once their occupants took their seats. The conversations resumed. Clarissa leaned close. "I hope I did not spoil the surprise, my lord."

"Mother," Eamon said louder, but their mother ignored him.

"No, it was a great surprise, my lady," Aiden said.

"Mother?" Eamon lost his patience. Potatoes flew across the table and hit Emilia at the base of her neck. The potatoes crumbled into chunks and sprinkled across the table.

Everyone focused on Aiden's mother, awaiting her reaction. Aiden saw the shift happen before it did. The room chilled and silenced. The lords and ladies stopped eating and conversing. Emilia rose up. Her shoes clicked against the floor with her determined steps around the table. Everyone held their breath, save for Aiden. He knew it was coming, and he would not let it.

Emilia yanked Eamon off the chair. The boy squirmed in her grasp and pulled against her fingers digging into his hair.

She raised a hand above her head.

Aiden reached her. His fist slammed her stomach, forcing her to stagger off—not quickly enough, however, as her open hand slapped Aiden across his cheek.

"You leave him alone," Aiden shouted at his mother. "He's only a kid."

As his mother took a step toward him, Aiden shoved her backward. Whatever she was doing, she would not harm Eamon.

By the table, Lionel's expression closed up. The previous smile was erased, and he stared at Aiden disapprovingly.

"Jarred," Lionel uttered.

Jarred, standing in the corner of the room, left his task and approached. His fingers shut around Aiden's arm, squeezing the skin tight.

"Jarred, let me go." Aiden squirmed against the grip, but the thrall refused his request.

"Bring him to the cellar." Lionel moved toward Emilia and ignored Aiden's plea.

Aiden shot a glance at his mother. Instead of pure fury and anger, she radiated with sorrow. She turned her gaze from him and rubbed the spot Aiden had struck.

"Mother, I'm sorry."

The dining hall disappeared behind a corner. His dress shoes slid on the stone floor as Jarred dragged him along. "Jarred, stop. I . . . I command you to let me go."

The thrall did not answer. But his face said it all. Every muscle of his face twitched to hold back the tears gathering in his eyes. Whatever was happening would not end well for Aiden.

"Please, I won't do it again. I . . . she was going to hurt Eamon. Hutton told me not to let people get hurt. Eamon's my little brother. Please."

They passed the kitchens, where smoke and heat from the burners escaped. Sonya and Nyle peered at them after hearing Aiden's plea.

A short trip down a flight of stairs beyond the kitchen led them to the cellar: a cramped corridor with boxes, crates, and burlap sacks lined up.

"I know I crossed a line. P-please, let me go."

A door swung open at the end of the hallway, and Aiden was thrust inside. He skidded on the floor but got up just as fast. The door slammed shut on him, locking him inside. Aiden tugged at the doorknob, but it refused to budge.

"Let me out. Please, let me out." His tugs turned to thuds. He slammed his hands into the door long past the point when his hands throbbed. A couple of receding footfalls reached him. "Don't leave me."

No light surrounded him. Utter pitch black stared at him from all sides as if there were thousands of Nightbringers studying him. Aiden turned back to the door and rattled the doorknob. "Mother? I'm sorry. I'm sorry. I . . ."

Complete silence resided here. Each little sniffle and croak he made turned to screams against the silence. Smooth stone greeted his fingers. Tiny crevices between the stones scratched his skin, and he let his fingers guide him. He traced the dark with his shaking hands, counting the steps. Five, six, seven. Seven and a half steps before another wall stood in his path. The same amount of steps to the other sides until he found his way back to the wooden door.

I only meant to help my brother, Aiden repeated to himself. He wiped his cheeks from tears, tickling his skin.

Again the door rattled with his attempts. "Please, let me out! I'm sorry. Father. Mother. Anyone!" His throat grew thick as gravel at the screaming. The floor chilled every part of him. He leaned up against the door, hoping and praying they would release him or at least come and speak with him. He gathered his legs and hugged them with his skinny arms, envisioning getting a loving hug from someone. All the while, he pounded against the door.

Snoring and sleeping people surrounded Leah in the gloomy room of the Rosses. She curled up into a ball in her bed and stared out the window. She was unable to fall asleep for hours, probably because of the burn mark she had on her chest. It itched so much, but she was unable to breathe every time she touched the raw skin because of the pain. Cidron had warned her that it would hurt, but not this much, and not days after it happened.

She hugged herself tightly, pretending that it was her mother's arms that held her. The anklets of her mother and sister were always close because of the necklace Cidron gave her. But it was never the same as seeing them or hearing them speak.

It wasn't easy for her to speak with the other thralls. At meals, Leah often found herself eating alone in a corner. Even when surrounded by others, she didn't dare talk to any of the rest, who were often much older than she was.

"Mind if I join you?"

She jumped by the disturbance. Leah used the back of her hand to rub away tears. The boy, Gil, with reddish-brown skin, shaved head, and calm gray-blue eyes, took a seat on her bed. Up close, she noticed his lower lip being a little off to the side compared to his upper lip.

"You're . . . ?"

"Leah," she sniffled.

"Right. Well, I don't want you to be alone when you're sad. What's wrong?"

"I'm . . . my burn hurts and itches." She yanked the sleeve of her shirt to let the skin breathe and not stick to the fabric.

"I've got a trick for that. When I want to scratch mine, I scratch a different place instead, like my arm or my hand." Gil demonstrated by pressing his nails deep into his elbow. "It doesn't help every time, but it's better than scratching the brand."

Leah scraped the palm of her hand, soft at first, but soon leaving scratch marks. "You sing very good," she said to keep him by her side.

"Thanks, I like doing it. But I only get to do it every other night. Gotta work bringing in water to people. Kind of boring. What are you working with?"

"I don't know. Cidron said I'll go to Riverview and work for a judge. But I'm scared. I don't know how to work," Leah said with a shrug of her shoulders, but was reminded not to by her aching wound.

"It'll be fine. Try not to think about it in a bad way, Leah. Riverview is beautiful, by the way."

"Maybe."

"And you're not alone. I'm here, right?"

Leah bit her lower lip, which tasted salty from her tears. The lump in her throat disappeared as she nodded. He was right—he was there, and she didn't feel as alone anymore.

"How did you know you were good at singing?" Leah smiled.

"Well, just sort of started doing it, and people liked it, I guess."

"Cidron liked it too?"

"Yeah. He even paid for my lute." Gil held up a strange-looking instrument. Strings stretched across the stiff wooden board. She'd seen him playing and somehow making it sound good; he was like a magician making wood sing.

Gil seemed to notice her awe, and placed the lute in her lap. He directed her fingers and pressed the hard strings down on the instrument's neck. A soft ring came from the lute, joined by another, and another.

An unexpected giggle left Leah as she plucked the instrument with Gil's help. He cleared his throat and sang quietly.

> *"Watch your wandering eyes, she called*
> *you may not know when you're enthralled*
> *With the crowd's dying cries*
> *all I could do was look to the skies."*

A grunt carried inside the room. "Shut up, Gil," a thrall called.

"Go to sleep, Berry," Gil said. Though his words were biting, his tone was not. He took the advice and grabbed the instrument from Leah with a smile. "Just something I'm working on."

"It's pretty. What's it about?"

Gil shied his eyes for a moment. "Just a person I liked. Wanted to make hi—her happy. But I don't think she'll hear it."

"I think she will. You'll be the famous singer from Keelheart." Leah nudged Gil's side.

"That sounds great. And you'll be . . . a famous, something?"

A faint giggle left Leah. "A famous something."

"What are you good at?"

That was a question she'd never asked herself. Playing with her sister and going to the Halls were things she loved to do before. All the other girls at the Rosses' worked as thralls to clean and take care of people. But she'd failed at taking care of her mother and sister. The lump returned to her throat. "Eh . . . I don't know."

"Come on."

She shrugged. "I like the Halls and the Keeper."

"The Keeper? Well, maybe you'll be a Guide, helping people?"

A Guide. That didn't sound that bad, actually. If she could work in Keelheart, she would be close to her family, where their ashes lay beneath the oak tree in the sanctuary. She could help others who were afraid and alone.

"One day, I'll write you a song," Gil said. "Are you feeling better?"

She gave him a nod.

"Get some sleep, and we'll talk in the morning. It's nice to have a friend here." Gil said, and snuck back to his bed a couple of windows farther into the room.

～❀～

The entire journey up Levent, Leah kept her eyes glued on everything the carriage passed by. The houses became prettier the farther up the street they traveled. Here, the red facades had been smoothed, making the houses look soft and inviting. Markets filled with people, and stalls had colorful garments that ladies and men bought. They passed a stall where a long dress swayed with a breeze. The fabric flowed like water by the wind; it even looked like clear water. Had they not been on their way, she would've stopped to touch the dress. For now, she gazed at it longingly.

They neared the last leg of the journey, passing a couple of guards standing by rough cliffs rising above the street. She peered backward and lost her breath.

Below her, the houses she'd passed were tiny dots. Was this what birds saw when they flew above the city? Small specks, some moving and some standing still? In every direction, Levent grew into the grasslands beyond the protective walls.

The houses at the very top, in the area called Riverview, were as big as ships. She counted some five, six, and even seven stories tall, white buildings surrounding her. Compared to home, the houses had large open areas between them, where plants and grass grew.

Ladies and lords walked along the carriage. The dresses the women wore were even more beautiful than the ones she'd seen before. One of them carried a dark green gown that hugged all of her tight. She looked like a tree walking along the street.

The carriage halted, and a woman dressed in the same sort of beige rags as Leah did not waste any time. "Are you Leah?"

Leah stepped off the carriage, her bottom sleeping. "Yes."

"I'm Karly, your supervisor. Come with me."

Karly held part of her dress up as she hurried down the street, toward one of the massive buildings. Leah ran after, holding a nibbled on piece of bread in her hand.

"You'll work for Lord Judge Dahle and his estate."

Beyond a steel fence, a huge mansion stood. A garden with pink, purple, and blue flowers stretched from the street to the double doors. The house itself was U-shaped and stood at least five stories. Tall windows reaching from the bottom floor to the fourth floor glistened in the sunlight. Leah squinted as she headed toward her workplace. Did just one person really live here? How was that even possible?

Karly led Leah into a massive hall. A single staircase reached through the house, from the entrance, connecting four floors. The white walls with wooden trimmings were covered with drawings. She had seen perhaps one or two drawings back with the Rosses, but there had to be at least fifty hanging on the walls here. Landscapes, portraits, and animals were drawn everywhere.

"Do you know how to clean?" Karly asked.

Leah tore her gaze from the wall. "Kind of."

Karly pulled the ends of her shirt to straighten out any pleats to the fabric. "Alright . . . well, take a bucket of water and a piece of old linen and wipe whatever surface you see. You're one of the thralls in charge of keeping the mansion clean."

Leah's eyes widened. "Do I clean all the drawings?"

"No. But the floors are to be cleaned, and the bookshelves, tables, and such. Anything you can reach." Though Karly's explanation was hurried, she had a certain calmness to her voice. "When you need to take care of your personal hygiene, you do so in the privy down by the thralls' quarters." She pointed to the right where a corridor lay. "When other thralls show up outside with water, you need to help out and bring the water inside the mansion. You will be fed. The Rosses do not need to send bread with you. When you hear a tiny bell in the house, that's when you get to eat with the other thralls. However, this is important: If you've begun a task or if you're in the middle of one, you are not to leave until it is completed."

Karly turned to Leah, giving her a first close look. The woman had to be older than Leah's mother, perhaps thirty or forty. Some lines wrinkled her broad forehead. But most clear was a mole on the right side of her crooked nose. "Do you know how to give a lord proper respect?"

Leah shrugged. "You bow?"

"Exactly. Show me."

Leah bit her lip. Thankfully, Gil had showed her how to do a bow earlier that day. Her right leg slid backward as she lowered herself in front of Karly. The shiny floor almost blinded her.

"Hmm . . . that will do just fine." Karly rubbed her fingers together. "Once you see a lord or lady, you must show them respect. You will work a little after sunrise until the toll of the bells in the evening. Oh, and if you feel sick, you cannot return until the sickness is gone. The lord is not to fall ill, since he is a busy and important man."

The bread in Leah's hand rained crumbs on the floor. She shoved the last piece into her mouth to avoid making a mess.

"A few hours and there will be food." Karly actually smiled down at Leah.

Then, without warning, the woman's face drained of color.

A man with white and gray hair combed out of his face and a dark gray dress-like robe walked toward them. Karly immediately took a bow, and Leah followed. She gawked from her hunched-over position as the man stopped before them. His claw-like fingers drummed against a bundle of papers. Leah swallowed the dry bread and felt it force its way down to her stomach.

"Good morrow, Karly." The lord's voice was quite bright for a man but surprisingly satisfying to hear.

"And to you, my lord." Karly changed from earlier. Her posture had slacked some before the judge appeared, but now her shoulders rolled back as she puffed out her chest. Leah tried to do the same.

The judge's eyes fell on Leah. At first, his gaze was cold as an eagle, but it soon softened with a smile. "By the Almighty, Karly . . . you dare keep such a beautiful girl hidden from me?"

"My apologies, my lord. She only just arrived."

The lord's hooded eyes refused to leave Leah. "What do I call you?"

"Leah, my lord."

"That is a beautiful name, is it not? And where are you from?"

"K-Keelheart."

"How old are you?" The man was not at all what she thought. Her mother had made lords seem like the Almighty, strong and judgmental, but the man standing in front of her was just a man, with nicer-looking clothes. He seemed really kind, actually.

"Nine, but I've been with the Wanderer five years, my lord," Leah replied.

Again the man's fingers drummed the papers. "It is a pleasure to meet you. We will meet again. Meanwhile, Karly will make certain you are acquainted with Riverview."

The judge took his leave and strolled up the staircase. His dress kissed each step.

"Let's get you ready to begin, shall we?" Karly said.

CHAPTER TWELVE

Nightbringers

Silence rang in Aiden's ears. A high-pitched chime lingered even as he slammed his palms over his ears. He had fallen asleep, once or twice, on the cold floor. No one had come to set him free. No matter how hard he kicked the door or how loud he screamed, no familiar footsteps approached. The silence terrified him.

There was no lock to be picked. It seemed like it was on the outside, out of his reach, which was a shame since he had a lockpick tucked away inside his shoes, just like Hutton had instructed.

Ravenous black eyes stalked Aiden in the dark. Never blinking, but ever watching. They encircled him, moving ever so slightly. It reminded him of a pack of wolves, their slow but calculating manner of approaching a wounded deer. Although he put his back into one of the corners, he could not escape the spying eyes. *They're not real. There's no such thing as monsters.* No matter how much he tried to convince himself, the eyes refused to leave.

His throat and eyes itched. Once he found a damp crevice in the stones, he licked whatever water he could from the dusty surface. Sand stuck to his tongue, worsening the itch. After ages of sitting in the dark, nothing was able to distract his thoughts. Not the feeling of running through the corridors at home or playing with Ayla in the woods. All his mind showed and repeated were the screams of the Eckrosie man as Berric harmed him. And now, he was supposed to join Clarissa's family? The mere thought filled his throat with bile. Life, his life, could be so much more if only the responsibilities left him. Ayla brought laughter and friendship, while Thorne's Town brought misery and heartache. This was not the place for him to be.

"Aiden." A voice called to him from beyond the opening. It was his father. Aiden rushed to the door, where a line of light leaked into the gloom. The eyes surrounding him pulled back at the sight.

"Father, please," he managed to croak despite the dry throat. The gnawed wood barricading Aiden from his father scratched against his fingers.

"What you did to your mother was wrong," Lionel sighed.

"I didn't mean to." Aiden pressed up against the door, expecting to hear it rattle and open. But it did not. It remained sealed.

"The Unborn has blessed us with another child. You're getting another sibling. When you hit your mother, you hit your sibling. Do you understand why that is bad?"

Why doesn't he open? I wanna get out of here. Aiden wet his lips. "I'm sorry. Please let me out."

Another voice, a wheezy and creaky voice belonging to an old lady, spoke to him. "Lord Aiden, have Nightbringers visited you?"

The eyes glared at him, waiting to eat him. "No . . . I don't think so." Aiden hesitated to answer. He had no choice but to lie to get out.

"Then why did you harm your lady mother, who is under the Unborn's protection?"

She was going to hurt Eamon . . . how is what she did any different from what I did? "I don't know . . . I'm sorry. Mother was going to hurt Eamon. A soldier does not allow innocent people to get hurt. Father, please don't leave me. I'm thirsty."

The lady spoke again. "Your brother insulted your lady mother. She brought you life. By disrespecting her, you disrespect the Unborn. Do you understand why your mother had the right to punish your brother?"

Not really. The rules are strange and unfair, he thought, but seeing the flickering light outside, he pressed up against the door. "Yes. I shouldn't have done it."

"The Unborn protected your father during the wars to ensure that your family came together. She watched over your mother and saved her from sickness. Family means everything. We cannot question the Almighty's decisions."

"Aiden," Lionel said, "we are simply concerned about your wellbeing. Nothing means more to us than keeping you and Eamon safe. But Nightbringers and the Beast will do anything to try to make us fight within our family."

Aiden sat silent. What else was there to say? What could he tell them that would make them open the door? He had begged. He had screamed at them. He only wanted to get out. A sniffle left him.

"Little lord, will you raise a hand against your mother or father when you do not agree with them?" the old woman said.

I will, he thought. "Never."

"Are you angry that they locked you in?"

"N-no," Aiden shivered. He was. Everything he did and wanted, his parents disagreed with. Or at least, they would if they ever found out about it. He thought the whipping of Nyle was his fault at first, but why would it have been? He might have held the whip, but it was his mother who forced him to use it. It was merely a matter of time until another such moment would arise. He had to get out of their reach. For a little while . . .

The door shook, and a spark lit in Aiden. The flicker of a torch forced him to squint at his father and an older woman with a gray robe. The robe reached from her hunched-over shoulders and brushed against the floor.

Aiden ignored her and threw himself into his father's arms. He could not arouse suspicion. "I'll be good. I promise, Father."

Aiden glanced behind his father and saw another figure, his mother. She stood dressed in a violet gown, but instead of standing in the middle of the passage, she cowered against one of the walls.

Aiden approached his mother. Her green eyes peered discouragingly at him. As she pulled back from her son, Aiden stopped. "I swear by the Almighty, Mother, I shall never raise a hand to you again." *I won't need to.* His dirty palms reached for her. Her hand rested in his. "I am sorry for hurting you."

"I know, my son," Emilia hunched, her dress folding itself on the ground. She let him near in another embrace.

"Is it true? Is my sibling in there?" Aiden glanced at his mother's belly, which hid in the bulked-up fabric.

"It is. Your little sister or brother lives there."

He sniffled, and his face lit up. But not from joy—it was another sibling for him to protect. "I didn't mean to hurt you."

"I know. You are my son. You will carry our name into the world and make us proud, dear Aiden." Emilia pinched his cheek and smiled. "Are you hungry? You must be famished. Spinach and mushroom soup is waiting for you."

She gripped Aiden's hand tight and strolled back up into the light of the mansion. The delicious scent of the soup being prepared in the kitchen heated his soul. "Also, Jarred will no longer be in charge of your safety."

The fear crawled right back. What did they do to Jarred?

"I know you liked him, but he was hurting you and tried to take you away." Emilia brushed his hair out of his face while trying to corrupt his thoughts.

"Did you kill him?" Aiden stuttered. His heartbeat increased.

"No, he will just stay away from you for a while. In the meantime, one of the Holdens' thralls will watch over you."

He had to leave. At least for a little while. It was simply a matter of time before he would be unable to keep up the facade of following their will and wishes. Others would get hurt if he stayed at their side.

Aiden waited for the night to fall. His mother came to tuck him in for the night, which he let her do. He could not give any hints about leaving. She read him a story from a book of heroes and heroines. None of it told a tale of how the protagonist whipped someone or let their friends get in harm's way. It only told the stories of their bravery in facing the unknown lands of Caldril. Aiden was nothing like those heroes. He was the opposite, the villain they had to face.

Once the mansion slept, the candles and lights were snuffed out. He lit one in his chambers, where he started packing a bag. He shoved trousers, underwear, shirts, and jackets into it quickly, filling it up and emptying the cupboard of nicely folded clothes. His favorite book, *The Adventures of Caldril,* found a new home in his bag.

The corridor held no signs of life, except for his brother, who slept peacefully in the bedchamber across from Aiden's. He paused to look at Eamon, who drooled on his bedsheet. The pillow had been tossed to the side. Could he really leave his own brother?

Aiden took a step toward the room but stopped. He could not drag Eamon along. Besides, they would not be separated for long. At least, that was what Aiden told himself. Also, Eamon was just a child, a young boy who could not care for himself. Dragging him along would endanger his baby brother more than doing him any good. Aiden swallowed the lump that settled in his throat.

Knowing that the entrances to the estate's front and back would be guarded, Aiden snuck into his father's study. Scrolls and envelopes lay in neatly formed piles on the heavy desk. By the mantel, Lionel's sword twinkled in the presence of Aiden's passing candle.

The window swung open, and Aiden climbed into the chilly night. Soft grass greeted him. Already, dew droplets stained his boots. Farther down the facade to the left and right, flames flickered, and the silhouettes of guards danced with a soft breeze, chilling Aiden.

Without light, the travel to Ayla and their village would be difficult, but he had to do it. He darted off into the gardens leading up to the mansion. He avoided any paths and cut through a gathering of lavender growing nearby. It was nearly too easy to clear the walls and leave without being seen.

Thorne's Town shrank behind him. He found his way to the trail he and Jarred always traveled on to get to the camp. As he'd never ventured through the night alone before, everything around him felt strange and dangerous. Every little twig snapping beneath his boots; every gust of wind felt like being back in the cellar. After all, Nightbringers got their names from the night. Once the sun disappeared, they crawled out of the shadows, seeking out any prey. This helped hasten his steps. As Aiden walked, he could make out some shapes in the looming forest. Treetops touched the sky with scrawny fingertips.

He found rest in the giant roots of a tree. Stories did not explain how uncomfortable it was trying to sleep on the ground. No matter what he placed underneath, it felt like sleeping on a bed of rock, and even if he found a comfortable position, a sound rattled him.

He dozed off many times, until the shadows made way for light once more. Heavy clouds covered the burning sky, which danced in reds and oranges. Aiden was quick to his feet and headed to the brook, where he found his path to the Eckrosie settlement.

The people slept as Aiden stepped into their territory. Or at least, he assumed they did. No one came to greet him, so he sat down in the glade on the outskirts of the settlement, watching the everchanging clouds. Crisp firewood lay heavy around him, but no pillars of smoke rose from the wagons.

Someone shook him, and he sprang awake. Ayla's wide smile warmed his cold and frightened core. "Aiden here?"

Aiden gathered his thoughts. He must have slept through the morning as the sun stood high. She handed him a bowl of mashed-up blueberries, which he shoved into his mouth. For some reason, whatever this was tasted even sweeter and better than the thralls' treats back home. He threw himself into her arms to give her a long and needed hug. She hugged back, rocking him in her embrace.

Her beady amber eyes watched him lovingly and calmed his mind from spiraling. She was there. That was all that mattered. She would never ask anything dishonest or mean of him. With her, nothing could go wrong.

～❖～

Gil writhed in the careless and rough grasp of a merchant. The man marched with a commanding clasp around Gil's neck all the way from Main Street over to Keelheart. Whenever Gil asked a question about what he was being punished for, the man grunted and kept going.

Only a few days had passed since Gil had stepped into the merchant's care as a thrall. His clothes weren't all that expensive, which made commoners flood to his tent to purchase a new pair of wool pants or shirts. Gil's obligations had been to run across town wherever the man sent him and to sell more garments to patrons, more than they had thought about purchasing. But suddenly, as Gil had been speaking to a couple of patrons, the merchant had grabbed him and forced him to the Rosses to have a word with Cidron.

Cidron turned to face them as the merchant shoved Gil through the entrance with such force it nearly knocked him over. A scruffy-looking woman at Cidron's side scattered away, leaving them alone, the upset merchant panting hastily. Gil wished to stay clear of Cidron's cold stare but forced himself to find courage to face his fear head-on.

"Caught the thrall staring at men visiting my shop. You allow 'is kind of sick behavior?" The merchant's hoarse yell scratched Gil's ear. That was what it was about? Him just looking at a man? It was just like Zahna said . . . he had to be careful of who watched him.

Cidron tugged at a belt keeping his slacks around his belly. "Since when is looking at someone a crime, dear sir? Especially for a child."

The man didn't listen. His words left him in quick puffs of air. "I've half a mind to head 'ver to the Halls and have the Guides care for 'im."

Cidron raised an eyebrow at the man's complaints. "Why didn't you, sir?"

The old gentleman with a plump nose firmly planted on his flat face squinted back at Cidron. "They're your little things. You've gotta keep 'em in check."

Things? Gil would've given the man's words some worth, but upon seeing Cidron's eyes roll in their deep sockets, he felt validated.

Cidron enveloped his arm around the merchant's shoulder and ferried him farther into the estate. "Sir, let me assure you, I will see to this matter immediately. Please, step into my study where we can discuss this in private out of earshot of the child."

A large lump in Gil's stomach grew once the door to the study shut. Again, he was left out of the decisions about his future. However ... last time, Zahna and Dorian had left him out of it for his sake. Cidron could be doing the same thing, although Gil worried about getting his hopes up. He did have a knack for screwing things up for those he cherished.

Why the merchant was speaking about this with Cidron, though, was beyond Gil. In what ways had he gotten upset with Gil's behavior?

The door swung open and the merchant stepped through. The way he'd peered down his thick nose at Gil previously had vanished. Instead, he cast a quick glance at the boy and then wandered away down the hallway, leaving Gil alone with Cidron.

Gil pulled at his shirt, making sure the hem didn't ride up his belly. "I'm sorry, Cidron."

"Stop worrying." Cidron placed a forceful hand on Gil's shoulder, squeezing it tight. "We don't choose who we fancy. We can't choose who we care for. We are a family here, and we respect each other, no matter what."

"Did I do something wrong?"

"No. But the world is a cruel one for those who stray from its light. You simply needed a nudge back onto the track."

"Thank you, Cidron," Gil said.

"Now, get some supper in that belly of yours and I'll find somewhere more suitable to send you. Hopefully one with less ... distractions." Cidron smiled.

Another day. Another chamber to scrub clean. Knees to the floor and back hunched, Leah scrubbed the hallway on the third floor. The bubbles in the bucket of water took many shapes. Like studying clouds and laughing at the strange forms they took, this was just the same. But without her mother and sister.

Drops of water disturbed the surface of the bucket as Leah squeezed a piece of fabric dry. In the large mansion, no bookshelf was to be left dusty. Leah pulled out another book to clean behind it. The tome nearly fell out of her hand as she held it.

She looked over her shoulder to the surroundings. No one was with her, it seemed. The other thralls had prepared food and placed it on a long table in the hall's center. Tall windows looking over the city let the sunlight fall on the food, where heat rose.

Something about the leather bindings told her to look inside. She placed the book on the stone floor, and the bindings creaked open. Within, strange symbols and lines marked the pages. The ink had been etched into the paper. She ran her finger up and down the carvings.

"Girl? Leah?"

The lord of the house, Judge Dahle, was standing on the other side of the room holding a glass of wine in his hand. Once she noticed she was alone with the lord, she got up from the floor and took a bow. The man's slow steps brought him closer.

A knot tied in her chest. She bent down to the open book on the floor and placed it back into the bookstand. The bindings slapped shut, which she disguised by coughing and continuing to wipe the shelves from dust. Of all the people to get caught by, the lord was the worst. She prayed that he hadn't noticed.

"I witness worse crimes than a thrall hoping to read, child. Trust me, Crimson Wights will not visit you. No harm will come from being curious," the lord said with calm to his voice. He stood next to her and pulled out the book she had been studying. "Although this read would be quite dull. *Noble Lords and Ladies of Vesilia.*"

"It . . . looked pretty," Leah explained as the judge spread the book bindings apart. The beautiful circles and squares appeared again.

"There are prettier books than this, with drawings. Your name is Leah, is it?"

"Yes, my lord. I'll leave you alone."

The judge placed a hand on her shoulder as she turned to go. "No need for that. I enjoy the company. Being a lord can, at times, be lonely."

"But you have visitors all the time."

"I do." Dahle raised an eyebrow. "Though tedious. Riveroaks, Holdens, Tallstags—even the Thornes are not the companionship I enjoy. Yet it is my responsibility, I suppose."

The water in the bucket rippled when Leah accidentally bumped into it. She reached for the cloth, but yet again, the judge stopped her. "I will teach you to read if that is what you want. These shelves are clean enough."

Leah crooked her neck to look at the tall man. "Why is that good to learn, my lord?"

The judge's eyes squinted with his smile. "Secrets hide in these pages. Information that only those who can read can see. Think of it as a treasure that only a few can find. You are a smart girl. It will be easy for you, like running."

Seeing what others could not? That sounded fun. The books around her suddenly did not look as mysterious as they had before.

"Actually, I have a book in my private chambers, one I believe you will enjoy. What do you say about following me there?"

Leah wiped her nose clean. "Okay, but it's alright that I don't clean?"

"Oh, do not fret. Karly will understand. Besides, it would be rude not to accept a lord's request."

Don't say no to a lord or lady, Leah's mother's words reminded her. Leah smiled. Learning to read would be great.

"But first." The judge nudged Leah forward. "I am famished, and you get to eat as well. What do you say?"

"Okay." Leah nodded and followed him to the large table. "Thank you, my lord."

The judge served her food. A spoon of mashed potatoes and some sort of red meat found its way to her. Having not eaten anything since the day before, Leah didn't want to ignore her growling belly.

The mashed potatoes were like nothing she had tasted. A creamy texture coated her tongue. Fresh milk made the potatoes taste divine, and the meat . . . it melted in her mouth. She smiled up at the judge, who observed her dining on his food. "What does a judge do? No one tells me."

The lord rolled his shoulders. "You know how there are things that are right and wrong? I make sure people are punished for doing wrong or bad things. Laws must be followed."

"Do you make the laws?" Leah accidentally spoke with her mouth full. She silenced herself and slowed down.

The man's fork scraped against the porcelain. He cut into the meat. "I am one of the people who creates the rules, yes. The great dome outside, the Precedent's Court, is where I work."

Something tingled Leah's throat, like a piece of food stuck in her throat. She cleared her throat, but it stayed. Leah let go of the utensils. "Could you make a law against dying?"

The judge's grip of his fork lessened. "There are laws against killing each other if that is what you mean."

Her throat burned at the thought of her mother and sister. What if she forgot what they looked like? How they talked? "But

Nightbringers, why don't they get punished? They made my sister and mother sick."

"Come here, child," the lord offered, and slid his chair out from the table, his lap ready for her to climb into.

She snuggled in, and the judge greeted her with an embrace. The arms squeezed a fraction tighter, and Leah breathed a bit slower as her sadness melted. His robe smelled of books and dust, like a stuffy room. But it gave her comfort. It reminded her of the attic and the stuffy smell lingering there.

"Sometimes, the Wanderer is unable to stop the Beast, but that does not mean that the Wanderer forgets to punish the Beast and the Nightbringers."

She collapsed in his embrace as sobs muffled into his shoulder.

"There, there." His big hands stroked her back. "Life is unfair business to beautiful souls like you. But I will protect you. As long as you are with me, nothing will harm you."

He buried his nose in her tousled hair and breathed slowly near her ear.

Hurried footsteps carried through the massive dining hall, and a heavyset man appeared by one of the doors. "My lord," the messenger breathed heavily as if he had run for hours.

"What do you want?" The judge's kind and soft voice turned cold and unwanting.

The short messenger took a deep bow. "I apologize, but the king requests your presence in Thorne's Town as soon as possible. Matters of the security of the nation."

The judge nudged Leah off his lap. His gray dress-robe covered his leather shoes gliding over the floor to the stressed man. "I cannot leave Levent every month to meet the king. Levent is under my protection, and I thought he understood this."

The messenger gulped. "He knows, but he urged me not to disclose these matters. He fears that the Following will get wind of the goings-on of the nation, which is why he gave me as little information as possible."

"Fine. Inform Karly of departure. We leave tonight."

The lord turned around to Leah. The sun lit up his smooth but wrinkled cheeks. "It seems I have to leave for Thorne's Town. And I do not wish to leave you in this state. Would you like to accompany me and meet the king of Vesilia?"

Meeting the king? What? she thought in bewilderment. She had never stepped outside of Keelheart before a few weeks past, and now she could maybe even leave Levent?

"Uh . . . yes. If Lord Ross lets me leave, I would be happy to, my lord." Leah beamed at him.

"Cidron Ross has no say in this matter, but I agree, you should let him know you are accompanying me on my trip. Inform him that I shall see to it that all additional expenses will be reimbursed once we return."

Leah grimaced. "Tell him what?"

"Oh, tell Cidron I will pay for new clothes you will need to wear, and for the food."

"I . . . I can get a dress? Like the ones ladies wear?"

The judge smiled. "Certainly. Now, off you go. I will send my men to come and get you later tonight."

Leah squealed with delight and skipped out of the room to hurry back to Cidron and give him the news. She was going on an adventure.

"Jaida—that was your mother's name, was it not?" Cidron asked. His hands were deep in a large bowl of ground beef. The meat squished and slobbered as he stirred. Alone they stood in the dying light shining into the Rosses' dining hall.

"Yes . . ." Leah lowered her head.

Cidron scrunched his nose. "What did she look like?"

What did this have to do with anything? Leah had told him about the judge's plan, but he'd changed the subject. She sighed. "She was the most beautiful in the world. Her hair was brown and really big sometimes. She didn't have ugly freckles like I do."

She couldn't see Cidron's eyes but heard a loud sigh, and his shoulders tensed. "You'll stay here, Leah. And I'm sending you to a merchant in the morning."

"But why? I wanna go," she protested.

"I'll send someone else to escort him. Trust me, those trips are boring, and nothing for a little girl like yourself to go on."

"Did I do something wrong?"

His ugly mug peered down at her, sweat dripping down his brow. "Not really. But I've made up my mind."

"But I wanna go."

"You signed a contract with me. You will do as I tell you, or you will be punished. Now, leave before I get pissed off," he scoffed, and returned to the bowl.

Leah marched off to the bed she claimed as her own. No one had returned from the day's work, as the bells of Riverview hadn't rung. She rested her head on her knees and let out the anger with loud scoffs and sighs. Of course Cidron wouldn't let her go. He didn't care about anyone else. He was a selfish bastard who wanted to make others sad.

The days with Ayla were like Aiden had hoped. No one questioned his presence. Sheila was the only one who asked where Jarred was, but Ayla jumped in to explain that he was sick.

He was offered pies and large bowls of cabbage, tomatoes, and other exciting food, which he gladly accepted. When he questioned Ayla about them not eating meat, Ayla explained how the Eckrosie couldn't risk smoke from fires revealing their presence. They ate meat and cooked food once the sun set and everything settled in a gloom.

Ayla peeked her head from one of the trees she was hiding behind while playing peek-a-boo with other children and Aiden. "*I will show Aiden something tonight, something out in the forest that only I know about.*"

"*A secret?*" Aiden hid in the shrubbery at the sight of a blond-haired girl their age beginning to search for the other children.

"*Is Aiden afraid of the dark?*" she teased.

Aiden's eyebrows furrowed at the question. Who would not be?

Ayla's huge eyes widened in surprise, and she ran out into the open, revealing herself. She threw herself into an approaching woman's arms, nearly toppling her over. Aiden followed.

"Ayla," the young woman said. Her clothes were eccentric in comparison to the others in the village. Big hoop earrings dangled in a thick growth of black hair. The dress she wore was decorated with circles and white flowers. A certain resemblance between Ayla and her became evident from their broad glistening smiles.

"*I have missed you, Zahna,*" Ayla said, a little tremble accompanying her beautiful words.

"*Not as much as I missed you, little bird.*"

Ayla pointed at Aiden. "*This is my friend, Aiden.*"

Aiden stopped himself from bowing or greeting her with any other form of courtesy. He cocked his head to the lady instead.

"This is my sister, Zahna. She has been away for a long time."

"*Happy meet you,*" Aiden said in Eckrosie.

In the beginning, Zahna looked surprised by Aiden's Eckrosie, but a grin soon replaced her confused look. She ruffled Ayla's wild hair, and twigs and moss fell out of it. "Of course you taught him Eckrosie, you little squirrel. I'm gone for a year, and you found a friend."

Unlike other Eckrosie Aiden had met, including Ayla, Zahna's accent and any hesitation in Vesilian had washed off entirely.

"Where were you this time?" Ayla got on her knees to listen to her sister's story.

"I went back to Levent and worked as a performer. Why not live hundreds of lives instead of one, I figured. But I missed you, so I came back." Zahna pulled Ayla close and ruffled her hair again. Ayla's face flashed red, and she shied her gaze away from Aiden.

Cloth wrapped around her slender hand, and Aiden could not help but notice traces of pus leaking through at the back of her hand. "Are you hurt?"

Zahna placed her other hand to cover the damaged one. "No, it's fine."

Ayla did not buy it. She yanked it loose and inspected it against her sister's wishes.

"It's not that bad. Me and my friends were marked because we were not careful enough. One of our plays was politically incorrect, and well, we paid for it. So I traveled with Rudy to get here, but . . ." She crossed her arms over her chest. "Soldiers attacked, and he stalled them to let me get away. I—I don't know if he made it."

Shit. Aiden cursed to himself. Rudy had to be the Eckrosie prisoner at camp, and Zahna probably the woman who escaped. He lowered his gaze.

Ayla must have reached the same conclusion. "But you are safe with us. We are together now."

Zahna gave a half-smile, breaking her concerned frown. "*That we are, little one.*" Zahna turned her focus to him and studied his clothing briefly. "You said your name is Aiden. Where are you from?"

Aiden stuttered, but calmed down when locking eyes with Zahna. The time of lies and deceit needed to end. He gathered the courage to tell her about his heritage, a heritage he had never had to be ashamed of before. "I'm Aiden Riveroak. I live in Thorne's Town and met Ayla on my way to camp Wintersmore a couple of months back."

A barrage of words escaped the sister's mouth at such a rapid pace, Aiden could not follow along, though he doubted her conversation with Ayla was positive. At times, he heard his family's name thrown into the discussion.

Despite the heated argument with her sister, Ayla kept her calm.

"I swear, I would never harm any of you," Aiden said.

Zahna ignored him altogether.

"I left my family to come here. No one followed me."

"And you believe a lord, nay, *the* son of a war hero will not be sought after?" Zahna remarked in Vesilian, and showed the brand on her hand. "You asked about this mark. We did a play where we apparently besmirched your father's repute, and because of that, they branded my friends and me. All because of a silly little joke."

Zahna stood up and pulled Ayla along to the caravans, and spoke loudly to the inhabitants. He could make out a few sentences, and realized quickly they were moving their encampment. People rushed back and forth between the wagons to gather their belongings on the outside. A few minutes went by, and the horses were let out of the pens to lead the wagons farther into the forest.

"I—I haven't told anyone. I wouldn't do that," Aiden shouted after Zahna. "I left because . . . I have nowhere else to go."

As the caravan moved, Ayla tore her arm loose from her sister's grasp. *"Zahna, stop. Aiden will not hurt us. I know we need to move, but do not leave Aiden. He is not his father."*

"What if he is? I will not lose another family," Zahna huffed with her hands on her hips, gazing back and forth between Aiden and the moving caravan. Her mouth snapped shut.

"Never forgotten nor forgiven," Ayla said.

Aiden blinked at the familiar saying—the words he had last heard from Clarissa's thrall.

At the sound of it, Zahna slouched. Her defensive demeanor rolled off her, and she held out her hand to Aiden with an apologetic smile tugging her soft features. "Aiden, I'm sorry. Ayla is right. You are not your father. Everyone deserves a second chance."

Aiden embraced her hand while throwing quick glances at Ayla. Whatever she said, it switched the conversation on its head. "What does that mean, *never forgotten nor forgiven*?"

The wagons rocked across the uneven forest floor, leaving Ayla, Zahna, and Aiden alone in the glade. Only a few markings upon the ground told the tale of their earlier presence.

Zahna sighed. "It's a . . . reminder, a horrifying reminder of what happened to Eckros. Some people, however, hide behind the saying to justify their violence against anyone who isn't Eckrosie. It used to just be 'never forgotten,' but recently people have added the 'nor forgiven' part."

"Are . . ." Aiden tripped on the words. "Are you going to hurt me?"

Zahna enclosed his hand in hers and squeezed it gently. "Never. Ayla reminded me of giving everyone a chance and not judging people for the acts of their peers. We are a family here, and Ayla trusts you, which means I need to do the same. The expression is something we have chosen not to follow. But I will ask of you to never speak of us to anyone."

Aiden bobbed his head. The thrall back with Clarissa . . . perhaps he was working up the courage to escape her family? Was that why he'd said those things?

Zahna and Ayla went around the glade, hiding the traces of their settlement by turning over wads of moss. Aiden followed their example and later walked farther into the forest with the other settlers. An hour or two through the thicket, the carts and wagons found another glade to stop in and resume their day.

The day passed with laughter, play, and joy. No one told him what to do or how to act, which was a welcome change from having to stand in line at the camp or having to court and entertain people he did not care that much for. His thoughts wandered to his brother, whom he'd left behind.

Evening arrived. Aiden sat together with Zahna and Ayla, preparing dried wood to light a campfire beneath a rain shelter that had a single chimney rising into the sky.

"Why did you live in Levent?" Aiden asked Zahna. "Why would you ever want to live anywhere else, especially if they'd want to hurt you?"

"Out there—" She bobbed her head to the north. Bracelets clanged against each other as she brushed her hair out of her face. "Out there, I get to show people that I'm just like them. Vesilian, Eckrosie, Drelorian, Burrousie . . . it doesn't matter in the end. In Levent, I'm a performer, and people listen to me. They don't fear me because of the language I speak."

"But you're hiding. You can't tell people who you are, can you?"

"That's true. If I did, they'd kill me. But maybe, just maybe, I'll come across someone who will see me as a person and not as a threat or an animal. Hopefully, that person can make a difference for all the Eckrosie living in hiding."

Given what his father and the captain said about Eckrosie, he doubted anyone would change it. But he wanted Zahna to be right. One day, perhaps, he could bring Ayla with him home to his family, and they would accept her. But at the moment, that was just a dream.

Ayla grabbed his hand. "Come," she said. His bowl of soup spilled at the disturbance, and he let her guide him.

Together they headed into the forest. The canopy greeted them, and the birds' songs of the late evening dwindled. "*Where are we going?*" Aiden panted.

Mosquitoes and flies bumped into him, searching for things to feed on. He swatted down on them before they got to take a bite. One of the letdowns of the evening was the insects and crawlies emerging.

Then a foul reek nearly made him throw up. Nearby, Ayla stopped to study a half-eaten corpse of a stag. The pelt gaped open, revealing messy red meat underneath. Its eyes . . . were gone. Only big, hollow eye sockets gazed to the leaves above.

Ayla sat down only feet away from the corpse. She folded her arms and legs to fight off the chill creeping up on them.

"Do you want to turn back?" Aiden asked, dumbstruck by the situation. "Or . . . why are we here?"

"*Waiting for the things.*"

"*Waiting for what?*"

She patted the ground next to her to invite him to sit. "*I want to show you the animals. They only come at night, and they like food.*"

Wolves? She was waiting for wolves?

"*But . . . we do not have any weapons to kill them.*" Aiden took a seat next to her.

"*Silly. We do not kill. We watch them and talk.*"

Dusk discolored the surrounding trees in grays and browns to make way for the dark. Every sound coming from the forest made him twitch, but Ayla did not seem to mind. She held on to his hand, keeping him safe and near. He discouraged himself from speaking, although he wished to say something.

Stiffness began to prickle his feet like tiny ants, and Ayla twitched her fingers. A smile burst over her face, and she stared at the corpse of the stag.

A cloud of mist approached, or smoke . . . It twirled through the dark as if caught by a strong wind. But there was no breeze, nor wind. The smoke moved on its own, nearing the stag.

"*Do not be afraid. I saw a stranger do this. Relax, Aiden,*" Ayla comforted him.

No matter what she said, he could not shake the great unease grabbing his soul at the smoke's presence. Whatever light still existed was swallowed and consumed by the haze that swelled around the stag. Like thousands of bees, it swirled. That was when he noticed claws, teeth, and eyes . . .

They're real? This—this can't be true. Fear made him freeze at the sight. *It's not true.* Yet there they were. The Nightbringers he'd heard stories and dreamt nightmares about—the servants of the Beast, who collected souls for consumption. Like snakes, the Nightbringers slithered through the air, without trouble or pause, closing in on Aiden and Ayla.

Ayla squeezed his hand. "They won't harm you. Listen to them."

Aiden's rugged and strained breath puffed into the night. The creatures swirled along him. A wet and cold chill spread from them, similar to a dawn's thick mist. Aiden closed his eyes, trying to hear anything else besides his rising heartbeat.

A rumble from far away. Another one . . . and another. Aiden believed it to be thunder, but it lingered longer and interrupted itself. Aiden buried his nails into Ayla, wishing she would stay.

A flash of something appeared before him, not actual light, but a memory or a thought. He concentrated on it, wanting to see it. The rumble around him remained.

Dank moss and a putrid reek stung his nose. He felt wet stone lick his body as he crawled down the sides of a pitch-black cave. A ravishing hunger threatened to eat him from the inside. Suddenly, trees and leaves caressed him, and he saw a stag on the ground. The smell of its rotting flesh brought saliva to his mouth. Nearby he saw both of them sitting together. Aiden saw himself shaking and talking with Ayla.

"*It speaks,*" Ayla said, and the vision faded.

"*What?*" Aiden whispered.

"It's showing me their home." She switched to Vesilian. "It's afraid because you're afraid, Aiden. Tell it you're not here to hurt it."

"And how do I do that?"

"*Think, and it will see.*"

Aiden let out a dry chuckle. Then he thought hard about wanting to get out of there by grabbing Ayla and running away.

The rumble stopped, and the creatures pulled back to the corpse. A sticky and wet sound reached them as teeth and claws tore meat from the bones of the carcass.

Ayla caressed Aiden's hand. "*They thank us . . . I think. Maybe we should leave them alone.*"

She did not have to ask twice. He pulled her with him and rushed through the forest, back toward their home. Either fear or shortness of breath narrowed his sight. His feet pounded the ground hard with each landing. He did not have to think about moving; his body did it for him. Anything to put distance between them and those . . . creatures.

The familiar and comforting sight of the clearing and the caravans showed itself. Under the dark sky, fires were lit, but the light was suppressed by panels to not give away their position. Aiden collapsed in the meadow to catch his breath.

"Are you always this reckless? What if it wanted to hurt us?"

Ayla giggled. "Silly one. To discover, we must make changes. That's how we met."

He opened his mouth to argue but could not find the words. "You said you saw a stranger do that? Do what exactly?"

Ayla pulled her jacket tighter. "*One night, I saw a man in a cloak sitting in the forest. He was alone, and the animals danced around him. He was speaking to them. I saw them, and he saw me. His eyes were the bluest I have ever seen. And he had a red line over his eyes.*"

"*What did he do?*"

"*Nothing. He sat still, letting them touch around him. He said they would not harm us if we did not look like food. I found the stag and thought they would show.*"

He blew out his cheeks to release the tension, keeping his body stiff and ready to run. Maybe the things he believed he saw in the cellar when he was locked up were real. Sure, they had made him scared, but they'd never hurt him . . . not like his own parents had.

"I can't believe we just saw Nightbringers," Aiden said. Ayla cocked her head to the side, looking like a curious puppy who did not understand what he was saying. He continued, "The servants of the Beast . . . you know? They bring souls to the Beast for him to eat."

"Why? You can't eat souls," Ayla said, and rubbed her forehead.

"No, but the Beast does."

"There's no soul after death."

Aiden flinched. "What do you mean, no soul? Of course there is."

"We live, we die. That is all. The story of a person's life stays after we die. Zahna tell me about Eckros and houses of stories where the dead go. The story only matters."

"What do you mean?"

Ayla guided him back to the gathering of people in the village. At night was when the meadow sprang to life. Women and men gathered together around the fires, where they munched on cooked meat and vegetables. As they joined, a plate filled with food found its way to Aiden's lap. The dinner was nothing like the ones he attended at home. No one waited for a specific family member to start. Instead, people enjoyed the food once it came to each person's lap. Spices were in short supply, it seemed, but they had managed to bring out sweet flavors of the food regardless. The meadow filled with conversations and laughter and even an occasional song in both Vesilian and Eckrosie.

He asked Ayla if they were celebrating, but she smiled at his ignorance and let him experience their lovely dinner, speaking to her sister instead.

"*I told him how story is the only thing that matters. But he does not understand.*" Ayla scootched closer to Zahna and got under a blanket like a baby bird would its mother's wing.

"*That is because they worship the Wanderer, a thing that protects them from the Beast, who is death and evil. We do not believe in the Almighty. We believe in stories. Each person lives a story. Life is all that matters and is what is important. Nobody's story is more than another's; everyone needs to be remembered.*"

"What do you worship then?" Aiden switched back to Vesilian to understand better.

"We worship life. That is our faith. We don't believe in greater powers where evil and good fight over souls. When someone passes, the living must tell about the dead person's life."

"Ayla said something about houses of stories?"

"The Towers of Remembrance?" Zahna wrinkled her nose with a grin. "I've never been there, but . . . I dream that one day, when Eckros is restored, we can rebuild them once more. There were libraries of Life Books, as we called them—one person's entire life written down in a book. Many years ago, there were people we called tellers who went to a deceased's home where they collected stories and memories about the dead in a book. The book was sent to the Towers of Remembrance. You have the Halls where you worship your Almighty. We had the Towers where all the lives of people lived on."

Aiden barely noticed how his mouth gaped wide during her explanation. Kale dropped from his mouth. Why did Vesilia not have such a beautiful thing? He envisioned thousands of books in a vast tower where he could read about people's stories all day. What would his story say when he died? His stomach churned. Would it read that he harmed Nyle?

"Do you know where the Towers are?" Aiden asked. He had to see it for himself.

"There are none left. They were destroyed during the wars," Zahna said. "But one day, we'll have them, won't we, Ayla?"

"*I am going to be a teller,*" Ayla said. She straightened her back and neck to appear taller. "*I will travel to other Eckrosie and build a Tower.*"

"*Can I be one too? A teller? Or do I have to be Eckrosie?*" Aiden said.

Pitter-patter twinkled across the tarp. One raindrop followed by the next. The heavens poured down on them and on the meadow. The sweet return of water made them smile.

"*Anyone can do it. Come with me and see the world.*" Ayla extended her hand to him.

Rain poured as they praised its return. Dry grass moistened under Aiden's feet as he followed Ayla, pulling his hand. The rain chilled his skin, and mud slobbered up his boots. She guided him through the rejoicing crowd, away from the fire's heat and back into the forest.

"*Water makes everything liande,*" Ayla said, gazing to the heavens. The sparse light glistened in the water drops rolling down her skin.

Aiden listened to her words, unable to understand one of them. After some consideration, he repeated her words.

"Water makes everything happy." Ayla chuckled at Aiden's failed attempt at speaking Eckrosie. "*You're getting better, but much to learn.*"

"*I am not that bad. You seem to understand.*" To tease her, he nudged her arm close. Raindrops splashed onto his forehead and wriggled against his scalp.

"*I hold you,*" Ayla said. She grabbed Aiden's hand and brought it to her chest, where she pressed against her skin. "*I hold you.*"

Hold you?

Like always, Ayla spotted his confusion. "*You make my heart sing. I never want to spend a day without you. I want to see you forever. This means I hold you.*"

"Oh, love me." Aiden blinked at the word. *She loves me?* He gulped loudly. "Y-you love me?"

Their lips connected, if only for a second. A rush of adrenaline thrust beneath his skin, and a strange tingle sprang to life in his belly. A current yanked him toward her, and he let it sweep him away.

Aiden leapt in for another kiss. She greeted him. Again their lips touched, but they did not pull away. He wished to feel her warm breath lick his skin and to taste her lips. The kiss blew his thoughts away, emptying his skull of worries and questions. He could not tell if he was succeeding or failing, but he did not care.

Their foreheads touched, and soon, so did their hands. They filled the gap between each other. At first, Aiden had a hard time understanding what to do, but Ayla guided him. Her lips brushed against his, and she pulled him in tighter. Unlike with a hug, he felt every part of her press against him. Aiden closed his eyes once Ayla closed hers, allowing him to focus on the taste, smell, and feeling of staying near her.

He did not wish to pull away. Neither, it seemed, did she. But once they did, they smiled lovingly at each other. It was hard to tell in the dim light, but he heard it as she chuckled that she blushed. So did he.

"*I hold you,*" Aiden whispered back to her. He placed her hand to his heart, which pounded hard at her touch. He actually did love her. Whatever this feeling was, it was one he longed to hold on to. A day would not pass without him wanting to hear her laugh, to watch her dance and smile. She meant everything to him. The stories he studied did not come close to describing the tingling feeling and the desire that spread through his soul.

They lay in the grass. The rain cleared, and the stars lit up the heavens. For once, the dark did not make him uneasy. With Ayla at his side, nothing did. His world narrowed to Ayla. He could not wait to spend the rest of his life adoring her.

CHAPTER THIRTEEN

Teller Riveroak

A thick cloud of ash woke Aiden up. Next to him, Ayla stirred at the same strong smell. It clogged the lungs. Together, they had fallen asleep beneath a large oak tree that now rustled in a strong wind, carrying more of the scent burning their nostrils.

He barely had time to rub the sleep from his eyes before they sprinted toward her home. The thick canopy shielded the sky. But as they neared the village, he understood that something was terribly wrong. Worry fueled his steps.

The meadow stood ablaze. Fire pillaged the caravans, with several of them wrapped in flames. The heat warmed his shivering skin, an invisible wall knocking into him. The smoke and ash brought tears to his eyes, obscuring the horrific sight taking form. Crimson streaks smeared the fresh grass. Underneath a silver and blue banner, soldiers wearing plates of armor thrust their weapons down on screaming Eckrosie.

He shot out his hand to stop Ayla, but she was already sprinting toward her home.

"*Ayla! Stop!*" he cried after her.

It seemed the people had been awoken by the fire only to be cut down at the entrances to the wagons, where soldiers waited. The Eckrosie never stood a chance against the Crown's men, and neither would he, nor Ayla. He had to get her out.

Ayla knocked into a soldier, who was slashing a blade at a man on the ground. The soldier stumbled to the side but snapped his fingers around the bottom of her neck.

Aiden thrust himself into the soldier, bringing him off his feet. All around him, an orchestra of sounds clouded his thoughts. Screams from soldiers and Eckrosie shattered his insides, while the fire cracked whatever it touched. Metal screeched in his ears, and people yelling orders in Vesilian.

Ayla and Aiden found their way to the middle of the village, where a familiar sight of long black hair sent a nasty shiver down his spine. Ayla turned to her sister, who followed limply. Strands of Zahna's long hair were glued to her face by blood, obscuring her closed eyes.

"Zahna . . . what happened? Why are you . . . ?"

Aiden froze by their side. He felt the urge to help, to do something, but he only gazed upon Ayla, who nudged her sister to wake her. How did the Crown find them? Had someone followed Aiden on his way to the village? He thought he'd made sure that night, but as everything collapsed around him, he was uncertain. Helms shrouded soldiers' faces from him, making it impossible to tell if they came from the camp or Thorne's Town. A few brave Eckrosie men and women stood to face the army, with nothing more than sticks and rocks to protect themselves. Was this what his father had done? Harm unarmed people and call them dangerous? Was that why the king praised him?

As expected, the soldiers overpowered the Eckrosie, and blood rained.

"*Ayla, please, we need to run.*" He tugged at her stained shirt, but she refused to budge.

A sticky and cold surface slid across his throat . . . He was going to die.

"Wait! Stop!"

The blade faltered but pressed against Aiden's exposed throat. A person squeezed against his back, making it impossible for Aiden to get out of the deadly hold.

With a cane thumping into the soft ground, Lionel's blazing eyes stared at Aiden. The Riveroak sigil decorated his chest with black and blue, his old uniform from his fighting days. But there he wore it, in all its glory. Old bloodstains mixed together with fresh new ones.

"Father? What are—"

"Lord Riveroak, is this your boy?" a strident and disembodied voice asked behind Aiden.

Lionel bowed his head. "Yes, my Lord Thorne. He is my son."

The blade left, and Aiden threw himself on Ayla to get her out of there. Rough hands yanked them apart just as quick. Aiden kicked and wiggled in the grasp to get loose, but they were too strong for him.

"Soldiers, take the little lord away. He doesn't need to see this," Serril Thorne said.

But Lionel was fast to cut him off. "He needs to stay, my lord. Bring them."

Ayla fought against soldiers who dug their hands deep into her hair. They steered her from Zahna as though she were a misbehaving pony, then did the same with Aiden.

"*Aiden, what is happening?*" Ayla grunted as they were forced to just outside the range of the raging fire and the fresh corpses. He wanted to reply, but he knew as little as she did.

"*I . . . we will make it out of here, I swear.*" Tears spilled on his cheeks after he told the lie. His nightmares were upon them.

Lionel stopped just short of the surrounding trees, which swayed in a strong breeze. Next to him, Serril Thorne lined up to gaze at Ayla and Aiden. He wore a long blue cloak and silver plate mail with golden streaks outlining a two-headed hawk.

"Let us go." Aiden pulled against the hands keeping him in check.

Ayla spat at Lionel and Serril. She was trying to be brave, but Aiden noticed a quiver in her lips, the same one he had.

Serril ignored it to focus on Aiden. "I did not recognize him, but you are quite a son to have. The son of the hero of Riverview, and here you are, the hero of Thorne's Town. My brother should be wary of the Riveroaks' heritage." Serril laughed.

Aiden shook his head. "*I did not know . . . I did not bring them here, I swear, Ayla.*"

"Even speaking like them?" Serril spread his hands in amazement. "You are a little lord full of surprises."

Lionel did not partake in the celebration. Instead, he kept his eyes fixed on Ayla. He sneered at her, utter disgust pulling the corner of his lips into a snarl.

"This one will do fine as a thrall, or . . ." Serril uttered, but was cut off by Lionel, who dragged Ayla with him. The sword from the mantel he had not used in years caught the light of the fire behind them. Ayla squirmed in Lionel's grasp as he shoved her onto the ground and placed the blade at her neck.

Dread twisted Aiden's gut and weakened his legs. *No . . . no, you can't kill her,* his mind screamed.

"My lord, that is not necessary," Serril urged Lionel.

Ayla shivered beneath the weapon.

"Please stop! I love her." Aiden screamed at his father. "Father?"

"You are not my son," Lionel said. His eyes were cold, unforgiving, with no remorse coating his iris. At that moment, Aiden felt the words cut through him. He had lost his father. An imposter looking like the father he knew stood at the ready to take the only thing Aiden cherished.

Lionel moved the edge of his shining sword at the base of Ayla's neck.

"*Ayla,*" Aiden screamed.

A surge of energy exploded within his chest. The hands holding him back faltered at the force spewing from his muscles. Aiden pulled the men with him for a few steps before they collided with each other with a loud thud and clang. Free from their grasp, Aiden rushed to Ayla. Another soldier stepped up, his blood-drenched sword drawn. It swayed to the right, wide and sloppy. Aiden snuck past the man's line of defense and twisted the soldier's grip on the weapon. The soldier gasped and groaned to fight against the tug-of-war for the hilt.

Don't stop, Aiden. Save Ayla no matter what.

The tip plunged into the soldier's leg. He keeled over and stumbled out of the way. Wherever Aiden got the boost of energy from, it powered his footsteps. He was going to make them regret endangering Ayla and killing her family . . . his family.

A blow to his cheek knocked him off balance and blinded him. Dirt, grass, and blood coated his tongue and stung his nostrils. He had to get back on his feet, but when he tried, his vision narrowed, and everything faded to gray. The surge of energy from before evaporated, leaving him defenseless. His muscles that had burst with power now turned sour.

Hands and knees crushed Aiden's aching bones to the grass. Fingers clutched his hair and yanked it to the side, where his eyes connected with Ayla's.

The sword still rested against her tiny body.

"Take me instead," Aiden pleaded.

But his appeal fell on deaf ears. Lionel kept a firm gaze at Aiden, filled with disgust and disdain.

"*I hold you, Ayla.*" Aiden begged for a smile from her, anything to make this go away. He wanted to see her gorgeous face glisten with joy. He ached to kiss her, to be near her.

The sword disappeared for a moment before it fell.

Aiden closed his eyes.

"Stop!"

How he ended up in a prison cell, he barely understood. Things bled together to form a horrific nightmare. The flames licking the carts and caravans, the sickening smell of blood, and Ayla's limp body . . . it was too much for him to remember, and it pulled him into a bed of knives and blades that tore into his soul.

After the surge of energy had vanished, he'd lain limp. The ache was similar to a growth spurt, but many times worse. Every muscle strained and protested whenever he moved. Only now did he gain control of his body as he huddled up into a ball in the far corner of a tiny cell. Two fully grown men, that was all that would fit in the space.

Soldiers had tossed him inside a cell after a long ride back to Thorne's Town, once the fire settled and the corpses burned. Children, men, and women from the village piled on top of each other before the soldiers burned them. Ayla was placed last on the pyre. He had turned his gaze away as the fire consumed their skins and clothes, but Lionel had made sure he would watch every moment of it by placing his son on the grass with his head turned to the pile. The guilt he felt after harming Nyle paled compared to the fact that he got all these people killed. He had not swung the blade, but the moment he met Ayla was the day he betrayed them.

Every part of him wanted to join them in death. He provoked everyone near in the hopes that one would grant his request, but they refused. His own tears drowned him in a lake of sorrow and guilt.

But he did not deserve to die. Not yet. Their conversation the day before reminded him. Their stories would go unspoken, untold if he joined them. They had to be remembered, and he would make sure they were.

Someone nearby cleared their throat. He spun his torso on the ground to give the surroundings a glance. Three people stood outside the metal bars keeping him separated from them and a corridor. His mother, dressed in black, held her hands on her belly where his sibling lived. Next to her, Lionel gazed into the cage where he kept his son. He leaned against his cane, his good leg looking hurt as he put all his weight on the aid. A third person, a man with long gray hair combed behind his ears, joined them, also staring at the Riveroak's son. He wore a long, black robe—strange attire for a man.

"*Leave me alone,*" he scoffed in Eckrosie.

Emilia's face paled, and she darted her eyes at Lionel and the other man as if trying to make sense of the words. She rubbed a hand across her face and muttered, "What . . . what language is that? Is it . . ." Her words trailed off, and she turned to her son and spoke more clearly. "Aiden, this is Lord Judge Dahle. He is here to help you."

He sneered at the newcomer and spat at his feet, one of the worst insults he could think of. "*I have nothing to say to you.*"

"Do you want me to hurt you? Do that again, and I'll . . ." Lionel threatened.

"*What? You'll kill me?*"

Another puddle reached the judge as new spit rained. But Lionel's threats were unfounded. His son knew that. The fingers around the knob of the cane whitened.

"My apologies, my lord," Emilia was quick to say.

"Please, my lady, all I see is a confused boy. I will not take any insult personally," the judge said, and knelt to stare straight into their son's eyes, washed with tears. "My Lord Aiden, you are frightening your lord father and lady mother. Perhaps you should be proud of your accomplishments. We are proud of you."

Proud. Of course . . . that was what they wanted him to be. Any ounce of self-respect was beyond his reach. "*You destroy everything, and you killed Ayla,*" he growled at his father.

"I have never seen anything like it, my lord," Lionel said to Dahle. "He lifted a longsword and used it as if it were a feather. Nothing about it was normal."

"You don't believe . . ."

"No. The Wanderer is not inside him. If so, I would not be standing."

He could not help but roll his eyes. The Wanderer . . . an Almighty who watched and allowed defenseless people to die. Whatever Almighty it was, he would not worship something like that. He tore at his ankle, at the cuff wrapped around it. The bindings came undone, and he threw it at the judge, who recoiled like a frightened doe.

Emilia whispered her son's name and took the anklet into her hand. "Did Jarred do this to you, my son?"

If he was not mistaken, tears danced in her brown eyes. "Or did the captain speak to you of these things? Why . . ."

"The captain would never do that, Emilia," Lionel assured.

"Then, where does this behavior come from? It cannot be as simple as Jarred claimed."

"By the Almighty, Emilia. That doesn't matter. This isn't our son!" Lionel roared. His voice carried within the confines. "We need to bring him back out and stop this whimpering child from tearing down our legacy."

Emilia crossed her arms to fight off the onslaught. "Then what do you propose? That we keep him concealed here until he changes his mind?"

Lionel leaned forward as though stifling off a stomach cramp. "I . . . I don't know."

"There is always Nedox. Though it might be a tad extreme," the slimy, gray-haired man whispered as though he did not mean to speak his thoughts out loud.

Lionel cocked his head.

"In the mountains, there is a place for the Crimson Wights," Dahle said.

Emilia removed a loose strand of hair from her face. "My lord, it seems you misunderstand our intentions. He is still a Riveroak."

"Of course. No, he will remain a Riveroak. The place I have in mind is one not often spoken of, and known only to the king's council."

"Lord Dahle, cut the crap and tell us," Lionel snapped. His usual calm exterior had vanished.

Dahle rubbed his hands together. "Crimson Wights are created in Nedox. They have, on occasion, reformed certain criminals there as well. Send Aiden there, and within a year or two, he will obey your every desire without protest."

Emilia caressed the bump on her stomach and rocked back and forth. "This needs to be contained. We cannot afford this rumor spreading with storytellers besmirching our family name."

That was it.

Teller was the name he had been searching for, ever since Ayla suggested he choose his own. A name that defined him and his life. A teller spoke of stories and history. If any story deserved to be told, it would be of Ayla and her family. He would make sure it was heard loud and clear throughout the kingdom. Lionel had taken everything from him. The least he could do was to destroy Lionel's reputation.

"I chose a name," he said, switching to Vesilian so they would hear his defiance.

Three pairs of eyes locked on him. He pulled himself to his feet using the metal bars.

"Aiden's dead. You saw to that when you slaughtered his family." He sneered at Lionel through the metal barricade. "My name is Teller, and I'll drag your name through the very dirt I'll bury you in."

Lionel's eyes blazed with utter disgust, precisely what Teller desired. Teller stood in the ashes of the man's manipulated son. "You might want to rid yourself of me now, Lionel. 'Cause if you don't, there's nothing you can do to stop me."

Emilia's piercing brown eyes bore into Teller. "Can you arrange it as soon as possible, Lord Dahle?"

At the utter disregard for her son, Teller scoffed. Just like with Lionel, Emilia held no empathy or care for those she claimed to love. *Poor little thing,* Aiden thought at the sight of her caressing her belly. The sibling would grow up in the same cold and unforgiving environment he had. Well, perhaps for a time.

"Within a day, my lady. I will admit, though, that there will be substantial changes to his mind, and . . ."

"Whatever you choose will be within your right," Emilia interrupted, and tore her gaze away. "Make sure he lives and can function in important aspects. He has a lady waiting for him."

Another scoff followed upon hearing her words. They would send him away, to a place where he would be tortured into obedience, but they would fail. Beneath the sole of his foot, the lockpick remained stashed away and hidden, clammy against his skin.

Hasty footsteps echoed through the corridor with Emilia's stride. She simply did not care what happened to her son. The knife, already in him, delved deeper with his mother's indifference. But he did not let it show. Whatever hopes lingered within snuffed out like a flame caught in a storm. The flame did not disappear, though, it simply changed, feeding a ravenous inferno deep inside Teller's being.

"Rumors have undoubtedly reached the king's ear," Lionel sighed once Emilia left them alone.

"The king holds your bravery high at court. I doubt anything his brother might divulge will be sustained. Your son is a hero who befriended the enemy and led our forces to their home. He is the hero who slew vicious Eckrosie." The judge gave Teller a fleeting glimpse.

"He was ready to die for that girl," Lionel said.

That girl. That girl? Was that all she was? Teller bashed his hand against the cage. A throb pulsated his skin. But that was all he could do. What else was there? Lionel had killed Ayla, and they acted as though Teller was the real issue.

"You have seen the effects these things take on certain men at war," Dahle said, ignoring Teller completely. He placed a hand on Lionel's shoulder and escorted him away. "This is merely indoctrination on their part. Aiden is still alive. We simply need to pull him back out."

Their conversation grew farther away as they left Teller on his own. Stone walls greeted his lonely gaze. They were sending him to

Nedox, to what? Be tortured? To see their way again? He would not let them. He had to make his own path and grow up to be big enough to bring them all down.

Teller removed his right boot. His fingers searched the sole for the lockpick he had managed to conceal for months. Who knew? Maybe Hutton had predicted this would happen, that Teller would need to escape the Riveroaks' clutches. Anyway, he was grateful to feel a warded lock on the other side of the metal bar. The lockpick slid inside, and the lock clicked. Teller made his escape.

"Aiden . . ." A weak voice caught his attention.

Trapped in a neighboring cage and chained to the ceiling, Jarred hung. His toes only nudged the floor as his arms raised above his head to keep him dangling.

Wasting no time, Teller unlocked the gate and stepped inside. A ghastly pool of blood shimmered in the torch's light. Cuts and bruises marked the thrall, who barely was able to look at Teller through swollen eyes. The bloated mess looked nothing like Jarred. The constant glimmer in his eyes had been snuffed out, leaving a broken shell in its wake.

Teller reached out to touch his friend, but stopped so as to not cause him any more pain. "What . . . what did they do to you?"

"I truly am . . . sorry. I . . ." Jarred mumbled in a drowsy, half-awake voice.

A latch kept the chains taut above Jarred's head. Teller searched the area for aid to raise him to it, but it stayed out of his reach. Only a tall adult would be able to undo the latch.

"I didn't want to—but I couldn't take any more."

Teller circled around Jarred's back and was greeted by a gory canvas. No patch of skin was left unharmed. Curtains of blood wept down the thrall's spine.

Teller ignored his instincts and placed his hand on Jarred's back to climb up and grab the latch. "It's not your fault, Jarred. I'll get you out of—"

"No . . . I want to stay," Jarred said with some force. "I'll look after your siblings."

"I . . . I need you."

"Please . . . stop."

Aiden gave up his attempt and returned to face Jarred.

"You need yourself. You cannot let your family get you in their grasp again. It will be the end of you. Stay as far away from the Riveroaks and Thorne's Town as you can. Do you understand?"

Teller clenched his fists. "Yes."

Strings of saliva fell from Jarred's mouth each time he spoke. "You listen well. If they catch you, they'll make you their slave. No matter what, you stay away."

"Did they hurt you because of me?" Teller could not help but ask, though he knew the answer too well.

Jarred's broken lips turned upward, or at least it looked like it. "You need to disappear. Go to Goldfork or Levent. No one will find you with all those people."

Tears welled up Teller's eyes. He had to disregard his emotions if he was to survive. He forced the lump in his throat down his gullet. There would come a time and place for it. Now was not the time.

"Wait . . . in the gardens, beneath the far eastern hedge, you'll find things to help you. Dig them up and run."

Jarred's brows drew close, and his lips trembled. What more was there to say? For whatever reason, he wished to stay, to be tortured. Teller wanted to bring him, pull him out of harm's way, but he had to respect his friend's wishes.

With an embrace, Teller bid farewell. "Thank you . . . for everything."

The moon shone brightly over Thorne's Town. A man stood outside the barn-like prison cells as Teller stepped out. The guard gazed upon the moon and held a flickering torch by his side.

Teller trapped air in his lungs and let his feet tap the dirt lightly. Holding the torch nearly blinded the man from what lurked in the shadows. Teller took the opportunity to sneak around a corner. The Riveroak estate rose into the night's sky in a frightful silhouette. Some candles flickered in the windows, creating a monster that grinned at him tauntingly.

Walking up to the main entrance would not work. Guards patrolled and kept the family safe. There was, however, always the path he took a few days ago over the walls.

Teller reached the mansion's gardens. He snuck in the dark to the far eastern hedges Jarred spoke of. Teller touched and felt around the soil to find any tampered with dirt without any light to guide him. A strange, moist bump greeted his fingers, and he started digging.

Two bags met his reach. One was stuffed with clothes, shoes, a knife, a waterskin, and dried meat; the other, somewhat smaller yet much heavier, carried whatever silver and necklaces Jarred seemed to have found in the estate. The man must have known this would happen eventually. Teller stopped himself from heading back and going against the thrall's wishes.

The grass tickled Teller's bare ankles. He gazed to the north, where the moon shone near the horizon. It was a long journey ahead of him. If he was to make ground before they came after him, he could always take Adventure and ride. However, the stables were not unguarded. It had been a big enough risk to enter the grounds. He could not chance it.

The long journey began with a couple of unsure steps into the darkness.

CHAPTER FOURTEEN

The Library

"I shouldn't have to teach you how to sew, not after I've already explained it." The woman snatched the cloth from Leah's grasp and threw it to the floor. "Garments cannot have more holes than they had coming into my shop."

The tailor's store stuffed Leah's nose with the smell of old clothes. Shelves and racks of dresses, shirts, skirts, and boots covered every space of the cramped shop on Rose Lane. Leah cursed at the needle that pricked her already-bloodied finger. No matter how many times the lady showed her how to thread the needle, the sharp edge pierced her skin.

"I'm trying my best . . ." Leah said hesitantly. She always tried to do a better job than the day before, but it never worked.

"Stitches need to be light, precise, and graceful. They cannot steal the attention from the garment. Think of it as a face. If you have a blemish, it will steal focus."

Leah gulped. She understood the point the tailor made, but her fingers ignored everything as the needle poked through the fabric.

"I don't want to make you sad, Leah, but this is bad for my business. You have one last chance. Stitch this gap together, and I'll let you stay."

The lady disappeared behind a curtain to greet customers at the front. With a heavy sigh, Leah returned her focus to work. A pair of beige pants with a ripped seam at the knee—she was supposed to stitch it shut.

Leah poked the thin fabric, and the needle snuck out on the other side. She pulled the thread, guiding it through, and jabbed the needle again. The beige thread disappeared into the trousers. If only she had something she liked to do at the Rosses'. Gil had his music and singing. What did she have? When she felt like playing, there were no other children around to join her. And during the days, she was busy working as a thrall, which stopped her from visiting the Halls.

Everywhere they sent her, she was met with no, no, no. Tailors, jewelers, and maids, all of them rejected her work. She missed being in Lord Judge Dahle's company, where he respected and enjoyed her work. She was afraid to speak with Cidron directly each time she explained why the employers sent her back to Keelheart. When she began to suggest going back to the judge, her words died in her throat.

Finally, they sent her to a stable near Main Street by the Ember Gate. She loaded piles of manure onto carriages, but that was actually the first place they didn't complain and snort at her lousy knowledge. The owners, two grumpy men in their late years, ignored her as they put beautiful new horses into the pens. Leah was only there to clean up.

The work was hard but worth it, as she could spend time with horses from all over the country. They were gentle giants who never grunted or rolled their eyes at her. The only thing they cared about was the buckets of water and bags of hay she brought.

Almost every evening after the bells rang all over the city, Leah came home to find Gil in the large dining hall, singing to people. The boy's happy charm made her smile and laugh, which she had never believed would happen again. He even wrote a song about Leah— "The Girl in the Corner," he called it.

The tailor sent her away, and so did the grumpy men. She ended up in Cidron's study, where he put his feet on the desk and inspected her.

Leah folded her hands in her lap, keeping her head low. She didn't want to tell Cidron of another person sending her away from their service. But Cidron sat silently behind his desk, waiting for her to speak.

"I gave the horses too much food. They said I am not good," Leah squeezed out.

Cidron put away a parchment and a quill, focusing only on Leah. He leaned his elbows on the desk. "I think we can agree that you're not the best at doing girly things. You can't sew, you can't dress, you can't nurture anything . . ."

Leah shrank deeper into the chair with his words.

"But . . . there's a library that needs cleaning. It's a two-person job, and I'm sending you and Gil there together."

Leah glistened back at the man. "With Gil? Really?"

"Yeah." Cidron let out a long sigh. "He's getting overworked, and I've seen you guys hanging out together. Maybe you'll be better at it if you've got a friend nearby? You'll do what you did for the judge. You'll wipe desks, and floors, and keep it looking nice for visitors."

Leah leaped off the chair. "Thank you, my lord."

"Haven't I said not to call me that?" Cidron commented.

"Yeah, you did. But thank you so much," she said, and went searching for Gil.

~❖~

Gil heaved a bucket of water from Lake Ember onto a carriage where at least twenty other buckets splashed. He grabbed another empty bucket standing at the lakeshore and lowered it into the shallows. The water gathered and spilled once he brought it back to the cart. His hands and feet numbed with the chilly water. Winter only brought rain in copious amounts, making his clothes stick and itch his skin. It didn't help that part of his work had him step into the lake to bring water into Levent and sell. He could not remember the last time his socks had been dry during the day. Once he returned to the Rosses', he found a pair of dry socks and smiled.

The city guards overseeing the Ember Gate gave him lazy gazes as he ventured through it with his horse and carriage, just like other days. After two new moons of him passing in and out of Levent, they finally trusted his reasons for doing so. Despite him showing a folded parchment, signed by Cidron Ross, they scrutinized him until they realized that he was, in fact, only delivering water into the city.

Inside Levent, his normal route took him from the base of Main Street all the way to the first walls separating Riverview from the rest of the red clay houses below. Fifty buckets went fast in the summertime, but not during winter, since the heavy rain filled whatever barrels the shop owners and people had. Still, he managed to sell all he was able to bring.

It was hard labor, lifting water and carrying it inside the patron's homes and estates, though he counted himself lucky. He could have ended up working as a thrall taking care of the waste of the city. During the early hours, when Gil headed outside the city's walls, he came across the reeking wagons of waste leaving the city as well. They worked throughout the night.

Friends were harder to make than he'd believed. Most of the people sleeping in the same quarters he did were quick to get out of bed and hurry to their workplace. Many of them were  boring as well. Whenever he sang to them, they shrugged and tried to hush him to get some shut-eye.

He had now spent more time with the Rosses than he had with the performers. He missed traveling with Zahna and Dorian throughout Levent. True, this way, he had a permanent bed and food coming his way, as well as a crowd to perform for. But the crowd didn't appreciate anything more sophisticated than drinking songs and shanties.

Thankfully, it seemed as if Cidron had noticed Gil's struggles working all day with heavy lifts before singing for hours to the lord's friends. Cidron informed him and Leah that they would work in a library together. Upon hearing this, Gil rushed to Leah's side and burst out in a joyous squeal, like friends meeting again after being apart for a long time.

The library, located on a parallel street next to Main Street, looked warm and cozy. The tan stones soaked in the morning light. A few square windows had been placed just below the roof nook. The tall, rectangular building smelled of dust, candles, and books. Endless rows of bookshelves created paths inside the house, with occasional breaks where chairs and tables squeezed together. Entering the library, they noticed it only had one floor. Together, Gil and Leah took hesitant steps into their new workplace.

A scrawny man with sparkling, excited eyes, set wickedly within their sockets, scurried to them, the first guests of the morning. His stubby fingers fiddled against each other nervously. There was something crazy about him—perhaps it was his attitude. His high-pitched voice suited his personality, at least.

"Be thee the thralls we requested?" He licked his lips.

"Yeah," Gil nodded. "I'm Gil, and this is Leah."

"Great." The man snatched them by their hands and dragged them into the library as if there was no time to waste. At the far back was a closet filled with brooms, buckets, and cleaning cloths, so stuffed the door couldn't quite close.

"Me name's Vince, a librarian. Clean the shelves, wipe the tables, fill the inkwells, and put books back on the shelves. Get it?"

"Where do the books go?" Leah asked.

"The shelves, Vince told you as much," Vince uttered.

Gil stepped in to stop the manic man from losing his calm. "We shall get it done."

"Good," Vince commented, and rushed back to the entrance where merchants and rich people were stepping into the library.

"I . . . I can't read, Gil," Leah mumbled into the closet.

"Neither can I," he admitted. "But we'll just put them on the shelves, right?"

Leah bit the inside of her cheek. "Okay."

～❈～

Levent was enormous. As Teller reached its southern gates, he gaped wide in awe at the walls looming above. Against the rapid clouds, the walls looked to be caving in over him. His traveling companion, Maric the farmer, did the talking, thankfully. Ever since Maric had found Teller, passed out on his fields north of Thorne's Town, he had been nothing but kind. Despite his humble roots, Maric had a smile close by to defuse every situation, reminding Teller of Ayla. The boy did all in his power not to watch the smile spread on Maric's aged, wrinkled lips.

"This my boy, Teller. Need to bring him to meet the merchants I do trade with." Maric squeezed Teller's shoulder tight to show him off to the Crown's guards at one of the gates.

"Right. Well, sir, you and your boy have two days to conduct your business. By nightfall tomorrow, you need to leave."

"Actually, kind sir, my boy need to stay behind. You see, with my age, I'll need him taking over the farm, and there are a lot of responsibilities he has to learn, and . . ."

The guard rolled his eyes and waved them through. Teller rocked on the cart pulled by a slow but steady horse that pulled them across the seas of grass leading from Thorne's Town to Levent. People, an endless crowd, occupied the busy wide streets. Like ants, they moved through the space in organized chaos. Men, women, and children gathered at a merchants' square just inside the city's walls. In Thorne's Town, people had distinctive features—or rather, there was enough time to study each face before the next came along. Jarred was right. In a city, he would become no one, just another face in the crowd.

At the top of the red-clay city, a white beacon shone above them like a second sun. The Precedent's Court. He remembered Sonya's stories of the enormous building where the library of law, judges, Crimson Wights, and prison cells all resided at Levent's top, Riverview. The district his father defended, as the stories went . . . but Lionel was no hero.

Too kind for one's own good—that expression could easily apply to Maric. Even though Teller had been allowed to travel with him for two days, Maric had insisted on giving the boy room and board for the first night in Levent. He never pried into Teller's affairs, though the old man more than willingly shared some wisdom.

That night, Maric sipped on ale while Teller munched on salty meatloaf.

"You sure you wanna stay here? The offer stands if you change your mind and want to live at my farm. We could use an extra pair of hands." Maric wiped froth off his unshaved beard. "These city streets are quick to turn on good people, I've found."

"Thank you, but I have business to attend to here." Teller cursed at himself. He needed to get rid of fancy phrasing to blend into a crowd and not stand out. Luckily, despite Maric probably figuring out Teller's background, or at least guessing at it, he pretended as though he did not.

"Well, you know where to find me if you'd change your stubborn mind."

After a relaxing evening and some good night's rest, Maric and his horse, Sky, left. The old man rocked back and forth on his carriage, wobbling over the cobblestones. Teller hoped he had made the right decision to stay behind.

It did not take long to realize he was no one in the grand scheme of things. Every person shoving past him on the streets had their own life in which Teller was an extra, a faceless person in the masses. Just what he wanted. Yet leaving a household where his every move was observed and entering a place where no one cared was not the relief he thought it would be. No one cared or bothered about his presence.

Though he carried riches in one of his bags, he refused to step into a tavern or inn. If he was going to survive Levent, the money needed to supply him for years to come. Therefore, he found shelter in a back alley of a cluster of houses. The sky above reminded him of the night with Ayla, when she told him she loved him. Her touch and the taste of her lips lulled him to sleep.

A massive downpour jolted him. His neck, and back, and well, every part of him ached in the uncomfortable position he'd slept in. Here, no one seemed to have noticed him in the rain. He gathered his bags and took off to the streets once more, uncertain where he was heading. Joining the Crown's forces did pop up as an alternative, but he smothered the thought just as fast. The foul things that happened to the Eckrosie were because of the Crown.

He peeked into bakeries and taverns, where food enticed his hungry belly. He could always see if they needed an extra pair of hands. After all, he did know a thing or two from working in the kitchens with Sonya and Nyle.

No. He had to get his priorities straight. A library that housed books of all kinds would guide him. If wanting to learn more about the Eckrosie and find ways to bring his parents down, books could help. If indeed he was to be a teller, he wanted to learn more.

After hours of searching for a library, merchants and locals led him to a giant clay building housed between tiny red abodes. He pulled the bag straps tighter and entered.

Aiden had always loved Lionel's study, but entering this place was something entirely different. Teller lost his breath, gawking at what had to be a collection of thousands of books.

"Good day to you, boy," a strange man with crooked teeth burst out from a counter right inside the wide doorway.

"Good day. Eh . . . I want to read books about the Eckrosie." Teller approached.

The wrinkled old man's face contorted. "'Bout the wars, you mean?"

"No, I mean about their culture."

"Listen here, boy. This a library with historically accurate books. We don't house illegal writings, so scram."

Illegal? Teller blinked but regrouped his thoughts. "Oh, I meant, of course, about the wars."

"Aha . . . and you read?"

Teller rolled his eyes and caught a glimpse of a sign above one of the shelves. "That one says 'geography' and the one behind it reads 'economics'."

The man hissed. "Fine. Be on your way. The texts about the wars you'll find at the far back." He wafted his hand dismissively.

Teller gave awkward bumps of his head to acknowledge every adult standing between the wide bookshelves, studying the writings inside. In the far-off corner, a gathering of desks and comfortable chairs wedged between bookshelves and the wall. His fingers brushed against the leather bindings squeezed tightly together. *The Great Wars, History of Vesilian Leadership, The Duties of the Crown,* and *Burrous — The Enemy to the West* were all titles his eyes sought out. *The Great Wars* seemed like a good starting point. He disturbed the order and staggered off to a table with the heavy book.

It was what he thought.

Barely two pages in, the screams, the pleading, the taste of blood coated his tongue and mind. The library disappeared, and he found himself in the glade. The book swirled in a disorienting haze where he relived the horrid morning. He had hoped that the nightmare would leave along with his old name. But it refused to leave and instead kept gnawing at the wounds.

Teller yelped at an unexpected touch. His clothes dripped with sweat.

By his side, a young boy with dark skin and a shaved head greeted him with a concerned smile. Next to the boy stood a girl with fiery curls framing her adorable puffy, rosy cheeks, which were adorned with freckles. She tugged at the ends of her sleeves, which cleaved with many loose threads tickling her wrists. She cradled an unlit candle, seemingly to replace a burned-out candle at his desk with.

"Are you alright?" the boy managed to croak. "Leah here thought you looked ill."

Teller combed his hair out of his face. "Yeah, I'm good. I . . . just had a nightmare."

"When you're awake?" Leah whispered.

What business was that of theirs? They would not understand anyhow.

"Do you know how to read?" the boy asked, his head tilted to the side, looking down at the open pages.

Teller leaned back in the chair. "Yeah." He sized them up. The way they awaited an answer seemed too curious for someone else who could read. They wore dirty beige robes similar to the thralls back home.

"Are you thralls?"

"Well, I'm Gil, and this is Leah. But yeah, we're thralls. We're supposed to clean and sort books, but . . . the librarian doesn't like how we sort the books."

Teller focused on Leah, who shied at Gil's side. "You're in trouble?"

"Nah." Gil waved dismissively. "Kind of. He said we'd be replaced if we don't get better."

A knot tied in Teller's stomach. Replaced. That was what Emilia had said about Jarred, and he was tortured. He would ensure they were safe.

"You know, I can help you guys. Bring the books that need to go back into the shelves, and I'll show you where to put them."

Their faces lit up. "You'd do that?" Gil asked.

Teller affirmed with a nod.

"What's your name?" Leah asked in a half-whisper.

"Teller."

Gil scratched his freshly shaved head. "Oh, why did your parents choose that name? Is it from a famous storyteller or something?"

A shadow fell on Teller, and he shielded his eyes. "I . . . I chose it myself."

"What? You can do that?" Gil said.

"Didn't like the one those bastards gave me, so I picked a new one."

Leah gave a slight grin at the curse, making her cute face squint.

"So why pick Teller?" Gil leaned against the desk, entranced in their conversation.

"Actually, in Eckros, tellers told the stories of every person who died, about their lives. And also because my mother hates bards and storytellers. But I've always liked them. They sing and talk about brave people."

Gil snickered. "I'm a bard. Or gonna be. Before I came here, I performed with a troupe."

"You did? What happened?"

"The Crown put an end to it. Said we weren't following restrictions." Gil rolled his eyes.

"You mean you said stuff you're not supposed to?"

Gil gave a half-smile Teller's way. "I guess. But one day, I'll get up on the stage again, where people will cheer me on. Sure, they already do that over at the Rosses', but I wanna perform plays and stuff."

"You should hear him sing, Teller. Gil's amazing. He even made a song about me."

Gil nudged Leah's side playfully. "But let's not forget Leah; she's an incredible friend."

The girl's face washed red at Teller's and Gil's faint chuckle.

Shit. Teller washed the smile off his face. *Don't get close to them. You know what happens to people who you like. Nyle, Jarred, and Ayla never stood a chance once you met them.*

But he could not help it. The entire day he spent with the happy pair, helping them out with their chores. It was difficult to explain, but a weird pleasure came from keeping the two thralls away from punishment.

The bells of Riverview marked the end of the day, and the library's visitors left. Gil and Leah scattered off to the strange man at the counter. That was when Teller took a risk.

Carved into the wall stood a closet with cleaning supplies. Gil and Leah opened the door every so often to get their brooms. Having spent all day with them, he had not found the peace to read. He dived into the mess of the closet and shoved his bags between brooms, buckets, and fabric. Then he bundled up and peered past the half-shut door. Their voices echoed in the hall, but after a few minutes, the large doors shut, and he found himself alone.

Chapter Fifteen

Singers and Brawlers

Each morning when Leah and Gil entered the library, Teller had somehow arrived earlier. It did not take Gil long to figure out the strange-named boy's secret hiding place in the closet. He and Leah brought biscuits and bread to keep the boy fed, as he didn't think about it himself.

Every day, Teller stacked a pile of books at the desk, claiming them as his own. He devoured the texts, hiding his warm beige oval face in the pages. Long, ruffled, sandy-brown strands of hair draped his face, falling just short of his ears. Beneath the concerned and stern expression he gave them, a young boy with crow's feet and dimples revealed a happy life, another life. But like Gil and Leah, Teller's innocence was smothered beneath the crushing hands of reality.

Gil had a hard time understanding where Teller had come from. A literate child who lived on the streets? He had spoken of his parents, cursing them with every opportunity given. He could be a merchant's son, or even higher. Regardless, both Gil and Leah came to rely on and even enjoy his company. One day, Gil would figure him out.

Luckily, Vince stayed oblivious to the goings-on at the back of the library. As long as the tables and bookshelves were clean, he had no complaints to give Gil and Leah. Not after Teller arrived.

Gil huffed as he brought over a tall stack of books. The books toppled onto the desk, and Teller gave a teasing smirk at his failure. Next, Leah approached, with not even a quickening breath as she placed an even larger stack of books beside Gil's toppled tower.

"This letter is an . . . ?" Teller pointed at a circle on a book front.

Leah traced the circle and bit the inside of her chin in deep thought. "An *o*?"

Teller beamed at her with the kind of smile that vanquished one's concerns. Gil's stomach tickled whenever it sought him out.

Heavy footfalls emitted behind them. Before they noticed, a large, bulky man set his palms flat on the desk. Cidron Ross looked down at the children. Gil and Leah jumped in surprise. Whatever the reason for him being there, it couldn't be good.

"Relax." Cidron rubbed his forehead at the sight of their fidgeting. "You guys worry too much, you know?"

"What are you doing here?" Gil managed to croak.

"I visit my customers every now and then, Gil. Especially when they all of the sudden report improvements overnight," Cidron remarked, an odd judgmental stare falling on Teller sitting on the opposite side of the desk. But Teller didn't flinch. He stared confidently back at Cidron, probably having faced much more threatening men than him.

"Books returned to the appropriate shelf," Cidron continued. "Would be quite impressive if you'd learned to read on your own. But logically, you had someone helping you."

"Actually, books returned to the appropriate *shelves* is the correct wording, sir," Teller said with a sly drag.

Leah excused herself quickly. "We're sorry, we didn't wanna lose this job."

"You've got nothing to apologize for." Cidron dismissed Leah. "I must ask, however, who are you a thrall for, boy? Is it the Gladstones? They're to stay in the western parts of Levent."

"I am not a thrall," Teller said.

The intensity of their glare and dialogue cut through everything nearby. Teller stood up against Cidron as though he were the bulky man's size. But this was a battle of wits, it seemed.

"Oh really?" Cidron clicked his tongue. "Show me your shoulder, right now."

The chair nearly toppled over with Teller's defiant rise. He pulled at the collar of his faded green tunic and revealed the top of his shoulders. Nothing out of the ordinary showed, to Cidron's disappointment. Or was it to his joy? The man's rough features were difficult to read.

Cidron jammed his hands in his front pockets and huffed lightly. "Apologizes, sir. Or perhaps you're a little lord from Riverview?"

For whatever reason, Teller tore his gaze free and fiddled with the closed pages of a nearby book. In a way, the sudden shift in behavior brought Zahna to mind. When she stood on stage, lost for words, she fidgeted and stalled for time. It was pretty clear that Teller wasn't a thrall, especially now that Cidron had pointed out the signs for them.

"I've never seen you before, my lord. Are you new to this city? Visiting a cousin or a relative?" Cidron spoke while taking a seat on the opposite side of the desk. "If you don't mind me asking, of course."

"I . . . I'm visiting my uncle, Lord Dahle."

Leah's lips tugged into a suppressed smile at the mention of the judge. She often spoke about him and how she wished to go back.

But Gil understood the reason for Cidron not sending her back. Leah was perhaps too young to see it herself, or just inexperienced, but Cidron protected her.

"Oh, welcome to Levent, my lord. I'm Cidron Ross. Your uncle and I have quite a lot of business together." Cidron's eyes searched through the stack of books in front of Teller. "Ah, glad to see you're helping him. Studying the Leventie uprising and the Eckrosie, it seems like."

Teller knocked over the stack of books, spreading them on top of the others. It would take a fool to miss the apparent signs of Teller's lies.

Hurried footsteps carried through the echoing library—hurried yet uneven, belonging to Vince. The old man joined the table, and all three children froze.

"Cidron, I'd discuss with ya the—" Vince stopped mid-sentence and rubbed his nose where several hairs sprouted out. "You, boy. Trying to sneak 'hind me back. The boy looking for trouble, looking for something illegal. I've half a mind to get the guards and let 'em have ya."

Cidron turned his attention to the crazy old man. "Please, Vince, surely curiosity at this age is to be encouraged."

But Vince kept speaking to Teller. "I've got keen eyes. There's no way to trick Vince. Now, you've 'en sleeping here and you ain't got answers. So off ya go."

"Vince, dear friend." Cidron rose from his seat and placed a hand on Vince's crooked shoulder. "Perhaps you'll find it in your heart to let the boy stay a while, seeing as he's been nothing but help. Also, he is a little lord."

"Nah, rules are rules. It ain't Vince's fault he's paying for two thralls who can't read. Now, away you go. This place ain't for sleeping." Vince pointed an accusatory finger at Teller, who seemed to see no other way out than to follow the old man's advice.

Teller released his stare from Cidron and retrieved two bags from under the desk. Vince pushed Teller forward, not even giving Gil or Leah a chance to say goodbye. He dragged his feet and glanced at the books longingly.

Soon the library fell silent.

Cidron shrugged, seeming unbothered by the ordeal. "Looks like your jobs got a lot harder. I'll see you tonight." With that, Cidron left Gil and Leah alone.

～❖～

Rain pounded the street outside the library, as the doors slammed behind Teller once the librarian tossed him out. He would get back inside, somehow. At the very least, he would stay nearby and talk to Gil and Leah once they were done for the day. Although Cidron had come a bit too close to figuring out his heritage, he seemed like a kind person, protecting those who worked for him.

Teller hurried across the street to a merchant's stall, where other people were huddled up, sheltering from the rain. His clothes were too fancy. If he wanted to disappear and stay hidden from his family, he needed to find better clothes.

" . . . that Eckrosie whore will get what she deserves."

Teller stopped in his tracks to glance back at two men talking by a nearby corner. They stayed clear of the downpour beneath a slanted roof hanging over the street.

"Say that again," Teller growled at them with surprising ease.

The older boys, probably young men even, jerked their hands to him to urge him away. "Mind your business, kid."

But Teller wasn't having any of it. He traipsed toward them, hands on his hips. "What does it matter if she's Eckrosie? You have a problem with Eckrosie?"

One of them, the talkative one, with a high brow, crooked teeth, and lazy eyes, sneered at Teller. "Who doesn't? They're the bastards destroying our country. Now shut your trap and bugger off."

There was no plan behind his approach. He clenched his fists tight. "And who gives you the right to decide what others deserve? Huh?"

Teller shoved the tallest boy and jumped the other to hit him in the groin. He managed to punch the talker and grab his hair to keep on beating, but something tore him loose.

Before he could react, he fell to the dirty, muddy road. Water splashed on his face and soaked through his clothes. Forceful hands spun him around. He reached for a knife from his bag, but a flurry of hits to his face left him disoriented and confused. The two people on top of him swirled from one side to the other.

His nose crunched deep into his skull, and a red veil covered his sight. Thick blood coated his tongue with its iron taste. Teller clenched his jaw to stop himself from biting through his tongue with each thrust that knocked him back to the hard ground. His body craved for a respite, but he refused to plead. He would make them stop.

"Messed with the wrong guys, bastard," someone shouted nearby. A high-pitched ring dazed Teller with a throbbing headache.

He reached deep within himself to find the source of power he'd attained when he tried to save Ayla. To bring out the fire that burned, he focused on his filthy father, standing above Ayla with a sword ready to slice through her. These bastards didn't care about Ayla or the Eckrosie. To them, they were disposable creatures . . . and Teller would not have it.

Again, a surge of energy exploded within his chest and into the rest of his body. It came alight in a furious inferno. Teller's fist connected with something soft. With his punch, he felt things break to make room for the force smashing into it. A loud scream echoed before things turned gray around Teller.

What am I doing? I'm going to die if I . . . Ayla can't be forgotten . . . Teller thought. Whatever he was fighting the guys for was not worth dying over. His hands trembled at his face, trying to shield himself from the onslaught.

"Oi . . . oi! That's enough. You've made your point."

Raindrops smashed his bloated skin. Everything from his head to his toes throbbed. He gazed at the mournful weeping sky.

A gray shape danced into his field of vision. "Hey, can you see me?"

It wasn't the same voice from earlier. This was different. Hard, but the words were caring and full of concern. "Let's get you on your feet."

The sky disappeared; instead, he caught a glimpse of a crimson street. Blood dripped from his nose and mouth. Everything felt wet and sticky, and a heavy scent of iron lingered in the damp air.

"Woah . . . alright, let's get you to a healer."

"My—my bags . . ." Teller mumbled through lumps of blood at the back of his throat.

"Ey, make way," the voice called. Though Teller kept asking about his bags, the person did not reply.

Things passed him before he was able to react to them. He noticed gravel rolling underneath his boots, the call of loud merchants, and flights of stairs.

"Andyr, I know we ain't on the best terms, but I found this boy beaten half to death. Could you help him?"

A rough touch, with fingers pulling and nudging his skin, made Teller grin from pain.

"I ain't doing it for you. I'll do it for the boy. What's your name?"

"T—Teller," he finally squeezed out to the featureless faces. In a way, they swirled like Nightbringers, fluid and smoke-like. But they didn't show him things. They insisted on talking though all he wanted to do was sleep—a cloud, fluffy and soft, snuggled Teller.

"Teller, I'm Andyr. I'm a healer. You have a broken nose and possibly a cracked skull."

Someone opened Teller's eyelids. "I need to set your bone straight in your nose, and it'll hurt. Cidron, pin him down."

A snap moved the bones in his face. Teller screamed with an unbridled intensity that spurred the ringing in his ears to swell. Time flowed differently. One moment he lay on the ground, hearing the assailants' punches echo through his skull. Another moment, he lay on the bed, listening to two men speaking in the distance.

A lone candle flickered with a shape's passing. The bed yielded to make room for a hefty fellow. Teller blinked to rid his eyes of the dark, but it seemed to be nighttime.

"You've got some spirit, Teller," the man with a harsh croak said. The edges of his round head glowed from the candlelight. A bald man with misaligned lips, eyes, and nose stared back at Teller. If ever someone looked like a former brawler, this man fit the description perfectly.

"It ain't easy to impress me, but . . . the way you broke that guy's jaw? Never seen that before." Cidron handed Teller a cup of water.

Teller accepted the water and quelled his thirst. "I broke someone's jaw?"

Cidron rubbed his chin. "Yeah. I'd expect that from a bigger guy but not really from someone as scrawny as you. No offense."

So the thing he'd done back at the settlement had happened again. Somehow, he found the strength of a fully grown fighter, but whenever he did, he lost all power just as fast . . . He shook off the riddled look on his face to hide it from the stranger studying him.

"Thanks for getting me out of there," Teller mumbled.

"No worries. You'd do the same if you saw a couple of guys jump me, I'm sure. Good thing the Crown wasn't there, though, or you'd have been taken to prison."

Teller squinted. "Why would you think that?"

Cidron scoffed. "Looking into books about the Eckrosie and picking a fight with people talking shit 'bout them . . . question wasn't if you'd be attacked, but when."

The bags . . . his bags. The square room only held a bed and a single chair. A pile of his bloody clothes was gathered at the end of the bed, but no sign of his bags. Teller's palms moistened, and his skin heated. Did those bastards steal them? His possessions that Jarred sacrificed so much to provide him with?

"Easy there." Cidron hushed Teller's panicking thoughts. "The guys are two rooms to the right. How 'bout I'll go over there and get your stuff back? It's the least I can do."

"They're here?"

"You ain't the only one who needed healing. I'm just gonna check with the healer, and I'll head over to get your stuff."

Cidron stomped heavily out of the room, where he turned to the left to speak to the healer. But Teller could not let a stranger stand up for him and get his stuff back. Jarred had fought for those things, and Teller would fight to keep them.

The hallway wobbled and shuddered with Teller's walk. He held on to a coarse wall that kissed his fingers with a spiky tongue. He passed one door, and a second swung open at his push.

On a bed, the talkative man lay, while his friend looked up at Teller from his chair. His face drained of color at the sight of the boy, and he stuttered, "Hey, we don't want any more trouble."

"My bags. Give them back," Teller snorted.

" Just . . . take the bag and go," the man said, and approached Teller slowly.

Off to the side, one of Teller's bags leaned up against the wall. The clothes and essentials Jarred had packed for him were still there, though the valuable bag was not. Teller sneered at the shaking guy and at the man with a bruised jaw.

"I had two bags."

Alone, the tall but brawny guy did not seem as intimidating. And his friend, lying with a broken jaw, only gave a grunt or two in protest.

"Don't know what you're—"

Teller grabbed the man's wrist and twisted it behind his back, one of the many tricks the captain had taught Teller. Without much effort, Teller held power over the squirming guy.

"Alright, just take it . . . it's by the bed."

If he wanted to, he could have snapped the wrist. Teller considered it, but let go and snatched the heavy bag. Both men stared blankly at Teller as he walked out of the room.

Not until he stepped out did he realize his heart was thumping loudly enough to cloud his thoughts.

He did not know how, but somehow he found his way back to the first room. Cidron sat by his side on the bed again. "What do you say about putting those skills to use and earning a bit of coin to fill that bag even more?"

Teller shielded the bag from Cidron's greedy hands. He was not losing it a second time.

The lord pinched the bridge of his crooked nose. "I've got a fighting ring where you'd be competing if you want to put those skills to use. It gets you off the

streets. You'll get a bed, food, and you never got to worry about basic things. Lets you focus on things that matter."

Teller played with the straps of his bag. The jewelry and silverware would last for a while, but not for too long. He was determined to only use this power when it was a matter of life or death. He could not use it for simple things such as food and board.

"You've got someone or something you need to get revenge on, am I right?" Cidron caught a whiff of Teller avoiding his gaze. The man leaned closer. "Trust me, I get that. But you need to grow, get stronger if you're to beat any of 'em. Stay with me, and I'll give you all of it. Also, your new friends, Leah and Gil, they work for me."

Teller fidgeted.

"Well, I've got to head out. Nice meeting you, and say hi to your uncle." Cidron marched out of the room.

Was this a chance he would never have again? Would he turn down the offer of a person who'd saved his life? Where was he going to go? Teller bounced from the bed to follow the man, but he stumbled and tripped. He crawled the last feet to find Cidron walking down the corridor. "Wait!" he called.

Cidron turned, looking like a vast mountain glaring at him from above the clouds from his position down at the floor.

"I'll do it. Please take me with you."

A wide grin from ear to ear erased Cidron's stern features. "Let's get going."

~❈~

Sticky and stinking sweat reeked once Gil stepped into the cellar beneath the Rosses' estate. Spilled ale and other beverages joined the intense odors. He was following Cidron, reluctantly going farther into the crowded space where men and women stood shoulder to shoulder, watching something and screaming. They encircled the middle of the basement, held up by chubby columns.

Gil cradled his lute close to avoid the unruly crowd. Cidron cleared a table in one of the dark corners of the room and wiped it clean with a fell swoop of his arm. Cups and glass rained to the ground and shattered. Wasting little time, Cidron grabbed Gil and tossed him onto the table to see above the adults' heads.

The large group encircled an empty square in the middle of the room. Adults he had seen before in the dining hall hollered and chanted while waving their hands enthusiastically. From the table, he noticed two thralls throwing themselves against each other, to the crowd's delight. They were cheering on the fight, and there seemed to be bets going around.

"You'll sing and perform here for the night, Gil. Especially in between fights. Keep the crowd going. Don't let it get quiet," Cidron instructed. But his tone was anything but suggesting. This was an order.

Gil gave a silent nod, readjusted his instrument's hold, and started playing a quick and upbeat tune. While the fight was going on, he saw no reason for singing, as his scrawny voice would drown in their cheers.

Boys and girls stepped into the ring to fight and brawl. At first, young adults seventeen or eighteen years old grabbed each other's hair and wrestled. They strained and fell to the floor, where the loser bashed their hand against the floor to submit. Some never got the chance, as they were knocked unconscious. When the blood started flowing, a sickening pit grew in Gil's stomach. Some children gazed at the adults pleadingly before being attacked and forced to submit.

A sickening crack made Gil stop playing, and a pained scream followed. A young woman clenched her jaw, which looked dislocated. In the crowd, Cidron's hard stare pierced Gil. The boy's fingers slid on the lute's neck and played another joyful tune while the woman was carried outside.

There was a certain coldness to Cidron, something Gil hadn't seen emanating from him before—a disregard for people's wellbeing. Up until this point, Cidron had seemed to do all in his power to see to others' needs.

Thankfully, Gil didn't have to step into the ring, and neither did Leah. Or at least, he hoped that was the case. However, his heart sank when a boy his own age, twelve or thirteen, stepped into the fray. Bruises, black and blue, disfigured the boy's features. Bashed-up eyebrow, busted lips . . . this kid had taken quite a punch. Still, there was a fire burning behind his emerald eyes, one Gil hadn't seen in a long time.

"Our newcomer, Teller, fights Gerry," a female announced to the crowd. "Place your bets if you haven't."

Although Gil wished they would have reunited under different circumstances, he couldn't help but feel a spark of hope light at the sight of Teller. Both Leah and Gil had wondered what happened to the intriguing boy after he was kicked out of the library, and now he showed up once more.

People exchanged money and placed their bets. Gerry, a heavyset fellow with stubby black hair, swayed back and forth in front of Teller, anxiously awaiting the fight about to begin. Although the fire burned brightly behind the boy's eyes, he wilted and cowered in the face of danger. He wasn't there for a fight. He was there to get hurt.

Gil's grasp on the lute tightened at the realization, but he was too late to intervene. Once the announcer started the fight, Gerry rushed up to Teller. Teller didn't stand a chance, and toppled over to the ground after Gerry slammed his fist into his temple. Scattered applause filled the basement. Cidron stood with his mouth gaping wide, not noticing that Gil was silent.

Each meaty swing sent blood gushing out of Teller, who did nothing to protect himself. After some unnecessary punches, Gerry backed off the boy, who blinked emptily on the ground. As the onslaught stopped, everyone looked to Cidron, whose jaw tightened and face reddened.

A grunt left Teller as he tried to rise. He got onto all fours, doing his best to find his bearings. Instead of harming the boy, Gerry simply pushed Teller back down onto the floor. Just as determined as before, Teller got back up to his feet.

"Finish him off, Gerry," Cidron said through gritted teeth, and exited the basement.

Late that night, once the fighting stopped, Gil was sent to his bed in the chambers, where Leah and the rest of the thralls were asleep. Gil, pumped with the adrenaline of watching the brawls, could not seem to join their snoring and calm breathing. Instead, he tossed and turned while sentences for a new song danced and taunted him.

Floorboards creaked nearby. A shape snuck into the room until it found an empty bed waiting to be laid in. A candle flickered and fought against the dark, casting long, frightening shadows on the walls and a boy's skin.

Teller sat on the bed, gazing out the window. The fire that had burned in the haunting eyes now dwindled; instead, a soft shimmer settled in them. There was a sadness and pain to him that was hard to understand. Although the room filled with people, he seemed to be alone, as though he stood solitary on a hill without a living soul for miles. He was lost, and Gil felt the pain.

Gil approached the boy, although his feet wanted to head back to the comfort of his bed. Teller needed company. He needed to know that he wasn't alone. He was the newcomer, like Leah and Gil had been, and he needed to feel welcomed.

"Hey. Mind if I . . . ?"

Behind the bruises and bloated skin, Teller seemed to recognize Gil, and smiled. He scooched over to let Gil take a seat.

"Saw you when you . . . eh," Gil said. While speaking, he looked for what to say next, the way Zahna did when she struggled with a play script. "You just arrived?"

Teller winced, shifting his position to favor his left. "Yeah."

"How did you end up here? We thought you'd left Levent."

"Yeah," Teller grunted. "I got in trouble, and . . . Cidron said I could be with you and Leah."

"You're a thrall too?"

"No. Even if I were, I'd never sign those papers," Teller said.

A stone sank in Gil's stomach. The papers that he'd signed? "What do you mean?"

Teller sighed. "Papers on Cidron's desk. He brought me to his study to help sort things out and let me heal."

"Joining the fighting ring helps you heal? Didn't seem like it." Gil leaned his head on the palm of his hand. "You're not really a lord, are you?"

Teller's battered nose crinkled and he winced with pain. "Not really. I don't know, to be honest. I just said I was Dahle's nephew, but that isn't true. I don't think Cidron bought it even, but he hasn't said anything about it."

"So, you get a bed to sleep in. Are you leaving us already?" Gil asked, fearful of the answer.

Teller shrugged. "I'll stay. Don't have anywhere else to go."

A silent sigh of relief left Gil. Another friend would stay near his side. Sure, they had not spent a lot of time together, but he had a good feeling about Teller. "The papers . . . what did they say? Leah and I, we, well, you know, we signed. He said it was just like a text that said we have to work for him and not with other places, and we need to go where he tells us to."

Teller sighed. "Sorry to say, but Cidron will make you do anything he wants you to. You can dream about performing, but he owns you."

"What do you mean?" Gil's eyebrows brushed against each other.

"That paper you signed . . . that's a contract. Once you sign the papers, you belong to Cidron. It says you owe him money for staying here. Don't know what amount you owe him, but the one I saw had to serve five years to pay it back."

Five years? I've got to stay for five years? Gil thought. *Sure, I don't mind the food and the bed or anything, but . . .* "How do you know that?" he asked.

"I read it on the paper. Everything. How he grants you food and shelter in return for your servitude, and how he can send you wherever he chooses. He has total control over all of you. If you break the contract . . . I don't know what happens."

If what Teller said was true, that Gil and Leah owed Cidron a debt. He had been lied to from the moment he stepped into the Rosses' house with his broken lute. He should have known. He should have known that this was too good to be true. Gil's gaze traced through the dark room across the beds where others slept. All of them had been lied to, and now slept soundly. He wanted to be annoyed, frustrated even, at Cidron but as of yet, he did not suffer in Cidron's care.

"I'll help you get out of the contract," Teller whispered at the sight of Gil's flickering gaze.

Gil scratched his dry scalp. "Why?"

"Because you shouldn't belong to anyone. You're a person, not property," Teller said.

Gil gave a dry chuckle. "Well, it feels good to have another good friend here who can help us out." Gil nudged Teller, who flinched, then gave him a lackluster smile.

"Look, I'm exhausted," Teller said.

Recognition dawned on Gil's face as he leaped off the bed. He was getting too close to Teller. Like always, he came on too strong. "Yeah, sure, sure . . . well, good night."

Gil hurried back, and the linens hugged him tightly. He stared at the ceiling, in deep thought. Teller had chosen his name because he hated the old one. Gil uttered his name, letting it slip past his lips. No, it was alright. He liked it. Gil the great. Gil the performer. One day it would come true. Somehow, he would find himself on the city's stages instead of the small ones Cidron put him on. His voice would travel over the massive crowds once again. With Teller's help, he would be able to get the opportunity he didn't know had been stolen from him by Cidron.

CHAPTER SIXTEEN

The Following

Once more, Cidron glared at Leah from his desk. "You're a very good listener, and once you start a task, you carry it out better than most other thralls."

Leah glanced up at him. She didn't know what she was expecting, but hearing him say good things about her wasn't it. Her lips inched upward at his words.

"You ain't going back to the library. You'll be my personal thrall," Cidron said.

She understood it might be too late to ask, but she had to. "Can I work for the Guides?"

"They don't allow thralls," Cidron blurted.

"Can't I work for the judge? He liked me, and I was good at it," Leah pleaded.

Cidron paused, and Leah's eyes widened. Was she asking too much of him? The man leaned his elbows against the desk. "You want to work for him? He didn't . . . hurt you?"

Hurt me? He never hurt me, she thought.

"The judge doesn't get my best thralls. I need them myself. Don't worry. It'll be good."

"What do you want me to do, my l—I mean . . ."

"Everything. You'll bring me food when I'm hungry, you'll follow me to meetings, and you'll do what I ask. And again, don't call me lord."

Leah played with her hands, unfolding them and folding them nervously. "Sorry, my . . . sorry."

"So this is what I'll need you to do today. We're going to the lord judge's estate in Riverview. I have a meeting with him, and I want you to be there with me. Go to the tailor in Rose Lane, where you worked, and buy a dress for the evening."

A pouch of money settled on the table. Leah blinked at it. All that money . . . was for her? To get a dress? The kind of fancy clothing the ladies of Riverview wore? Tears glistened in her eyes, but she was quick to wipe them away. She left her home, walking determined through the slums of Keelheart and across a river to make it to Rose Lane. She hated going through the slums on her own. At every corner, it felt like adults tried to stop her or persuade her into stopping. But as soon as she hurried across the river, the houses and the people didn't frighten her.

Returning to the tailor's shop, she saw the dresses and clothes decorating every space of the shop in a new light than she had when she worked for the bitter lady, Gizelle. The materials caught the afternoon's sun in different shines. Some fabrics swallowed whatever light was cast on them, but others glistened like Lake Ember on a sunny day. One such dress caught her eye, a deep blue one with a long train at the back. But that was for the fancy ladies, not for someone like Leah.

Gizelle appeared from drapes shielding the back of the store. She halted in her tracks once she witnessed Leah touching the soft and soothing textiles.

"You're not supposed to be here. I have another thrall now," Gizelle sighed.

"I'm here to buy a dress," Leah said, and put the pouch of coins on the counter. Gizelle peered into the pouch and counted the coins within.

With a raised eyebrow, she gestured to the shop. "What is it you're seeking?"

"I'm going to Riverview with Cidron Ross, and he asked me to get a dress," Leah said.

"Well, then." Gizelle squeezed past Leah and pulled a few items off their hinges, then placed them on the counter for Leah to look at.

Three short dresses spread out on the desk. All three had the same fabric and look, but in different colors—one blue, one red, and one green. Each had long sleeves with straps at the ends, and the same style at the neck. Leah pointed to the blue one and let it hug her body as she tried it on. The thick and somewhat-coarse material touched her skin but didn't sit too tight. The weight rested on her shoulders. It fit perfectly.

Back home, Cidron presented her with another gift. A white-and-brown pony used to pull one of the carts filled with thralls to different districts stood waiting for her together with Cidron. The pony's reins were tied to a larger horse's saddle.

She got on, and shortly after commanded the pony to stop. Or at least she tried to. She squeezed her feet against the animal's fluffy belly, but it refused to listen to her and continued its trot until the reins connecting with Cidron's horse pulled tight. Thankfully, Cidron paused and gave her a short lesson on how to ride before they made their way up Main Street and into Riverview. It was hard at first, speaking with the pony in a language it would understand. Still, once she realized the different positions of her heels, the journey was exciting. Her feet didn't hurt from a long walk, but her calves did as she sat and strained her muscles to not fall off the cute, chubby animal.

A thrall from the Dahle estate gathered their horses and brought them to a smaller building off to the side of the gates of the mansion. Last time she'd visited the estate, the garden had bloomed with colorful flowers and smelled sweet. Now, in the wintertime, green leaves covered the gardens, and the flower buds were absent.

Leah straightened her dress after seeing Cidron brushing something off his doublet. "I need you to remember what the judge and I are talking about. I know you can't write or read, but when we get back, you'll speak with a thrall who can. I like to record what has been discussed and said during my meetings with the judge."

Leah picked her nails and gave a quick nod. They stepped into the hallway of the enormous house. She kept an eye out for Karly, the head thrall of the estate. But only new, unfamiliar faces found her as they guided Cidron and Leah to the dining room where Leah had once cleaned the bookshelves and floors.

By the high windows, reaching from the floor to the roof, the lord judge observed the city below. His gray-and-white hair lay combed behind his ears. He closed the bindings of a book and turned to face his guests.

"Ah, Lord Ross. Welcome." Dahle extended his hand to Cidron, who shook it. "And who is this?"

Leah peered at the judge, who looked the same as he had a few weeks earlier. His hooded eyes widened after taking another look at her. "You brought her back?"

Leah smiled and took a bow. "Yes, my lord."

"Well, that is quite a delightful sight, I must say. Thank you, Lord R—" Dahle said, but Cidron cut him short.

"She's my personal thrall since she returned to my service."

The judge's soft gaze hardened. "Good for you. Please, take a seat."

The long table seemed to stretch over the entire room. Leah sat down by it, barely reaching up with her arms to it in the cushioned chair. A thrall served the gentlemen drinks, wine it looked like, and Leah got a tall cup of water, which she gulped down fast.

"Your absence from Levent was undeniable. Where were you, if I may ask, my lord?" Cidron asked.

The judge moved his wine glass in his hands, making the wine swirl. "I had business with the royal family in Thorne's Town, and some other people I had to meet."

"And now you return to meet with a lesser lord such as myself," Cidron said. He sipped on the wine.

Leah stroked her dress, pressing the pleats to go away.

"Am I right, Leah?" Dahle suddenly said. His kind eyes stared at her as he brought her back to the moment. She smiled widely.

Cidron threw a gaze at Leah. "You want her as a token of good faith? I would accept ... though your latest Following-favoring policies and taxes have created problems for my business. Some thralls are simply too valuable for me to depart from."

"The Following has grown increasingly bold, but the taxes were something I could not go up against without upsetting the king himself. This city rests on thin foundations between you, the Following, and the Crown. Upset one, and the city will crumble."

"With all due respect, that sounds like your problem, and a problem you enjoy sustaining to keep yourself in power."

"I will admit, the view from these windows is spectacular and quite a perk. Perhaps you should move here as well, my lord?" Dahle pointed toward the windows. Hundreds of lights glowed in the dark, almost like fireflies. Leah gawked at them, but then focused on their boring discussion again. She had to listen.

"Listen, I will be blunt," Dahle said. "Our arrangements have not changed with this tax and with the policies. It is a tug-of-war. At this moment, the Following needed leeway, or they would start an uprising. We can both agree that such a thing would not serve anyone."

Cidron picked his teeth while the judge spoke. He didn't seem impressed with the conversation. "I didn't come all this way to hear you rant. Also, I hope you're not forgetting that I have a large say in this conversation, and upsetting me, and my interests, is not something to look lightly upon."

The judge put down his glass. "Fine, speak freely. What is it you want?"

"Shut down the three merchants competing with me. Ulric in Northrun, Patty in River's Brook, and Tyler in Westview. It's the least you can do. You'll find they are . . . less inclined to aid your efforts."

"Consider them dealt with. The thralls who work for them shall be sent to you and your establishments," the judge agreed.

Cidron scratched his nose. "And . . . keep the city patrol clear from Keelheart."

"My lord, keeping clear of an entire district is not something that rests in my hands."

Cidron clicked his tongue. "Sure it is. And you'll make sure that happens. Do this favor, and I'll do my best to find an Eckrosie girl for you as a deal well struck."

Whatever they were deciding, it seemed to work. The judge and Cidron shook hands. Cidron got out of the chair and instructed Leah to follow him, leaving the other man behind.

"Oh, before you leave," the judge said. "The Lord and Lady Riveroak, their son has disappeared. If he happened to end up under your nose, your cooperation in bringing him to me, letting me reunite the family, would be greatly rewarded."

Cidron kept his back to Dahle. "Disappeared, you say? I heard he ran away."

"Phrase it as you wish . . . just keep an eye out."

"Will do," Cidron spoke over his shoulder, and guided Leah back to their mounts outside. A light drizzle fell upon them during their quiet journey. Leah did her best to protect the dress from getting wet.

Cidron and Leah didn't have time to enter the Rosses' estate before a thin man stepped up to them. Sweat glistened on his forehead—strange, since it was kind of chilly in the air.

"Eh . . ."

"Spit it out," Cidron said.

"The boy did the same act today."

"Where is he?" Cidron rolled his eyes and mumbled.

"Asleep."

The scrawny man took off as Cidron marched into the sleeping quarters. Heads, arms, and legs poked out from blankets lying over the sleeping thralls.

Cidron snatched the ashen, brown-haired boy from the bed. He looked like a puppy in the large man's grasp. Leah left room for Cidron and Teller in the narrow doorframe but followed fast. Teller clawed and struggled against being dragged by his hair.

"Let go," he pleaded, but Cidron threw him into a tiny room without windows, where stacks of barley and wheat stood.

With a dull thud, Teller slammed into a barrel and onto the floor. Before he had the opportunity to get up, Cidron put the bottom of his boot across Teller's throat.

Leah blinked and drew closer to the defenseless boy, but froze when Cidron roared. "You put my reputation on the line. I thought I made that clear—you don't fuck with me, boy."

Leah hadn't seen it on the way back home, but maybe Nightbringers had managed to get to Cidron. This amount of anger and hatred washing over Teller from the man was something Leah had never seen before . . . he was like a monster. A horrifying monster, harming Teller.

The boy gasped for air, clawing at Cidron's feet. His skin turned deep red like blood, and his eyes stared at the man.

As Teller's eyes began to shut, Cidron stepped off him. "Get him up, Leah."

Her hopes of staying invisible to them vanished. She rushed over to Teller and gently nudged him to his feet. He coughed violently at her side, almost unrecognizable as the boy she'd met at the library. His tanned skin had been overtaken by bruises and cuts.

Cidron clutched Teller's head and brought him close, almost as if leaning in for a kiss. "What did you do wrong? Tell Leah what you did, so she understands why you're making me do this."

Leah croaked. "He doesn't have to . . ."

"Shh." Cidron shot a glance at Leah before returning to Teller. "Go on . . . tell me."

But Teller bit his lips, staring at Cidron.

"Maybe force doesn't work with you. Is that it? Hmm? You're happy to take a beating. But what if I say that if you don't answer, I'll take it out on Leah?"

Teller blinked, and his stern face was replaced with a frown. "Fine, I . . . I didn't fight back . . . in the fighting ring."

Cidron grasped Teller. "So that's your thing. You don't care if it hurts you, but if you get someone hurt . . . that's unbearable." The man placed a hand on Leah. She couldn't help but feel an aching tingle spread from where his hand touched her. "Don't worry. I'd never hurt you, Leah. That's the judge's way, not mine. Come, let's get you to bed while we leave Teller alone to think about what he did."

The door shut behind Cidron and Leah. He locked the door with a key and slid it into his pocket. "You do understand why I hurt him?"

Not really, she thought, but gave him a nod.

"Now . . . Leah, I hope you learned much today and that you enjoyed following me around. You did well, kid. This type of thing is more suited for you, don't you agree?"

Even though he had just hurt Teller and locked him up on the other side of the door, she agreed. She did have a good time until now, so much that she didn't even notice her eyelids that felt like sand against her eyes. Because of Cidron, she'd finally felt the gentle touch of a fancy dress over her skin. Although she had just been shown Cidron's bad temper, she was thankful not to have disappointed him.

Cidron nudged her along the hallway. "I would never hurt you. I hope you get that, Leah. What I said in there was to scare him. He's been causing trouble."

She turned to him and gave a weak smile. The smooth dress kissed her skin. "Can . . . I keep this?"

"It's yours. And trust me, that's just the first one you'll get."

Cidron was wrong. All of them were wrong.

Teller's windpipe ached from where the man's boot had crushed against it. Darkness stared back at him like it had in the cellar at home. But it did not frighten him. He had seen Nightbringers with

Ayla, and they did not hurt him. What harmed him were the people walking in broad daylight. Adults loved to speak tales of monsters and creatures wanting to do harm. Yet they always avoided speaking about the monsters roaming among them.

Every part of him throbbed with pain, though it faded in comparison with the sickness tearing him up inside. Once he came to stay with Cidron and the Rosses, he went against Cidron's wishes. After reading the contracts on his desk, contracts that bound people to the man, Teller could not help but feel obligated to help out against him. His practices left desperate children no choice but to enter legal slavery. Sure, they signed a contract, but without understanding what they were agreeing to. Teller had been unable to help Nyle and Jarred—perhaps he could help Gil and Leah. At least the thought of actually helping someone calmed the storm within him.

Cidron, without question, wished to see the brutality Teller had displayed outside the library again. But no matter the threats or the yelling at him, he refused to fight back. For some reason, it felt good taking punch after punch. He knew he deserved it. Every bit of it.

After what had to be at least a good hour, Teller searched his worn boots for the lockpick. He dragged his fingers along the door until he found the lock, which clicked with his first try.

He did not quite know where he was going. His stomach was crying out for food. Perhaps taking a bite of some stale brown bread could satisfy him. Just one bite, then he would head back to the room and lock himself in. Someone else would not get the blame for his absence . . .

"Boy," a tired voice called from a room.

Teller stopped in his tracks to look at Cidron, sitting by his desk. A harsh light strengthened the already-bulky features of his face. "Take a seat."

There was no point in running or returning to the cage. Teller sat down in a cushioned chair opposite Cidron.

"You can sell that to others, but I see what you're doing. Don't think I don't, boy," Cidron said. Ink marked a paper with sharp thick lines beneath his stubby fingers.

"Sell what?" Teller asked. His eyes searched the cluttered desk, where piles of papers and inkwells lined up. Within his reach lay a dagger.

"I know a fighter when I see one. You won't make me any profits by being a punching bag, or whatever it is you're getting off to." Cidron eyed the dagger as well. "Tell me what you want, Teller."

"I don't know." The boy avoided his hard gaze.

"If you wanted, you could have killed me. But that's not what you want. You agreed to get into the fighting ring without hesitation. Selling me the bullshit of you being the judge's nephew . . . well, that was cute, seeing as Dahle doesn't have any siblings. But it's obvious that you are of the higher class and not some merchant's boy."

Beads of sweat pricked Teller's skin. The thin clothes seemed to get tighter with each of the man's words.

Cidron continued his speculation. "Now, what would a nobleman's son be doing in Keelheart with me? I guess you can't go back home, since you avoid your family's name like a plague. There's only one boy I know of who's on the run from nobles—would that be you, Aiden Riveroak?"

The chair shackled him at the sound of that name. Teller shrugged to keep his composure, but whatever he did, Cidron saw straight through it. "It makes sense. You've got nowhere else to go. Rich folks near Riverview would recognize the son of the hero of Riverview in a heartbeat. But in the slums . . . surrounded by poor people . . . well, that's better. Unlike the poor suckers living here, though, you've got no clue how to survive, so why not accept the offer of living beneath my roof?

"What I don't get is why you're letting yourself get beat down. You know how to defend yourself. I wanted you to become the best brawler we've seen, but you just take one punch after the next. Quite disappointing, and perhaps a call for help. I think the only right thing for me to do is inform the lord and lady . . ."

Teller flew forward in the chair, almost toppling it. "Please don't tell anyone. I—I can't go back."

The quill found the inkwell, and Cidron moved over to Teller's side of the table and put a determined hand on Teller's shoulder. "Your secret is safe with me, kid. It's not like I'm one of the nobility, not really. In fact, I'm going to reward you and put your skills to good use."

Teller dried his aching cheeks with the cuff of his sleeve. Reward? Why would Cidron give him a reward for breaking out and going against his wishes?

"That's not the first lock you've opened, is it?"

"Not really," Teller sniffled.

Cidron towered above him like a guard on a wall, staring down at him. "You know how to read, and you've been trained in social skills. You're not a regular kid. Therefore, I want you to spy for me. There's a group of people I need you to keep an eye on. Inform me about their activities. Do this for me, and I'll keep your secret safe. It will stay in this room, and I'll make sure the Riveroaks won't find you." Cidron extended his hand to Teller. "Deal?"

A hiding place and someone who could keep his name secret? He did not want to agree, but what other choice was there than to accept? At least, this way, he didn't have to hurt people.

Their hands embraced.

"Good. Alright, they call themselves the Following, and I need you to spy on them at Rose Lane. There's a lady named Elara Averil. She's what they call a Presider, which is a leader in their ranks. She comes from a family of great wealth and uses slaves instead of thralls. You'll try to get as close as you can. Learn what she's up to, who she meets, even what she eats."

At the mention of the Following, his body tensed up. Those were the people who had risen up against Canden, and fought against Lionel. But what was the real reason for Teller growing tense? Was it the remains of Aiden that came back to haunt him?

"But what about the fighting, or Gil and Leah?"

Cidron clicked his tongue. "What about them?"

"Can I meet them and stay here?"

"You'll stay where the Following allows you to stay. And with regards to Gil and Leah, they'll stay here, where they belong."

"You promised me a reward. In that case, I want you to promise that neither Gil or Leah fights in your stupid games."

Cidron's upper lip curled into a deceiving smile. "This is your reward. You damaged my reputation. So I can't promise you that."

"Fine, then I won't do what you asked."

Cidron scratched his chin, covered with stubble, deep in thought. The way Lionel did. "Deal. They won't fight."

"And you stop the fighting pit completely."

Cidron crossed his arms. "Don't push your luck, kid. I've given you more than you deserve."

It was worth a shot at least, Teller thought, but was happy to hear that Gil and Leah would escape that fate. No kid should have to beat up another for adults' amusement.

"How am I supposed to get close to Elara?" Teller asked.

"It's simple—I need you to be Aiden. Go to Rose Lane, and look desperate. Once she learns you're the son of the hero who fought against her leader, she'll have to keep you close."

Teller tapped his feet to the ground. "But I'm Teller."

Cidron slouched closer to him, making his presence even scarier. "Teller isn't useful to me."

"But they'll send me back to my parents if they find out."

"Trust me, they won't. They'll keep you as close as they can, perhaps even from Keelheart and me. But we'll make sure you can come to report to me."

The plan felt even worse. What if the Following sent him back to Thorne's Town? What if they killed him? Everything about it felt wrong. "I don't want to do this."

Cidron's face hardened. "I didn't want to say this, but . . . if you're thinking about running away or doing anything against me, Gil and Leah die. You don't want their deaths on you, would you?"

"You—you can't . . . do that," Teller stuttered.

A grin showed on the man's face. It was the kind of expression that said, *Do you really want to test me?* A couple of bones cracked with Cidron's stretch. "I don't need your friends, and they're easy thralls to replace. But the son of the hero of Riverview? That's pretty rare. Now, do we have an understanding?"

It did not look like it, but Cidron's mansion was a prison where meanspirited men decided the paths of others' lives. He did not know how, nor when, but Teller was going to free Gil and Leah from Cidron's filthy hands.

～❁～

Rose Lane differed from Keelheart in every way. Instead of narrow, reeking streets, Rose Lane had wide and often fair-smelling alleys and roads. Bushes and trees stood in front of the red clay houses, making it feel like a small village trapped in the city's walls. The buildings stood intact, with polished facades.

Cidron did not give Teller any more details on who to search for to find Elara Averil of Rose Lane. So, Teller walked the streets in search of anything that could help him. The occasional patrol of city guards passed him. He was quick to turn his head away, even if the chances of them being able to identify him were slim if not near impossible. Barely able to see through the swelled-up lids of his eyes, he would probably not recognize himself even.

The dull call of a bell rang near. Unlike the morning and evening bells signaling the beginning of trade and marking the end, this was at midday. People walking beside Teller stopped to listen to it ring before carrying on with their business. Some, however, began walking in the opposite direction. Teller followed.

He overheard a conversation. "Another one? They're getting busy, aren't they?"

"It's gotta be that arsonist they caught a week ago."

"You think a Crimson's gonna be there?"

A Crimson? A Crimson Wight? Teller had never seen one as of yet, but the stories he'd heard were enough to thicken his blood and ice his fingers. A morbid curiosity wrapped around him, and he continued following the crowd. Whatever was going on, it would be worth watching.

Teller wedged his way past the cramped gathering, in search of a vantage point. Above him stood a statue of the famed explorer Keldra. Teller grabbed onto it and climbed well above the sea of heads, grasping tight to the flat stone, which warmed his fingers.

The mass of people gathered in what was used as a marketplace. The sellers' colorful stalls full of wares had been moved to make space for the horde. Still, they seemed to be able to  sell their goods despite lining up along the surrounding houses' walls.

Up ahead, near the oddly shaped building known as the Halls, a timbered plateau peered over the market square. Teller's eyes went straight for the mystical beings he'd heard tales about. There, amid city guards, a herald, and a prisoner, stood a Crimson Wight. A bright white cloak wrapped the entire person from head to toe. Where the face would have been, a blank white mask, void of expression, disguised the Crimson. As with the Nightbringers Teller had met with Ayla, the sight of the Crimson sped up his heartbeat and moistened his palms. He was not alone in this, it seemed, as he listened to other people gasping and whispering.

The Crimson held onto a chain linking it together with the prisoner, an older man with gray hair and a slouched demeanor. The herald, dressed in blue and silver, the Crown's colors, stepped forward and called out.

"The district court of Rose Lane brings you a heinous criminal. The prisoner attempted to burn a local tavern, known as the Laughing Rooster. Luckily, he was apprehended and is therefore brought before you today. It is the will of the court that Caleb, the arsonist, be sent to Nedox and the Beast's Gate to serve until the day the Beast claims him."

A sudden wail echoed through the crowd. Probably a friend or relative to Caleb, the arsonist . . . but was he? He had tried, but had not succeeded. Did that make him an arsonist? Teller scratched his head. It seemed like a steep price to pay for something that had been prevented.

"As is custom," the herald said, and gestured to the Crimson, "the prisoner will be branded with the years he is to serve. May the Wanderer pull you back from the shadows."

The prisoner screamed and struggled against the Crimson, who pushed him forward. It kicked Caleb's knees, making him fall with a heavy thud. Guards pinned him down, and a thin shirt was pulled over the prisoner's head to reveal his back.

An iron found its way to the Crimson, who applied the sizzling-hot brand to the man's skin. One brand would have sufficed, but the Crimson did not stop after one. For each brand, Caleb twitched and called out in pain. Even at this distance, Teller could feel the heat of the brand on his skin . . .

After twenty, maybe thirty brands, the prisoner silenced, probably passing out from lack of air. The crowd clapped as the people left the stage.

"Seems as though Dahle listened to your request, Lady Presider," a person said nearby.

Five people surrounded a tall woman. Parts of her long, golden hair combed back behind one of her ears, while the rest was left flowing freely in the harsh breeze. As Teller managed to squeeze past some of the retreating onlookers, he caught a glimpse of her scarred features.

One intense blue eye sought the crowd, sweeping past Teller. Her left eye, however, had been replaced with damaged skin patching up the hole. A horrific scar cut her angular face, from her left eyebrow, across her nose, and down her right cheek. Still, she was quite attractive despite her disfigurement.

She stood tall among the others, despite her slim stature. Although her appearance spoke of a hardened and grizzled woman, people around gazed upon their leader with admiration, the sort of admiration Teller held for Captain Hutton. Her fairly short-sleeved leather jacket creaked with age. Many creases and discolorations marked the coat, reaching from a cloth shirt down to the beginning of her simple and comfortable pants. There was no doubt in his mind. This had to be Elara Averil.

"Hey! Elara," Teller shouted through the crowd, and climbed down to shove his way to her.

"Get away, boy." The strong and deep voice belonged to a lean man dressed in padded armor covering his clear, olive skin, and he pointed at Teller. His sleek, raven-dark hair, tied into a tight knot, made his stone-gray eyes pop.

"Joren, enough." Elara put a hand on the man's chest to stop him from closing in on Teller. "This boy won't harm me, will you?"

Teller gazed upon the Presider. *No, but if I wanted to . . .* he thought. "No, I just—I just need your help."

"Besides, you look like you have fallen off a horse. How can I help you?" Elara said, empathy gleaming behind her one eye.

What was the point of waiting? Cidron was clear with what he wanted Teller to do.

"I'm . . . my name is Aiden Riveroak." Teller subdued a bulk of food, rushing up his throat by uttering his old name.

Elara and Joren exchanged looks, riddled with concern. "Riveroak?"

"But please, call me Teller. I don't want to hear my old name," he added.

Elara blinked as she searched for words. "Riveroak, as in the son of Lionel Riveroak? The bastard of Riverview?"

At the sound of the bastard of Riverview, Teller could not help but smile broadly, going against the ache to his lips. Finally, someone understood and even said what he wanted to hear about that monster. The smile disappeared just as fast at the thought of what she would do to him, though. Now that she knew ... would she chain him up and send him back, or worse, kill him?

Elara knelt before him. "I would never hurt a child. We don't choose our parents, my lord," she said in a sweet and somewhat-hoarse voice. Her intense blue eye peered at him gently.

"I'm not a lord, so—" Teller shrugged.

"Lady Presider, you do not mean to talk with our king of this?" Joren uttered with a bewildered glare at both of them.

"What's he gonna do with a child, Joren? Huh? Use him to bargain with? Teller will accomplish more good for our cause simply by staying by our side and besmirching his family's reputation. Lord Haven will learn about this in due time, but he'll agree with me."

While Elara told him off, Joren reached into the pockets of his loose-fitted trousers and pulled out a paper. "Prove you're a lord. Read this sheet of paper and tell me what it says, word for word."

Rushed handwriting etched the paper with sharp strokes.

"There's no need for ..."

"Lady Averil, the Presider of Rose Lane, requests an audience with you ... audience is misspelled by the way." Teller peered from the scroll at Joren, who simpered at him. "Apple pies are delicious, why don't we make more of it?" Teller chuckled at the sudden shift of the text.

"Fine. What is the color of your estate's roof?" Joren probed further as he shredded the parchment.

"Red or orange depending on the sun."

Elara rolled her eyes. "What? You're not asking him about his favorite color?"

Green, Teller thought on instinct, but stood quiet.

"I simply need to know." Although his words had been sharp, his voice did not fill with threats. In a way, he spoke in a manner like

Ayla had. "My lady, please consider this: why would the son of the most famous person in Levent find his way here, to you? I hold the utmost respect for you, but you place your faith in people too quickly."

"I don't," Elara huffed.

"Really? You do not think this is another attempt to get into our ranks by Cidron Ross?"

"I came here on my own," Teller lied, a bit too quickly.

Joren crossed his arms. "In that case, how did you know the Presider's first name? You shouted her name before we spoke."

"I, uh . . ."

"Save the questions for later, Joren. In the meantime, you should really have someone look at you," Elara said. Teller realized then that his nose had begun bleeding once more. The woman's lips drew back in a concerned snarl. "Andyr will get to look at that before it kills you. Joren, take him to the healer, and then I want him to join me for supper at the Rooster."

"But my—"

Elara raised her hand to silence Joren. "That's my decision, and it's final."

"As you wish," Joren exhaled.

Chapter Seventeen

To the Sound of a Drinking Song

"I cannot let him out of my sight, the Presider's orders," Joren said to a familiar healer.

Andyr, a man in his early forties, sat on a stool in one of his practice's simple rooms. The healer's hairline was retreating like a crater on top of his dark scalp. Although summer had gone, Andyr's brow glistened with pearls of sweat. Hiding beneath bushy eyebrows, hazel eyes rooted in his deep eye sockets, glaring at Joren with all patience snuffed out. Teller recognized him as the man who had healed him not many days ago.

"Come on, Joren." The healer rolled his eyes in a full circle. "I don't have time for this. It's not like this kid can jump out the window with wounds like these. He's safe with me."

Joren judged the situation, his silver eyes jumping between Teller to Andyr. After some thought, he marched through the door and closed it gently behind him.

Alone, Andyr went straight to inspect Teller's wounds. Using a couple of tweezers, he dug through a reeking scab across his slit eyebrow. Andyr did not seem like a talker, but once he started, the words cascaded past his lips, making it hard to make out what he was trying to say. "This kills just as well as swords and cuts, but slower. Don't let dirt live in wounds, that's why it's infected," Andyr slurred, and reached into a casket by his feet. Bottles rattled against one another as his stubby fingers roamed through the necks.

The aching wound on Teller's face itched with new fire. If what Andyr said was true, was his own body trying to kill him too? "Really? You can die from this?"

"Yes," the healer mumbled.

Alcohol reeked with its strong presence as Andyr poured it over Teller's infected skin. A sore white pain bolted through his skull, coursing up his neck, leaving his head numb.

"Why?" Teller managed to get out.

"Well, it's . . . it isn't good for the body. Why, I don't know, but dirt or stuff that shouldn't be inside the body is pushed out. If not, it corrupts the body until the body gives up," Andyr said.

Andyr presented a neatly pressed linen to Teller's wound and rubbed it against his flaking skin. Teller bit the insides of his cheeks to keep his composure. "So if you get your ear sliced off, you survive it if you make sure that dirt doesn't touch it?"

"Precisely."

For whatever reason, Lionel had survived both a cut-off ear and a lost foot. If this was as dangerous as the healer implied, and Lionel still survived, was he guided and protected by the Unborn? Was Andyr, the healer, really a servant of the Unborn? He did not want to ask, but he had to know.

"Are you . . . are you a servant of the Unborn, sir?" Teller hesitated.

Andyr gaped wide and tossed the rag to a corner. The fabric turned yellow and red from touching the wound. "Nah. I'm an old grump wanting to keep death away. That's all. Your nose is healing just fine. You've managed to stay away from getting hit there again?"

"Yeah," Teller said. Keeping death away sounded otherworldly, like something the Almighty could do. But here he was, healing and stopping death. In a way, he was more powerful than any person with a blade, even more powerful than Captain Hutton. At the quick thought of the Captain, Teller sulked, wishing to visit him once more.

Andyr put fresh linens around the cleaned wound. Then he wrapped a small band around Teller's forehead and his neck. "How's your head? Any headaches?"

"Yeah. And I'm tired all the time."

"That's because of your skull. Last time I saw you, it looked like you fell off a horse. You haven't vomited?" Andyr asked.

"Sometimes. But that's after a fight." Teller shrugged. Thankfully, his days of fighting for Cidron were over.

"You shouldn't get into any more fights," Andyr sighed. "But if you're in one, make sure you end it quickly."

"How do I do that?"

The healer scoffed. "I don't know anything 'bout fighting."

"But you know about the body," Teller persisted. "Should I hit the head?"

Andyr fell silent, tying the last knot of a bandage. In silence, his face contorted as if speaking. Every muscle that pulled his boney skin to grins and faint smiles told a story to Teller.

"If you wanna to kill someone, then maybe . . . I mean . . . no, that's something you shouldn't do," Andyr finally spoke. "Besides, you'll eventually break the bones in your hand if you hit something as hard as a skull. The throat, right across the airways, that'll at least leave someone stunned . . . but no. That's not what I—you shouldn't harm others. So stay away from that."

Teller interrupted the healer's mumbling and hastening blabber. "Of course. I'm not looking for a fight. They usually find me. I just wanna know how to defend myself like you said."

"That's what happened then? Cidron brought you to me after a fight had found you?" Andyr peered at Teller from under his bushy eyebrows.

"Yeah . . . well no. People said things about Eckrosie that made me angry," Teller admitted. "People keep assuming that they're evil or trying to take down our country, but that's not true. They're being hunted and massacred even though they're nice people who are just like us."

Teller kept talking, kept speaking of the Eckrosie, and how wrong everyone was. If Andyr was judging him or not did not matter. Teller needed to start telling their story. Ayla's story.

The healer put a hand on Teller's knee, making Teller's words stop. "Look, I respect what you're saying . . ."

The hurry in his voice disappeared as if Andyr suddenly had all the time to spare. Teller waited for a "but."

". . . But you need to watch your words, Teller. People who share your opinion and speak out, they disappear. Don't know if you're Eckrosie—if you are, the Following will hide you as well as possible. But you cannot speak about these things freely."

"Why not?"

"It's against the law. Keeping Eckrosie and their culture in a favored light is not allowed, and many suffer severe punishment as a result. So, at least for now, keep those opinions to yourself."

What did he know? Andyr was just an old man who lived in Levent. The chances of him meeting an Eckrosie were slim, if even possible. Teller crossed his arms as the healer spoke, suddenly wishing for the uptight man, Joren, to return.

"Keep it clean, and meet me here if anything changes with that wound," Andyr said, getting off the stool, which he placed up against the wall. Bottles clanged together from his disturbance. Before heading out the door, he faced Teller. "I know Cidron sent you to spy on the Lady Presider. Whatever the man has told you, don't believe him. The Following cares. Unlike the Rosses, they don't accept torturing little boys."

How did he know? Teller gulped, and his feet tapped the floor.

Andyr's eyes sparkled with concern. "Cidron has tried many things to get into their ranks. I ain't surprised that sending you into the Following was his next move. Unfortunately for Cidron, I understand how his operation is run. He'd never disband or release a thrall from their contract after a few days. You'll see why the Following adores their Presider, and once you do, I pray you haven't caused too much damage." The healer shut the door behind him.

It seemed clear that Cidron did not care about Teller and his health at all. If what Andyr said was true, and the wound could have killed him . . . what did that say about Cidron in the end? Teller could not leave Gil and Leah in those brutish hands. He'd already left two people, Jarred and Nyle, to fend for themselves. Even his own brother. That was not going to repeat itself. If not for the other thralls, for Leah and Gil, he would do anything to stay with the Presider. But once again, the lives of those he cared for rested in the palms of his small hands. There was no chance of this ending well. It never did. Hordes of bad things always accompanied good things. That was the only certainty to life.

Nothing Cidron had claimed about the Following seemed to be true. Elara introduced Teller to one nice person after the next. The only one he felt remotely uncomfortable around was Joren—Elara's Protector, as they called him. Over the weeks that followed, Joren kept a watchful eye on Teller. Like a hawk observing its prey. In a strange way, it felt comforting knowing that Joren watched over Elara and the Following, protecting them from any harm Teller might come to inflict on them.

The Laughing Rooster, an inn and tavern owned by the Following and also the home of Elara, became Teller's home. Although Joren objected, Elara quickly trusted Teller and gave him his very own room on the second floor of the inn. However, she agreed not to let Teller accompany them at the meetings held at the Rooster. Compared to the Rosses' house in Keelheart, where people of all ages walked, Teller was the only child. No thralls were working there, only free men and women.

The fear of the Following using his family name and his heritage lessened little by little. To them, he was Teller, a friend. Which hurt even more, as he used every opportunity to listen in on their conversations, where potential useful information could come from. It never did, though. Not in Cidron's opinion, at least. Teller would sneak out of the bedroom under the cover of night and return to Keelheart to speak to Cidron. Unsurprisingly, the brute threatened Leah and Gil if he did not return with more useful information.

One evening, rain drizzled against the tavern's dirty windows. The Presider brought her guests farther into the house, down a corridor, and into a secluded dining room. Teller leaned his chin on his hand, listening to the patter outside and the conversations around him. Travelers and visitors of the city gathered by the bright fireplace to dry their soaked clothes. Traders, merchants, and farmers like Maric visited the popular tavern and inn. The innkeeper, Loira, a

woman with a captivating smile always ready, rushed between rows of tables to bring the guests food and beverage. One would be forgiven for not seeing their business being run as a cover for the Following's activities. No banners or signs of defiance against the Crown hung on the walls of the large, rectangular room that smelled of charred wood and freshly cut onion.

The house itself, quaint much like the thralls' quarters of the Riveroak estate, stood on Prince Street a few blocks away from Rose Square and Keelheart. Inside a set of double doors, a grand hall with benches and long tables greeted its visitors. To the left of the doors, a corridor leading to the secluded dining room also brought people to the Presider's study and a staircase where fifteen bedrooms lined up. The first night, Teller found a perfect hiding place for his bags inside of the room given to him. A couple of loose floorboards covered the dent in the red clay floor.

Teller used Loira's disappearance into the kitchen as his distraction. He snuck off to the Presider's study. Their meetings were often long once the doors of the dining room shut. To his surprise, the door swung open with his touch and revealed a pleasurable sight.

Books lined four tall bookshelves reaching from the floor to the ceiling. Seeing the amount of writing in the cramped shelves surprised him. The stuffy yet comforting smell of dried paper calmed him.

A desk poked out from a window, separating the room in two. The rain pattered the glass with increasing force, drowning the sounds from the tavern. If he would bring information to Cidron, snooping would be the way to do it. That did not stop Andyr's words of wisdom from interfering with his conscience. *I pray you don't cause too much damage.*

So did Teller.

Rifling through neat piles of papers, his fingers did the work as gently as possible. Mostly, there were deeds and greetings to people unfamiliar to him. Something about a pleasure house and the name Amabell popped up a couple of times. Maybe that could be used.

He stopped at the sight of a freshly written note.

Dear Guide Ida,

I hope and pray for your wellbeing and the wellbeing of those who seek your guidance in Keelheart. These are challenging times, with Nightbringers trying to corrupt and destroy. Yet in these dark hours, even the Keeper may prevail in striking them back.

Our dearest ally and friend, Silas, will need your aid within the upcoming moons as he, on my behalf, seeks to expose the Rosses and their practices in Keelheart. When the time comes, we ask you and the other Guides to protect and safekeep him in your Halls until we may bring him safely to Rose Lane.

As a token of our appreciation, please accept these funds.

Regards and best of wishes,

Presider Elara Averil, Rose Lane

This was precisely what he needed. He read it three times to remember the writing, deciding it best to leave the letter be so as to not raise any suspicion from the Following.

The door swung open, and Teller moved the letter to the side. Teller gazed upon the bookshelves behind him to avoid whomever was entering suspecting him.

"Teller, what are you doing?" Elara asked.

He spun around. "Oh, I was just admiring your collection of books."

The Presider, dressed in her usual gambeson, stepped inside and took a seat on the opposite side of the desk. "It probably cost a fortune, but this was set up before my time as a Presider. Sometimes, I too come to read and relax."

Shit. She knew. She had to know, the way she leaned back in the chair with arms behind her head.

Teller pulled his earlobe. "Well, I . . . I'll leave you alone."

"No, no. Please stay."

Teller moved up to the desk, putting it between him and Elara. Beneath the piles of papers, a letter opener gleamed, and Teller closed his fingers around it. He pointed the blunted tip toward her. "Please don't hurt me."

Elara's one eye blinked away sleep. "Hurt you? I'd never. This"—she gestured to the desk—"was unfortunate but unavoidable."

Teller trembled, even though Elara sat exposed entirely to trauma. No anger or disappointment lingered in her intense eye as he'd expected it would.

"I knew Joren was right, that you serve the Rosses. This doesn't surprise me." Elara looked at the table and her own scribbles. "What did you find more than who is working for us by the Ember Gate?"

"Nothing," Teller lied. Even he heard the clear tremble in his voice.

"Like I said, I won't hurt you. Let me guess—Cidron sent you to me because he knows I would take you in. He has threatened you that he will send you back to your parents in Thorne's Town. You can always stop doing his work, Teller. He hasn't branded you or made you his thrall. I will protect you from him if that's what you're worried about."

What point was there in lying? She figured everything out anyhow. Teller put away the letter opener and slumped into a chair. "I want to stay with you, but he's got . . . people I care about, and if I don't bring back information, Cidron will kill them."

"I understand. Growing up in Keelheart or Stonelake is dangerous. Sure, I didn't have to worry about ending up in Cidron's hands, but had he offered me a place to stay, I would have accepted it."

"You didn't have thralls when you were little?"

Elara raised her eyebrows. "We did, but people went to houses of rich families on their own. It wasn't like it is today, with brutes looking for poor desperate people to exploit."

Teller let out a loud sigh, expelling the tension from his trembling body. "You have a last name, which means that you are a lady of higher standing. I haven't seen your family crest or anything like that."

"Maybe—or rather, in most people's eyes, I'm not a lady." She turned her gaze to the window and its curtains of rain. A veil of pain concealed the easily accessible smile she wore. "I enfolded a lady who was from a noble family, the Averils. In that sense, I am a lady, but her family shunned us by sending us to the Halls to get rid of Nightbringers they claimed lived with us. Being a woman who refuses to get pregnant isn't something society looks kindly on."

"I'm sorry to hear that," Teller said. "But you're together now, right?"

Elara's shoulders slumped with a deep sigh. "She died. I've asked Andyr what he thinks happened, and well, when they cut out Thora's eye, the wound got infected."

Teller gaped in shock. "They cut out your eye because you enfolded a woman?"

She rubbed her shoulders. "Quite a wonderful world we have, don't you think? They didn't cut out our eyes because we were enfolded. They cut out our eyes because we didn't want to bed any men and fulfill our duties to the Unborn." She tore her gaze from the window and back at Teller. "Anyway, what information did you get? I need to know so I can get on top of this."

He raked his fingers through his hair. "I saw information about an Amabell. And something about a guard at the Ember Gate."

"Ah, well, that was bound to leak. Anything else?"

Teller shook his head. If what she said was true, and the Halls were responsible for killing her wife, why would she do anything to help the Guides with funds?

"Next time, just tell me what you need, and I'll help you out, Teller."

The weight became too great for him to carry. He winced and muttered, "I . . . I saw this note too."

The note slid forward with his push. The corners of Elara's lips rose. "Thank you."

~⁂~

Another night, the same songs. Gil's body ached from the day's work, but he kept on going to give the crowd what they wanted. One more collection of drinking songs.

Leah's wild, red curls beckoned Gil through the rowdy crowd. She bopped her head along with the beat of the clapping adults, looking like a tired little bird as she did. During his performances, they managed to have little inside jokes at the drunk people's expense. They cast glances at each other, smirking or rolling their eyes at the childish behavior going on around them. For whatever reason, adults turned sloppy and stupider with each ale they consumed.

A young woman pushed through the double doors and moved up to Cidron's table. Her hands clenched a bag at her back, and her short, straight blond hair bounced with her. Gil couldn't hear what they spoke of, but it was clear that she was upset. Her pale skin flared red and hot, and her catlike features hissed at Cidron.

Gil stopped his song. The rest of the crowd silenced with him little by little to listen to the woman speaking up against Cidron.

"I refuse. I'm not going back to that house or any other place you'll send me. I don't care what you do, but I'm leaving." The woman's high-pitched shrill filled the quiet dining room.

Leah, sitting near Cidron as usual, wrapped herself into a tiny ball to escape the heated argument.

"Nora, take it easy." Cidron shook his head in denial of her words. He took to his feet and crossed his arms. "You know you can't do that. You signed a contract and still owe me servitude for at least another year."

Nora faced Cidron, ignoring the eyes studying her every move. Defiantly, she leaned closer to Cidron, who towered above her. "I don't owe you anything. I'm not letting another filthy man get his hands on me and rape me. I'm not your property."

Cidron remained calm despite her accusations. The same kind of accusations Gil had heard Teller speak of before he had to leave for Rose Lane. "As I've said, it's unfortunate that he harmed you. I will try to find . . ."

Nora screamed at the top of her lungs, turning her face crimson. "I don't care! You don't control me, Cidron. Had I not worked for you, the district courts would punish all those filthy bastards who put their hands on me. But you just let your friends use us and torment us because it gives you coin. We both know you'll just send me to another customer who'll do the same thing! That's why I'm leaving, and you can't stop me."

The hall waited for Cidron's answer. Gil could tell that Cidron bit his tongue, letting Nora speak her mind. She did have valid points, and so did Cidron. But given the nature of her argument, she had grown tired of this place despite it being a sanctuary and a safe haven for them.

Once Nora took hurried breaths and marched to the wide doors, Cidron nudged his head to a couple of people nearby. "Very well. Silas, Cyle."

Their chairs toppled over, and their boots scraped the hardwood floor. Nora bolted for the doors but was knocked into the wall by two large men, whose heads seemed too small for their bodies. Nora hit the floor before being flung back into the hall, where Cidron stood waiting with a glimmer in his eyes. Gil gasped along with Leah at the situation suddenly unfurling before them.

Nora placed her hands on the ground to get up, but Cidron swiped them away from underneath her. "You want to leave, to go back to the streets where you'll get raped, robbed, and killed? I took you in and gave you a home when you came begging me for it. Is this how you decide to repay me?" Cidron's voice stayed calm, yet forceful as always. "All I ask in return for my protection is a little gratitude. You agreed to let me send you wherever I decide, and you won't get hurt unless you deserve it."

Throughout Cidron's discourse, Nora crawled toward the door where Silas and Cyle waited.

Cidron took a couple of commanding steps closer, his boots striking the wooden floor with one thud after the next. "But defiant bitches like you . . . you just have to complicate things, don't you?"

The shift happened in an instant. The care and concern Cidron had shown Gil and Leah washed away. Replacing it, a ferocious beast gnawed through the reins keeping it at bay. A tidal wave of unbridled rage swept through the hall, and each part of Gil told him to grab Leah and run.

Bystanders darted out of their way as a scuffle began, or rather a beat-down. Nora managed to keep up with the two attackers for a few moments before Cidron slammed his fist into her face. The thump reverberated loudly, and a mist of gore exploded.

Cidron was enjoying it. He had to be. The spark in his eyes looked like pleasure. "Since actions speak louder than words, why don't I give you a fucking lesson?"

Gil put down his lute and approached the commotion through the seated crowd. A couple of people whispered to him not to go near Cidron, but Gil's feet moved anyhow. Cidron sat on top of her chest, obliterating her features with each punch.

Gouts of blood attacked Gil's nose with sick iron when he stood near them.

"You . . . don't own us." The weak retort left Nora.

Cidron's hands slipped on her skin as he pulled her near. "I do, and I'll do whatever the fuck I want with you."

It was just like Teller said, and Cidron was definitely not denying it. He owned the thralls. They were his to do with what he pleased. The fact that the room was silent except for a gurgle and the forceful thuds made it absolutely clear. Cidron was an Almighty. He was the judge and executioner. What would happen if he turned his attention to him, Leah, or Teller? What would happen once he didn't see any use for keeping them around? Well, Gil saw the horrific answer staring him dead in the eyes.

"I'm . . . sorr . . ." Nora spat blood at Cidron. Her reactions grew sluggish and weak.

Opposite Gil, Leah gaped at the master and the thrall, just as petrified. The girl pushed through the confusion and the alarm to reach Gil. She shook her head at him, knowing very well what he was about to do. But he couldn't let this go on.

"Cidron, she's had enough," Gil squeaked.

Cidron was quicker than ever. Before Gil finished his sentence, Cidron's large hand clenched Gil's tunic and yanked him close. His reeking breath cascaded on the boy. "You want to take her place?"

Gil wriggled in his grasp, blood smearing his clothes. "No, I . . ."

"Keep singing." Cidron shoved Gil away and continued hurting Nora.

"But she can't breathe," Gil retorted. Nora lay in a puddle of her own blood. Her steady breathing had turned into a gurgle and silent cough.

Someone pulled Gil back toward the stage, probably saving his life by putting distance between him and the raging hound. Gil blinked, and his hands grasped his lute. The words refused to come, and his fingers trembled along the lute. This was the first time he'd watched someone die.

Wanderers clung to the belief that the Wanderer could inhabit a person. He had yet to hear tales of the Beast doing the same, but watching Cidron unloading on the woman, it sure looked as though the Beast was inhabiting the man.

Cidron rose from the ground and dragged the mutilated body of Nora to his seat. He sat down on an empty bench while planting his feet on what remained of Nora. "Sing," Cidron grunted.

Cidron was a servant of the Beast. A shadow-walker who thrived in darkness and pain. Seeing him swigging mead while pressing his feet on the motionless woman revealed him for what he was. A relentless monster. Sure, some others saw it too, but they seemed almost used to it, numb. This was what Teller spoke of. Cidron held no real concern for any of the thralls.

"When darkness falls across the Halls,
beware the Bringers crawling the walls."

The room filled with song. But it wasn't because of Gil. Scattered voices obeyed Cidron's command, while Gil was unable to understand what he just saw. Nora died to the sound of their song.

A drinking song.

CHAPTER EIGHTEEN

The Forgers

"They have some sort of arrangement with an Amabell and a pleasure house," Teller told Cidron, who leaned up against his desk and glared at the boy.

"Fine. What else?" Cidron grunted, his crossed arms bouncing on his belly as he spoke.

"They have a guard they pay off at the Ember Gate," Teller said.

"Got a name?"

"Not that I could discern."

Cidron snorted. "Then that information is useless. I've got paid-off guards there as well. No name doesn't help. What else?"

Teller found the cold and calculating stare similar to his mother's, and he caved to it right away. "Silas works for the Following."

"How do you know that?" Cidron huffed.

"I . . . I saw a letter."

"Addressed to?"

Teller looked down on his folded hands. Elara trusted him. He could not destroy what little friendships he had.

"Aiden," Cidron said with a menacing drag. "Let me remind you of your friends. Gil can easily fall into a very deep sleep if I find you're lying or keeping things from me."

The lives of Leah and Gil were too important. This information would not kill anyone, hopefully. "It's addressed to a Guide in the Halls of Keelheart. Elara paid for them to let Silas stay there until it's safe for him to go back to Rose Lane."

Cidron clicked his tongue for a good while. "Good. I'll expect more information soon. They didn't catch you, did they?"

Teller was quick to shake his head. "I snuck into her study while the Following had a meeting."

"Do whatever you can to get to sit with them during a meeting. But for now, head back to them right away."

"Yes, sir," Teller said, even though he made up his mind to stay in Keelheart to meet with Gil and Leah. Cidron did not inspect the bedchambers. He left the study and hurried past any of Cidron's associates to find a bed to occupy.

～❖～

"Fuck you," Silas spat at Cidron.

Inside Cidron's study, Leah shrunk into a ball in one of the corners, watching Cidron throw an equally large and bulky man into a wall. Two of Cidron's friends stood in the room, ready to help if needed. But they seemed more surprised than Leah. Minutes earlier, they enjoyed a late meal when Cidron suddenly threw himself on Silas and unleashed a storm of punches on his friend.

Cidron clicked his tongue and hunkered in closer to the other man's, their faces nearly touching. "Oh, you tried. Thanks to your daft Presider putting your name in writing, you'll never get the chance to do anything against me."

How surprised could she be, though? In the time she'd served as Cidron's thrall, listening to his knuckles pound others had become a mundane routine. A normality. Still, whenever his ugly mug shone bright with his evil smirk, Leah hid.

"What are you doing for the Following?" Cidron tossed Silas's head against the wall. A hollow thud followed. "Hm? Plotting to kill me? I've known you for a long time, so why do you choose to go to the Following?"

Silas, a scary-looking man with oily brown hair draping over a round and plump face, wiped blood from his mouth, where several teeth were already missing. He used his sausage arms to push himself off the ground. "I ain't with the Following. Whatever they said . . ."

Cidron kicked Silas in the chest. "What did she give you that I didn't? Huh? I took you in, gave you all of it after Nedox. You swore to be by my side. What happened?"

"I'm telling you the truth. I ain't with the Following. But I'm seriously considering it seeing as you kill children now."

Unable to see Cidron's expression, Leah could only guess it. But knowing the man, he was smiling from ear to ear and enjoying the beating. "Since when did you grow a conscience? Was it when you started sleeping with a Guide? You found your faith? How about this? I'll make sure you find faith again."

The floorboards creaked with Cidron's walk. The green carpet decorating the floor of his study flung a cloud of dust over the dimly lit room with Cidron's command. Hidden from sight, a trapdoor revealed itself and groaned. A pitch-black pit met Leah's wide gaze.

"You know what they do to prisoners in Nedox, Leah?" Cidron's fingers locked around Silas's hair, and like steering a horse, he tugged him with him. "People think other prisoners are the problem, but no, the place crawls with sick bastards holding the whip. I've seen men crack, becoming willing puppets after years of beatings."

Using incredible strength, Cidron got Silas to his feet, inches from the gaping hole in the floor. He leaned into the man and continued. "That's what I'll do with you, Silas."

With a loud bang and crack, Silas vanished through the floor. A high-pitched screech followed, but Cidron kept speaking, only louder. "I ain't killing you until you beg me, or once the Following gives up on you."

The hatch clicked and made Silas disappear. With a lazy nudge of Cidron's foot, the green carpet covered the hidden cellar. The cushioned chair creaked, and the man sat down at his desk.

The two other brutes awaited Cidron's command, standing with their arms crossed.

"Go to sleep, Leah. We've got much to do in the morning."

He didn't need to ask her twice. As soon as Cidron finished his sentence, Leah darted to the bedchambers.

How could Cidron do such things? Was beating someone to death or locking them up under houses good and allowed? She remembered what the judge had said, and how he made sure that people doing bad things were punished. Was what Cidron did not bad?

She pulled the bed linens tight to protect herself. Sure it was dark in the bedchambers, but she was terrified to think about what Silas saw . . . or what he didn't see. What if Nightbringers were surrounding him and tried to eat him?

"Hey, Leah."

A squeak left her at Gil's sudden appearance. "Teller's back."

Her head jerked fast as she followed him past resting thralls. Hopefully, speaking with Teller and Gil would help her forget what she just saw.

The bruises and cuts Teller had worn weeks earlier were all gone, replaced with new and smooth skin. The bags under his eyes were gone, and as he saw them approach, he surprisingly looked glad to see them. He slid to the side of his bed, letting Leah sit next to him. The linens trapped the heat from Teller. She snuggled in it.

"Welcome back," Gil whispered.

"Where've you been?" Leah said. Sitting next to him, she realized how much she'd missed him. Of course, Gil stayed, but something seemed off when the three of them weren't together.

"Rose Lane and the Following. Cidron put me there to spy on them."

The Following? The thing Cidron was talking about just now and what he spoke to the judge about? "Are they bad?" Leah scratched her head.

"What? No, they're—" Teller paused in search of words. "They're very kind. Their leader is fantastic. But I don't know how long I'll be with them. How have you been?"

Leah avoided Teller's gaze. What was there to say, especially after the other night, when Cidron killed a thrall for trying to leave?

Gil whispered. "You can help us, can't you?"

"Help with what?" Teller grunted.

"Getting us out of here."

The bedsheets wrinkled into Teller's fists. "Has Cidron hurt you?"

"No. But . . ." Gil shook his head. "A couple of days back, Cidron beat a thrall to death."

"What?"

"I was singing, and this woman was about to leave, and Cidron killed her in front of everyone. Who's to say that won't be us next time?"

Leah lowered her head. Would they judge her for the things she had done? Although the blood washed from her hands, it felt like it still stuck to her skin. She rubbed her thumbs over her blue knuckles, which poked her back with an ache. "He made me hurt someone. I don't know who, but Cidron said that I had to or he'd hurt me."

Her chest rose and fell with her rapid breath. Something in her belly twisted and hurled when reminded of the tied person in Cidron's room she'd bashed her knuckles into. The person had pleaded underneath a bag pulled over their head, and begged her to stop. When the thrall whimpered something about never looking at another man like that again, Cidron sneered at Leah with disgust and told her to kick the defenseless person. She regretted not listening to the thrall to stop.

A hand found her—Gil's hand. Instead of squeezing tight, he only caressed it, the way her mother did. She dared to raise her chin and saw him smiling back at her.

"I want to help, but I don't know how," Teller said.

There had to be a way. Leah bit the inside of her cheek. Papers and contracts were things Cidron liked to talk about every time someone spoke up against him. Maybe that was important. "You can read. If I give you the papers that Cidron has, could you destroy them?"

Teller drew in a long breath, and if she wasn't mistaken, a broad smile dawned on his pretty face. "I'll do better than that. Thank you, Leah."

"What did I do?" Leah said, confused, although she felt a flutter of happiness spread from her stomach.

"You gave me an idea. My—" Teller paused and forced out the next word. "My father purchased lands and taught me the wording. If we forge papers of ownership, making it look like the Following has bought you, then you'll be free."

Teller caught wind of Gil's and Leah's confusion. "What I mean is that if I can get into Cidron's study, I can write new papers that say that Cidron has sold you to the Following. He won't own you."

"Why would that work?" Gil said. "He'll just come and get us back."

"He won't," Leah stepped in to explain. "I was with him and the judge in Riverview, and they were talking about keeping the Crown, the Following, and Cidron happy, and something about not starting an uprousing?"

"An uprising?" Teller's lips widened. "That's great. That means he won't be able to touch you. Because if he does, he'll start a war. The Following hates Cidron, and they'll protect you."

"But I don't want to be a thrall for them," Gil said. Leah couldn't resist nodding in agreement.

Teller combed his long curls behind his ears in a rushed swoop. "I promise, you'll never be thralls again. Their Presider, Elara, is fighting to stop Cidron, but she hasn't found a way yet. I need to get into that study, without Cidron there."

"He's usually there if he isn't drinking or meeting people at inns. Or sleeping. And he locks the door."

"That's not a problem," Teller said confidently.

Leah grimaced in deep thought. "What if I keep him busy? How much time do you need, Teller?"

"I don't know. But I'll write the papers with the Following and bring them here, where I can write everyone's name and sign it. It shouldn't be hard to find two papers."

Gil shook his head. "Not only two. Look around. We can't leave without them."

"But I don't know everyone's name, Gil," Teller said. "And this is only one sleeping quarter. There are a lot more thralls than this, I think."

Sitting on the floor with his legs crossed, Gil scootched closer to them. "Then write as many as you can. Your friend Elara can take care of the rest, right? While you do that, I can try to get as many of these people to come with us."

"How do you do that?" Leah asked.

"I've got my tricks," Gil said with a wink.

"Alright. I think we can do this. The only time I get to come here is when I tell Cidron about the Following's plans. I'll speak with Elara and let her know about this. In one week, I'll come back and we'll set you free."

A few days more. Only a few days, and Leah wouldn't have to stand by and watch as Cidron harmed someone. And maybe, just maybe, she could decide for herself who she wanted to play with and spend time with. She grabbed the boys' hands and chuckled.

"What did you tell him?" Elara asked. Her fingers wrapped around a quill that scratched ink into a sheet of paper. Next to her, Joren sat on one of the chairs of Elara's study in the Rooster. Teller twisted and turned to rid his butt from the stiffness of sitting too long on chairs.

"I didn't want to, but he threatened to kill my friends if I didn't," Teller stuttered. "I . . . I told them about a letter regarding Silas."

There it was. The sight of disapproval and disappointment. Or was it worry? A crease appeared between her delicate eye sockets. She took in a hard breath. "Oh, Teller."

A flush crept up his face, heating his cheeks. "I'm sorry, I really didn't want to, but he is going to kill my friends."

Elara gave a silent chuckle. "Don't worry about it. We wanted to test you. Silas isn't working for us, I just wanted to see how much faith he places in you."

"So . . . he's not getting hurt?" Teller mumbled.

"You mean Silas? Hopefully. He's been causing a lot of problems for us lately."

Joren, who stood arms crossed, clenched his jaw at Elara's swift forgiveness. Teller did not understand entirely why, but Joren did not seem interested in getting past his first impression of Teller.

"I need your help," Teller blurted upon seeing Joren taking in a sharp breath. "My two friends and I, we . . . we want to escape."

"Of course you do. I would too." Elara slid a sheet to the side and put aside the quill.

"No, I mean, we are doing it, but I need help from the Following. I need help from you." During the silence, Joren gave a dismissive wave of his hand. Teller gritted his teeth. "If you help, I'll do anything you wish."

Elara raised her chin. "Easy there. Those kinds of promises are not to be made lightly. I mean, I don't . . ."

"I think we should aid them, Lady Presider."

Both Elara and Teller glanced at Joren with his sudden shift in tone. "You said it yourself, you have been looking for opportunities to make Cidron hurt without upsetting the beehive too much."

Elara brimmed brightly at Joren. "I was wondering where you had run off to, you rascal. Welcome back, Joren. Yes, I agree. We will help you, Teller."

"You will?" Teller shuffled forward in his seat, excitedly. "Thank you."

"Do you have a plan?" Elara said.

"Is it possible to forge letters of ownership?" Teller said.

"I suppose it is." Elara shrugged. "What do you have in mind?"

"All thralls are made to sign a contract with Cidron. It says that they owe him a certain amount of work before they're released from it. Is it possible that the Following could buy thralls from Cidron?"

Joren tied his hands together and rested his elbows on the table. "We cannot buy anyone. Besides, it is illegal to trade in human lives. But if we were to pay off this supposed debt, we are in the clear."

"But do you have that money?" Teller interjected.

Elara spoke again. "No, but as you suggested, we'll forge letters, but make it look like we compensated the money that Cidron has planned to make off the thralls. We can write those papers together and send you to Keelheart, where you'll sneak in and sign the papers and leave them with Cidron. Quite a surprise, wouldn't you say?"

Teller brightened. The Presider and Protector of the Following were listening and considering Teller's ideas. Hundreds of thoughts clouded his mind in a strange blur. "Shouldn't we also have those papers? In case someone comes around asking about it?"

"Indeed." Elara pointed her finger at Teller. "That makes sense. When are you planning this to take place?"

"I only get to return if I have information about the Following or you. As soon as I get there, Cidron questions me. I'll make up some stuff," Teller said.

Elara rubbed her temples. "Cidron isn't a simpleton. He sent you for a reason, and if we're to pull this off, we need to make some sacrifices. I'm sure he could learn of some activities that are bound to be revealed soon anyhow." Elara's one eye focused on Teller. "Let's get started with the papers."

～❀～

The only functional house of Keelheart looked like a fortress to Teller. Big, watchful, and impregnable. Although he had not given Cidron cause to suspect him, walking through the doors of the Rosses' estate raced his heartbeat. Together with Leah and Gil, he was taking Cidron down. An invisible touch on his shoulder, the support of the Following, strengthened his fleeting mind and ensured that he stayed on the path to the enemy's camp.

The bells of the city rang. Hopefully, Gil did not have to perform this night, and hopefully, Leah was in Keelheart with Cidron nearby. A lot of their planning could turn sideways if circumstances were against them. But he hoped they were not, and carried on.

As expected, Cidron's brutes let Teller pass, and he took a seat across the hallway from Cidron's study. Before he did, however, he cast a quick glimpse to the dining hall. Gil flashed a wide smile his way and kept singing a song to the tired crowd just entering for supper.

Teller stared at the shut door. Cidron's gruff voice grew muffled, but Teller was certain it was him. Dry sheets of paper, the forged letters he, Elara, and Joren had written, dampened against his sweaty back. Hopefully, the ink would stay dry and the papers wouldn't rustle once he met with Cidron. To stay calm, Teller listened to Gil's joyful, almost celebratory song.

Heavy footsteps came, and the door swung open. A young man, dressed in drab and oversized robes, left the study.

"Ah, Teller, join me," Cidron said. The gruff voice remained, but something was off about it. Perhaps it was the way he greeted Teller—he seemed genuinely pleased about something.

Sitting nearby in a corner was Leah, her wild red curls hiding her face, though Teller could still see it fill with color at the sight of him. She turned her head to her folded hands in her lap.

"Seeing how the last information you revealed turned out to be accurate, I can't wait to hear what you've learned of the Following today," Cidron said, and rubbed his stubby hands together.

Oh, I've got information for you. But you won't like it when you figure it out in the morning, Teller thought. "The Presider has made allies with the city patrol. Especially with Captain Ivory. They struck a deal where the Crown will stay clear of Prince's Street and Rose Square."

Cidron got out of his chair and leaned on his desk to glare down at Teller. "That was a matter of time. I ain't surprised. What else?"

"At the next meeting with you, Lord Haven isn't coming. They don't think you're worth the time."

Cidron's good mood vanished. His eyes turned cold and filled with a bitterness Teller could almost taste. Teller savored the moment, as he believed that was the face he would give once he realized what Gil, Leah, and Teller had done.

"Fine. If there's nothing else, grab some supper. You're going back to Rose Lane after that," Cidron said.

Crap. He'll keep an eye on me and won't let me out of his sight. Teller threw a quick glance at Leah—hopefully she had a plan to distract him. Using the scraping boots of Cidron to cover the rustle, Teller moved past the bulky man. Not knowing if the papers were exposed underneath his shirt, Teller hurried to cover his back. Leah and Cidron followed after the door clicked shut with a couple of keys. He caught a glimpse of the lock. It looked simple and would easily fall for the lockpick Teller kept hidden in his boots. By now, he had grown accustomed to having it beneath his feet. The lumpy and hard curves of the metal poking his soles did not bother him.

Like always, Gil managed to get the crowd to cheer, but Teller could tell from the way Gil lazily strolled from one side of the stage to the other how fed up he was. The twinkle in his eye had been extinguished, and a tedious eye roll replaced it. It was clear Gil had done this many times before. Thankfully, he would not have to much longer.

Teller slouched down beside a couple of other thralls, still working on their supper. A couple of empty stares met him before returning to their potato stew. Cidron, accompanied by Leah, took a seat closer to the stage Gil occupied. All Teller had to do was wait.

Leah chugged another cup of juice, a thing she soon regretted when it rocked inside of her. She could just as well have swallowed all the water of Lake Ember. She forced another gulp down to join the rest.

Cidron sat nearby, like always, next to his companions. As the evening went on, they started singing along with Gil. She hoped this would last for a long while, but as time went by, and Teller was still sitting there, waiting for something, she grew worried. She had no way to control when Cidron wanted to go back to his study.

After what felt like forever, she cast a glimpse to the entrance and Teller's table, only to find him gone. She counted Gil's songs. Six songs later, Cidron's jug of mead stood empty. The time was running out as the man rose and headed toward the door.

Teller needed much more time.

Leah followed Cidron. "Let me fight," she let slip.

Cidron continued his march. In desperation, she snatched his slake clothes to make him stop. "I wanna fight, and you can teach me how."

One of Cidron's eyebrows bent with curiosity at her. "Why?"

"Because . . ." She tripped on her words. What would he respect and not question? "Because you're strong, and I wanna deserve to be with you."

"Right now?" Cidron placed his hands on his hips. Clearly, he was interested in her suggestion—he hadn't run off.

"Yeah. You don't have anything planned for the night, and I just really want to. Right now."

"Fine. Clear the room!" Cidron shouted to the crowd. "We're getting ourselves a fight. This little girl wants to brawl. Who wants to go up against her?"

Gil stopped his singing and stared at Leah. But what else was she to do? Cidron's attention had to stay locked inside this room, far away from Teller. Whoever stepped up to fight her, Leah had to beat. If not, Cidron would leave.

Leah rolled up her sleeves and stepped into the square forming within the crowd.

Teller shut the door. Luckily, Cidron had left a lone candle flickering on the desk. A window peered into the back of the estate, a risk he could not take. He rushed to a couple of drapes and pulled them shut to conceal his presence from curious eyes.

Sitting behind the desk—simple, but still a desk like the one Lionel had—felt a tad strange, to say the least. Especially in the cushioned chair, where his feet dangled a bit away from the ground. The last time he'd sat like this, Lionel had watched over his shoulder and helped him read and write. This time, Teller was putting those skills to use.

He placed the dampened documents on the table. His and Elara's scribbles marked the pages. All that needed to be added were names and Cidron's signature at the bottom of the contracts. Teller's fingers leafed through stacks of papers on the desk in search of the thrall contracts. He remembered Cidron scribbling his handwriting at the bottom, signing it himself, and there were two sets of the same documents. That meant they were important.

Important papers should always be hidden. Never leave them out in the open for unwanted eyes to gaze upon, Teller heard Lionel comment in the back of his mind. *Right.* Teller searched nearby drawers and chests, all while keeping a keen ear, listening to the singing nearby. On each occasion, when a song came to an end, Teller froze, but resumed his search once it continued.

Thick leather bindings surrounded a stack of papers, filling the drawer with a harsh aroma.

"Found it," Teller told himself.

One page after the next was filled with Cidron's handwriting, and the pleasing sight of the brute's own name written out brought out a brief grin to Teller.

Four important papers, the most important, moved beneath his fingers. Leah and Gil's names repeated. *Gil the Great,* it said on Cidron's record. Knowing that details mattered, Teller scribbled it down on the contracts he, Joren, and Elara had forged.

The door rattled.

Teller leaped under the table.

"Lord Ross? Are you in here?" a voice called from the opposite side of the door.

Luckily, though the handle creaked, the door remained locked. He thanked himself for remembering, although his entire body shivered with fear. They were only going to get one chance at this. If they were found out, there was no telling what Cidron would do to either of them. Or to him.

The singing stopped, and it remained silent. Teller hugged his knees tight on the carpet under the desk. The person by the door must have moved, but what worried him now was the lack of singing. Objects scraped in the distance, and commotion came from the dining hall, not ceasing for a while.

Teller returned to the inkwell and the papers.

"Nah, Leah, you don't get it. Sure, you've got the force and the power, more than most girls, but you don't know how to use it," Cidron slobbered once she returned to his side. Mead reeked with his foul breath.

Leah clasped her ear, pushing back at the aching ring eating it. She'd held on for two fights before a beefy young man knocked her over her head with a powerful jab. She never stood a chance. Luckily, Cidron had decided to stay and watch.

He wrapped an arm around her and pointed at a couple of thralls brawling. "Sure, you know what to do to hit someone, but you've gotta keep your guard up."

"My guard?"

"Yeah, you've gotta protect your head." Cidron raised his elbows and placed his arms just in front of his face, peering at her from behind them. "If an attack comes, I can stop it quickly. Think of your arms as both a shield and a weapon. Try it."

He brought her arms up to keep them protecting her head. His fist came her way, but instead of hitting her head, it slammed into her arm. Her wrist ached from the blow, but she was still standing. Without thinking about it, she thrust her left fist at Cidron and rammed it into his belly. He was knocked over, lying like a turtle on the ground, on his back and . . . laughing.

"That's it. You're a quick learner, aren't you?" Cidron dabbed a finger at her. "But you know what? I'm heading off to the sack. Gotta wake up early in the morning."

Leah sought another distraction. But the room was full of it already, and he wanted to leave. He got up to his feet, barely able to stand straight. "You keep on doing what you're doing. I'll see you in the morning, Cyle," he said, and staggered off.

Leah followed, keeping him standing.

"You know what, Leah? I fucking hate this . . . shit. It's the same thing, over and over again. You know, the worst thing about Nedox was how boring it got. It was the same thing every day. This is like Nedox. Boooooring."

Cidron dragged to the right, but she steered him to the door. She'd stalled him as long as she could. If Teller wasn't done by now, there was nothing she could do.

"I don't even have a woman. It's not like I don't want one, I do. It's just hopeless, you know, to find someone who cares 'bout you. I mean sure, I went to your mother and others like her, but that's only for a couple of hours."

Leah stopped. Her mother? "What do you mean?"

"Yeah, she was an Almighty in bed. I'd save up a lot of money to touch her. Surprised she didn't have more kids than you. Gonna be interesting to see how you turn out when you get older. Hopefully as great as her. Some people can't wait, like Dahle. He's a real sick bastard, that one. Good, I kept you away from him, right?"

Cidron marched into a doorpost. But Leah couldn't care less about his loud grunt. Had her mother really let Cidron touch her, be near her? Why?

"Oh, right, you didn't know? Yeah, your mother made me promise not to tell you, but I mean, she's not here to make sure I don't. She was a trollop and had sex with people. She didn't want you to be that, so that's why I'm keeping you away from Dahle." Cidron chuckled. "And people say I ain't got morals."

Before she could register any of it, Cidron managed, after a couple of tries, to open the door to his study. But instead of worrying about Teller and the papers, she stared at nothing. That was why her mother didn't want her or Miya to find out. Jaida had been ashamed of what she did. What little Leah knew about trollops wasn't that bad, though. So why would she be ashamed of that?

The desk rattled at Cidron's harsh nudge. He propped his chin in his hand.

If Teller had been in the room, she couldn't tell. Everything looked the same as when they left. She let out a harsh breath.

"People don't think I care 'bout others. But I do. Maybe that's why everyone are assholes. To be honest, I'd like to live in Riverview with those pompous asses dressing up and whatnot. But . . . I've got my status to maintain, don't I? I'm the prisoner of Nedox. Nobels don't want that kind of people dining with them, just because I did some stupid shit when I was younger. Mark my words, Leah. No one cares 'bout who you are. They judge you by shit you did before or where they come from. You're a trollop's daughter and a thrall. You ain't gonna be anything else. Just accept that."

He waved his hand at the door. "Shut the door when you leave, I've gotta . . ."

Cidron paused and looked beneath his desk. Before Leah or Cidron could react though, someone knocked Cidron off his chair. A powerful thump left the ground as Cidron toppled over and hit the back of his head.

Leah leapt forward to see the attacker. Teller rose up above Cidron, pummeling the dazed adult with all of his might. Thrust after thrust—like what Cidron had done against Nora.

"Teller," she squeaked like a frightened mouse. But she felt invisible to him, as if she didn't exist. Teller kept punching Cidron bloody, his knuckles turning red with gore.

At first, Cidron seemed to be enjoying the beating. A smile and chuckle followed his attempts to get to his feet, but then he rolled over to his side, where Teller proceeded to kick him. Even if she felt like he deserved some of the beating, Leah couldn't help but want Teller to stop. He hadn't seen the real anger that Cidron could set free if he wanted to. If he didn't stop soon, Cidron would make him regret it.

Leah ran into Teller, to get him out of Cidron's way. It was enough force to knock him off balance and leave Cidron bloodied on the floor.

"You bastard." Cidron spit a mouthful of blood at their feet. "You're as good as dead."

The heel of Teller's boot stomped Cidron's face, silencing him. Leah gasped, but followed Teller's pull to the door. They left the adult behind and locked the room.

~❖~

Candles snuffed out, and night began. Other thralls in the large room found their beds and slipped beneath their bedsheets. Gil clutched his sheet, crinkling and folding it. How would he convince them to go with him to Rose Lane, and to different people he wasn't sure they could trust? Teller trusted them, but there was still a gaping hole in Gil's chest, and it was growing with uncertainty.

His belly tickled and ached from mixed feelings. It was just like a performance, but this one was the biggest one of his life. It was a matter of life and death. Teller and Leah were doing their part, and it was time for Gil to do his. He knew they were waiting for him.

He threw the blanket to the side and rose to his feet. The light outside the room was long gone, a perfect opportunity for him to make himself heard. He grabbed his lute in one hand, to make sure he wouldn't lose it.

"Aren't you all tired?"

Gil took one heavy step after the next to advance into the room. A couple of heads turned to follow his thought. "Aren't you tired of going to sleep, marching off to work someplace they'll beat you and humiliate you, only to come back home and sleep? Aren't you angry that the bed where Nora used to sleep now has another thrall in it, as if she never lived?"

"Shut up, Gil," a frustrated call came from farther down the rows of beds. Gil knew that voice. It belonged to an older boy called Chip. Gil moved closer.

"You'd better cover your ears, Chip, for I've only just begun. You see, I'm leaving. This house and Keelheart. I'm leaving all this behind at the end of my speech. And I want you to come with me." Gil did a sweeping swirl to point at all of them. Some heads left the comfort of their pillows to listen to Gil. He saw no point in stopping.

"You're leaving? You can't do that," another voice, female, said in the dark.

"I can, and I will. Teller and Leah are making sure, while I speak, that we get our lives back. The thing Cidron made us sign, that was a paper telling everyone that he owns us. We are his property. He can do whatever he wants with us. Sure, we get his food, we get a home . . . but we don't have any freedom. Teller is a nobleman's son, which means that he can read and write. Right now, he's changing the papers. He's giving us freedom if we choose it."

"I don't want to go with you. I like it here," Chip called out. Gil smiled. *So Chip is listening?*

"What do you mean, you like it? You like being a thrall, getting beaten up, working for these assholes? You're nothing more than coin to them."

Chip still wasn't convinced. "It's better than living on the streets where no one looks out for us."

Although uncertain how to proceed, Gil kept letting the words slip out. "I beg to differ."

"Nora said the same stupid things you are. She even tried to escape, and look at what happened," Chip said.

Gil's heart sank. The thick smell of iron, and the sound of Nora's face cracking beneath Cidron's fist, came back to haunt him. "Yeah. I was there. I was there, and I saw what Cidron did to her. The entire room was full of people. No one stood up to Cidron while he killed her. I will regret not helping her enough, till I die. He tricked me, like he tricked all of us into believing he cares about us. But the truth is that Cidron is terrified of us leaving."

"They'll hunt us down and kill us if we leave," the girl said.

"They won't and can't. Not once Teller is done with the papers. We're going to Rose Lane, to the Following. They are buying our freedom, and they will never hurt us. Because they'll help us find good places to work and live."

"So, we're serving someone else?"

"No. Not unless you choose to. They are not buying us. It's something to do with papers that makes it look like the Following buys us. But they won't own us. I promise," Gil explained.

Chip spoke up. "Where you're going ain't gonna be any different, mark my words."

"It will. I refuse to be the next thrall, the next Nora, who dies. Usually, a person responsible for beating another person to death faces the law and the Crimson Wights and gets justice. But Cidron owns us. He can do whatever he wants with us. He can kill us and replace us with a new kid. We are not replaceable. We are not animals. We are not property."

Some of the onlookers tilted their heads, interested, while others crinkled their eyes in frustration. Gil prodded along the crowd to hold their attention.

"Our lives are not in our hands. At least out there, we choose for ourselves." Gil pointed to the windows. "Out there, we decide where we sleep, what we eat, what fights we get into. Here, we live by Cidron's rules, his orders, his will. He tells us what we should be, places us into neat little crates, but if we speak up against it, what does he do? He hurts us. Belittles us. Beats us. I say, no more. I'm sick of being told who I am by someone who doesn't know me, but owns me.

"I won't force any of you to join me. I won't tell you what to do or who you are. I am, however, daring you to take control. Take control of your own life. Take control for what you stand for, what you want to be, because I promise you, Cidron won't give you any of it. Let's march out together and show Cidron and the world that we are not animals. We are not replaceable. We are not property."

Once he finished his speech, he marched to the door, refusing to look behind to see who joined him. If what he said had not swayed them, then nothing would. His heart thumped against his ribcage. He was doing it. He was leaving the Rosses and Cidron. He wasn't their property. They couldn't decide what to do, what to sing, or anything. He was joining his family. His real family. Teller and Leah were the brother and sister he searched for, and he would not let them go.

Gil reached the front door without difficulty. The hallway lay desolate. Though he knew that wasn't the case right outside the front door, where at least two people were waiting. His stomach cramped, but he ignored it. If anyone was following him, he had to show them what courage looked like.

A deep inhale, and Gil swung the door open. A chilly wall enveloped him. He leaped forward to take down one of the people outside but met nothing but air.

On the ground, two grown women lay in the gravel with two very recognizable people sitting on them. Teller and Leah smiled at Gil and his wide eyes. "You . . . you've finished?"

"Yepp." Teller flashed an adorable smile. A pile of papers spread from a stuffed bag, and he pulled it closer. "How did it go on . . ."

Ten, even fifteen other thralls stepped outside the Rosses' estate. Girls, women, boys, and men of all ages followed with their belongings cradled in their arms. Gil was fast to disguise his surprise, not wanting to put it on display for them. But for each person stepping out his heart skipped a beat, especially when Chip joined.

"Right, let's go," Teller said to the crowd, and led the way through the night. Leah brought a lantern hanging from the wall of the house and guided them. Like moths drawn to a flame, they followed the glowing outline of Leah and Teller. It hit Gil how far the three of them had come. Although his legs were getting wobbly with fear, Leah guided him to safety, just like the Keeper with dying souls.

Keelheart offered little resistance. Only a couple of people walked the streets, at least the streets Teller guided them along. The lantern Leah carried pushed the night away, revealing the weathered houses and shelters of the slums in an even more frightening manner than during the day. The few they met pressed against the walls, trying to become one with the shadows. He couldn't blame them. To the naked eye, they could as well have been a gathering of an angry mob.

The narrow alleyways opened up to reveal a bridge connecting Keelheart to Rose Lane. On the opposite side of the river, torches and lanterns welcomed their arrival. A large gathering of tall people stood at Rose Lane. The thralls murmured words of concern, and their confident walk dwindled at the sight of the large crowd. But Teller stepped over the bridge, turning to face the thralls.

"These are our friends. They won't harm us," Teller spoke to them, and Gil couldn't help but suppress a sigh at the lackluster delivery. Gil pushed his way to the front, where he lined up with Leah.

"Are you Cidron's property? Are you his thrall? Or are you a strong person in control of your own life?" Gil hollered. "This is our chance. Will you be brave and cease it, claim it as your own?"

They were scared. He saw it in how they shifted their weight back and forth, how they shuddered at every sound and breeze.

Well, I'll try to convince you one last time, Gil thought. "Look, I'm as terrified as you. I'll probably not get a proper shit for a month after this, but this is important. This is something we have to do. Life isn't safe, but it'll be a lot safer without Cidron deciding it. So let's send him the message by walking into our futures together."

Gil grabbed Leah's hand tight and tugged her with him. They had done all they could for the others; it was up to them to act on it.

Her hand tightened around his as they neared the unknown people on the other side of the bridge. As they closed in, however, the lanterns and torches separated to let them pass. Together, Gil, Teller, and Leah stepped into Rose Lane and left Cidron and Keelheart behind.

CHAPTER NINETEEN

Rascals and Kings

On the other side of the bridge, in Rose Lane, men and women smiled at Leah, spreading joy. She was free from Cidron. Even though her heart pounded with fear, she held Gil's hand tighter than a blanket that she refused to let go. At the end of the bridge stood a lady, whom Teller was quick to approach.

"Elara, these are my friends, Leah and Gil," Teller said.

The tall woman with combed-back hair on one side and wild curls on the other squinted against the harsh light of the lanterns and torches.

"Pleasure to meet you, and welcome to Rose Lane," Elara said. "You should be proud of yourselves, getting this many to follow."

Other thralls brushed past Leah, all of them making sure to leave Keelheart behind.

The Presider turned to the gathering of adults. "Escort them to the Rooster, and we'll take it from there."

In the corner of her eye, Leah noticed a bright flicker. A crowd emerged between the house shapes of Keelheart. The Following and thralls whispered to each other while Leah grabbed Teller's hand and shrank behind Elara from the approaching hoard.

Walking shoulder to shoulder, Cidron's brutes, strong-looking and brawny, stopped on the other side of the bridge. Cidron's friends and companions who enjoyed drinking and singing with him studied the enemy. Leah trembled at their gaze.

Cidron squeezed past and marched onto the bridge. It seemed that he had cleaned himself off from Teller's attack earlier, as no blood covered his rough features. With both hands on his hips, he called out to the thralls. "All of you get back on over here."

The water flowing beneath the bridge splashed.

Elara took a few slow steps toward Cidron and Keelheart. "You don't own them," she said.

Papers rattled in Cidron's hand as he presented it to them. "These documents that your little friends left behind? You think Dahle will believe this?"

"I do, and apparently so do you, my lord. Is it just me, or are you looking a bit feverish?"

Cidron neared them. "Step aside," he threatened.

The other Followers closed in on Elara and Cidron as well. But Elara kept her head held high, making sure Cidron saw her determination. "You don't make demands this side of the river."

Cidron gave a bitter laugh. "How 'bout we fight it out? You and me? I know my guys want to see a fight."

"Absolutely."

A knot tied in Leah's stomach. Having seen Cidron shatter and break so many people before, Elara wouldn't stand a chance.

Cidron threw the papers to the nearest of his friends. He rolled up his sleeves. "I win, you hand them over."

Elara wrapped a curl around her finger, not moving into position. "Oh, but my Lord Ross. You already signed the papers, and I've made no deal as to let you take anyone back."

The sly smile on Cidron's misaligned face washed away. Elara knew that fighting him wouldn't amount to anything. Whatever Teller and the Following wrote on the papers, it worked against Cidron.

Cidron turned his attention to Leah. Her shoulders and body slumped beneath his gruesome glare. "Leah, have I not cared for you? Isn't it better to be with me, a person you know, instead of a murderer? With me, you're more than a whore's daughter. With me, you matter."

A whore's daughter? Was that all she was to him? Leah waited for someone to speak for her. But no. This was her moment to speak up. Because of Cidron, she'd been forced to harm others, and now he dared to speak badly about her mother. No more. She had to stand tall for the other thralls behind her, those who followed them. Gil and Teller stood beside her. The anklets of her mother and sister radiated with warmth against her chest. She wasn't alone. But more importantly, she stood beside a powerful woman, Elara, who refused to let Cidron have his way.

Leah clenched her fists. "I'm staying here."

Quicker than Leah could speak, Cidron faced Gil. "And Gil? You think they'll accept you once they learn you enjoy the company of men? Trust me—they'll hand you over to the Halls the first chance they'll get. They won't let you spit the Unborn in her face by fucking men."

Gil's jaw tightened, and the eleven-year-old looked to be at least twenty with his hardened features and shaved head in the sparse torchlight. The normally kind and loving gray-blue eyes glared with hatred at Cidron.

Before Gil got to spit words at the man, Elara spoke up in his defense. "The Following won't punish someone for who they love.

The fact that you bring that up speaks more about your repute than ours."

Cidron ignored her and let his eyes rest on Teller. As they did, however, a wound across his left eyebrow opened, and a string of blood rushed over his cheek. "And Aiden Riveroak, of course. Let's not forget about you. Judge Dahle is looking for you, and I've kept you hidden. Stay with the Following, and I'll make certain the judge marches in with a Crimson Wight to bring you home. Come back to me, and I'll protect you and your secrets. I'm sure you haven't told them about your Eckrosie friends you helped slaughter? You are the hero of Thorne's Town."

Leah glared at Teller. Aiden? He was the boy the judge was searching for. Was he a nobleman's son? It didn't really matter to her if he was or not. The boy she knew was Teller, a sweet and caring person.

"I don't know who you're speaking of, but Teller is one of us, and we protect our own," Elara said, still not letting Cidron affect her.

"Mark my words," Cidron grunted. "You'll regret this and pay for it."

Elara wrapped her arm around Leah's shoulder, shielding her from Cidron. Leah squeezed tight to the gambeson covering the woman. "But today, I celebrate with my new friends."

It could be because of the chill of the night, but Leah swore she felt tiny shudders from Elara. Was she as afraid as Leah was?

Cidron slithered closer to Elara. The Followers nearby exposed their weapons slightly, and so did those behind Cidron. But he stopped inches away from Elara, their faces nearly touching.

"Enjoy it while you can," Cidron threatened. "And keep a wary eye on this one." He pointed his chin at Teller standing next to Leah. "The little Lord has a knack for getting his friends killed."

"I think you should leave, dear Lord Ross," Elara said with a strange calm, not right for the situation. "Thank you for your business."

Cidron's watchful eyes sought Leah, Teller, and Gil out. Leah didn't know why, but a grin spread across her face. He didn't have any power over her. He didn't decide. Although Elara was a stranger, Leah felt the care and concern spreading from the woman's embrace.

With a scoff, Cidron turned heel. Several of the scary-looking people grunted loudly, but they followed their leader. Their torches flickered with their departure and shrank to specks.

"You're free." Elara embraced Leah and collected the boys to join them.

"Thank you, my Lady," Gil mumbled into Leah's shoulders.

"No." Elara kept them near. "You three are the ones who should be thanked. Because of you, the other thralls are free, and so are you."

She turned to other figures nearby. "Keep an eye out. Cidron has a temper that blows over fast, yet violently. Let's make sure we survive the night."

A man nearby spoke. "Northrun, Main Street, and River's Brook have sent people to help us. They're already keeping a close eye on Rose Lane. If anything happens, you're the first to know, my lady. Also, if they attack Rose Lane, they'll have a war on their hands. The Following will not lose ground to the Rosses."

Not until Elara hunched down and put her hand on Gil's shoulder did Leah notice the missing eye. The color drained from Leah's face at the sight.

"What do you say about getting you something nice to drink?"

As Gil entered the tavern, known as the Laughing Rooster, through an old, creaking wooden door, jumbled conversations and the smell of a dying fire welcomed him. Chip and other former thralls spoke with grown-ups. It was just as charming inside as it was on the outside. Squared wooden beams supported the ceiling, with candles hanging from them. It was the middle of the night, perhaps even early morning, but the tavern was packed. Elara escorted Gil, Leah, and Teller to a couple of benches, where they took their seats.

In silence, they listened to the surrounding discussions while waiting for Elara to bring them some hot beverage. For the first time in forever, Gil breathed without concern. They'd successfully broken free from Cidron and the Rosses. And the best part of it: Leah and Teller remained by his side. They had not left.

Elara placed three mugs with steaming water on the table as a gentleman approached. Well-groomed, salt-and-pepper stubble covered a cheerful face. Deep dimples in his etched, sandstone-kissed skin told tales of an easily attainable smile. Something was enticing about him. A kind of unforgettable presence, but not menacing or threatening like Cidron's. Quite the opposite.

Elara bowed to the gentleman. "My king."

King? I'm sitting down in front of a king? The king? Gil's eyes grew to twice their size, and he rushed to his feet. He patted down his drab clothing and bowed, still holding his lute tight.

Leah followed Gil, bowing to the king like she was taught. Both Gil and Leah peered at Teller, who sat with his back straight in defiance. Did he not understand how important these things were for the nobility? Gil dug his nails into the palms of his hands, hoping that the king would ignore it. However, the king chuckled and took a seat next to Elara. A long taupe cape swung from the man's back.

"Presider Averil tells me you are the three young heroes I should thank for dealing a devastating blow to the Rosses. What do I call you?" the king said.

Gil was quick to answer. "I'm Gil, this is Leah, and this is Teller, my king."

Teller scoffed. "You don't have to call him that, Gil—he's not a king."

"Teller," Leah barked.

"What?" Teller said. "Canden sits on the throne, you're not Canden, and you've never had a crown. Your sister is the one with a crown."

Surprisingly, the man only chuckled at Teller. "That's true. People call me king because they choose to, not because they have to. So Teller is right. You don't have to call me your king. Call me Rick."

Gil shrugged. "Whatever you say, my king."

Rick chuckled even harder. "I wish I could have seen Lord Ross's face when he realized what you little rascals did. Would you like to join us in the Following?" Rick's eyes widened and darted between them. "Not now of course. I mean, when you're older."

"Didn't your rebellion fail?" Teller said.

"Oh, it did. Thanks for reminding me." Rick gave them a misplaced smile. "But we've only gotten started. War is a long and dreadful affair, with many ups and downs. Losing to your father in Riverview was definitely one of the downs."

Gil glanced at Teller, whose gentle and kind demeanor had turned threatening and condescending. His father had fought against Rick? How much did Leah and Gil know about Teller, really?

"How did you survive?" Leah asked.

Elara leaned in closer to Rick. "My lord, you don't have to reply to—"

Rick waved his hand dismissively at Elara. "I didn't—not that part of me, at least. King Thorne has a flair for the dramatic and vile. Instead of sending me to the Beast's gullet, he killed my lady and children and cut off my manhood before throwing me to the streets."

Rick threw his arms wide. "This is my family now. Blood isn't all that unites us. We stand against the Thornes, their wars, their tyranny, and their murders. Because of Canden Thorne, people such as Cidron Ross exist. The Following stands up against all of it. By joining us, you'll be part of a large family who resents the way our leaders are using their power."

Gil brushed his hands together. "That sounds good to me. I'm in."

Rick and Elara chuckled at Gil's enthusiasm. "Glad to hear it." Rick stood up and brushed his cape to the side. "I won't overstay my welcome. We'll have many opportunities to get acquainted. Now is your night to celebrate. Thank you for everything you have done. The Following is grateful."

With that, Lord Haven disappeared into the diminishing crowd. Not long after, Elara showed Gil, Leah, and Teller a second floor of the inn, where a corridor of adjacent rooms lay. A large bed, fitting at least three grown men, stood inside the simple abode.

"I wish you a good night's rest. In the morning, we'll discuss your future here in detail if you choose to stay. Good night, my little heroes."

～❖～

The Rooster was quiet. Gil and Leah breathed silently in the twin-sized bed while Teller sat at the end of it. No doubt, they'd managed to achieve something great together. Because of Gil, Leah and Teller, the rest were free. But why did the gaping hole within Teller's chest continue growing?

He could not linger. Staying at the Rooster, with the Following, felt right, but he could not. Somehow, Cidron would make good on his promise. Someday, a Crimson would come to collect Teller, and when it did, he wanted to be as far away from people he cherished as possible.

Teller maneuvered around Gil and Leah's limbs spreading out across the bed. His weight shifted the bedding, but he managed to reach the cold floor. He glanced outside. The sky was bright, with the moon gazing at him.

Thankfully, he came prepared for quick getaways. The valuables in his bags clattered with his disturbance. The thickest coat Jarred had stuffed in Teller's bag wrapped around his shoulders as he snuck through the door and down the pitch-black corridor. Using his hands, he let the touch of the wooden panels guide his way to the staircase. On the first floor, dying candles flickered. He waited for any noise, but nothing reached him. The double doors leading from the large gathering hall to freedom greeted his touch.

"Teller." A voice penetrated the dark veil. With his hand on the doorknob, he watched Elara emerge from her study. A candle flickered at her side. "You're not leaving, are you?"

What more could be said with his appearance?

"Please, grab a bite with me before you go," Elara insisted, and directed his attention to a nearby table. She placed herself on the bench and waited for his arrival. The cold feel of the metal brushed against his fingers, making it clear for him that the chilly night was waiting on the other side of the door. Staying a bit longer would not hurt.

Elara spread butter on a stale piece of bread and handed it to him. "I wanted to thank you."

"You already did." Teller set the bags at his side.

"For show, yes, but this is my sincerest appreciation. As promised, I'll do all in my power to ensure they find great homes. Gil, for example—tomorrow, I'll invite him to stay here at the Rooster with me."

"What about Leah?"

"There something she's good at in particular? Gil showed his talents tonight, so it wasn't difficult to find him a place. But Leah, I don't know. Northrun and River's Brook have a lot of places they need filled, so she'll probably find something there."

"Don't separate them," Teller demanded. His heart throbbed hard against his chest at the thought of them parting ways.

Elara clicked her tongue and combed loose hair behind her ear. "I have to. Rose Lane doesn't have many opportunities to let former thralls in. I was making an exception for Gil."

"So you're saying there's no one who wants an extra pair of hands? Not a bakery, an inn . . . no one?"

"Not really."

This was a matter of life and death. Leah leaving Elara's sight would be devastating. Cidron would find a way to get the girl back. Although the treasure at his side bestowed him with some much-needed courage, he knew this was what he had to do.

A loud thud and clatter emanated through the silent room as Teller placed his bag of valuables on the table. Even though this was not what Jarred had intended, it was the right thing to do. Hopefully, the man would understand.

Elara separated the tired flap of the bag to reveal the glimmering pieces of silver and gold hiding within. "What's this?"

"Leah doesn't leave Rose Lane unless she says she wants to. If it's a question of money, hand this over. Andyr needs an extra pair of hands, and I'm sure there are others. This will cover her living costs for at least four years, right?"

"And what about you? Where are you going?"

I don't know. Please make me stay. Teller suppressed his worry with a shrug. "It's a big city. I'll find a place."

Elara removed the bag to catch an unobstructed view of Teller. She grabbed his hand, but he quickly moved it aside. "Teller, you have a home here in Rose Lane. Whatever Cidron said tonight about your past, it doesn't matter to me. I hope you understand that."

It didn't matter? What part of it did not matter? The fact that he'd harmed Nyle, leaving him alone in the care of his parents, or that he'd gotten Ayla and her family killed? The door he kept closed in the back of his mind, holding his guilt in check, sprang open and he glared at Elara. "Why wouldn't it? All that Cidron said is the truth. I get my friends in danger. It's only a matter of time until . . . until another one gets hurt."

Elara refused to let her one eye falter from Teller. "Life is never certain. Sometimes we win, sometimes we lose. Whatever happened in Thorne's Town is not your fault. Look at what you did tonight. You saved fifteen people, people I wouldn't have been able to reach without you."

"How can you even say that it's not my fault? You don't know me. You don't know that because of me, an entire Eckrosie village was massacred. That's on me. I'm not staying to watch you guys get killed as well."

Teller swung one bag over his shoulder. She would not understand. No one would. He was alone, and everyone would be happier with him gone.

"It's not your fault," Elara insisted. She rushed in front of Teller, placing herself between him and the door.

"Yes, it is!" Teller screamed at her. "They're dead because of me. My father killed Ayla because I loved her. Everything I hold close to my heart disappears. So get out of my way."

She refused. He did not want to hurt her, but unless she moved, he would have to.

Make it stop, please, Teller pleaded to a force clutching his chest with its searing pain. His skin itched and burned. His fingers trembled along it, ripping and tearing it asunder. It became harder and harder to breathe. Death came for him with razor-sharp teeth, tearing his flesh into shreds.

Right then and there, he stood alone in the glade. The settlement, ablaze. The piles of those he cherished melted before him. Their black, fair, and red skin turned to charcoal while their clothing soared into the sky as smoke and ash. The lifeless stare from Ayla's severed head refused to leave his sight.

A cavern collapsed, trapping him beneath its weight. Above him, thousands of Nightbringers swirled, twisting and turning while their wide grins spread fear. They exposed his betrayal and sliced his skin with indisputable truth. Whatever pain they put him through, he deserved. He would welcome it even though terror ensnared, crushed, and suffocated him.

"Hush." Elara yanked him back through the void. "Crawl back to me, Teller."

Why would he? He deserved to lay buried beneath the Nightbringers. It was his true home and where he deserved to be—locked away in a hole. A sickening stench of blood shoved him deeper into despair. The Nightbringers heeded his cries for help and mercy but ignored them. His pleas fell on deaf and unforgiving ears.

"Teller, you're not alone," a voice called.

He wanted to answer, but the weight of the rocks squeezed the air from his lungs. He was dying. The Nightbringers killed him while smiling at his demise.

"Buddy," Gil's calm and friendly voice uttered from afar. "We're right here. Me and Leah."

The soft touch of their hands brought him comfort. A little comfort, but enough for him to cling to. He was not alone. Leah and Gil drew breath, and he would do all in his might to keep them alive.

He opened his eyes. A calming scent of leather washed over him. He pressed against the Lady Presider in a loving embrace. The kind of embrace that spoke of care and concern. He was not alone. Tears spilled, and Teller cracked. His sobs turned to pained wails once his breath returned, and Elara snatched him from the pile of rocks.

"I'm really sorry you had to live through all that horror," Elara said. For once, someone cared and listened. For once, Teller listened to himself.

Other hands caressed his back while Elara grabbed him tight.

"Stay with us," Leah said behind Teller. "We need you."

She got it wrong. They did not need him. He needed them.

Elara grabbed his chin to make him look at her. "You have my word. I'll never ask you to do anything that goes against your will. And when the time comes for you to do what you need to against those who wronged you, I won't stand in your way."

"I'm scared," Teller mumbled.

"I am too." Elara brushed his tears away. "We all are. The important thing is to face our fears together and not head toward them alone. Stay with us at least long enough to help Leah find a home."

"You can't leave us. We're a family," Gil said. The usual cheer and positive tone of voice was replaced with distress and sorrow. "A family helps each other through the darkest of times."

"Besides," Elara stepped in, "you're not a lonely rebel. The Following is full of rebels. That's what we do, and we do it together."

"I don't want to forgive or forget what happened," Teller sniffled. The words of the Eckrosie spoke clearly to him.

"You won't. Those you've lost live inside of you, and once you're older, you'll make the aggressors pay for what they did. Like I said, I won't stand in your way."

Leah extended her hand, a small but comforting sight.

Together, she and Gil brought him back to the bedroom and they lay down beside each other.

CHAPTER TWENTY

Welcome Home

The bells of Riverview marked the beginning of the day, and the other bells came alive and woke Leah from her deep sleep. Next to her, Gil slobbered on a pillow while Teller snored on the other side of her. She listened to the sound of them sleeping.

Rain patted a small window over the broad bed. Veils of droplets smeared the window and cast a strange light into the bedroom. A part of her was waiting for someone. For her mother, to step in through the door, bringing sunlight with her. But Leah knew Jaida would never do that again. Yet as she gazed at the shut decorated door, she felt eyes on her. Invisible eyes. The eyes of someone looking out for her. Her mother and sister were there with her, watching over her.

A knock at the door jolted Leah. She rubbed the boys awake.

"Breakfast downstairs," Elara called to them.

"Thank you," Leah was quick to say.

Downstairs, a long-table pushed against one of the walls. On it, bread, jugs of milk and water, pork, and other meat teased them as they joined Elara and what seemed to be patrons of the Laughing

Rooster. The tables filled with people, hunched over and shoving food into their mouths.

Leah squeezed Teller's hand tight, to make sure he didn't run away. Gil seemed to have the same idea, with his eyes flickering between Teller and the door. They approached the table while Elara presented them with plates and dining ware.

"Where are the others?" Teller said to Elara once they sat on a bench and tasted the great food.

"The other children? Main Street, River's Brook, and Northrun's Presiders have taken them to their districts and found them homes. Unfortunately, you three are the only ones we can house here at Rose Lane."

Gil chewed loudly at Leah's side. "What do you mean?"

"Well, Gil, you have a place right here at the Rooster—that's of course, if you want to. We need someone like you to boost morale. I've heard of your singing, and our king thought you ought to stay here."

"And Leah and Teller?"

Elara clicked her tongue. "We'll find somewhere. There's a couple of places nearby you can present yourselves to. The bakery near Rose Square, Ellswood's smithy, and a tailor by Main Street. They might not want help, but I think you should ask. Oh, and Teller, Andyr demanded that you meet him once you're done."

"As long as they get to stay nearby, then I'll stay here." Gil gulped on some milk.

"I would expect nothing less," Elara said.

The rain was unforgiving and never-ending. Within a few steps outside the inn, Teller and Leah walked with drenched clothes sticking to their backs. Her boots squished and bathed her feet. She followed Teller, who was less talkative than usual along the street, stretching toward Main Street from the Rooster.

Teller pointed to a sign outside a narrow house. A chimney spewed a dark cloud into the rainy sky. Two stories high and shaped like a box, the house looked to be nothing special except for a sign with some funny-looking shape. They hurried to the door, and Teller banged on it.

No answer.

Teller knocked on it twice.

"Maybe they're not home," Leah whispered to him.

Despite the heavy downpour, they heard a couple of massive footsteps approach from inside as if belonging to a giant. Leah grabbed Teller by the hand again.

The door swung open on tired hinges that creaked with a hulking man's push. The man towered above them. A tunic hung loosely from his rounded shoulders and covered up a heavy stomach. The clothing was stained with black and gray spots but revealed small spots of creamy white, what seemed to be the original color.

From where Leah stood, the man had to tilt his head to see her from behind his puffy cheeks. His face also carried the black and gray dirt. He wiped his thick nose on a dirty napkin.

"What?" He grunted. In many ways, he was scarier looking than Cidron.

Leah pulled Teller with her, but Teller stood his ground. "We're looking for Davon Ellswood."

"Found him," Davon snapped back. "Patrons always walk through the door. They don't knock."

"We're not patrons. Lady Averil sent us," Teller explained.

Rain rolled along Leah's back, making her want to turn back to the comfort of the inn.

"Spit it out." Leah was jolted by the blacksmith's temper.

"She said you might need some extra hands, and well, Leah needs somewhere to live. I brought you this to pay for her."

The bag Teller insisted on carrying made it to the  cobblestones. Metal rattled, and silver and gold glimmered. Where did he get that?

Davon leered into the bag of treasures Teller exposed. "Where'd you steal this?"

"I didn't," Teller said.

The door slammed in their faces.

Pay for her? Leah gaped at Teller. Was she still a thrall? Probably not.

"Sorry, sir . . ." Teller said to the door. "I stole it from my parents."

The door cracked open again. "I don't work with thieves."

"I swear to you, sir, she isn't a thief. We simply want to give her a place to live."

"And you thought a girl such as her would swing a hammer and sweat in a smithy all day? Shouldn't she be sewing or singing or whatever?"

Singing or sewing? Leah rolled her eyes and shoved Teller aside to stand up for herself against the huge man. "Excuse me, sir, but I'm stronger than I look. And I hate all the things you just said."

"Right, common." Davon wobbled toward a raging fire farther into the shop. They passed a counter where iron and silver works lined up. Everything from candelabras to knives glittered beneath the candles heating the room.

Leah hurried behind the grumpy man, although Teller dragged his feet.

Davon withdrew some sort of metal from the furnace that sizzled red. The air vibrated with the heat. He grabbed a hammer and handed it over to Leah. "Strike the metal for as long as I tell you. Not all in one place, but spread it out evenly."

Leah ensnared her fingers around the oversized hammer that pulled her shoulders down with its weight. Droplets of water ran down her cheeks, and she wiped it off to concentrate on the task Davon presented her.

"Leah, if this doesn't . . ." Teller began. But that was enough. No one thought she could do anything for herself; no one thought she was good enough. Her teeth gnawed her lips in concentration.

Sparks flew from the hammer striking the hot iron. She followed the blacksmith's instructions perfectly, and with each impact, her entire body juddered. She didn't know if what she did was right, but it didn't matter. With each thrust, the metal spread little by little. It felt powerful, bending and forming steel with her bare hands. The iron flipped over to the other side, and Leah kept hammering until it left her sight and made it back to the roaring flames.

If she wasn't mistaken, Davon raised a seared eyebrow with surprise. "I've seen better. Your thrust needs work. But sure, you'll do fine."

"You'll have me?" Leah stuttered.

"I've got a bedroom upstairs for you. I'll teach you my way, and you'll accept that. Whatever you're thinking about the Following or the Crown, I never wanna hear it. That crap stays outside this house, you hear?" Davon grunted.

Leah nodded, and Davon snatched the bag from Teller, who looked at her with a gorgeous smile creasing his green eyes. She was staying near her friends and Rose Lane. She was free from Cidron's clutches, and she was going to learn a craft.

"You coming or not?" Davon said from the other side of the house by a couple of rugged stairs.

Leah spread her arms wide to embrace Teller. She whispered to him, keeping the lump in her throat at bay. "Thank you, Teller."

Teller and Leah left Gil alone with the Lady Presider.

"Actually, I had an idea," Elara said. "The Rooster needs your aid, but I think you should go to Amabell's brothel."

"A brothel? Why?"

"Trust me. Go there and find out on your own. Ask for Lady Hillgloom, and tell her you're interested in working for her."

Work at a brothel? The Lady Presider surely had hit her head the day before, but he wasn't about to talk against her. Not after leaving Cidron.

He followed her instructions. Outside the Rooster, he took a right and headed through a couple of alleys before reaching Rose Lane's marketplace. On the far corner, the octagonal shape of the Halls distinguished itself from the red clay houses, but he quickly found another odd house, a three-story building that rose above the market. From the outside, the house looked cozy and intimate. Spruce wood kept the clay together. Eight-sided windows with painted glass gave little, if any, insight to the ground-floor. The other floors had normal-looking windows gaping wide open, drapes fluttering with the wind.

A line of patrons waited to enter the brothel. Gil patiently stood there as well, observing the merchant stalls. It hit him—the last time he'd visited the market, the caravans of the Shields of the Moon had been lined up, ready to travel to Main Street. The barrels where Gil sat, anxiously awaiting Zahna and Dorian, were still there. Hopefully, Zahna had found her family and lived a good life in Rostain. And Dorian, well, he would find him, someday.

The door opened for him. The brothel was a different world. Sweet and potent perfumes mixed with the lovely smell of roasted beef fighting for his attention. Candles decorated every table and countertop, but instead of the usual orange light, something made the light turn purple and deep red—nothing he had seen before.

A large room opened up inside, revealing a grander room than he'd thought would greet him. It extended like a long L. A staircase made of marble led upstairs. Multiple stone statues of naked men and women decorated the luscious space. A large gathering of odd chairs and tables filled the room, and in the far corner, to the right of the entrance, a plateau where three musicians played a joyful tune welcomed him inside.

"What ya here for, good sir?" someone uttered next to him. Gil tore his eyes from the stage and raised a confused eyebrow to a woman right beside him.

"Oh . . . I'm . . . I'm here for Lady Hillgloom."

The woman dressed in an evening gown, as fine as those that ladies of Riverview wore, leaned into him and whispered, "Don't let her hear you call her that. Amabell is fine. Far left corner."

Gil followed her finger. Behind circular tables of couples watching the show, a beautiful woman was sitting with her legs and arms crossed. Like the woman by the door, Amabell wore an emerald evening gown, which complemented her skin, as red as Lake Ember's clay.

The closer he came, the more features popped out to him. Sweeping brown curls reaching just below her earlobes framed the angular shapes of her face. An artist would undoubtedly seek to study her, and apparently, so did he. But she already knew that given the sly smirk she gave him with his approach.

"Good morning, my lady," Gil said, and took a bow to her. "You look fantastic."

"Good morning, fair stranger," Amabell said with a silky and seductive drag to her words. "Who might you be?"

Gil wiped his sweaty palms on his trousers. "Eh . . . Gil. Gil the Great."

"It's clear it's your first time here. What is it you wish for, Gil?"

Gil blinked at the offer. She rose from her chair and grabbed his hand. "No, I'm seeking work with you . . . here."

Amabell stopped and winked before sitting down. "Oh, well, please sit. I don't accept thralls from the Rosses."

Joy seared through him at the realization. He wasn't anyone's thrall. "No, I'm not a thrall. I work over at the Laughing Rooster. A friend recommended I seek you out. I'm here of my own will."

"Elara sent you, did she not?" Amabell plucked grapes from a bowl on the table and gestured a hand to offer him the same. "I don't see a reason to hide my connection to the Following, especially with you. She told me grand tales of you, and I'm already impressed by your talents. I saw you perform with the Shields of the Moon. Dorian has been looking for you."

Gil stopped himself from taking a grape. His gaze darted across the room in search of his old friend. "D-Dorian?"

"He works for me as a performer, among other things. He's asleep at the moment, though," Amabell said. The music dwindled, and the room erupted with cheers. "How old are you?"

"Eleven."

"Well, sadly you'll be the only child here, but I hope that's fine."

"Would I get to sing and perform?" Gil asked.

"Of course. Look, Gil, this isn't like any other brothel. This is an experience, a magical night for patrons to remember and have fond memories of. Singing and performances are part of what makes this place special. And I want you to be one of the bards."

Sounds too good . . . there's gotta be a catch. There's always a catch, Gil thought, running his tongue along the rows of his teeth.

"Let me stop your pondering. Is it too good to be true? It's not. This place is real. How about this—you work and live with us. However, the Rooster will be able to ask for your help whenever they need an extra pair of hands. Write me some catchy and cheeky songs to perform, and we'll put you on stage by the end of the new moon."

"Really?" A genuine laugh left him. All this was within his reach? Having never been in a fancy home before, he couldn't see how nobles of Riverview had it much better than this.

"When you're ready, let me show you your room." Amabell zig-zagged between her patrons, walking in beat with the musicians' song. A room? Was he getting his own space as well? Everything he'd wished for and dreamed of suddenly presented itself to him. All he needed to do was reach out and claim it as his own. Even Dorian had stepped back into his life. Hopefully, this wasn't a trick created by an Almighty, looking to pull the fantasy from his grasp and laugh at his expense. Why would it be, though? Had Gil not suffered enough? The Halls had kicked him out. The troupe was disbanded, and he'd ended up in Cidron's hands. Was this not his chance to turn it around?

Gil felt a smile coming on, and he let it grow. His lips pulled apart to reveal his wide grin to anyone near. This was his family, and this was his time.

～❀～

Andyr's practice wept beneath heavy clouds. Though the rain persisted and nipped Teller's skin raw, there was a sort of contentment resting in his chest at last. Leah and Gil were looked after. Sure, Davon did not come off as the best person, but the way

Leah grinned as she struck the iron gave him the confidence he needed in order to leave her. For some reason, leaving the bag with them was not as difficult as he'd thought it would be. It was liberating in a way, although he would have to find a way in Levent, dirt poor.

Teller stepped into the practice. A puddle gathered on the stone floor beneath his clothes. The entrance held at least twenty people, waiting for Andyr's care. They gathered on benches stowed away by the walls. Teller took his place.

Not long after, Andyr sought Teller out. "Teller, come with me," the healer blurted.

They passed the rooms on an inside balcony overseeing the entrance below. Upon reaching the farthest room, Teller entered, but the healer kept on walking along the barricade. Confused, Teller peeked behind the door to see where Andyr was heading and found a couple of ragged stairs that waddled with the adult's walk. Teller followed.

At the top of the stairs, a dusty yet tidy room greeted them. Bookshelves leaned against the walls, and there was even a desk filling the room beside a bed. A window gazed out at the street below, three stories up.

"What do you think?" Andyr asked.

Teller racked his brain for a compliment. "Yeah ... this looks good. A bit difficult for injured people to get up the stairs, but sure I ..."

"This is yours if you want it."

Teller blushed. "What?"

"There's too much for me to do, and I'll need an assistant," Andyr rushed.

At the offer, the bedroom did not feel as foreign. Bookshelves waiting for books, the bed waiting for a visitor. Teller bought himself time to think by saying nonsense. "But I'm—I'm just a child, and I . . ."

Andyr crossed his arms over his chest. "Have other places to be? Yeah, I know. But you can't do anything against those people you're angry at right now. Stay here and work with me until you move on. This way, you'll stay close to your friends."

There it was again. The plea for him to linger. As soon as he heard the suggestion, his heart pounded loudly, not to be ignored. What if the worst happened? "I can't. I . . ."

"Look, I don't know everything that's happened to you, but your friends need you as much as you need them." Andyr smoothed down his shirt. "Think it over. I'll be downstairs while you do."

The dust clogged his nose as it whipped from the floor with Teller's disturbance. Underneath the gray coat, a birch desk greeted Teller. It was simple in its woodwork—sharp corners, and no unique carvings like Lionel's. But the circles created from the tree itself spoke of hidden sophistication and an old life. Perhaps living in Rose Lane would not be so bad after all?

Like the day before, a sticky and painful itch clutched his chest. How could he even consider staying, becoming complacent, forgetting Ayla?

The window swung open by his push. Vines used the house's facade to slither up, perfect for climbing. Teller's fingers trembled along the slick surface, and raindrops drenched him once more.

He stopped. Elara and Andyr were right. What was there for Teller to do while he was this, a young boy on his own in the streets? Cidron remained a threat to Gil and Leah despite what the Following or Elara believed. Somehow, Cidron would enact vengeance for his loss. With the Following keeping his back clear, this was the best opportunity Teller would get. Elara swore to protect him. The

Following held power with the higher-ups, and getting into trouble was nothing he would stop doing. Staying with the Following would keep him safe from Crimsons, and learning from the best healer in Levent would aid him. Besides, if he could become one of the greatest healers, he could earn money and buy books. Books where he could write Ayla's story.

Teller left his bag in the attic and hurried down the stairs that wobbled with his run. Five empty rooms threw the sound of his footfalls back to him until he reached one where Andyr stood, checking in on one of his patrons.

Teller took his place at Andyr's side, in his new home.

Meet the characters

Dear reader,

Do you want to see what the characters look like? Scan the QR code below to get a glimpse of character portraits.

Thank you for reading the first novel in
the Silver and Crimson series.

Sarah Eriksson is a gritty medieval fantasy author
hailing from Sweden but grew up across the Atlantic in
the United States. Other than writing, Sarah's lens
captures moments as a photographer and weaves tales
as a filmmaker. Her love for all things cute is
juxtaposed by her passion for metal music.

Want to see what else Sarah has written?
Be sure to join the Following on social media.
Sarah Eriksson
www.saraheriksson.com
www.silverandcrimson.com
www.facebook.com/writersaraheriksson
www.instagram.com/writersaraheriksson
authorsaraheriksson@gmail.com
#silverandcrimson #forgedincrimson